ANOTHER PASSIONATE GENERATION OF PAXTONS— ANOTHER SHANA CARROL BLOCKBUSTER!

First, there was RAVEN, the story of the first of the dazzling Paxton women, a black-haired beauty who leaves the peace of an English country estate for a pirate's life on the high seas, and who founds the Paxton bloodline in wild but forgiving America.

Then, YELLOW ROSE, a prairie-fire saga of love between spitfire Elizabeth Michaelson and lean, hard-driving True Paxton, caught up in the wild war of independence, struggling to root themselves in the raw new West.

And PAXTON PRIDE, a tempestuous novel about Texas-bred Vance Paxton and his bride from back east--Karen Hampton, elegant, city-bred, whose great burden and great reward is coming into womanhood on the brawling new turf of Texas!

AND NOW, *LIVE FOR LOVE* . . .

It is in the carnival setting of an English country fair that wealthy planter Tom Paxton first comes under the spell of the flame-like gypsy dancer, Adriana, whose midnight vision tells her they are fated to be lovers. Long separated, they reunite on a dangerous voyage that will decide the fate of future Paxton generations—and uncover a desire as stormy as the tropical seas they sail.

Shana Carrol

LIVE FOR LOVE

A JOVE BOOK

LIVE FOR LOVE

A Jove Book / published by arrangement with
Shanew Corporation

PRINTING HISTORY
Jove edition / January 1984

ISBN: 0-515-07385-7

Jove books are published by The Berkley Publishing Group,
200 Madison Avenue, New York, N.Y. 10016.
The words "A JOVE BOOK" and the "J" with sunburst
are trademarks belonging to Jove Publications, Inc.

PRINTED IN THE UNITED STATES OF AMERICA

∽ CHAPTER I ∽

Wind blew through the trees surrounding the clearing, rattling branches and carrying other night sounds—the whine of insects, the rustle of small animals moving about in the brush, the occasional whinny of a horse or growl of a dog. Parked around the large clearing were a score of Gypsy wagons so sturdily built that they were actually small houses on wheels. The wagons were decorated with colorful drawings of unicorns and flowers, wheels and stars, birds of every color and plumage, and were festooned with bits of bright cloth that fluttered like pennants in the breeze. The horses that pulled the wagons were penned nearby in a rough makeshift corral. Strong, heavy beasts that might once have carried knights into battle, they were content now to rest after their long day's journey. In the center of the clearing, where the remains of a large fire were banked for the night, coals winked like jewels and ghostly trails of smoke undulated upward to be whisked away by the night breeze.

Though there had been a great deal of activity earlier in the evening, tranquillity now settled over the clearing. Most of the Gypsies were asleep in their wagons and in tents that had been pitched nearby, for the wanderers were tired after traveling most of the day from Kent's Grove to the Chiltern Hills and then setting up their encampment. They would be well rested in the morning, ready to prepare for the spring fair and festivities.

All was not peaceful and quiet in one of the wagons, however. Both of its occupants were asleep in narrow

1

beds that folded out from opposite walls, but one of them rolled uneasily from side to side, restlessly tossing her head, tangling her long, thick auburn tresses. She was young but ripe with the bloom of womanhood, as was obvious when, moaning and writhing, she threw back her blanket, revealing a full figure in a thin night-dress.

The violent dreams that crowded in on her as she struggled and tossed filled her sleep with a fear so intense that her breath quickened and the blood raced in her veins. Even as she dreamed, she sensed that the cause of her fear was real and quite close, but it was so well hidden in the shadows of her nightmare that she could only cringe from the specter and never actually see its source. Violence and fear were not all that she sensed, though for there was a man, too, whose face she couldn't make out, but whose presence in the dream served as a calming influence. He had about him an aura of passion, of great strength; he seemed capable of both boisterous laughter and icy rage. She sensed that he was full of everything that made the pageant of life fascinating.

Who are you? she asked. *Who are you? Speak, I pray you!*

He gave no answer. Uninvolved, he seemed poised on the brink of her life, waiting for . . . what? The proper moment?

Then let me see your face, good sir, that I may know it when the time comes.

Her fear gradually departed, slowly dissipating like the last vestiges of an ugly storm. In its place, where the man stood, dark shadows rushed in to hide his face, then pulsed outward, soon dispelled by a glowing light that, increasing, became a . . . tree! A tree, tall and golden, entwined with golden brambles rising like a phoenix from the ashes of her fear.

What does this mean? I beg you tell me, what does this mean?

The image of the tree grew and swelled until there was

no room for anything else in the Gypsy girl's mind. A low moan escaped from her throat and she thrashed about more violently. There was nothing frightening about the tree, but a sense of overwhelming power flowed from the image, filling her dream and washing away everything else with the cleansing strength of a rushing river. . . .

"Adriana!" a voice hissed in the darkness of the wagon. "Wake up, Adriana! What is wrong?"

Adriana bolted awake and her green eyes snapped open. Powerful hands gripped her arms and relief flooded through her as she recognized the familiar shape of her brother, Giuseppe, leaning over her. She took a long, shuddering breath and willed the pounding of her pulse to slow. "I was . . . dreaming," she said raggedly, reaching up to clutch his hands and taking comfort from the grip of his blunt callused fingers.

"Do not worry, little one," Giuseppe said softly. "Your visions have never caused you harm. Nothing will harm you. Have I not always taken care of you?"

"Yes, Giuseppe," Adriana said, nodding as she sat up. The throbbing in her skull gradually subsided, and she put her arms around her brother and hugged him quickly. "I will be all right now. You can go back to sleep."

Giuseppe's dark square-jawed face betrayed his concern. "You are sure?"

"Yes," she promised. "I am sure. Just visions. For myself, I think, but I cannot tell yet."

He stood and rested a hand on her shoulder as he lingered at her side. "Your moan awakened me. I was frightened to see you in such torment—I thought perhaps you were sick."

Adriana shook her head and looked up at him. "At first there was fear and terror, but then came a man in shadows and a golden tree." She paused, realizing how little sense she was making. "Do not worry, Giuseppe. I will sleep now."

Giuseppe's teeth gleamed as he smiled down at her.

"You know best, little one. I am nearby if you need me."

With a nod, Giuseppe went back to his bed, and Adriana reclined once more on her thin mattress. Her eyes remained open, however, staring into the darkness. She lay quietly until she was certain that Giuseppe's breathing had settled into the deep, steady rhythm of sleep. Then she pushed her blanket back again, swung her legs out of bed, and stood on the wooden floor of the wagon. Despite what she had told Giuseppe, the vision of the tree and the brambles was still as vivid as if it had been printed on her brain. Moving soundlessly, she went to a small window set into one wall, pushed back the curtain, and peered into the night, as thick with shadows as her dream. This was not the first time she had had strange, unexplainable dreams. Usually something about them came true later on. The people who paid their shillings to have their palms read in her tent might scoff at what she told them, but often there was truth in her words. How she knew these truths, and why she had been chosen for this gift, were questions she could not answer. But she knew. She knew.

And now, as she stared out at the stars in the night sky, she wondered what this dream could have meant. There had been violence and fear in her life before: no Gypsy grew into adulthood without seeing things better left unseen. Gypsies had a vision of the world as a strange, dangerous, and magical place. Demons walked the land, fairies hid beneath the oak leaves. A wood sprite might steal your slipper but leave a guinea on the windowsill. The world was an endless display of mystery, life, and death. Hangings, floggings, scourgings, murder. She had witnessed infidelities and lust; jealousy, persecution, and death; and yet she herself had remained safe. Perhaps, because she had been so lucky, fate was waiting to surprise her with something worse in the future. Perhaps ill fortune was lurking there to pounce when she least expected it. But what about the man in the mists of the dream? He had been like no one she had ever known. Would he shortly come into her life and change it forever? Most important, what of the tree, the strange golden tree wound about with a thicket of brambles? The stars winked distantly, the night unwound in silence. Adriana sighed. Only time knew the answers to her questions, and only time would tell.

Fair time! It was spring fair time in Mumford, low in the Chiltern Hills, thirty miles from the city of London. The Gypsies knew what winter in these bleak parts did to the spirits of people who'd been cooped up in smoky hovels, eating a monotonous, starchy diet for six months. They knew, too, how to break through the sullen, oppressive air and elicit, along with laughter, the spare ha'penny and penny on which they made their livings.

The ritual was years old, and each and every man, woman, and child knew his task. The camp woke before daybreak, and within moments the previous night's communal fire was revived and water for tea was boiling. Women cooked while children tended the horses, milked the goats, and cared for younger brothers and sisters. The carcass of a wild boar was encased in clay and set to roast, to be cut up and sold that night. Women began the day-long process of cooking the sweets and puddings and meat pies they would peddle. By sunup, the men had staked out the fair in a plan that would not alter the year long, no matter where they went: a large central commons around which each family was alotted space, the best spots for the eldest and the tribe's leaders, the least desirable for the younger members. Like magic, tents rose and wagons became booths where food and trinkets and notions were sold, where a country lad could try his hand at a game of chance, and where craftsmen plied their trades.

The first fair of the season was always the most exciting, for the Gypsies, too, were tired of the boredom of winter. The day couldn't have been better. Already a cuckoo had called three times, signifying good luck that surely was increased by the discovery of a gold earring that one of the women had lost the year before. The luck held when the sun rose hot and bright, burning off the early morning fog and chasing away the chill of the night before the first customer arrived. Though it was tempered by a vague premonition she attributed to her dream of the night before, Adriana, too, felt the luck as she stood under the sign of the palm over the entrance to her tent. The tent was not large, but it was colorful and eye-catching. Its sides were dyed in alternating vertical bands of red and white, and on top a red pennon flapped languidly in the breeze that rustled the new leaves on the trees. In comparison to the efforts of many of the others, Adriana's preparations had been minimal. The tent had been erected in a matter of minutes, and Giuseppe had carried a bright red rug from their wagon and covered the hard-packed ground inside. On the rug were placed a small round three-legged table and two chairs of lebanon cedar, arranged opposite each other. A pair of unlighted candles in an ornate brass holder completed the decor. Later, the candlelight, heightening the air of mystery inside the darkened tent, would fall on the palms of those who came to have their futures told.

"The demons of night have fled, eh?" Giuseppe said, coming around the tent from where he had been helping the tinker set up his booth.

"You've been helping Saul again?" Adriana asked.

"The leather on his bellows cracked. I told him before we left winter camp that he should replace it." Giuseppe shrugged good-naturedly. He was short and compactly built, and his teeth gleamed remarkably white against his dark features as he smiled at her.

"Saul listens only when listening pleases him," Adriana said.

Giuseppe suddenly scowled. He had seen Adriana and

Saul making eyes at each other. Only that morning, while the half-dozen other eligible men in the tribe had sipped their honeyed tea and watched Adriana with hungry eyes, had she gone to sit at Saul's side. "He listens to *you*," Giuseppe said.

"He is a good tinker. The pots he mends stay mended. Would you have me a spinster? People talk already, Brother. I must choose a man one day soon, and as well Saul as another."

"A man who doesn't care for his tools can't be trusted to care for his woman," Giuseppe growled.

"Giuseppe—"

"Ahh, I know. I am worse than a father. I worry too much."

Fondly, Adriana touched his arm. "You are brother and father, so worry doubly. I do not mind, truly. But you must listen fairly to Saul if he comes to speak to you."

"It's gone that far, then?" Giuseppe asked. "I tell you—" He was interrupted by a child running into camp and announcing the imminent arrival of the first customers. Always the first customers of the first fair of the year stirred his blood. "There will be time for this talk later," he said, rubbing his hands in anticipation of the action to follow. "We have much to do. This will be a good fair, I sense it."

Adriana smiled warmly at him. "And I thought I was the one blessed with the power to see the future. Perhaps you would like to read the palms for me today?"

He shook his head. "I will leave that to you, little one."

"I am not so little anymore, Giuseppe. Must I keep telling you?"

Giuseppe grinned. "So my eyes and my friends tell me. Ah, Adriana, I shall always remember you as the little child with her hair in braids, running to me whenever something was wrong. You believed with all your heart, did you not, that your brother could set anything aright?'' His voice was soft with the fondness of the memory.

"And more times than not, you could," Adriana told him.

"Times change," he mused, a faraway look coming into his dark eyes. "You are a woman now, and less and less often need the aid of your brother. So I remember you sometimes as a child, the way you once were. But I love you always, as child, as woman, forever."

Adriana put a hand on his wiry arm. "And I love you, Giuseppe. You have been more than my brother: you have been all of my family for so long, and we have always been strong . . . because of you."

He shook his head, a solemn expression on his broad face. "The strength, the power—these come from you, Adriana," he said. "This is the way it has always been and always will be." He suddenly smiled again. "These things do not need to be discussed. They simply *are*. So enough. Are you ready?"

"I am ready," she told him.

"Good. I will be close by if you need me."

Adriana nodded. Giuseppe had taken care of her ever since that awful day when a mob of angry citizens inflamed by charges of Gypsy thievery had descended on the camp and had wreaked havoc, creating a hideous scene of chaotic carnage as they rampaged with clubs and torches, overturning wagons and setting fire to tents. A boy of ten, Giuseppe had saved his little sister by snatching her up and racing into the woods, where they watched in horror as their parents were beaten to death. Giuseppe's hand had covered Adriana's eyes, shielding her from the worst, but she had seen enough, and the sights she had witnessed had left an indelible impression. She would not have been able to stand the memories had it not been for Giuseppe. Mother and father and brother, he was the center of her universe, and though the time was nearing when she must take a man, she knew her love for him would never diminish.

The keen anticipation Giuseppe had felt raced through the fairgrounds. Men, women, and children busily made last-minute preparations. Gregori, the clan elder, made his rounds as he had for the last decade. Ancient and bent, he was so emaciated that his traditional colorful Gypsy clothing hung loosely on his skeletal frame. A white moustache drooped over his mouth, white wisps of hair clung to his mottled scalp in isolated clumps, and an age-blackened briar pipe was clenched between his gums. Taking the pipe in his gnarled hand, he pointed the stem at Adriana. "Ready, girl?" he asked in a quavering voice.

Adriana nodded. "I am ready, Gregori."

"Good," he said, replacing the pipe in his mouth. Without another word, he turned and ambled off, already intent on his next visit.

Adriana ran to Saul's booth for a bit of fire to light her candles, then hurriedly settled herself in the dim, cool interior of her tent. Soon she would be busy studying palms, telling farmers and miners and wives and servants what they most wanted to hear. This moment of introspection was important to Adriana. Quietly, she sat at the table and emptied her mind of distractions. Some—perhaps even most—of the Gypsy fortune-tellers she had met were shams who prattled nonsense that sounded wise and omniscient but signified nothing. Adriana liked to believe she was different. She was shrewd enough to dispense good predictions to those who so desperately wanted to hear them, but at the same time she could not and would not totally deny the mysterious gift with which she had been blessed. Many times, she actually did see something in the customer's palm. Sometimes what she saw was good, and she could then use this knowledge in what she told her subject. Sometimes, though, the future held something bad, and she had to decide whether to withhold the truth. There had been occasions when she had not told all she knew, and then wished that she had, but that was all a part of the great game. It was never easy knowing when to keep quiet. Honesty often brought trouble, but then trouble was part of being a Gypsy.

This was the only life she knew. She could not imagine being somewhere other than where she was, surrounded by Giuseppe and Gregori and all her other friends, traveling the English countryside, free of the responsibilities and cares that beset the farmers, soldiers, villagers, and city dwellers. And when the clan had its fill of England, there were always other lands, new people, new sights. She felt as much wanderlust as any Gypsy, maybe even more.

A low cough caught her attention. Adriana looked up to see a blocky man in rough clothes, clutching a grimy cap in his hands, peering into the tent. She smiled to put him at ease and beckoned. "Come in," she said in a low, husky voice. "I am Adriana, one with the spirits of the past, one with the shades of what is to come. Enter and know what the mists of the future hold for thee."

Adriana was glad to give the farmer what words of hope she could, and he, wanting to believe them, left well pleased. The day's work had begun.

As the morning went on and passed into afternoon, the clearing became more and more packed with people. The citizens of the area arrived in a near-constant stream, ready to break loose from the bonds of the winter past and enjoy themselves, however fleeting the pleasure. Gypsy and village children met and scuffled and played in gay abandonment. Women chattered in little knots and men gathered to dicker and discuss. Broad smiles and open laughter would come later, as everyone became more at ease. Of noise there was plenty. Sheep bleated, cows lowed, horses neighed, and dogs barked. Vendors hawked their wares in time-honored chants. Fiddles squawked and pipes screeched, discordant against the flat, regular clang of a smith's hammer. The air was redolent with an enticing assortment of aromas: beef roasts sizzling over open fires, spice cakes warming in pans, mulled wine and pungent Scottish ale flowing freely.

The Gypsies were busy, many of them displaying the entertaining skills that brought people back to see them year after year. A knife swallower casually inserted a twenty-inch blade into his mouth and down his throat to the accompaniment of startled gasps from the watching crowd, then pulled it back out to cheers and applause. A bald and tattooed juggler, naked to the waist, kept a dozen small flame-red and bright-yellow wood balls spinning through the air over his head. More wondrous yet, the sequence of red, yellow, red, yellow changed to six red and six yellow, then four of each, three of each, two of each, and back to the original one-and-one sequence in a dazzling feat of legerdemain. A pied piper leading a goat wearing a scarlet vest made for him by his owner and prancing about in time to the music emerged from a tent. Within minutes the piper was leading a troop of enthralled children around the grounds. Laughing onlookers dropped coppers into a leather sack that hung from the goat's left horn.

Not all the activity was strictly entertainment, however. Traveling merchants who trailed the Gypsies from fair to fair sold bright bolts of cloth and intricately carved figurines and painstakingly shaped utensils of copper and tin. A blacksmith with his forge and bellows filled the space beneath a giant oak tree, and close by, another man sharpened knives and scissors.

The crowd grew even more as the day waned. By dusk, most of the people from Mumford and the surrounding countryside had come for the first day of the festivities. They took advantage of the opportunity not only to visit with their neighbors, friends, and relatives, but to conduct business at the same time. There was buying and selling and trading aplenty. Men clustered in small groups, talking in quiet tones, frowning and rubbing their jaws as they concentrated on the offers flowing back and forth. From time to time, discussions became heated, voices were raised and emotions flared, but none of the arguments turned into actual fights. People had come to the fair to enjoy themselves, not to engage in squabbles. Besides, a bare-knuckles fight between two of the area's most strapping lads was scheduled for later, and that would be violence enough for one day.

There was a steady flow of customers through Adriana's tent. They were tenant farmers for the most part, poor people who had saved their pennies carefully in anticipation of this day, and who were spending them no less carefully. The men were all stoop-shouldered from work, with thick bodies and dull faces, and their women matched them, all looking older than they actually were. Laborers from the coal mines in the hills appeared too, their way of life evident in the permanent stains under their fingernails and in the creases of their skin. Life in the Chiltern Hills in this year of our Lord 1809 was hard for everyone, and Adriana kept her predictions light and cheerful, feeling no shame for telling these people things that she knew would never come to pass. For one small copper, a beautiful Gypsy girl would peer into their palms and look sultry and mysterious and tell them that they would soon be the recipients of bountiful fortunes. Most of them chose to believe exactly what she told them, if only for a little while. And those moments of belief and hope were worth the money that they spent.

"Adriana! Come dance for us, woman!"

Adriana looked up from the table in the tent as strident, eager voices called to her from outside. Night had fallen, and the candles cast flickering shadows around the interior. The day had been long. She'd had many customers in search of information about their futures, some steered to her by Giuseppe, others drawn by the sign of the palm above the tent entrance. More than one young man, she was sure, paid his shilling not to have his fortune told, but to have his hands held by her long, slender fingers, to regard with appreciation the honey color of her skin, to gaze deeply into her green eyes, and to listen to her voice, speaking low and soft to him alone. Now, after long hours of bending over the table, she welcomed the opportunity to get outside and move around. Although her readings were not finished for the day, she was glad for a break. As she pushed out through the flap of the tent, she was greeted with enthusiastic shouts and a burst of music from tambourines and fiddles and wooden flutes. Pleased by the attention, Adriana smiled and walked toward the large fire in the center of the clearing. The enveloping darkness made the light of the fire brilliant. Leaping and crackling, it illuminated a wide circle of faces that parted to create a narrow lane through which she could pass. The music became more urgent as Adriana entered the open space near the fire. Swaying just slightly, in movements barely discernible but promising much, much more to come, she slowly began the dance they were all waiting to see.

Simultaneously ancient and new, the dance, too, was part of the great game. The dance was freedom, a melting of mind and body into one sensual, exultant whole. Lost in rapture, Adriana whirled and darted, spun and dipped and leaped. Her hips swayed seductively from side to side and her skirt spun outward to reveal slim, muscular calves. With her head back and her eyes closed, her long, thick auburn hair dangled loosely behind her in a dance all its own. Her feet, in soft slippers, traced intricate patterns on the hard ground.

On and on the music went, wild driving rhythms that inflamed the blood of dancer and spectator alike. The night was cool, but a fine sheen of perspiration dampened Adriana's face, the droplets beading and rolling down her neck and chest until they disappeared in the deep valley between her breasts. Suddenly, her movements slowed. She raised her arms until her breasts strained against her blouse, then crossed them over her head before slowly, sinuously lowering them until she reached a point where she paused and stood absolutely still for several beats. Then, without warning, she was dancing again, even more wantonly than before.

The dance reached out to every man present in a powerful, primitive way. Amid cries of appreciation, the applause increased in tempo to match the music. Everywhere were grinning faces, the long winter's hardships forgotten as spirits rose and cares fell away. The Gypsy girl was spring, the essence of a world awakening to eternal youth and promise. The heat of the campfire was forgotten, unable to compare with the blaze burning from within.

Adriana was well aware of the effect she was creating. She did not necessarily think of herself as beautiful, but she knew that the country people who watched her did, and had become accustomed to their looks of ill-concealed jealousy and desire. For the most part, these did not bother her, wrapped up as she was in the dance. . . .

An icy finger of warning ran up her spine. Still dancing, Adriana turned and saw a uniformed man standing at the inside edge of the crowd. She recognized him from previous Mumford fairs, and knew instantly why she felt uneasy. The man's name was Trevor Bliss, and he was the youngest son of a wealthy and powerful local family with extensive coal holdings. He wore the uniform of an officer of His Majesty's Navy, and had a reputation as a man who acquired whatever struck his fancy. There was good reason to fear Trevor Bliss, for his position conferred on him an immunity to punishment that no Gypsy enjoyed. In his latest escapade a year before, he had become drunk and belligerent and had tried to molest a servant girl from the local squire's household—and then had tried to throw the blame on Saul. The consensus of the Gypsies was that he was one of the most unaptly named men in the world, unless one included a sour disposition and a harsh temperament among the attributes of bliss.

The young officer was resplendent. A plumed hat rode proudly on his tightly curled sand-colored hair. His lieutenant's uniform, consisting of a blue jacket, tight white breeches, and high white boots, was set off with a sword, ribbons, sashes, medals and epaulets. The combination of boots and hat made him appear taller than he truly was, somewhat less than six feet, and few men or women present dared meet the hard brown eyes that stared contemptuously from his narrow, pale aristocratic face. Those eyes were now watching Adriana intently, and Bliss was taking no pains to conceal the unbridled lust that the Gypsy girl's dance had aroused in him.

The music rose to a climax. Adriana whirled faster and faster until, with a crash of cymbals and drums, the music stopped and she collapsed, arms spread and head bowed to the tumultuous applause. The crowd cheered and threw coins, which the musicians' children darted in to retrieve. Slowly, Adriana rose and curtsied deeply around the circle, taking care to avoid Bliss's eyes, lest her discomfort show. At last, flushed and still breathing deeply, she allowed Giuseppe to take her arm and escort her through the sea of grinning faces and grasping hands.

Away from the crowd, the breeze was cool and invigorating. "Did you see him?" she asked, wiping her face with her sleeve.

"The one who caused trouble last year? Of course."

"He frightens me," Adriana said with a shiver.

"Do not fear, little one. Only remain in your tent until I come for you. I have business to attend to, but I won't be long."

Leaving his sister alone, Giuseppe melted back into the crowd. Adriana sighed and headed for her tent. She was tired, and the closing of the fair for the night couldn't come too soon. There would be more palms to read, though, for inevitably her dancing inspired a half-dozen or more local lads to seek her out. Perhaps afterward there would be time to sit and talk, to share a moment with Saul and listen to him flatter her with reasons why she should be his woman. She smiled secretly. Who knew? Perhaps tonight, if he was eloquent enough, she would let him . . .

A stare burned into her back. Adriana caught her breath and kept moving. Trevor Bliss had to be the source of that searing stare, and she knew that she dared not turn to meet it. Perhaps if she ignored him he would go away. The strategy seemed to work, for a moment later she sensed that he was no longer watching her. In any case, the anticipated line of young men waited outside her tent, and the next half-hour passed peacefully and quickly. The young men were polite, their dreams written on their faces. Each was content to stare avidly while she held his hand, studied his palm, and hinted of wealth, beautiful women, and adventure.

The signal for the end of the day's festivities sounded just as Adriana's last customer, a moonstruck cobbler, left. Adriana sighed and stretched, feeling the weight of the coppers in the pocket of her skirt. The morning's good luck omens had been correct: the first day of the first fair of the year had been a good one. Just as she leaned forward to blow out the candles, the tent flap was swept aside and Trevor Bliss swaggered through. "Not closing just yet, are you, lass?" he asked mockingly.

Also part of the morning's premonitions, Adriana thought fleetingly. "Yes," she said, trying to conceal the nervousness she felt in his presence. "You will have to return on the morrow."

Bliss carried a pair of white gloves in one hand, and he slapped them lightly into the palm of the other as he stepped to the table. "But I want my fortune told tonight, Adriana. That is your name, isn't it?"

She bridled at his familiarity, and was repulsed at the way his eyes ran over her body and lingered on the low scooped neckline of her blouse and the swell of her breasts.

"You see," he continued offhandedly, "I remember you from other years. Strange that I never noticed until tonight just what a lovely woman you've become." His smile held no humor, only menace. "Blossomed over the winter, eh? Smacks of witchery to me."

He was close enough that she could smell the strong scent of ale exuding from him. To judge from the faint flush that suffused his face and the slight sway in his walk, he had been drinking heavily, perhaps from the moment he had arrived at the fair. "I'm sorry, sir," Adriana insisted politely, "but you will have to come back again some other time."

Accustomed to subservience, Bliss was galled. Tucking his gloves behind his belt, he pulled back the customer's chair and sat at the table. "Well?" he demanded haughtily, his eyes intent under his plumed hat. "Are you going to carry on with your business, Adriana? Or are you afraid you'll be found out?" His lip curled in a supremely confident sneer. "I know about you Gypsy fortune-tellers. You're all charlatans. You spout cheap generalizations in low, mysterious tones, pass off blather as wisdom, and then complain that you're being persecuted when persons of substance run you off as you so richly deserve. Now, do as I say."

Ridicule and contempt came too easily to this young English officer with the superior attitude, and Adriana controlled her temper only with effort. "It is customary to pay first," she told him in a low, cool voice, less concerned now with being careful not to offend him.

"Of course." Bliss reached into his jacket pocket and produced a shilling, which he flipped into the air.

Adriana caught the coin and dropped it in her pocket. "Give me your right hand," she commanded, sitting opposite him. Bliss extended his hand toward her. She took it in both of hers, turned the palm upward, and spread his fingers slightly. Bending forward a bit, uncomfortably aware that she was exposing even more of her breasts to Bliss's view, she carefully studied his palm. Bliss leaned forward too, so close to her that she could feel his breath on her face. "I see," she began at last, tracing with inward reluctance one long line on Bliss's palm, "a great fortune that will come your way. Perhaps only wealth, perhaps even more." That seemed to be a safe enough statement, given the holdings of the Bliss family. Surely at least a part of their fortune would come his way someday. "You must be watchful and ever careful, but not fearful, and you will succeed only if you are bold, energetic, and cunning, for though the rewards are great, the opportunities are few, and you must snatch them before they evaporate as quickly as the morning dew." That was a standard part of many fortunes, but Adriana hoped that if Bliss heard what he wanted to hear, he would leave without causing any trouble.

Bliss's smug face told her he wasn't being taken in, not for a second. Perhaps if she could appeal to his vanity. . . . Solemnly, she bent his forefinger and made a show of counting a series of tiny lines in the first joint. "You have been three times in great danger of death," she declared confidently. "I see—"

"More often than that," Bliss interrupted with a laugh. "Death is an old companion of mine. But I must tell you, he fears me more than I him."

"Only three times has the threat been real," Adriana insisted, "although if it pleases you there will be other times."

"Bosh! Is that all you have to tell me?" Bliss asked in disgust. "The meanest beggar in London could do as well, girl!"

Adriana held her breath and swallowed the angry retort that threatened to burst from her. "No," she said when she dared to speak again. She folded his hand into a fist and looked directly into his eyes. "One thing more. A lady of great beauty will change your life."

Bliss slapped the table sharply with his free hand. "You're just telling me things any man would want to hear," he taunted. "But I am not just any man. Tell me something specific if you can . . . if you dare."

"Very well." Adriana's lips curved in a smile that wasn't entirely pleasant as she opened his hand and leaned forward again. An ominous silence filled the tent. The only sound seemed to be Bliss's breathing, made fast and slightly harsh by the ale he had consumed. "Very well," Adriana repeated finally. "I will reveal to you what your palm reveals to me. Many times have your passions involved you in great trouble. You are a hot-blooded man, and your pursuit of pleasure and vengeance will lead you to greater trouble in the future. Your courage is a sham, and you will always be denied the wealth and power that you crave—"

Bliss's face clouded with anger and he jerked his hand out of Adriana's grasp. "How dare you!" he spat. "You damned Gypsy wench! Does my palm also say that I intend to have you for my own—that I *will* have you?"

Adriana stood and glared down at Bliss with eyes that had gone as hard as emeralds. "Never in a thousand years," she vowed, furiously tossing caution to the wind. "The things I saw in your hand are no fault of mine. They are truths that you, not I, must face. Now, leave my tent!"

Bliss stood so abruptly that his chair tipped over behind him. His face tight and red with anger, he stepped around the small table. "Who are *you* to order *me* about, girl?" he demanded fiercely. "You're nothing but a Gypsy. A Gypsy whore, if I don't miss my guess. And say what you will, but I'll have my shilling's worth of you!"

Where was Giuseppe? He should have returned to the tent by now to walk her back to their wagon. Trapped, Adriana searched desperately for a way out of her predicament. She could hear the muffled clamor of voices protesting the closing of the fair, and knew her own screams wouldn't sound much louder to anyone outside

—and they might possibly only antagonize her assailant even more. The tent was too tightly pegged down to allow a quick escape under its edge. Bliss now stood between her and the brass candleholder, the only possible weapon close at hand. "Get away from me," she hissed.

"Get away from me," Bliss mimicked mockingly, his eyes glittering with lust as he backed her into a shadowy corner. "Not likely, wench."

Feinting to his left, Adriana ducked and tried to dart under his right arm. Bliss's hand shot out, caught her arm, and roughly jerked her toward him. Before she could shout or scream, his mouth had found hers and was pressing against her lips in a cruel semblance of a kiss. When she tried to drop out of his grasp, his left hand cupped her buttocks and, his fingers digging into her flesh through her skirt, he pulled her lower body against his.

The evidence of his lust was sickening. Enraged, Adriana bit down hard on Bliss's lower lip and tasted blood. Bliss grunted in pain and, backing away, slapped her across the face with enough force to knock her against the wall of the tent. "Bitch!" he growled, wiping the blood from his chin. "Want to fight, eh?" He advanced upon her, grabbing a handful of her blouse and tearing it from her. "Think you have a chance, eh?" He seized her again and jerked her roughly to him. "Too good for Trevor Bliss?"

"Swine!" Adriana spat his own blood into Bliss's face.

Bliss froze, then slowly wiped the spittle from his face as Adriana tried to cover her breasts. "You've done it now, wench. You've gone too far." The anger had faded from his voice, replaced by the quiet determination of a man who has slipped into madness. "Fight if you want, but little good it'll do you. And I don't mind a bit."

The only defense against a madman was madness itself. With a bloodcurdling shriek, Adriana leaped at him, her fists bouncing futilely off his chest, her fin-

gers searching for his eyes. Bliss backhanded her and
knocked her down, then immediately dropped on top of
her, tearing at her skirt with one hand and restraining
her free arm with the other. Adriana almost gagged as
his tongue thrust into her mouth. She whipped her head
from side to side and tried to twist away. Bliss thrust
one knee between her legs, and in the process loosed her
right arm. Swinging blindly, Adriana's fist caught Bliss
in the throat. Gasping, Bliss loosened his grip, giving
her the slight space she needed to drive a knee into his
groin. Bliss grunted and fell back. The advantage momentarily hers, Adriana slashed out with her nails, and
then tried to crawl past him toward the tent's exit.

Blood welled out and flowed down Bliss's cheek. His
groin throbbed and his breath whistled in his throat.
Beside himself with rage and pain, he lunged after
Adriana and pinned her against the floor. Helpless, she
lay numb and weeping beneath his weight, tasting the
salt tang of blood on her lips, unable to cry out.

He had won! His pain forgotten, dizzy with anticipation, Bliss pushed himself to his knees and fumbled at
his breeches. The fight had excited him beyond measure; seldom had he been harder. His, by God! She was
his, and well worth the price paid, to judge by the sight
of her. Oblivious of everything else, he lowered himself
toward her.

"Whoreson bastard!" a voice roared.

Bliss's head jerked around and he tried to climb to his
feet. Giuseppe, a blade glinting in his hand, caught Bliss
by the collar and dragged him off Adriana. Wanting
only to escape, Adriana rolled into the far corner of the
tent and huddled defensively.

Giuseppe circled Bliss to place himself between
Adriana and her attacker. The knife inscribed a small
circle inches from Bliss's face. "Tell me why I shouldn't
kill you now, son of a dog," he hissed. "Tell me why I
shouldn't carve your face to ribbons and castrate you
like the swine you are."

"What's happening in here?"

Giuseppe looked up to see old Gregori framed in the entrance to the tent. The momentary distraction was all Bliss needed. Before anyone could stop him, he bowled Gregori over as he bolted from the tent.

"Giuseppe!" Adriana cried.

Stopped by her voice, Giuseppe hurried to kneel at her side.

"No, Brother," she gasped. "He did not take me, I swear it." She gripped his arm and wouldn't let him rise. "Do not try to stop him. He will only bring more trouble down on us. Stay with me, please. Help me to the wagon."

Giuseppe retrieved her shawl from the back of her chair and arranged it over her breasts. "I should have killed him," Giuseppe said, his rage turning to sorrow as he cradled his sister in his arms. "I am not a man. I should have killed him where he knelt!"

A loud, metallic click punctuated his sentence. "You should have," Bliss said from the entrance, "but you didn't."

Giuseppe had never used a firearm, but he knew the sound of one being cocked. "Hush, little one," he said, gently releasing Adriana. Careful not to move fast, he turned slowly toward Bliss and the twin-barreled pocket pistol that was aimed at him. "If you shoot, Englishman," he said calmly, "you will die. For my knife will find you . . ."

He was a blur of motion. His hand dipped to the sheath on his belt, rose smoothly, and loosed the deadly blade. At the same instant, Bliss fired. The shot was followed by a solid, sickening thump as a lead ball tore through Giuseppe's chest. His fingers clawing at the mortal wound, Giuseppe grunted in surprise and doubled over.

Bliss, smiling triumphantly, backed out of sight as Giuseppe collapsed.

"Oh, God!" Adriana sobbed, trying to stem the flowing blood with an embrace. "Oh, God, please!"

"Little one? Little one?" Disbelief written on his

face, Giuseppe stared up at his little sister. "I'm sorry," he rasped, and then he slumped wearily. The light in his eyes faded and flickered out, like a candle in the wind.

Her own pain was forgotten. "Giuseppe!" Adriana screamed, shaking him, trying to bring him back to life. "Giuseppe! No!" Dropping him, she half-crawled, half-ran to the entrance. "Murderer!" she howled into the night. "He murdered Giuseppe!"

Aroused by the sounds of the shot and Bliss's horse galloping away, men ran from every direction toward the tent. Old Gregori, momentarily dazed by the blow he had taken from Bliss, staggered to his feet and into the tent, now filled with acrid powder smoke and the stench of blood.

"Giuseppe is dead!" Adriana cried out in anguish to anyone who would listen. "My brother is dead!"

And then the world tilted crazily. Too late, she realized that she was falling. Footsteps pounded the earth around her, voices were raised in fearful questioning and alarm. There was an inviting pool of blackness in front of her that promised peaceful oblivion and escape from grief. Without hesitation, Adriana dived in, and slipped gratefully all the way to the bottom.

Gregori's voice was quiet and soothing. "Revenge is useless," he said. "There is no justice for the Gypsy in the courts of the English. You know this, Adriana. Giuseppe himself would tell you as much."

Adriana rested beside the wagon that until tonight she had shared with Giuseppe. She stared up at the stars, and made no reply to the elder's statement because she knew he was right. The Gypsies were tolerated in England because of the pleasure and diversion their fairs brought to normally dull lives, but they had no legal standing in a country where law and justice were rooted in a system based on ownership of real property, a concept completely foreign to her people. Attempting to bring charges against Bliss would be useless. And, deserving of vengeance though he was, killing him would only bring harm to the whole tribe.

"One day this man—this demon!—will go too far," Gregori continued when Adriana did not speak. "His deeds will catch up to him, I swear it! Now, you must come away with us. You must go on with your life, Adriana, and put this terrible crime behind you. Giuseppe would want—"

Adriana whirled to face the old man, the icy control and calm she had demanded of herself ever since she had come up from that black pool of unconsciousness finally shattering. "Stop telling me what Giuseppe would want!" she blazed. "Giuseppe wanted to *live,* as we all want to live, but he is dead, and none of us can change that! All we can do for Giuseppe now is avenge his murder." The Gypsies were readying to leave this place where death had visited them with his ghastly grinning countenance. Middle of the night or not, they were leaving after only one day of the fair. It was for the best, Gregori had decided. "Go with your people, old man!" Adriana said to him.

"They are your people, too," he told her in a quavering voice. "You will take a man . . . have children. Life goes on, child!"

Adriana shook her head. Forgotten was Saul, forgotten the ties of blood and tradition that bound her to the tribe. "So it does, and so I shall," she said with a voice as cold as a winter night. "But not here, for there are things I must do, and I have no wish to harm my people. The path I take can only be traveled alone."

"You mean to kill this Lieutenant Trevor Bliss." Gregori's words were a flat statement, not a question.

"I mean to avenge my brother's death."

"But, child . . ." The old man was pleading now. "You know no other life."

Adriana took a deep breath and looked to the stars again, her green eyes searching. "Then, perhaps," she said, "it is time for me to learn another."

~ CHAPTER II ~

"Tell me, lass, and be true, for it's my future you hold there."

Work-worn and weather-cracked, the man's hand lay palm upward under Adriana's unwavering gaze. Cold seeped through the shuttered and rag-chinked window, hovered around the table and chairs set close by the hearth. Outside, the sky was dark with clouds and the ground with soot-stained snow. London in January was a dreary place.

The man across the table from Adriana was a tall, spare, hard-bitten sea captain in his mid-thirties. His hair was covered with a black knitted cap and his close-cropped beard trimmed his jawline with a fringe of brown shot through with white. His brows were thick, his eyes dark-brown and stern. Deep lines etched his face, which at one time might have been considered kindly, but by the year of our Lord 1810 could only be called hard and careworn. His name was Isaiah Hawkins, and he was desperately in need of counsel.

Isaiah had expected to find a withered crone when he set out to seek the Gypsy rumored to possess powers beyond those of the ordinary fortune-teller. Angel Street, where she lived, was lined with dilapidated buildings that housed charlatans who existed to cheat poor salts out of their hard-earned wages, and harlots who enticed the unwary to squander whatever money they had left for a moment of love and a lifetime of disease. Number 17 leaned precariously, and its front door was stuck open. The hall stank of an excess of unwashed

25

humanity. The banister was missing from the wooden second-floor landing, which was decorated with the half-eaten, frozen carcass of a foot-long rat. When Isaiah's knock was answered, his surprise had been total, for—bundled though she was against the cold— there could have been no doubt that the Gypsy was anything but a crone.

"I see a white bird," Adriana said at last, breaking the trancelike silence into which she had fallen. "A stately fowl that glides across the water."

"A swan!" Isaiah gasped. "My ship, the *Swan of Yorkshire!* She rides at dock along River Street."

"But not for long," Adriana said. "The swan is free under a fair sky . . ."

"Aye, free. A comely brig, she is, eager to leave this black city in her wake. And if she never returns, it'll be soon enough for me."

It required no seer to sniff out the despair that haunted him, the bitterness that poisoned his soul. "You've had troubles—more than your share," Adriana murmured sympathetically.

"Troubles, hah! Yes, I'd call them that. A man is bilked of his profits by a lord of the realm. On the next voyage he springs so bad a leak he has to heave overboard a whole cargo of rice or be split in two when the damn stuff swells. And then I return from a hard nine months of dodging pirates and bring to port a load of prime tobacco, only to find the price is down and my creditors are trying to attach my beautiful *Swan*. And if that's not enough, my wife's run off with a tanner!" His face reddened and his eyes bulged. "A tanner, mind ye! A brown-handed, stinking landlubber of a tanner!"

"Perhaps you're better off without her," Adriana suggested.

"And my cottage, too? That I worked and slaved for, and half-built myself with these two hands? Ahhh . . ." He stared at his hand a long moment, then suddenly pulled it free of Adriana's grasp. "What's the use? My course is set no matter what you say. The future's fairer elsewhere. I'll sneak some cargo aboard and sell it where I may. I've got plans." He took out his purse, extracted a shilling, and dropped it on the table. "That's for your time and trouble, lass."

Adriana slid the coin back to him. "Very little time and no trouble," she said with a smile as warm as the room was cold. She stood and took two mugs from the mantel. "I'll not take money I haven't earned. Neither will I send a man into the cold without a spot of something hot to warm his stomach. Will you have a cup of tea with me?"

Isaiah stared quizzically at her, at last let himself lean back and relax. "Aye," he said, his face softening, "it's been a long time since anyone's refused to take my money or offered me something for nothing." His eyes crinkled with a rare smile. "I'll take that tea, lass, and gladly."

The tea was hot and strong. Adriana warmed her hands on her mug and sat looking into the fire. "I wish you well, you know," she said, her voice soft against the hiss of the fire. "It's not easy when the world turns against you."

"No, it's not." Isaiah propped his feet on the hearth, felt the tension drain from his joints. The coin lay untouched on the table. The girl's hair spilled silk-soft and deep-auburn from under her kerchief. Her lips, full and sensual in profile, invited kisses. Her emerald eyes—he could close his own and see them—had the power to delve into a man and set his soul to singing. His mouth dry, he glanced at the coin and then back to Adriana. "You could earn it yet," he said.

Adriana sighed and looked around the apartment. The single room, not even her own, overlooked Angel Street. It was furnished with a broken-down chest of drawers and a rickety bed large enough for two, a table with one broken and splinted leg, a ladderback chair, and a stool. Three age-cracked wooden truncheons were

propped on the mantel next to a small box that held four
pewter spoons and a bone-handled knife. A candle in a
rough wooden candlestick stood at each end of the
mantel, and a third sat on the table, providing the room
with its sole source of illumination. The only bright spot
in the otherwise somber interior was a torn and threadbare multicolored quilt that covered the bed.

And so it comes to this. . . . But what man, under
the circumstances and considering the surroundings,
wouldn't try to buy her? God only knew that others had
tried, though usually—the comparison amused her—for
much more than a shilling. "I don't want your money,"
she said with a shy smile meant to ease his embarrassment.

Her quiet, unassuming dignity shamed him: he had
offended her, and cheapened himself. Isaiah's face reddened. He lowered his eyes and then, realizing that he
was staring at the soft line of her breasts under her
heavy shawl, averted them altogether. "Your pardon,"
he stammered. " 'Twas an ill-conceived notion. I mean
. . . oh, damn it all, what've I come to? I knew you
weren't no tart. The apology of a fool carries little
weight in this world, but it's the only kind I can offer.
I'll not take the shilling, though," he said adamantly.
He stood and once again slid the coin toward her, then
froze as she reached out and covered his hand with her
own.

"Gypsy women give freely of themselves for pleasure
or love, but not for money. I hold no ill will toward you.
It was an easy enough mistake to make. Angel Street
tends to do that to a man. And who knows? Perhaps if
we'd met under different circumstances . . ." The room
was cold and bleak, but her smile made it a cheerier
place. "I'd guess a woman could expect many a pleasur-
able hour with a kind, handsome man such as yourself."

Pleased by the compliment, Isaiah straightened his
shoulders and smoothed the wrinkles out of his waist-

coat. "You ought to quit this place, you know. Get yourself somewhere decent, with clean, fresh air and trees and sky." The idea struck him so suddenly that he blurted it out without thinking. "Come with me, then! Quit this whole bloody black island. I've room for a fair lass like yourself aboard the *Swan of Yorkshire*. And no demands, either, save perhaps you read a palm or two for my lads."

"Come with you?" Adriana asked, taken aback.

"Have you ever been to America? Or the Caribbean? They're far fairer places than this hellhole, by m'oath."

Adriana almost laughed, but stopped herself when she saw his proposal was serious. "You're very kind," she said gently, "but I can't. I couldn't possibly until . . ." Her mood darkened. "There's . . . something, a task I've got to finish. I'm sorry."

"Ahhh." Isaiah waved away her apology, pulled on his overcoat, and started for the door. People had their secrets, and there were some things best left unknown. *"Swan of Yorkshire,"* he repeated from the open door. "If you change your mind, we sail the day after tomorrow on the morning tide." He looked down as a calico cat, its fur ruffled against the cold, glided between his legs and padded into the room. "Remember . . . River Street, the day after tomorrow."

"I will," Adriana promised, picking up the cat and cradling it in her arms. "Godspeed, Captain Hawkins."

The door closed and she was alone with the cat and the fading sound of footsteps on the stairs. *And why not follow him? Why not sail off to a far fairer place?*

"Free, kitty," she whispered, her cheek warm against the calico fur. "But not of Giuseppe's ghost."

Damn Trevor Bliss! Damn his soul to eternal hell! It was he, not I, who wrote his name in blood and sealed his fate.

"And mine, too," she told the cat. "My fate, too."

The dream ended in cold. She stood at one end of a

long hall carved in ice. The light was dim and blue, and at the far end, a laughing Trevor Bliss mocked her and beckoned to her. Half-mad, she ran toward him, only to discover that the gap between them never closed no matter how fast she ran. And how Bliss laughed to watch her try and try, and run and run and run. . . .

Adriana stirred under the quilt and the tumble of patched blankets and looked up as the door to the apartment creaked open and closed. She glanced at the window and saw light through the cracks. "It's morning already?" she asked.

Her only answer was a noncommittal grunt, followed by a puffing sound. Seconds later, a candle flared, illuminating the room. "You were out all night?" she asked.

An old man with scraggly white wisps of hair poking out beneath a wool cap set the candle on the table and squatted to hold his hands over the coals in the fireplace. "And you let the fire go out," he rasped.

He looked as if he lived in his thick, baggy wool coat. In truth, he wore the garment all fall and winter. Only when spring came did he take it off and begin to peel away the layers of clothing underneath it. As the weather warmed, off would come a thick sweater, a vest, and two shirts, right down to the ragged, stained undershirt he wore during the heat of summer. A gold earring gleamed in his ear. His teeth—the five he had left—were yellow and cracked. They were also a source of constant pain, a pain he endured rather than risk his life with one of London's barbers, who had been known to extract chunks of jawbone in the process of pulling teeth. He was as thin as a reed, he limped, and he reeked of the cheap tobacco he continually smoked in an ancient clay pipe, which was, considering the years he had gone without a bath, a blessing. He looked as much a discard of the human race as a man could, and still be alive.

Paolo Belisarrio was also a magician—or had been at

one time. He had left Adriana's tribe when she had been an infant and had gone to London to seek his fortune. He had been forty at the time, and his dark good looks, long and wavy hair—more elegant than any wig—and his flashing teeth and deep laugh had attracted a high-born lady with a title. The lady's husband was in his dotage; Paolo was vibrant and alive, as well as wise and thoughtful in the ways of love. Charming her, he had lived a charmed life until, one day, the spell was broken and his brush with prosperity came to an abrupt end. Though he never again attained such heights, neither did he forget those he'd once ascended. Old, bent, frail, and decrepit he might have been, but his spirit lived on.

"It's bad luck to let a fire die down this far," he grumped, removing a handful of kindling from one of his pockets. "I let you sleep in my room, and what do you do?"

"Clean it," Adriana said, baiting him.

"Bah. You forget to log the fire." He blew on the coals and added the kindling stick by stick until he'd built a cheerful blaze. "And I must sleep in the street or break my back on the floor because you steal my bed."

"There's room for both of us, Uncle, if you'll only scrub off a half-dozen layers of dirt."

"You're an ungrateful child who'd have me freeze to death. So tell me. What else did you pilfer while I was gone?"

"Oh, it's a thief I am now?" Adriana asked, rising and handing Paolo a burlap sack she pulled from under the bed. "I ask you, what kind of thief is it who brings you cheese and bread and a jug of wine to fill that shrunken parcel you call a stomach? Uncle, your only virtue is ingratitude. It will make a poor epitaph."

Paolo snorted to keep from laughing, dug into the sack, and took out the jug of wine. Immediately, he un-corked it and drank, then gasped and lowered it to the table. "Whoresons," he croaked. "That's brewed from coals, not grapes. Live coals."

"Far be it from you to offer thanks," Adriana said with mock anger.

"Perhaps, perhaps not," Paolo said, his eyes twinkling. "Watch." He waved his hand and, fingers wiggling, plucked an imaginary scrap of paper from the air and held it out for Adriana. "For you. It's a note."

"A note?" Adriana asked, playing along and pretending to try to read it. "The light's bad. Perhaps you've read it?"

"I didn't have to," Paolo said, cackling. "I wrote it." He sat down, emptied the sack, and rubbed his hands in glee. "How unfair your description of me. Paolo the ungenerous, Paolo the ungrateful." He pointed a finger at the invisible note. "My gift may well prove your undoing, girl, mark my words. Still, it's the gift you asked for."

Breathless, Adriana sat across the table from him. "You found Bliss?"

"He's in London." Paolo carved a thick slice of cheese and tore off a chunk of bread. "But not for long. The press-gangs are filling out the crew for his ship, the *Druid*. As soon as men and provisions are aboard, he's setting sail."

Adriana paled. She couldn't let Bliss slip through her grasp. She had to find him before he embarked, or lose all hope of avenging Giuseppe. "You know where he is?" she asked.

"It is said he frequents a particular tavern. A wench there caters to his wants."

"The name, old man, the name!" Adriana snapped.

Paolo stuffed his mouth with bread, poking in a piece of cheese for good measure. "Written on the note in your hand," he managed to say, crumbs spilling from his mouth.

Adriana crumpled the imaginary note in her fist and threw it into the fire. "Curse the note and you as well, Uncle, if you withhold the name. He killed Giuseppe. I swear, my brother's ghost will haunt you as he does me if you don't tell me."

Paolo frowned, chewed deliberately, and appeared deep in thought. "Very well," he finally said, swallowing. "But first you must disguise yourself . . ."

Paolo had given her the news at nine in the morning. At ten, dressed in rags and a heavy, nondescript greatcoat, looking for all the world like an urchin, she had followed Paolo to the back door of the Cub and Calf and was introduced to the maid who had been Paolo's informer. Bliss was still inside, the maid had said, but there was no telling when he would leave. Adriana would simply have to wait. Her wait had been long, boring, and cold. A north wind that cut through the heaviest clothes brought snow flurries. If it hadn't been for Paolo, who brought her warm bricks from the hearth, and the maid, who let her sneak into the kitchen and warm herself every hour or so, she wouldn't have made it through the day. What the night would bring, she couldn't imagine.

The temperature plummeted with nightfall. Six o'clock came and went. A young man entered the Cub and Calf. No one left. Seven o'clock. Four more newcomers. Eight o'clock. A particularly frigid gust eddied through the recessed entryway to Ashley's Coffee Shop, where Adriana huddled across the street from the Cub and Calf. She dug her hands deeper into her pockets, stamped her feet to keep them warm, and then forgot the cold as the tavern door opened.

At last. She tensed, and gripped the handle of Giuseppe's dagger. *Let it be he before I freeze. Please, God. . . .*

Four gentlemen exited, cursed the brutal cold, and, hiding their chins in their mufflers, plunged down the street in search of a coach. Not one of them wore a uniform. Bliss was still inside.

Disappointment sapped her strength. Adriana beat her arms against her sides, sat disconsolately, and stared at the brightly lighted windows across the street. *How grand it must be to have one's pockets lined with silver, to revel over cups of hot buttered rum, to enjoy the toasty warmth of a well-fed fire, to feast on hot meat pies and sweet pastries!* The cold seemed even more intense. Paolo had promised to return with more heated bricks at eight, and was overdue. If nothing happened in the next few minutes, she'd have to go around to the back of the Cub and Calf again. *So cold . . . so tired. . . .*

The jingle of a harness and the clip-clop of hooves brought her to her senses. Edging away from the door, Adriana watched as a carriage slowed and stopped in front of the coffee shop, and as the driver climbed down from his perch. "That'll be four bob, sir," he said, opening the door and tipping his hat. "Hope you had a pleasant ride, sir. A nasty night."

The interior of the coach was lighted and looked warm. An elderly gentleman wearing a gray greatcoat, a thick wool scarf, and a fur hat dug in his pocket and paid the driver while his companion busied herself arranging her fur-trimmed cloak and slipping her hands into a fur muff.

If I only had a muff. A nice warm lamb's-wool muff. . . .

"Poor lad."

Adriana looked up as the gentleman stopped in front of her. "Evenin' to you, sir," she stammered, her teeth chattering.

"What's your name, lad?"

"Really, Sir Charles," the lady sniffed.

"Uh, John, sir."

Sir Charles peeled off one glove, found a coin in his pocket. "No pillow for your head this wintry night, eh? Well, here's a little treat, then."

"God bless you, sir," Adriana said, staring at the warm penny that lay in her hand.

"And God bless you, John," Sir Charles said. And then, warmed by his largesse, he waved his companion ahead of him and disappeared into Ashley's in search of conversation and a piping-hot cup of mocha.

A penny wasn't much, but at least Adriana would have something to give the maid to repay her for her kindness. The coach blocked her view of the Cub and Calf, but suddenly she was aware of bright light on the snow and a swelling of music and laughter.

"You there, coachman!"

Bliss's voice! Do you hear, Giuseppe?

"Aye, sir," the coachman called back as he settled into his seat high above the ground.

"If you're free, my friends and I will hire you."

Adriana ran to her right, peeked around the coach, and saw Bliss standing with two companions in front of the Cub and Calf. But how . . . ?

"I'm free, but for a fee, good sir," the coachman quipped.

"Better to pay a fee than freeze for free," Bliss shot back, to the amusement of his friends.

You may laugh now, Adriana thought, *but not for much longer.*

The coachman was looking toward Bliss and his friends, who were not aware of Adriana's presence. Giuseppe's ghost seemed to guide her. Warmth spreading through her, she padded soundlessly to the side of the coach opposite her quarry, turned the handle, and opened the door.

"Three bob to the Anacreon, sir," the coachman said.

Slowly, being careful not to rock the coach, Adriana eased her weight onto the step . . .

"A bargain, coachman," Bliss said. "Come along, lads."

. . . and into the coach. It was a coach fit for a gentleman, for a captain in the King's Navy, for a murderer. Polished mahogany gleamed in the dim lantern light. The smell of fine tobacco lingered in the air. The leather was soft and smooth to the touch. Adriana slipped Giuseppe's dagger free, blew into her hand to warm it, and crouched, ready to spring.

How many months had she waited? How many days, hours? Unbidden, the scene in the tent replayed itself. Her fear, her pain; Giuseppe's anger, his love. And then the hated face of Trevor Bliss as he stood just inside the tent flap, the ugly muzzle of the pistol, Giuseppe's warning, the flash and explosion and Giuseppe's life-blood warm on her hands. . . .

Everything happened very slowly. She heard footsteps approaching, saw the inside handle turn. She felt the slight vibration as the door began to swing open, the blast of cold air. She saw an expanding wedge of dark-blue fabric and above it the paleness of an as yet unsuspecting face. She felt the carriage sag as it accepted the weight, heard the sharp creak of cold springs, clearly saw the face before realization dawned . . .

"My God! You!"

Adriana lunged. Bliss fell backward. The carriage rocked and threw Adriana off balance and her dagger went directly up Bliss's sleeve, slicing a long, deep furrow in his arm.

"No!" he shouted, falling into the arms of his astonished friends. "Help!"

Like a cat, Adriana sprang, but lost her footing on the ice. She came up slashing before Bliss's startled companions could react. The blade ripped across Bliss's chest, but was turned by the heavy greatcoat. Screaming with rage, Adriana tried to stab him but lost her knife when it was torn from her grasp.

"I've got it! Stand back!" one of the men shouted.

Adriana heard the rasp of steel, saw the dim glow of light on a drawn cane sword, and barely avoided being run through.

"Foul play! Murder afoot!" the man shouted, pressing his counterattack.

Adriana leaped backward into the coach, rolled, and tumbled out the opposite door. The hatred that had driven her was replaced by fear. If they caught her . . . ! She had to escape.

She tried to get up and run, but one foot caught in her coat and she tripped, falling onto the icy street. Pain ripped through her elbow and she gasped with shock.

"Go around the back!" one of the men was shouting as the carriage rocked violently.

Another was coming straight at her, the third would cut her off from the rear. Desperate, she hauled herself upright on the rear wheel, stepped on one spoke, the rim, the windowsill, and finally hauled herself onto the roof.

"See here, now. What's all this about?" Awkwardly, bundled up as he was, the coachman half-rose and twisted as he struggled to cock a horse pistol.

Adriana sat, held on to the luggage rack, and kicked. One foot caught the portly driver in the chest, the other in the shoulder. Thrown off balance, he tottered and, arms flailing, shouted in alarm as he somersaulted through the air and landed with a bone-jarring impact, inadvertently discharging his gun.

The men who poured out of the Cub and Calf were too late to help. Already frightened, the team was off and running at the sound of the shot, leaving Bliss, his companions, the outraged coachman, and a dozen would be assistants behind. Adriana's cap was whipped from her head. Tears froze on her cheeks. She crawled forward and fell into the driver's seat where she could grab the reins before they were jerked loose by the panicked team.

She'd never handled a four-horse team, much less one that was bolting. The carriage bounced crazily across one ice-rutted intersection, flashed through a second, and almost collided with a dray. Adriana braced her feet against the footboard, hauled on the reins with all her might, and somehow forced the horses into a turn at the fourth intersection.

Iron-rimmed wheels struck sparks from bare patches of cobblestone. A blizzard of ice chips and blowing snow churned into the air in the carriage's wake. The horses swerved to avoid an oncoming coach, whose cursing driver was forced to pull his team onto the walk. Adriana clung to her perch and managed to stretch one leg toward the brake and jam the wooden lever forward. The carriage slued to the left and slowed the horses. The sharp edges of the wheels bit into the ice and stopped suddenly, tipping the carriage and throwing Adriana free. The carriage hit with an earsplitting crash; Adriana landed in a cushioning snowdrift, rolled, and smacked into a wood picket fence.

Snow had been forced up her sleeves, down the back of her neck, and into her ears and nose. The pain in her elbow was excruciating. The world spun, and only gradually slowed to a stop and righted itself. Adriana hauled herself to her feet and stared at the panting, wild-eyed horses and the coach that lay, wheels spinning, on its side. The accident was attracting a crowd. Sailors and their wenches spilled out of nearby taverns and, ignoring the cold, surrounded the overturned coach. "Anyone inside?" one called.

"I'll look. Gimme a 'and, there, Freddie. Well, I'll be damned, the bloody thing's empty—and on fire! Bring some buckets, lads! Let's 'ave some—" He stopped in mid-sentence and pointed at Adriana. "Wot's this? Hey, lad, were you drivin' this 'ere— Hey! Come back!"

Oblivious of the crowd's calls, and hoping the onlookers would be preoccupied by the fire and the still-terrified horses, Adriana darted down the street and into the nearest alley. A moment later, with no sign of pursuit, she emerged on the docks and slumped out of breath in the recessed doorway of a warehouse. Melting snow dribbled down her back. Her hands were freezing, her whole body ached. She had failed: Bliss lived. Worse, she'd been recognized, and Bliss would see to it that she was hounded until brought to justice. To remain in London meant arrest and incarceration, not only for her but for Uncle Paolo and anyone else who had extended a hand to her in friendship. She couldn't even rejoin the tribe in their winter quarters, for surely she would be sought there as well. Her only choice was to leave England.

I failed you, Giuseppe. Failed you, failed myself. What am I to do?

Never, not even on the night Giuseppe had died, had she felt so lost or alone. She'd had her anger then, and a purpose. Now there was only her failure and a sense of complete helplessness. She clenched her fists and tried to stop her tears. There was no time for weakness; there was only time for escape. Escape and survival until she could somehow, some way, find Bliss again.

You'll freeze. Keep moving. You can't give up. Not now, not ever.

Willing herself to her feet, Adriana stumbled into the open and started down the dock. To her right, black ships rode at anchor. Masts like spires jutted into the black night sky.

Spires . . . churches . . . sanctuary . . . escape . . .

She stopped, shook her head, and tried to remember.

A white bird . . . a swan . . .

A snowflake brushed her cheek, then another and another, until the air was thick with great silent fleecy flakes that obscured her vision.

River Street . . . day after tomorrow. . . . Dear God, but it's tomorrow morning now!

She trudged eight long blocks before she found River Street, then searched a half-hour before she located what she sought. At last, reeling from exhaustion and exposure, and hidden from prying eyes by the thickly falling snow, she stumbled up the gangplank and fell, half-senseless, aboard the *Swan of Yorkshire*.

⤮ CHAPTER III ⤮

Tom Gunn Paxton knelt on one knee. Slowly, he reached out to place a colorful bouquet of azalea and mountain laurel on the well-tended grave before him, then lowered his head and gathered Jenny in his memory.

An imposing rough-hewn slab of native South Carolina granite at the south end of the small cemetery proclaimed the family name: Paxton. Smaller headstones marked the individual resting spots of the tightly knit family, and it was in front of the newest of these that Tom Gunn knelt.

JENNIFER LOUISE
WIFE OF THOMAS GUNN

B. APRIL 18, 1788
D. APRIL 22, 1810

She had been twenty-two, just twenty-two, and had been gone six months. More than anything in the world, Tom Gunn Paxton longed to hear her laughter, to watch her face radiant in the morning light, to live again in the beauty of their lovemaking. The earth was warm to the touch, but not as warm as it had been when she was aglow with life. Six months. It seemed years since the fever, the pneumonia that was the old man's friend and the young man's bane, had stolen her from him. It had seemed impossible—she had been so young and vital and alive.

It was the second Sunday in October, and a heavy, moist heat shackled the day despite the early hour and cold weather of two nights earlier. So small was the secluded island glade where the Paxtons laid their own to rest that the sun had yet to penetrate the heavy foliage surrounding it. On all sides, swamp water lay smooth as brown glass. Nearby a towering cypress stood sentinel-like without a single leaf moving. On the western edge of the high ground, moss hung like fog from three ancient giant oaks. Nothing stirred; not even the faintest breeze. The only indication of the teeming life beyond the boundaries of the cemetery was the incessant humming and buzzing of insects and an occasional splash as a rotted twig fell or a small creature made its way through the dim and dangerous world where, sooner or later, all small creatures were eaten.

Sweat ran down Tom's face and plastered his shirt to his sides. Sighing, he cleared away a blade of grass that had grown over Jenny's headstone, and stood. As always, the few minutes of meditation had helped calm the deep anger that ate away at him. Jenny and he had been married just a few months short of four years, and there were too many good things, too many happy memories, for him to permit anger to rule his life. Softly, as on every Sunday, he whispered goodbye to his Jenny, and turned and walked down the narrow causeway that separated the cemetery island from the rest of the world.

Tom Gunn Paxton was a tall and rangy man of twenty-seven years, with a face that had known punishment. A black patch covered his blinded left eye. Thick black hair that he tied back when there was heavy work to be done hung to his shoulders. His forehead was high and broad over his one penetrating light blue-gray eye. His mouth was wide, and he smiled easily, somewhat softening his otherwise harsh features. His shoulders, back, and chest were smoothly muscled and deeply tanned from hours of hard work in the sun, and his hands, though broad and obviously strong, somehow gave the impression of a softness of touch that didn't match the rest of him.

The narrow trail threaded its way north before joining the main path that led inland to Solitary. A wrought-iron fence, more decorative than necessary, stretched across the end of the narrow path. Brushing the dirt from his twill trousers, Tom strode through, latched the gate, and untethered his horse. It was time to return to Solitary, say good morning to the twins, and get to work.

Reaching the main road wasn't easy, even if the path he had come along an hour earlier was the only way back. The nagivation required to prevent one from going astray—more a gut feeling for swamps than anything else—was no mean feat. If a person did lose his way, he could run in circles until he dropped and died of exhaustion if the snakes or the heat or the insects didn't get him first. Having a swamp-wise horse helped considerably. All Tom had to do was prod the clay-colored mare into motion, point her nose back along the path she'd negotiated for six months of Sundays, and sit back and relax. And, of course, swat mosquitoes, brush away low-hanging moss and fresh cobwebs, and keep an eye out for snakes that could spook even his swamp-wise horse.

Tom usually found a special beauty in the swamp, but this morning it was too oppressive and filled with death and decay, fueling his already dark mood. Only thirty-five years ago, the Paxtons had lived beyond the edge of the swamp near the Atlantic, where Jason Brand and the pirate Marie Ravenne, known as Raven, had landed a century earlier and taken the name of Paxton. Tom's grandfather, though, a careful man, had chosen to relocate farther inland during the War for Independence. In the years since, his grandfather and father, and now Tom himself, had built Solitary into one of the most impressive plantations in South Carolina.

There was no question but that the family had done well for itself. Tom had been running Solitary for the last two years. His father, Jason Behan Paxton, and mother, Cassandra-Colleen, who everyone called Colleen, had moved back to the family home in Brandborough, where Jason reigned as the town patriarch. Benjamin, Tom's younger brother, had ventured west three years earlier and sent back occasional messages that a man who knew mules could make a fortune—which he was doing—and that he was having the time of his life. Hope Elaine, Tom's sister, was married to a horse breeder in Tennessee. Tom hadn't seen Hope Elaine for over two years, but her letters indicated that she was happy and more than satisfied with her lot in life. And as for himself?

Ah, Jenny, Jenny.

Shadows washed over him in the hypnotic calm, the emerald twilight closeness of the swamp.

Jenny, Jenny. What did you say?

His mind reached back into the past to pick a memory out of a host of memories like a rose from a bouquet. He knew he would prick himself on the thorns, but didn't care.

Forever? The very word you used as we fled to London. Forever. . . .

Tom's visit to England in 1806 had begun as a business trip, but had turned into much more. Not only would he bring home a shipload of wool fabric and cutting tools and sundry other articles and goods to be sold and traded in Charleston, but a bride as well.

A heavy overcast had delayed the dawn. Inside the carriage house behind the Vincent country mansion, all was dark and still. Tom carefully felt his way through the building until all the doors were closed and the windows shuttered. Only then did he remove the hood from the lantern he'd brought and load his carpetbag and rifle into the small fast barouche he'd selected earlier.

The next step was riskier because he knew he couldn't avoid making noise. Working quickly, he selected the tack he'd need for the barouche and carried the rest to the stable, where he hid it under a pile of hay.

A horse nickered, another beat a tattoo on a stall wall. Tom held his breath, but the groom, who slept in a small room off the stable, snored on contentedly. Tom coaxed his favorite pair of bay geldings out of their stalls and led them into the carriage house, where he hitched them quickly to the barouche. Finished, he paused and took a deep breath. Everything was ready, and the minute Jenny arrived they could leave her father's country estate and make for London, there to board the Paxton ship that waited to set sail for South Carolina.

The side door creaked. Tom shielded the lantern and ducked out of sight.

"Tom?" a voice whispered. "It's me."

"Close the door." He heard the door close, then opened the lantern and hurried to meet her and help carry her bags. "You have everything?"

"I think so." Jennifer stretched up on tiptoe and kissed him on the cheek. Dressed in a simple beige traveling gown, her pale, narrow shoulders hidden by a lined lace shawl, and a bonnet covering her long honey-blond hair, Jennifer Louise Vincent looked absolutely radiant. Only eighteen, five years younger than Tom, she retained a simple girlish innocence, yet was far from being a mere girl. The master artist, love, had blessed her with subtly blushing cheeks which complemented her classically high cheekbones, pert nose, and full rose-colored lips that were sensual and yet almost regally demure. Most striking, however, were her eyes. Amethyst, they were widely spaced, frank, open, and compassionate; they drew people to her, as they had certainly drawn Tom the moment he met her. "We'd better hurry," she said, giving his arm a squeeze. "The servants will be up and about any minute. Someone may have heard or seen me as it is."

"They'll be too late to stop us," Tom assured her, leading her to the barouche. "I hid the tack, and I can't imagine your father riding bareback." He loaded Jenny's bags and helped her into the backseat. "Up you go. I'll get the doors and we'll be on our way."

Tense and a bit breathless, Jenny settled into her seat. Tom brushed his lips across hers, then shielded the lantern and plunged the carriage house into deep shadow again. He groped his way to the large doors that led outside and, wincing at every squeak and rasp, carefully opened them. The sky was lighter outside, gray instead of black, revealing a line of thunderheads sweeping toward them from the north. Tom ran back to the carriage and swung up onto the driver's perch. Restless, the horses moved back and forth in their traces and stamped the hard ground. "Ready?" he asked, looking over his shoulder at Jenny.

"I'm ready," she replied with a brave smile.

"Stand where you are!" a furious voice shouted from the open doors.

"Oh, Lord!" Tom groaned, his heart almost stopping.

"Father!" Jenny gasped.

"Light," the same voice snapped.

A second silhouetted figure stepped forward and uncovered a lantern. Bright light bathed a scene in which the players were frozen in place: Jenny, fright etched on her delicate features, in the rear seat of the barouche; Tom, looking hard and wary, on the driver's seat.

"Damn me for a fool, but they were right," Sir Theodotus swore, stepping into the carriage house. A man of medium height, his confident, almost imperial demeanor made him appear massive and threatening despite his almost comical nightclothes. Sparse white hair—he had forgotten his wig in the rush—ruffled in the amber light as a breeze swept through the doors. A full white moustache bristled under his large, bulbous nose as he glared at the elopers. "Give me the light, Pendergrast."

Pendergrast, the burly head butler, obeyed with alacrity.

Dressed in a nightshirt, robe, and slippers, Sir Theodotus approached the barouche. "Get out of that carriage, Jennifer Louise," he commanded, "and return immediately to your room."

Jenny shook her head. "No, Father." Her voice quavered, but she gained strength of purpose with each word. "Tom and I are leaving. We're to be married, and we're going to America."

"Nonsense," Sir Theodotus growled. "Paxton, is this how you repay the hospitality of a man who's invited you into his home? My God, man, we've done business together. We've eaten together. We've even *fished* together, and now you try to steal my daughter from me?"

"I asked you for Jenny's hand, sir," Tom reminded him in a deceptively soft voice. "We wanted your and Lady Eugenia's blessing, but you refused."

"Of course I refused," Sir Theodotus snapped. "You barely know my daughter, and she can't possibly know you. If she did, she'd never entertain such a ridiculous notion as this."

"We know each other well enough to be sure that we're in love," Jenny said defiantly. "I want to do this, Father, and I won't let you stop me. We *will* be married."

Sir Theodotus took a deep breath and jerked his head toward his servant. "Help my daughter out of that carriage, Pendergrast, and escort her to her room."

Pendergrast took a tentative step toward the barouche. "Miss Jennifer," he said, keeping a wary eye on the grim-visaged American, "why don't you do like your father says?"

Not hurrying, Tom picked up his rifle and let the barrel drift toward Pendergrast. Quailing at the sight, the servant stopped in his tracks. Brawling with the American was one thing. Getting killed was quite another.

"My God, Paxton! Put that weapon away!" Sir Theodotus said, shocked by the threat of violence.

"When we're safely away from here," Tom replied in the same soft voice. "I don't want to hurt anyone, but we're leaving, just as Jenny told you."

"I cannot allow that!"

"You'll have to allow it, sir. You have no other choice."

"You, sir, are a . . . a . . . barbarian!" Sir Theodotus sputtered through his moustache.

A ghost of a grin played across Tom's face. "Maybe," he allowed, "but if so, I'm a barbarian who's deeply in love with your daughter."

It was obvious that further argument with Tom was pointless. Confusion, frustration, and fury mingling in his voice, Sir Theodotus turned to his daughter. "Please don't do this, Jenny," he pleaded. "Your mother and I. . . . Well, damn it, you just can't be serious!"

"But I am, Father," Jenny replied gently. "More serious than I've ever been in my life."

"You'll be miserable. The colonies are no place for a young lady of your breeding and refinement. Think of all those savages and ruffians roaming about committing depredations and all manner of vile—"

"I might remind you, sir, that this is 1806," Tom interrupted. "The colonies, as you call them, have been free for over twenty years. And Jenny is going to be free there, too."

Sir Theodotus looked forlornly at Jenny, but she only nodded in agreement with Tom's statement. His face sagged and his shoulders slumped. "Since I can't reason with my daughter, it doesn't appear that I can stop you, Paxton."

"That's right, sir. You can't." Holding the rifle in one steady hand, Tom gathered the reins with the other. "So if, under the circumstances, you'd like to reconsider—"

"Never, damn you!" Sir Theodotus swore.

"Very well, then." Tom snapped the reins and the

horses bolted forward into the morning light.

"Paxton!" Sir Theodotus roared after the departing lovers. "This isn't over! You'll pay for this, I swear it!"

Determined to put as much distance as possible between the barouche and Sir Theodotus as quickly as he could, Tom whipped the horses into a fast trot. Ahead, the sky was clear and bright. Behind, lightning-filled clouds gathered. As long as they stayed ahead of the storm, they could outdistance any pursuit. Still, not until the Vincent estate was more than a mile behind them did Tom heave a sigh of relief and slow the team to an easier pace. Several miles later, Jenny called for him to stop, and climbed up beside him.

"You all right?" Tom asked, slipping one arm around her.

Jenny huddled against him. "It was awful," she finally said.

"But it's over, now. All we have to do is head for London, and then on home."

"Home," Jenny murmured. "South Carolina. And we'll be husband and wife."

"We certainly will. Until death does us part."

"And we'll love each other forever," Jenny whispered. "A beautiful word, forever. Forever and ever . . ."

With thunder rumbling far behind them, the carriage rolled on toward London.

Forever, Tom thought bitterly as he turned onto the broad wagon road that connected Solitary to Brandborough. *Forever. . . .* Only four years. It was strange, though, how he never felt alone when he visited Jenny's grave. Somehow, he could sense her spirit there—feel it as palpably as he could when he sat or played with or simply watched the twins.

The horse broke into a ragged trot as the land rose out of the swamp. The road widened and cut through a meadow lush with a third growth of hay that was ready to be cut if the weather held, then narrowed again, squeezed between towering rows of cane. Farther along, a large fenced field reserved for mares and their foals was dotted with huge shade oaks, two of which had been made into giant ornamental fence posts that marked the entrance to Solitary. Tom's pulse always quickened when he entered the long wide drive and saw the plantation house his grandfather and father had built. The sprawling two-story structure, its white-washed sides gleaming in the morning sun, was surrounded by trees, the most prominent a pair of venerable white oaks so enormous that no two men together could circle their trunks with their arms. The breeze cooling his face, Tom urged the clay-colored mare into a gallop, then reined in sharply by the hitching posts set in the ground on either side of the steps.

"Morning, Lavinia," he called, sliding off the mare and looping the reins around one of the posts. "Hot enough for you?"

"Sho' nuff, Mr. Tom." The black woman standing in the open front doors grinned back at him. "Goin' to be a real swamp swizzler, if'n yo ask me."

Tom raised an eyebrow at Lavinia's latest expression. "Where's Vestal?"

"Right here, Mr. Tom!" A young black boy, lean as a whip and moving just as fast, came tearing around the corner of the house. "I'll take care of her."

"She'll want a rubdown and some cool water. Hot and close in the swamp today. She must've sweat ten gallons. I know I did."

"Mind you be careful with that horse now, Vestal!" Lavinia called as the boy clambered onto the mare. "You *walk* it, you hear?" She handed Tom a tall glass of mint-flavored tea and watched him fondly while he drank. "I swear, that boy . . . !"

Dressed in a bright-red blouse and a long sky-blue skirt, with a red kerchief tied over her curly black hair, Lavinia was an impressive figure. Her sleeves were pushed back to reveal thick forearms that were not strangers to hard work. Her strong hands could deliver a resounding smack to the backside of a mischievous boy, too, Tom knew, for Lavinia had supervised the household and taken care of the Paxtons for twenty years. Now in her mid-thirties, though her waist was thick and lines were beginning to appear on her face, she was no less in charge than she had been when Tom was a boy. "Visitin' Miss Jenny again, Mr. Tom?" she asked, knowing he had been and watching intently for any sign that he was relapsing into the deep depression that had gripped him for weeks following Jenny's death.

"I took some flowers out there," Tom replied. Aware of her concern, he flashed her a quick grin to show that he was coping with the vestiges of his grief. "Stole them out of your garden again, I'm afraid."

"Shoot, frost'll get 'em soon anyways, so I'm glad you did. Make me feel like I'm givin' her somethin' too. Miss Jenny, she always did like pretty things."

"Speaking of which, where are those sons of mine? They weren't up when I rode out."

Lavinia's smile broadened, if that was possible. The Paxton twins were her special pride and joy. She was responsible for them when they were at Solitary, and it was more of an honor than a duty for her. She jerked her head toward the rear of the house. "They be around back playin' with Mr. Maurice. I figured it be all right, they like playin' with him so much."

"And he likes them too," Tom said. "Which is natural, I guess, seeing as we're the closest thing to a family he's got."

He strode along the verandah to the corner, hopped down, and walked rapidly through the side yard to the rear of the house.

A mountainous moccasin- and buckskin-outfitted man was whittling with a razor-sharp bone-handled hunting knife. Maurice Leakey sliced wood shavings off the stick for a moment, then held the knife and wood out to the boys. "Here ye go, lads. Which one wants to try first?"

"Me," the larger of the two said, clumsily grabbing for the knife.

"Mr. Maurice!" Lavinia yelled, bearing down upon them from the house.

"Now, Joseph, you got to handle a knife slow and careful," Leakey instructed, fitting the boy's hand around the handle and then hovering over him as he took a first awkward swipe at the wood.

"Joseph, you give me that knife this minute!" Lavinia ordered, snatching it away before Leakey could stop her.

"Now, look here—"

" 'Vinia took my knife, Uncle Maurice," Joseph wailed.

Lavinia stood toe to toe with Leakey and glared up at him. "You goin' to let that precious little boy slice his whole hand off with this thing!" she exploded, waving the knife in his face.

The two of them did make a picture, Tom thought as he held back and watched the confrontation. Two years older than Tom, Maurice had grown up more a Paxton than a Leakey, and the boys had run away to sea together in 1784. The next five years had been a time of pirates and shipwrecks and more dangers than most men faced in a lifetime. Maurice and Tom had been drunk together, fought together, womanized together, saved each other's lives a half-dozen times, and in the process had become closer than brothers. Tom remembered well the day he'd lost the sight in his left eye to the slash of a buccaneer's cutlass, only to have Maurice grab the pirate, lift him overhead, and snap his back like a twig. After the years of adventuring, the Paxton blood had finally drawn Tom home to help his father run the family business, business that had taken him to England, where he had met his beloved Jenny.

Maurice Leakey, in the meantime, had given up seafaring and had headed inland where the trackless hills and forests stole his heart forever from the sea. Ranging through Kentucky and Tennessee, he'd ventured all the way to the great rolling waters of the Mississippi before the news of Jenny's death, passed through no one knew how many mouths, had drawn him back. Not surprisingly, considering the imposing figure that he cut, Leakey dominated practically everyone with whom he came into contact—the exception being Lavinia, who wasn't impressed, and who didn't back down an inch.

"Take it easy, both of you." Tom laughed, stepping between them to break the stalemate. "Lavinia, give me the knife. The boys have to learn how to handle one sooner or later, and they're better off learning the right way from the right people. Besides, a nick now is a good way to avoid a serious cut later. We won't let them get hurt badly."

Lavinia looked skeptical, but handed over the knife. "Well. . . . Long as they don't lop off a foot or finger or somethin'. You watch 'em close, Mr. Tom."

"Don't worry. I will. Here you go, Joseph. Remember, *slowly*. And cut *away* from yourself."

Still dubious, Lavinia went grudgingly to the back door of the house and disappeared inside, where— Tom didn't doubt for one second—she would observe through a window everything that went on in the backyard.

"That woman's a holy terror," Leakey growled as soon as she was out of earshot. "Don't know that I'd put up with her, Tom."

"She just thinks we're all too incompetent to take care of ourselves," Tom replied. "And she's been right often enough to make her scolding worth listening to." He knelt and adjusted the way Joseph was holding the stick, then guided his other hand through a few cuts. "This way's better, see? The knife cuts the wood better, and it can't cut your thumb. And don't you think it's about time Jason had a turn?"

"No!" Joseph answered in a piping voice. "I'm whittlin'."

Tom let him make another few cuts and then gently

took the knife and branch away from him. "I know you're whittling, but it's Jason's turn."

Joseph's bottom lip started to quiver.

"I don't want you crying about this, Joseph," Tom told him sternly. "Fair's fair, and it's nothing to cry about."

"I don't care," Jason said. "I can whittle later."

Tom looked back and forth between the twins, then shrugged. "All right." He handed the knife and branch back to Joseph. "Here you go, son."

Straightening, he continued to watch the boys, as he had promised Lavinia he would. "There's something about teaching your sons to use a knife . . ." he observed, almost dreamily.

"You got a couple of fine cubs there," Leakey rumbled. "Take after their ol' pappy, they do."

"Joseph does, anyway," Tom answered in a low voice. "Jason's more like Jenny."

There was no great difficulty in telling the twins apart. Everyone had thought they were identical when they were born, but each passing month had revealed new differences. From an early neutral brown, Joseph's hair had become almost black, while Jason's had turned fairer. Joseph was bigger and stronger and more aggressive, while Jason was quicker of mind, naturally curious, and more sensitive. Now that Jenny was gone, Jason was more dependent than ever on Tom, more needful of being assured that he was still loved and that everything would be all right. It helped the twins that their grandparents lived in Brandborough and saw them often. The boys dearly loved staying with Grandpa Jason and Grandma Colleen. Frequent family visits also got the boys out of the way when work backed up at the plantation and Tom didn't have time to give them the attention they needed. Later on that day, in fact, he planned to take them to their grandparents' for Sunday dinner, after which they would remain in town for the next week, conveniently out from underfoot during the busiest week of the harvest.

One of Jenny's fondest dreams had been to be reconciled with her parents. She never ceased to hope that they would accept Tom and, someday, meet and love the twins. She had written frequently over the years—every Paxton ship that sailed for England carried at least one letter to them—but they had never responded. Nor had Tom fared better when he wrote to inform them of Jenny's death. The damnable part was that it was the boys who would suffer the most, and all Tom could do was try to think up a logical story for them when they finally asked.

"Well, I guess I'll eat something and then get ready to leave. You coming with us? There'll be plenty of food. You don't have to worry about going hungry."

"Your mama expecting me?"

"Not that I know of, but—"

"Naaah. We got an agreement that I send word ahead of time so she can have the cook make plenty extra. 'Sides, I don't feel too comfortable with all them buildings around. When you been away from civilization for a while, it gets awful stifling. Tell you what I will do, though. You tell your mama I'll come in next Sunday when you go to fetch the boys home. It's been too long. It'll be good to see her and Jase again. He still hell throwing a tomahawk?"

"He can still beat me."

A wolfish grin spread across Leakey's face. "Then you can tell him something, too: he better practice up, 'cause this time ol' Maurice is gonna beat him so bad he'll want to hide his head in a tow sack. And tell him to tune up that pianoforte, too. It's been a long time since I heard such pretty music as that man plays."

Neither spoke then. The two men stood together enjoying the shade and the lazy morning, and remembering, perhaps, that they too had once been boys for whom there was nothing in the world more important than learning how to whittle.

⤳ CHAPTER IV ⤲

Tom kept the team moving at an easy, sedate pace, the gait to which they were best suited. There'd been a time, before the path had been broadened to accommodate the heavy wagons necessary to freight supplies in and cotton and tobacco and other products out, when the way had been precarious and required a man's full attention. Now, though, the trip was nothing more than a leisurely Sunday drive that was occasionally disturbed by a snake and, when the weather was right, by hordes of mosquito hawks or other insects. Joseph and Jason sat beside their father on the seat. Tom's saddle horse, the clay-colored mare, trailed along behind, at peace with the line that tethered her to the rear gate. In the uncovered bed, two bundles containing the boys' clothing for their week's stay in Brandborough bounced lightly from side to side. As usual, Tom took advantage of the trip to further the boys' education.

"What kind of bird is that, Jason?" he asked at one point, indicating an ungainly-looking creature with spindly legs and a long, pointed beak.

Always desperate to please his father, Jason peered at the bird that waited patiently for the opportunity to spear an unsuspecting fish, then up at Tom. "A heron?" he asked.

"That's right. What kind of heron?"

"A blue heron!" he cried, startling the lanky, regal creature into an awkward run and, moments later, graceful flight. "Green heron's smaller, and greener."

"That's right," Tom said, ruffling his hair. "What

are you looking at, Joseph?"

Joseph already knew which of the swamp denizens to avoid, and could identify most of the others. "Water moccasin," he answered laconically, pointing to a snarl of logs poking out of the water at the side of the road.

"Where? Oh, yes." Tom pointed so Jason could sight along his arm to a spot of sun that filtered through the trees. "Old moccasin taking a sunbath. Getting ready to shed, looks like. See how dull and gray his skin is?"

It was a wonder how two boys born within a half hour of each other from the same mother could have such different natures. The contrast between Joseph and Jason hadn't seemed so obvious to Tom when Jenny was alive because he'd left the business of raising them to her and spent relatively little time with them himself. Since her death, though, he'd arranged to do less of the work at Solitary so he'd have extra time for the boys—time to teach them and love them enough for two parents now that there was only one. Running a plantation and being a father and mother for a rambunctious set of twins was no easy job, even with their grandparents and Lavinia to help; but, outside of missing Jenny so damned much, it was a role he had quickly come to relish.

Five miles west of Brandborough, the land rose out of the swamp and the road intersected another wagon trail that headed north to Brandborough and Charleston. One crack of the whip, and the mares broke into a brisk trot. "I wanta see Grandpa," Joseph said as he jolted against his brother.

"You will," Tom answered. "He and Grandma will be waiting for us on the front porch, I'll bet."

"Where's Uncle Maurice?"

"He's staying at home. Too many buildings and people in Brandborough. Not enough elbow room makes a man like Uncle Maurice nervous."

"What's elbow room?" Joseph asked.

"Well . . . space, I guess. He likes a lot of space around him."

"Why?" Jason asked.

" 'Cause he's used to it, I guess."

"Why?" he asked again.

"Well. . . . Because, damn it," he snapped, exasperated as usual by Jason's string of *why*'s that had a tendency to go on forever. "Get along!" he called to the horses, flicking the reins. "Move, Julie. Move, Ruth. Get along, now!"

The road rose to follow the crest of a long low ridge that paralleled the ocean, then angled off to the east toward Brandborough. The sun beat down on the treeless land. Questions, questions, questions. But why else did a boy exist if not to ask questions? Tom glanced down at his sons, pride lighting his eyes. Lulled by the heat and the motion of the wagon, Joseph had begun to nod. Jason, his mind full of unanswered questions, tried to fight off the drowsiness. Reins in one hand, Tom slipped his free arm around them both. They were handsome lads, he thought, a little drowsy himself. Fine lads. A man couldn't ask for better sons. "You did a fine job, Jenny," he said quietly, talking to her as he sometimes did.

"What?" Jason asked, half-asleep.

"Just talking to myself."

"Why?"

"Just because," Tom said. Along with the memories, the twins were all that was left of Jenny. Without them, his life would be a desolate wasteland. "Just because, son."

Sweat trickled from under the brown floppy-brimmed hat that shaded his face. He'd left Solitary without changing clothes, and his shirt was damp, his feet hot inside his boots. Their faces flushed with the heat, the boys were more asleep than awake by the time they drove past the first house that signaled the outskirts of

Brandborough. Soon they were moving onto the broad
hard-packed main street.

Brandborough had grown considerably from the
original four cabins erected a century earlier when
Marie Ravenne and Jason Brand and their crew had
first settled there. Expansion had been slow but steady
until the War for Independence, after which, fueled by
Paxton enterprise, the town had grown by leaps and
bounds. The Paxton Cotton Company, housed in a
sturdy whitewashed building with large gilt-embellished
letters on the front window, brokered cotton from as far
as fifty miles inland. The Paxton Tobacco Company,
three doors down the street, served a similar function
for local tobacco growers. The Paxtons' prime horses
were all raised at Solitary, but buyers and traders
gathered at the Paxton Auction House on the fairgrounds. The Paxton warehouses and ship's chandlery
were in Charleston, from which harbor the family's
ships set sail to ports all over the world—but the profits
eventually found their way back to Brandborough. As a
result, clapboard buildings lined a good hundred yards
of the main street where over thirty merchants, from
liverymen to milliners to gunsmiths, did business. Walks
made of wide planks, a necessity during the winter when
rain turned the street into a quagmire, ran in front of
the buildings.

Wealth and influence had their drawbacks, however,
so it was no surprise to Tom that not everyone in Brandborough held the Paxtons in favor. Some disliked the
founding family because it was the founding family;
others were jealous of wealth and influence in any form.
No one on the sparsely populated Sabbath street, however, failed to exchange greetings with Tom as he rode
through town: the Paxtons weren't a vindictive lot, but
one never knew, and no one wanted to be the first to put
them to the test.

Jason Behan Paxton and his wife, Colleen, lived in a

large two-story whitewashed house on the north edge of town where they could take their ease on the porch and gaze across a well-kept lawn and colorful beds of flowers to the sparkling blue bay and, in the distance, the Atlantic. The house had been built only ten years earlier, when Jason and Colleen had first started thinking about moving back to town from Solitary. Built on a site less than a hundred yards from the original Paxton cabin, their home had no rival in Brandborough. A drive of crushed shell led from the road to the front door. Boxed hedges, always neatly trimmed, gave the house and grounds a formal appearance that was mitigated by the cozy good cheer of open bright-blue shutters. Hickories, live oaks, and magnolias surrounded the house and shielded it with deep shade that, combined with the Atlantic breezes, kept the interior cool on the hottest day in the summer. Tom had seen, visited, and lived in houses in a half-dozen countries around the world. Some had been larger, some more elegant, but not a one, with the possible exception of Solitary, was as pleasant or comfortable.

"Wake up, boys," Tom said as the team turned onto the drive that led to the house. "Almost there. Shake a leg."

Joseph rubbed his eyes and looked around. "Can we go in the boat, Daddy?" he asked the second he realized where he was.

"You'll have to ask your grandpa. It's his. Well, damn."

"What?" Jason asked. Then, remembering the responsibility Colleen had charged him with, he added, "Grandma says you shouldn't say bad words."

A figure dressed in black was descending the front steps. Tom's mood turned sour and he ignored Jason's admonition. "Damn the luck, Reverend Caldwell Lewis is there. Now, you two be polite, you hear?"

With the journey nearly over, the twins were more in-

terested in getting out of the wagon than in being polite.
Jason tried to climb over Joseph, but Joseph pushed
him back.

"You hear what I said?" Tom asked, grabbing a pair
of arms and pulling both boys down to the seat.

"Yes, sir," the twins chimed in unison.

"Good. Whoa!" He hauled on the reins and brought
the team to a stop. "Reverend," he said, touching his
hat in greeting.

Dressed in black shoes, hose, breeches, coat, and
tricorn, the Reverend Mr. Lewis stopped on the bottom
step. "Good afternoon, Thomas," he said in the deep,
stentorian voice that had earned him his job in Brandborough. "Jason, Joseph. Good lads."

Tom still had hold of the boys' arms, and he shoved
them to their feet.

"Good afternoon, sir," they said, with Jason adding,
in the same breath, "Can we go now?"

"Yes. Just don't both of you jump on your grandma
at the same time. Take turns."

"Yes, sir!" There was no holding them. The words
barely out of their mouths, the twins were scrambling
down from the wagon and running past the Reverend
Mr. Lewis onto the porch and into the house.

With an indulgent smile, Lewis stepped aside to let
them pass. "A healthy-looking pair, Thomas," he said,
a little too jovially. He waited in silence while Tom
climbed out of the wagon and hitched the horses.

Tom walked around to the back of the wagon and
grabbed the boys' clothes. "Plenty of food, fresh air,
and exercise," he said, trying to sound friendly but
knowing he failed.

Lewis cleared his throat and, back stiff, stood in the
middle of the steps. "And you, Thomas? How are you
on this Lord's day?"

"Hot and thirsty, Mr. Lewis."

"Ah, yes." The preacher coughed nervously, but
wasn't to be deterred from expressing his concern for

Tom's spiritual welfare. "We see so little of you, Thomas," he went on. "How long has it been?"

Tom glanced quickly to make sure the boys were inside the house, then swung his attention back to Lewis. "It's been months and you know it," he replied.

Lewis slowly shook his head. "Thomas," he said, his tone simultaneously sorrowful and chiding. "Don't you realize how unfortunate it is when one of Brandborough's leading citizens never attends services?"

"I attended services six months ago," Tom said tightly. "Funeral services."

If Lewis recognized the dangerous undercurrents in Tom's voice, he chose to ignore them. "The Lord understands your pain, my boy. What He doesn't understand is why you've abandoned His divine mercy."

The hard lines of Tom's face and the dull fire glowing in his eye betrayed his bitterness. "Maybe if the Lord had been around when Jenny was busy dying," he snapped, "He would understand!"

The preacher flinched as if Tom had struck him. "I was just trying to be of some help," he said, shocked by the sentiment and vehemence of Tom's outburst. "If you only knew what a comfort God can be, even now—"

"If God wants to comfort me, let him come do so Himself," Tom interrupted. "Mr. Lewis, you've got nothing more to say that interests me, so if you don't mind, I think I'll wish you good day."

Lewis's knuckles were as pale as his face, and his hands trembled as he gripped his Bible. Without answering, he turned and walked away.

Tom watched with relief as Lewis retreated down the road. He'd had no wish to confront the man, and knew he meant well. The problem was that preachers always had the same advice, no matter what the tragedy: simply chalk everything up to God's will and go on. Go on, no matter how crippled. But Tom wasn't built that way. He'd been hurt, and he needed time to lick his wounds.

"Feel any better?" a deep voice said from the open door.

Tom looked up and saw his father on the porch. At fifty-one, Jason Behan Paxton was a few inches shorter than his son and still solid as a log. His gray hair grew as thick as a young man's. Dark and deep-set under his black beetling brows, his eyes were able to pierce the hearts and souls of those to whom he spoke. Tom's thoughts and emotions had always been an open book to his father. As a boy and now as a man, Tom found it impossible to keep a secret from him. Up the steps and past his father, Tom hurried into the house. "I thought you were with the boys," he said, pausing to toss his hat on a rack set just inside the door.

"I was with the boys, but found your conversation with Reverend Lewis more interesting." Jase pulled the mahogany-paneled door closed as he followed Tom inside. "Don't you think you were a little hard on him?"

"Reverend Lewis is a fatuous, self-righteous fool," Tom snapped. "Whether or not I go to church is no concern of his."

"But it is. Fatuous or not, he is concerned," Jase chided, placing a calming hand on his son's shoulder. "Look. I know how irritating he can be. Lord knows I've wanted to tell him a thing or two myself at times. But he had nothing to do with your trouble, and you have no right to take out on him your bitterness and hurt over Jenny."

Tom swung around to face his father. "If Lewis wants to be so damned quick to speak on God's behalf, he can sure as hell take some of the blame, too."

Jason Behan's mouth twisted in a momentary grimace. "I'm sorry you feel that way," he said, carefully controlling his impatience. "But you're just making the matter more difficult for everyone, including yourself."

"To hell with Lewis, and to hell with all the others in this town," Tom said in a harsh voice. "They never accepted Jenny, never gave her a chance. You heard the gossip. An impoverished title marrying American money, the local girls not good enough for a Paxton . . ." His voice broke, but he cleared his throat and made himself continue. "Well, damn their hypocritical sympathy and the smiles they paste on their faces when I drive through town. They aren't fooling me for a second. They didn't like her when she was here and they didn't give a damn when she died. And nothing you or Lewis or anyone else—"

"That isn't fair and you know it," Jase said angrily, then glanced up as tiny feet raced overhead along the second-story hall. "Come with me," he said, starting for his study.

"What you want to say can be said right here," Tom said. "Unless it's a lecture, in which case you can forget it."

Jase turned with the ease of a cat. His eyes were hard chips of flint that brooked no argument. "Your mother took the twins upstairs to change their clothes. They'll be down any minute. The choice is yours. We talk in private or in front of them. But, by heaven, we talk."

Tom started to shake his head, then closed his eye in resignation. When his father wanted something, when that steely tone appeared, there was no arguing with him. He never shouted, but his words carried too much weight to resist.

His boots echoing on the waxed hardwood floor, Jason led the way to a set of double doors made of thick mountain pine and adorned with heavy brass knobs. Inside, two walls were lined with enough books to make the Paxton library one of the finest in South Carolina. Two windows set in the east wall looked out onto the meadow, bay, and ocean, and a fireplace dominated the north wall. Arranged on these two walls were rifles and pistols with ornately carved stocks and grips, and swords and other cutting weapons both in and out of scabbards. The rapier used by Marie Ravenne herself when she commanded the pirate ship *Ravener* hung in a spot of honor over the mantel.

A massive black walnut desk was placed between the windows on the eastern wall. Jase settled into the chair behind the desk and gestured for Tom to take the one in front. "One month was reasonable," he said as Tom sat, "two acceptable, three within the bounds of reason, given the circumstances. The fourth month of unrelieved mourning is a luxury, the fifth month a bore, and the sixth an effrontery to the living *and* the dead." Jase slapped the shining desk top as Tom began to rise. Tom settled back in his chair. "Your mother and I and everyone else have been solicitous. I've dropped hints, I've intimated, I've insinuated, but you've been too damned stubborn and pigheaded to listen. Now, by God, you will, or you'll take yourself home and not come back until you're ready to."

Tom almost spoke, but clamped his mouth shut under the glare of his father's eyes.

"Jenny's dead, son," Jase continued in a gentler tone. "You don't like it, I don't like it, your mother doesn't like it, but she *is dead,* and you're going to have to learn to live with that fact. With the exception of your mother and myself and the few others at Solitary we all call family, the people who live in Brandborough are neither Paxtons nor Paxton property, and you can't expect them to predicate their lives on what happens to the Paxtons. Our trials and sorrows are our own. The people who live in this town have their own troubles, and they're not going to put ours ahead of theirs. No one in the world would." He lifted a finger and pointed it at Tom. "To expect them to, and to excoriate them when they don't, only aggravates the situation."

Tom's hands clenched into fists. What his father was saying made sense, but he was in no mood to acknowledge that fact. "So it's my fault now," he said, a little too calmly and quietly. "Well, do you know what I think? I think it's obvious that you never really gave a damn about Jenny either, or you wouldn't be defending them."

Jason Behan Paxton turned livid. "How *dare* you!" he roared. "I loved Jenny from the day you brought her here, and always tried to make her feel at home." He took a deep, shuddering breath, and when he spoke again, he'd regained his composure. "I won't let you put me off the track. What I really wanted to say to you is this: there's a fundamental truth about life, and it's time you faced up to it. Simply put: before God, the town drunk and Tom Paxton stand exactly equal. As for tragedy, no man can say when or answer why. Life is a mystery that's sometimes loving and sometimes cruel, and the way we respond to that loving, cruel mystery is brutally limited to two choices: we can accept, or we can go mad."

Tom stared at his hands and at Marie Ravenne's sword. He stared at his father's blurred reflection in the desk top. At last, he stood and started out of the room.

"Where are you going?" Jase asked.

"I've lost my appetite," Tom answered wearily without looking at him, "and since God's not going to treat me any better than anyone else, I'd best be getting back to Solitary. There's hay to be cut, and tobacco, cotton, and corn to be chopped."

"You're not going to stay the night?"

"That's right," Tom said dully, opening the library door and starting out. "I'm not. Jason? Joseph?"

Footsteps pounded overhead, and by the time Tom reached the foot of the stairs, the twins were on their way down the banister rail. "Guess what?" Joseph yelled.

Tom caught him, then Jason, and swung each in turn to the floor. "What?" he asked, gathering one in each arm.

"Grandma says Grandpa will take us out in the boat!" came the garbled double reply.

Colleen Paxton, at fifty, had gained a pound or two

around her hips but was still a remarkably attractive woman. Her eyes were exactly the same color as her husband's, but softer and warmer, and her face was lined more by laughter than by years. Because Jase liked her hair long, she kept it so, and in truth took pride in its length and in its deep, luxuriant brown that had never dulled. "They're such dears," she said, following them down the stairs. "We're going to have a marvelous time, aren't we, boys?"

The encounters with Lewis and then his father had completely ruined Tom's good mood, but he hid his anger with a smile as false as those he had complained of only moments earlier. "I'll bet you are too," he told Colleen. "Oh, by the way, Lavinia says they've about worn out and grown out of their last pairs of good breeches. She's patching them for play and letting them out, so if you could get Joe Luke to make them each a pair for good wear, I'll pay him when I come back next week. Well . . ." He gave each boy a hug and a kiss. "Wish I was staying for dinner," he said, rising. "You boys be good. Pay a mind to your grandma and grandpa, especially in that boat."

"But I thought you were spending the night," Colleen said, distressed.

"Something came up," Tom said, hoping he didn't sound too abrupt but not wanting to explain further. "I'm heading back right now."

Jason cried out in protest as he realized that his father was leaving, and Joseph joined in.

"Now, boys, there's nothing to cry about," he reassured them. He reached over, tweaked their noses, and held his thumbs between his first two fingers of each hand. "Got your noses. You quit that crying and I'll bring 'em back to you. You don't . . ." he said, looking terribly fierce and serious, "I'll feed 'em to that big 'gator we saw on the way over."

Joseph giggled. Jason took a moment longer, but finally joined in. Tom ruffled their hair, stood, and kissed his mother on the cheek. "You all take care," he said. "I'll see you next weekend."

"Take care of yourself, Thomas," Colleen said, hiding her disappointment.

"No need to worry about me." Tom retrieved his hat from the rack and started out. "Oh, yes. Maurice is back. I'll bring him with me next weekend, so you'd better see about buying an extra cow or bag of rice or something. His appetite hasn't shrunk any."

"Maurice back?" Jase asked from the door to the study, where he'd been watching Tom's leavetaking without comment.

"Got in last week. Said to tell you . . ." Caught somewhere between anger and love, Tom stopped mid-sentence and stared at his father. And for the first time, Tom realized how difficult the scene in the study had been for Jase. ". . . to tune up the pianoforte and get that tomahawk-throwing arm of yours ready."

"Oh, he did, eh?" Jase said. God knew it was hard raising a son. Funny thing was, even after a man figured he had his son all raised, along came something that made him wonder. But then, Jase thought with silent amusement, that wasn't so strange, because there were times when he wondered if he himself would ever grow up. A man never escaped the boy inside him: he might be a father but was always, in part, his father's son. "Well, you tell him I'm ready," Jase said, the twinkle returning to his eyes.

"I will." Tom almost relented, almost changed his mind, almost stayed, but didn't. "See you next week?" he asked, offering reconciliation if not absolute surrender.

"See you next week." Jase nodded, and added, as Tom put on his hat and started out the door, "And, son?"

"Yes?"

"You ride careful. And bring those boys' sniffers back with you when you come."

✒ CHAPTER V ✑

For a three-year-old, there is nothing in the world quite like being spoiled and pampered by indulgent grandparents. In the six months since their mother's death, Joseph and Jason had found a second home at Jase and Colleen's house. Sunday evening they were having a circus. They slid down the banister. They played rough-and-tumble with Jase. They feasted on molasses cookies and milk. They chased Spider, the long-nosed terrier, whose job was running a treadmill to turn the spit, but who vastly preferred playing with boys. They got away without eating their greens, turned up their noses at a rhubarb pie because it was too sour, and demolished a whole bowl of sweet cream and honey. And if neither of them liked bedtime, it was hard to resist a story told by Grandpa Jase and harder yet to keep their eyes open until the end, because Jase had a way of stretching his stories until they fell asleep.

Jase and Colleen had discussed in great detail how firm they were going to be during this visit, and though their resolve was great, it was difficult not to give the twins whatever they wanted. And later, after they'd blown out the candle in the boys' room and had gone downstairs for a cup of tea before turning in themselves, they rationalized their shameless indulgence with a very simple excuse: that was the joy of having grandchildren.

On Monday, as promised, Jase took the boys sailing on the bay. That night, though the October weather was brisk, they helped set up a tent on the north lawn and camped out like seasoned frontiersmen. On Tuesday, they accompanied Jase on his rounds of the Paxton offices and played aboard a Paxton topsail schooner that had put into the estuary the night before to load a half-dozen bales of cowhides. On Wednesday, Forbes, the butler, drove the twins and their grandma Colleen around the bay to the Atlantic shore, where they ate a picnic lunch and gathered seashells. That night, it was two exhausted little boys who lolled on the rug in the parlor and played lackadaisically with a set of wooden figurines that Jase had carved for his own children twenty-five years earlier.

"Time to go to bed, boys," Colleen announced.

"Awww . . ." Jason complained, while Joseph rolled over and pretended not to hear.

"You've had a long day, and now it's sleepy time."

Jase finished playing the tune, one he'd composed many years earlier, closed the keyboard cover and watched the proceedings, so reminiscent of scenes that had taken place at Solitary when Tom and Benjamin and Hope Elaine had been children. A great deal of time and painstaking effort had gone into the creation of his accurately detailed carvings. There were a dozen sailors, including a mate and captain, enough to handle his representation of the first Paxton-owned vessel, a barque-rigged ship that plied the coast as far north as New York before the War for Independence. There was a Yamasee Indian family: a chief, two warriors, two squaws, and three children, all resplendent in traditional tribal garb. A squad of uniformed British soldiers contended with a dozen buckskin-clad frontiersmen armed with long rifles. Last but not least were a half-dozen pirates, Jase's tribute to his forebears. Strangely enough, though purely coincidentally, one wore a black patch over his left eye and looked remarkably like Tom Gunn Paxton.

"Not sleepy," Joseph declared sullenly, breaking his grandpa's reverie.

"You heard your grandmother," Jase said firmly. "Up you go."

"He took my Indian," Jason wailed, snatching at the chief.

"Did not," Joseph said.

"Did too. Grandma!"

"Stow it!" Jase roared.

Wide-eyed, the twins froze.

"Enough's enough, by God! Now, you two mind your grandmother."

Jason sniffed. Joseph's lower lip quivered as he fought the tears.

"If you *don't*," he said, leaning forward and fixing them with a ferocious leer, "I'll see that you walk the plank tomorrow. Of course"—the leer became a grin and a wink—"if you *do,* maybe I'll take you to Charleston with me to spend the night, eh? What do you think of that?"

Jason giggled, and both boys brightened immediately, especially Joseph, who loved going anywhere. "Can I go to bed now?" he asked in all seriousness.

Jase stifled a guffaw.

"Will you tell us a story?" Jason asked in turn.

"No stories tonight," Colleen said. "Toys in the box, and then up we go."

One by one, Indians, soldiers, frontiersmen, sailors, and pirates were placed in the box Jase had made for them. "Care to lend a hand?" Colleen said to her husband as she stood and lifted Jason from the floor.

Joseph climbed into the chair behind Jase, wrapped his arms around his grandfather's neck, and rested his head on his shoulder.

"Sleepy?" Jase asked.

Joseph yawned. "No."

"I'll bet."

The house was quiet. The servants had finished with their after-dinner chores and most of them had retired. Only Forbes, who was never fully satisfied with the state of the house and was always watchful for something else that needed his attention, was still stirring. The hall was lighted by an argand lamp fueled with whale oil and mounted on the wall. Jase lighted a candle and led the way up the stairs.

"Daddy?" Jason mumbled sleepily.

"Hushaby," Colleen crooned.

Bedtime for played-out boys, a time Jase had missed all too often when his own were the twins' age. There'd been reasons enough, of course: land to till, a house and stables and barns and outbuildings to raise, businesses to reestablish after the ravages of war. Still, it was a shame that it took a man until he was half a century old to experience the softness of a child's breath against his neck as he carried him to bed. Candle in one hand, his other arm under Joseph's bottom, he stepped aside to let Colleen open the bedroom door, then again preceded her and lowered Joseph onto his bed before lighting the bedroom lantern and blowing out the candle. "Growing like weeds," he said, helping Colleen put Jason down. "I put 'em on the scale at the tobacco warehouse yesterday." He shook his head in disbelief. "Joseph weighed forty pounds, and Jason thirty-eight."

Colleen moved with an economy of motion that some women never learn and others never forget. Shoes and stockings off, then shirts, then breeches. Tiny bodies were lifted and covers turned down, then blankets tucked snugly under chins. "They're beautiful, aren't they?" she said, gazing down at first one and then the other. "Do you remember?"

Jase moved behind her and put his arms around her waist. "What?"

"One night when Tom was seven, Benjy was five, and Hope was three. It was late in January, and that steel-gray mare with the black eye that you liked so much had just foaled. I'd put the children to bed and you came in, still covered with blood and smelling like horse, and stood beside me looking down at them."

"I remember," Jason Behan said simply. He kissed the top of her head. "You told me I stank."

"I know. And you stalked out of the room. I was angry because Tom had been impossible and I was tired and you'd been too busy to help me."

"Those were hard days. I never held it against—"

Colleen turned in his arms and put two fingers against his lips. "I never told you how sorry I was for saying that," she said, her eyes moist with the memory. "I should have told you I loved you, but all I said was—"

"That was a long time ago, Colleen, and I did my share of saying the wrong things at the wrong time." He nodded down at the boys. "Look at them. Things worked out well enough. You ever see such a fine pair in your life?"

"You're partial," Colleen said with a low laugh.

"Nope. That's all those other grandfathers. I'm making an observation based on . . ." He paused. "What's that?" The front door rattled a second time. "Who'd be calling at this time of night?"

Colleen shrugged. "Forbes is still up. He can answer it. Someone needing directions, probably."

They heard the low rumble of an unfamiliar voice, the words indistinguishable, then the sound of the front door closing, followed by the tramp of heavy boots on the stairs. "Stay here," Jase told Colleen, keeping the alarm out of his voice.

The hair on the back of his neck prickling, Jase moved quickly around Jason's bed, snatched the pitcher from the basin on the nightstand, and then, the pitcher half-raised, stopped short and stared into the wide black mouth of a fifty-caliber flintlock pistol. "Who the hell are you?" he asked in a voice harsh with rage and surprise.

"I am Onofre Sanchez, señor," the man with the gun said. He swept off a black soft-brimmed hat with a long red feather in the band and, eyes and gun not wavering from Jase, bowed. "Regrettably not at your service."

Colleen watched as the tall, broad-shouldered man with the heavy paunch stepped through the door. Long black braids entwined with silver wires hung below his shoulders. A full black moustache dropped from the corners of his mouth in an oriental manner, and dark, bushy eyebrows gave his lean face a menacing cast despite his ready smile and the merry glint in his coal-black eyes. He wore a blousy white shirt and a red vest covered with ornate silver stitchery, and a matching red sash. Just below the sash rode a broad leather belt, from which hung a rapier with a leather-wrapped hilt and a brass hand guard. Dark breeches that hugged his legs vanished into high black boots that were polished to a bright sheen.

"Jase . . . Jase—" Colleen stammered.

What Sanchez wanted could only be limited to a very few things, none of them good. "It's all right, Colleen," Jase said, trying to calm her and simultaneously edging away from the beds so she and the twins would be out of harm's way if he saw a chance to use the pitcher. "What are you doing in my house?" he demanded of Sanchez.

Three other men, all bearded and roughly dressed, with kerchiefs bound around their heads, crowded into the bedroom behind Sanchez. "Waiting for you to stand very still, señor," Sanchez said in a voice that only a fool would take as friendly. "And lower your arm slowly and drop the pitcher before I grow nervous and, in my fear, accidentally squeeze the trigger, no?"

Arguing with a half-inch ball of lead was pointless, and Jase did as he was told. The pitcher bounced once on the rug, hit the hardwood floor, and shattered.

"Grandma?" Joseph asked, startled awake by the noise. Confused, he turned and saw Sanchez. "Who are you?" he asked, his eyes full of wonder.

"Step back now, Señor Paxton," Sanchez said, ig-

noring Joseph and still sounding as if he had nothing
more on his mind than a pleasant visit. "We wish to
hurt no one, but we have a mission which we must accomplish. Señora? If you would be so kind as to join
your husband?"

"I most certainly will not!" Colleen took two steps
and stood between Jason and Sanchez. "Not until you
tell us what you want."

Sanchez shrugged, and motioned with his free hand.
At his signal, the three men hurried past him toward the
beds. "Very well, señora. We are here for the children."

"No!" Colleen cried.

Jase suddenly broke to intercept the three pirates.
Sanchez jammed the pistol into Jase's stomach, effectively blocking his progress. "You're mad," Jase
wheezed. "Absolutely mad. I'm giving you ten seconds
to get out of here."

Colleen snatched Jason out of his bed, threw him
beside Joseph, and lay half-across them in an attempt to
protect them with her body. Awakened to pandemonium, the twins were crying. The three men hesitated.
Sanchez spoke sharply to them in Spanish. "I am sorry,
señor," he added with a soft disappointed clucking
sound. "I've told you that we have a mission, and I
must carry it out, so please tell your wife not to be such
a foolish lady."

Colleen clutched the twins to her bosom and clawed
and scratched with her free hand at the first pirate to
reach her. "Get away!" she screamed. "Get away from
me, damn you!"

The first pirate grabbed her arm, the second leaped
over the bed and caught her other arm. Together they
separated her from the boys and hauled her backward
off the bed. The third jumped over Jason's bed and
grabbed Jason's arm and one of Joseph's legs as the
boys tried to crawl after Colleen.

The twins howled in fear. Colleen raged as the two

men holding her unceremoniously dumped her on the floor and went back to help their comrade with the boys. Jase started at the gun and tried to gauge his chances.

"Bastards!" Colleen shrieked, scrambling to her feet and attacking the first pirate from behind.

The pirate cursed, turned, and pushed her back sharply, sending her reeling into a chair. The chair broke and Colleen fell heavily. Distracted, Sanchez looked to the side, and in that second Jase knocked his pistol aside with one hand and sent a fist at Sanchez's face. The pirate was knocked aside. Jase hurtled past him and headed for the closest of the other three.

Sanchez shouted a word of warning a fraction of a second before Jase slammed into the first pirate and sent him crashing into the nightstand. The second pirate thrust Joseph into the hands of the third and, before Jase could get his balance, pulled his cutlass. Jase made a desperate grab for the weapon, but his age was against him. The pirate dodged away, raised his cutlass, and could easily have lopped Jase's head off; but instead, on Sanchez's order not to kill him, he swept Jase's feet out from under him with a well-placed kick.

Jase grunted and went sprawling to the floor. He landed with a crack that everyone in the room heard. Face drained of blood by the shock, Jase rolled over, moaned, and tried to get up, but failed.

"Grandpa!" Joseph screamed, his cry cut off by a filthy hand clamped over his mouth.

"Jase!" Colleen half-crawled, half-ran to Jase's side and lifted his head into her lap.

"Get them out of here," Sanchez ordered his men in Spanish. "Wait for me downstairs. My apologies, señora," he said to Colleen in English as his men carried out the kicking, screaming twins. "I had hoped that there would be no need for violence."

Jase's face was pale, his forehead beaded with sweat.

His leg lay at an impossible angle. "Tom? Tom!" he called in agony. "Help me up, Colleen. Help me up, damn it!"

"Hush. Just lie still . . ."

Colleen cradled his head and rocked him as she would a child. "Why?" she asked Sanchez savagely. Tears streamed down her face and blood down her arm where the broken chair had cut her. "Why are you doing this? For money? What kind of monsters are you?"

"Wealth is the chief pursuit of every man, señora," Sanchez replied.

"Then we'll give you money! As much as you want, and anything else you want. Just release the children and leave us alone."

Sanchez shrugged apologetically. "I regret that I cannot, dear lady. We have already been paid, and we are honest pirates. Your money means nothing to us now. Only the children are important. Only they can fulfill the terms of the agreement with my employer."

"Who?" Colleen asked, her voice little more than a whisper. "Who would pay you to do such a wicked thing?"

"His name is Sir Theodotus Vincent."

"Oh, dear God, no!"

"Damn!" Jase moaned.

"I was told to tell this to Señor Tom Paxton, but I will tell you and you must tell him for me, do you understand?"

"Dear God!"

"You will say that he stole a man's daughter." Sanchez's smile was gone and he spoke very clearly so there would be no misunderstanding. "You will say that now the girl's father will have what is left of his daughter on this earth: her sons. You will say that the debt of Thomas Gunn Paxton is paid. Paid with the flesh of his flesh." With that, Sanchez wheeled about and strode out of the room without a backward glance.

"Wait," Jase called, struggling to a sitting position. "Come back, damn your hide!"

Stunned, unable to comprehend the enormity of what had happened, Colleen moaned and rocked back and forth. "They're gone," she cried, her voice choked with anguish. "Oh, dear God, they can't be gone!"

"Our room," Jase snapped, shaking her by the arm. "The gun on the wall. Get it!"

"We can't, Jase. You might hit—"

He was already dragging himself toward the window. "Now, Colleen, *now*. Hurry!"

Downstairs, a door slammed. The sound galvanized Colleen, who scrambled to her feet and ran for the rifle. The pain in Jase's leg was excruciating, but he forced himself up to the windowsill and threw open the shutter. He grabbed the useless leg and somehow got it out in front of him so he could sit with his left arm out the window to hold him up. The room spun; blood seeped from the corner of his mouth, where he'd bitten through his lip from pain.

A whinny. Hoofbeats from the far side of the house. *They have my grandsons! Have the twins. Can't pass out. Have to stay conscious.* "Colleen!" he roared. "Colleen!"

Colleen materialized at his side and, removing the ramrod, thrust the rifle into his hands. "It's loaded," she said, dropping the rod and pulling the stopper out of a powder horn.

Jase steadied the rifle on the windowsill and pulled back the flintlock. Colleen poured powder into the pan just as, below, four horses thundered around the corner of the house and headed down the drive toward the road. They would be out of range in seconds. Jase willed the agony of his leg from his mind. A single shot would cure nothing, but no one was going to steal his grandchildren and get away unscathed. At least one of the bastards would pay. . . .

The light was bad, the targets astride hard-running horses, and there was danger of hitting one of the boys. Jase inhaled, held his breath. *Steady . . . steady. . . .*

Sparks flashed, the rifle roared, a tongue of flame, followed by a gout of smoke, leaped from the muzzle and obscured the view momentarily before the breeze blew it away. Nothing happened. The riders slowed for the turn onto the main road, and were out of sight within seconds.

Colleen stood motionless, as if turned to stone. Wearily, Jase tried to pull the rifle in the window but it slipped from his fingers. "I missed," he mumbled as the rifle landed outside with a thud. His face felt sluggish. A black void opened before his eyes and expanded like a huge stain of ink on a blotter. The pain in his leg was a fire that consumed him. "I missed," he repeated and, unconscious before he landed, slumped to the floor.

Onofre Sanchez cursed his men in Spanish and commanded the dogs and sons of dogs to row faster. Moonlight twinkled on the calm water of the cove a mile north of Brandborough where his ship, tacking back and forth just offshore, awaited the return of its master and cargo. Too confused and exhausted to offer resistance, the boys lay quietly huddled in the bottom of the boat. The raid had been ridiculously simple, and all had gone according to plan. Sanchez had found horses and had discovered the Paxton house with equal ease. A shame the old man had to break a leg, but that made up a little for the loss of Fouchet. What exactly had happened to Fouchet, Sanchez didn't know. He had looked around after the shot and all three men were still following him, but only two had arrived at the cove. It was a pity. Not so much that Fouchet was missing and probably dead, for no man was promised tomorrow, but his loss meant that Fouchet's woman would get triple his share of earnings for this job, which meant less for Sanchez. Such mishaps were to be expected, though. There would be gold enough, and, more important, six months in which to do as he pleased without interference from the English. Not a bad wage for a few weeks of easy sailing and an hour's work.

The shallow water chop lessened beyond the breakers, and the small boat rose and fell over the deeper water's gentle swells. There, coming down on him, was the beautiful shape of his ship, the *Red Dog Song*. It would be good to be aboard and under way again, heading south. "Row, you miserable issue of fish-fed dogs!" he roared, steering a course that would intersect with his ship. "Row, scum, or I'll have your arms for breakfast!"

Yes, a shame about Fouchet. But then, death did come unbidden, like a thief in the night. *One thing I know about is thieves,* Sanchez thought, *thieves and death.* He looked down at the wet and frightened boys lying in the bilge. "But not yours, little ones," he said aloud, softly. "Not yours."

⌒ CHAPTER VI ⌒

The night sky was clear, the moon not yet up. The Big Dipper hung close to the horizon, and Cygnus, the swan, was winging his way toward the southwest through the haze of the Milky Way. It had been a good day. The corn and cotton were in, and the hands had started on the tobacco. The south meadow had been mowed, and the last of the year's hay would be in by Monday or Tuesday if it didn't rain over the weekend. All day long, Tom had moved from field to field, from job to job, working a half-hour here, giving advice there, making decisions, sharing a joke, and generally being a combination of friend, taskmaster, confidant, and overseer. All told, the day confirmed what he had known since he was a child. His pirate great-great-grandparents had been right when they had set free the first slaves they bought, and so began a tradition that had lasted almost a hundred years: that no Paxton would ever own slaves. The Negroes employed by the Paxtons worked for wages and of their own free will. That most were constrained by the very real fear that others might enslave them if they left was beside the point. One did what one believed was right, and if no single person or family could change the world, at least Tom could live with his own conscience. And if Paxton horses were better cared for and Paxton fields were more productive, so much the better. Freedom was right, but happily also profitable, as proved by the family's ledgers. The refusal to hold another human being as chattel was not only good for the conscience, it was good for business as well.

Maurice had arrived unannounced three days earlier, after having been gone for over a year. On his last trip he'd driven a herd of Paxton mules to Memphis, where he delivered them to Benjamin. There'd been little time for talk between Tom and Maurice during the past two days, but now that the corn was in, Tom felt he could ease off. It was well after dark when supper was finished, and he and Maurice decided that a dip in the pond, along with the jug of beer Maurice had hidden there earlier, was just the medicine they needed. "Where'd you say you put it?" Tom asked.

" 'Bout ten feet this side of the dock," the frontiersman said. "Should be nice and cool by now."

The pond backed up behind a dam thrown across the creek that ran through the south pasture. Slowly, taking their time, they stood at the water's edge and stripped. Years of hard work had honed Tom's body. Standing exactly six feet tall, he was lean as a whip, wiry, with each muscle sharply defined. Leakey was larger. Two inches over six feet, he was broad in the shoulders and chest and without an ounce of fat. His torso, arms, and legs were massive and chunky but smooth, giving the mistaken impression of softness. He was, in fact, one of those rare men who are not only as strong as mules, but endowed with a quickness that is seldom matched as well as stamina that keeps them going when most others have fallen by the wayside. There had been a time, when Tom was eighteen, that he had thought he could beat Maurice, and had said so in a contemplative sort of way. Maurice had invited him, in just as friendly a manner, to try. Tom remembered his shoulder digging into Maurice's stomach, but that was all. A half-hour later, he'd opened his eyes to see a concerned Maurice looking down at him and bathing his head with a cool cloth. He was sore for a week, and never tried again.

Leakey tested the water with one toe, tentatively stepped in, and felt around with his foot for the jug. "Here 'tis," he announced, hauling it out. "Feels about right." Easing gingerly into the water, he jumped up when his bottom hit. "Damn, this stuff's cold!" A white form streaked past him in the dark and hit the water in a shallow dive, drenching him. "Hey! What the hell . . . ?"

Tom swam hard all the way across the pond, rolled onto his back, and took his time returning. "It's not so bad if you jump right in," he said, propping himself on one elbow in the shallows.

"It's a shock to the system," Maurice growled. He passed the jug to Tom and lay back with his head on the bank and his legs floating in the dark, cool water.

"My system works just fine, thank you."

"Yeah? Well, it won't forever." Maurice shook his head. "A man oughtn't to work out in the heat of the day the way you do, Tom. You make me sweat just watchin' you."

"Then don't."

"Pretty hard not to, you slapdashin' all around the place." He took back the jug, drank deeply, and emitted a long, satisfying belch. "That's civilization, though, I guess."

"Yup," Tom agreed, contemplating his toes. "That's civilization. An honest day's work for a day's pay."

Maurice grunted and passed the jug. "Too damn much work, you ask me."

"Hell's bells, Maurice. I've seen you go for forty-eight hours straight on the deck of a ship that was pitching like mad in a storm. And I'd wager the mountains have offered you no easy time of it, either."

"Walked and trotted sixty miles in a day two months ago out in Tennessee with a bunch of heathen Cherokees after me," Maurice admitted, "but that was different."

"I'll bet it was."

"It sure as hell wasn't boring, I'll tell you. Hell, Tom. Think of all the scrapes we pulled each other out of, all them places we went, things we seen." He sighed and lay back again. "It plumb breaks my heart to see you all civilized and missin' so much fun."

"Fun for you," Tom said, laughing. "But not for any sane man."

Maurice found the polestar, let his eyes wander to the west, where a man was meant to be. "Well, now," he said softly. "I never did claim to be sane, did I?"

The beer was cool and rich, the water restful and refreshing. The smell of horses and freshly mown hay lay over the land like a blanket into which threads of cricket and night-bird song had been woven. A man could do worse than to lie in a pond and drink beer while he talked to a friend and contemplated the night and the stars after a hard day's work. "You know what?" Tom asked. "I was thinking about that time in—"

"Shhh!" The water sloshed as Leakey came to his feet. His skin white, he stood motionless; only his head moved, turning slowly until he pinpointed the direction from which the sound came.

"What is it?" Tom whispered, rising as quietly as possible.

"Rider. Coming fast for nighttime. Any ideas?"

"None that sound good," Tom said. "Let's go."

Taking no time to dry, they pulled on breeches, socks, and boots. Only Maurice had a weapon, a twelve-inch-long double-edged blade that he called his arkansas toothpick and that he'd laid close by on his shirt. The hoofbeats were close enough for Tom to hear now as the horse pounded up the long drive toward the house. Together, Tom and Maurice ran across the field.

"Tom! Tom!"

Lavinia's voice. It had to be bad news. Something from town. One of the twins . . . both of them. . . . Tom leaped the fence, ran unheedingly across the remnants of the garden. "Here!" he yelled. "I'm coming!"

A lathered horse stood in front of the porch. Its rider waited next to Lavinia on the top step. "What happened?" Tom asked, gasping, as he joined them.

Neither answered right away. Lavinia looked as if she'd seen a ghost. The man, Emory Pembroke, Jason's stable keeper, stared at Tom with an open mouth.

"Speak up, damn you!" Tom shouted. "What the hell's going on?"

"It . . . it's the twins, Mr. Paxton," Emory said. "They've been took, kidnapped by pirates, and Mr. Paxton's leg broke."

"What?" Tom asked, stepping back as if struck and almost falling down the stairs. *"What?"*

"It's true, sir. Kidnapped by pirates—"

Maurice took charge. He sent Lavinia to find Vestal and have him saddle Tom's clay-colored mare and his own roan gelding. He led Tom upstairs and saw he got into dry breeches and boots and shirt. Ten minutes after they'd received the news, he and Tom were galloping down the drive toward the meadow and beyond, into the darkness of the swamp.

Low in the saddle, racing past the great oaks, they slowed as the land sloped into the swamp. There, where the cypresses blocked out the starlight and the horses' eyes were more to be trusted than their own, they slowed to a walk. The pace was excruciating, but a wise man knows that a horse with a broken leg takes him nowhere. Not soon enough, but eventually, the land rose out of the swamp and the cypresses fell behind, and once again they were racing, now along the low ridge, now through Brandborough, and now, two hours after leaving the plantation, up the drive in a flurry of crushed shell.

It was one o'clock in the morning and Colleen was more exhausted than she knew. At Jase's bedside when she heard the horses and Tom's call, she hurried downstairs in time to meet him in the foyer as he burst through the front door.

"Tom! Thank God!"

"What happened?"

"They . . . they . . ." The firm hold she'd kept on her emotions during the long hours since the kidnapping dissolved. "They're gone," she sobbed, weeping openly against Tom's chest.

Tom hugged her a moment, then gently forced her from his embrace and held her at arm's length. "How?" he asked in a strained voice. "Who?"

"He said his name was Sanchez. Onofre Sanchez," she said, fighting for control. "He was a pirate and he had three of his crew with him. There was nothing anyone could do. They took Jason and Joseph. Without warning, came and took them away."

"They must be holding them for ransom," Tom ground out. "I'll give them a ransom they'll wish they'd never gotten."

Colleen shook her head. "He didn't take them for ransom," she told him. "He was paid to take them. By Sir Theodotus Vincent. He said—"

"Sir Theodotus!" Tom whispered. "But how? He couldn't—"

"Vincent?" Maurice asked. "Ain't that—"

"Jenny's father," Tom answered before Maurice could finish. "That *bastard*!"

"I'm sorry, Maurice," Colleen said, trying to collect herself. "I didn't even say hello."

"That's all right. It ain't time for hellos. What'd he say?"

"That he was taking the boys to Sir Theodotus because they were all that was left of Jenny, and that Sir Theodotus told him to tell you that the debt is paid, flesh for flesh."

"We'll get 'em back, Tom," Leakey said. A massive hand closed on Tom's arm. The thick fingers imparted strength and reassurance. "Don't you worry none about that. We'll get them boys back."

"Yes," Tom said as if from a long distance. "Yes."

A great emptiness gripped him, echoed meaninglessly through his mind. Gone? It was inconceivable, and yet . . . true, leaving him, for the moment, totally drained, incapable even of rage.

"You're hurt," he said in surprise, noticing for the first time the dark-stained bandage on Colleen's arm. "Just a cut," she said. "There was a fight . . ."

"And father?" Tom asked hollowly.

"In bed upstairs. Dr. Cleary finished setting his leg a couple of hours ago. I don't know if he'll wake up soon or not. A whole pint of corn whiskey . . ."

"Is he going to be all right?"

"I think so. I sent Forbes for help as soon as the pirates left. Poor Forbes has a lump on the head himself. Thank God they didn't slit his throat. Dr. Cleary says the break in Jase's leg was clean, and now that it's set and splinted it should mend well enough if he rests and stays off it."

It wouldn't have been beyond Jase to give his own life in an attempt to prevent the kidnapping, and Tom found himself grateful that his father had gotten out of the situation with as little as a broken leg. "Maybe I'd better go talk to him anyway," he said, starting up the stairs.

"Dr. Cleary says the leg will probably never be as strong as before," Colleen said, catching up to Tom, "but I'm still thankful. Tom, it was terrible. I was afraid one of Sanchez's men was going to kill him."

The master bedroom was brightly lighted. Jase was sound asleep and snoring loudly. Propped halfway up in bed, he was wearing a nightshirt. His broken left leg, splinted and heavily wrapped, was cradled in a row of supporting pillows. Tom stood by the bed, looked down at his father, and put a hand on his shoulder. "We're going after them," he said in a low voice. "Don't worry, Father, we'll get them. Maurice is back, and he'll go with me." Turning to his mother, he asked, "Anybody figure where they went after they left?"

"Sheriff McBride came over," she answered. "He went back home, but told me to tell you to wake him up when you got here."

Tom and Maurice exchanged glances. "Let's go," Maurice said, already on his way out the bedroom door.

"Tom? That you?" Jase blinked against the light, tried to sit up, groaned, and slumped back down again. "Oh, Jesus!"

"It's Tom *and* Maurice, Jase. They're both here." Colleen took a rag from the bedside stand and wiped his forehead. "But you have to lie still . . ."

"Wanna talk to Tom."

"I'm right here," Tom said, leaning over him. "Mother's told me everything, and Maurice and I are going to see McBride. You get some sleep. We'll talk in the morning."

"They went north, prob'ly some cove up the coast. Tried to stop 'em, but . . ." His head fell back on the pillow. "Oh, shit, I'm drunk and my goddamn leg *still* hurts." He tried to focus on Tom, gave up, and closed his eyes. "Got to get 'em back, Tom. Got to get 'em. . . ." With a sigh, he relaxed, and fell sound asleep again.

"Watch over him," Tom said grimly, "and try to get some sleep yourself. We'll be back later on." He took Colleen in his arms and held her. When he spoke, his voice was low and determined. "Don't worry, Mama. We'll bring them back somehow."

The drapes were drawn so the light wouldn't hurt Jase's eyes. A cloth dipped in cool spring water lay over his forehead. "I've had hangovers before," he said as Tom and Maurice settled wearily into chairs at the side of his bed, "but none like this. I told Cleary the next time he runs out of opium he'd better not come around trying to set any broken leg of mine. I'd've been better off letting him set it stone cold sober."

"Well, I've seen that done," Maurice said, "and it

ain't a pretty sight. The muscles pull up tight and you got to do a lot of pulling to get the bone—"

"All right, all right!" Jase interrupted. "I've seen it too, so let's just drop the subject. Besides, we've more important things to talk about. What'd you find out?"

Tom and Maurice had spent the rest of the night and the early morning hours with Sheriff Tom McBride, and had been back at the house only long enough for a bite to eat and a cup of coffee. "You were right about going north," Tom said. "We found three of Hugh Northrup's horses milling around at Bunker's Cove, and marks where they'd pulled a skiff to shore and shoved off again. Whoever this Sanchez is, he must know this part of the coast, because the bottom drops off pretty sharp there. He probably had his ship tack back and forth offshore and wait for him."

"Problem is," Maurice said, "where'd he take 'em once he got 'em on board? If we don't know that, we don't know where to chase 'em to."

"Somewhere on this side of the world, I imagine," Jase said. "I got thinking this morning after I woke up, and sure enough, the name Sanchez is familiar. One of our captains had a run-in with him about eight years ago just east of St. Kitts. Johnston it was, on the *Andrea,* that little fore-topsail schooner I got rid of a couple years ago. Anyway, Sanchez is a two-bit Caribbean pirate who I figured to be dead by now, except he isn't. The point is, I can't see him sailing to England, because I doubt if he has the ship or the intelligence."

"He could've had a rendezvous with another ship somewhere up or down the coast," Maurice suggested.

"Not necessarily," Jase said. "We don't know that Vincent is still in England. You've had no communication with him, have you, Tom?"

"Not a word. Jenny wrote and so did I, but he never answered. In any case, he has to know I'll be looking for them. What am I supposed to do? Take an army with— damn!" He got up so fast his coffee sloshed all over his breeches. "Come on, Maurice, let's get out of here."

"Where? Where you going?" Jase asked, alarmed.

"That one you hit last night. He—"

"I *hit* one of them?" Jase asked, amazed. "I thought—"

"They found him about a quarter mile up the road and took him to Doc Cleary this morning. He was still unconscious at sunup, and then I forgot about him in all the hullabaloo."

"Well, I'll be damned," Jase said. "I hit one of 'em!" Then he added, "Tom!"

"Yes, sir?" Tom asked from the door.

"Don't get your hopes up too much. I wasn't aimin' to wound—"

Tom didn't hear the rest. Followed closely by Maurice, he took the stairs in threes and was out the back door before Colleen could ask where they were going. Less than a minute later, riding bareback, he and Maurice were racing for town and Dr. Cleary's.

Cleary was half-dozing after a long night when they pounded on his door and then burst in without waiting. "Where is he?" Tom demanded, pulling the bewhiskered old doctor out of his chair.

"Who? Oh, it's you, Tom." Cleary shook his head to clear the cobwebs. "That pirate? He's back in my surgery."

"He still alive? Conscious?"

"Came to about an hour ago, but he's dying. The bullet's still in his chest somewhere, and there's no way to get it out without killing him."

"Can he talk?"

Cleary shrugged and led the way toward his surgery. "Only way to tell is to go see. Whatever you want to learn, you'd best learn quick, though. He's lost a lot of blood, and the infection's got a start."

The surgery was dimly lighted and smelled of unguents and salves and liniments. Cleary turned up a lantern and hung it next to a bed in the corner. The pirate was only in his early twenties, but pain had aged him overnight. His hair and beard were matted, his face and hands still covered with dirt from the fall he'd taken from the horse. A bandage that looked surprisingly clean was wrapped around his torso. "He doesn't look that good from the back," Cleary explained, touching the pirate's forehead. "I got him lying this way because the wound was bubbling. Pressure'll keep it closed so his lung doesn't collapse."

"He speak English?" Tom asked.

"Don't think so. What little he's said sounds like Spanish to me."

"We'll get along just fine, then," Maurice said with a death's-head grin. He stood over the pirate and bent low. *"De veras, amigo?"*

Cleary coughed. "Ah, if you don't mind," he said, a little nervously, "I think I'll let you ask your questions in private."

"That's a good idea," Tom said. "We'll call when we need you."

The door closed and the three were left alone. The pirate stared fearfully from Maurice to Tom and back. Maurice pulled up a chair, sat next to him, and thoughtfully changed the compress on his forehead for a cooler one. "Listen to me," he said in Spanish. "I'm going to ask you some questions, and you're going to answer them."

The pirate's eyes blazed with hatred and fever as he glared up at Maurice. *"Agua,"* he gasped, his voice raspy and tortured.

"There's the man who hands out the water," Maurice explained, pointing at Tom. "You tell us what we want to know, and he'll give you some."

The pirate focused with difficulty on Tom. "Tell you . . . nothing . . ." he croaked in Spanish. "Bastards . . . murdering bastards . . ."

"What'd he say?" Tom asked.

"Called you a bastard."

"You tell him," Tom said grimly, "that he helped steal my sons, and I want to know where they were taking them."

Maurice translated and the pirate shook his head weakly. "Can't say," he gasped. "Sanchez . . . would . . . kill me."

"What's that?" Tom asked. "What's he—"

Maurice waved him into silence. His lips drew back in an expression that was more a grimace than a smile. "My friend says he doesn't want you to die," he explained in Spanish, "that we have your best interests at heart." His hand moved and his smile became even broader as the lantern light played on the double-edged blade that suddenly appeared in front of the pirate's eyes. "You still have that musket ball in you, and my friend is so concerned with your health that he wants me to remove it." The blade dipped and slid between the bandages and the pirate's skin. "Now, if you'll just hold still, I'll cut off this bandage and roll you over, and I'll bet I can dig out that ball in no time."

The sight of Maurice leering down at him and the feel of cold steel against his chest were terrifying. Dying was bad enough, but dying in agony, a blade digging slowly through his back, was beyond thought. The blade moved, cut through the first piece of bandage, slowly sawed through the second. "San Sebastian!" the pirate cried, fear and pain overcoming loyalty. "Sanchez is sailing for San Sebastian!"

Tom needed no translation. San Sebastian was a small island in the Caribbean, part of the British West Indies, one of the Leeward Islands. He and Maurice had called at the port there during those wild years they had been at sea, and as he met Maurice's eyes, he saw that he remembered as well.

"Why San Sebastian?" Maurice asked. "Why was Sanchez taking the boys there?"

"The governor . . . the governor there. . . . He was the one who paid Sanchez. His name is . . . is Vincent."

Tom closed his eyes and took a deep breath. Sir Theodotus Vincent, the governor of San Sebastian. A lucky stroke, or had he wangled the appointment? In some ways, getting the twins off a tiny island would be more difficult than taking them from England. Only one port, an inhospitable shoreline. . . .

"Sanchez was taking the boys directly to Vincent?" Maurice was asking.

The pirate struggled for breath. "Don't know. Figured he would. . . . Oh, Sainted Mother, it hurts! I need a priest." He raised his head and fell back weakly. "I've told you . . . the truth. . . . Water. . . . Confess me . . ."

His head lolled to one side and his breathing became rapid and shallow.

"Won't get any more out of him," Maurice said, rising and slipping his knife back in its sheath. "We didn't get here any too soon. He'll be dead by nightfall."

"San Sebastian," Tom said, almost dreamily. "The boys'll be on San Sebastian, and that's where we'll be, too." He shook himself as if awakening, and headed for the door. "Well, let's get started."

The nearest Paxton ship was in Boston, and wouldn't return to Charleston for at least four weeks. Two more were bound for England and couldn't be expected before February. With the rest, the pattern was dismally similar. The only way to get to San Sebastian was to take the *Marie*, the small pleasure sloop Jase kept in Brandborough, around Florida to New Orleans and pick up a Paxton ship there—assuming one could be had. Tom and Maurice each wore a money belt stuffed with gold coins and carried identical copies of Jason's letter to Thad Barton, the head of the Paxton shipping office in New Orleans. It had taken time to make their preparations, and they'd had to take an extra day for provisioning the sloop, but they could hope, with luck, to be in New Orleans by the beginning of November.

"Damn, but I wish I was going with you!"

Jase, Colleen, Tom, and Maurice stood on the dock, Jase leaning on rough crutches, Colleen at his side with a hand on his arm. Tom shook his head. "There's no way we can take you and you know it," he said gently. "You did enough by hitting that pirate—and then getting out of bed to see us off."

"A lucky shot," Jase grumbled. "And any damned fool can get out of a bed."

"Right. Which is what you are, seeing as you're supposed to be flat on your back for another two weeks at least."

"I'll be the judge of that," Jase snapped. "You're sure there's nothing else you'll need?"

"Got everything," Tom said, patting the hilt of the rapier he had taken from the mantel. Forty inches of steel, the weapon had belonged to Marie Ravenne, the Raven with a silver guard.

"You watch out for hurricanes, now," Jase warned for the dozenth time. "You see the signs, you head for shore as fast as you can."

"We will," Tom said, laughing.

"I just wish you could leave for San Sebastian from here."

"I do, too," Tom replied, "but the boys should be all right. Sir Theodotus paid to have them delivered safe and sound, so the chances are he'll get them that way. Besides, we shouldn't be delayed for long in New Orleans. Well . . ." He extended his hand. "The wind's right, and all this talk won't get us there any faster."

Jase's grip was strong. "We'll be praying for you, Tom. Good luck, and Godspeed."

"Thanks. Mama?" He let go of Jase's hand and, in a gesture that dated back to his childhood, touched the hair at his mother's temple. "Keep him off that leg," he said, "and make plenty of Christmas cookies for us."

Jase turned to Maurice as Colleen embraced Tom and whispered a choked goodbye. "A hell of a thing for you to come back to, but I'm glad you're here, Maurice.

Take care of this son of mine, will you?''

"Sure will, Jase," Maurice said, shaking the hand of the man who'd been more like a father to him than his own had. "And don't worry about them boys. Like Tom says, we'll have 'em home for Christmas."

"I'm going to try to believe that, Maurice. I'm going to try very hard."

Tom leaped abroad the sloop and took the tiller and sheet. Maurice cast them off forward, then aft, gave the boat a mighty shove, and jumped across the widening gap.

"Christmas!" Colleen called as the wind filled the sail and the sloop picked up speed. "We love you both!"

Tom turned to wave once, then put his mind and back to the task at hand. "Ready about!" he called.

The first of many tacks. The sloop lost speed, the sail luffed briefly, then billowed as it caught the wind again. One more tack and they passed the lighthouse and hit the Atlantic chop. A mile out, the trees onshore blurred to a solid mass of green. Tom steered southwest by south, tied off the tiller and sheet, and walked forward past Maurice, who was on his way to the tiny cabin below decks to get some sleep.

The wind was quartering from the east-southeast. Long rolling waves lifted and dropped the small boat. Spray was flung across Tom's face. New Orleans was well over a thousand miles away, but the *Marie,* if not exactly suited to deep water sailing, was fast and sure. Pensive, Tom reached inside his shirt and withdrew the amulet he wore on a gold chain. The amulet, an heirloom precious to the Paxtons, was of pounded gold filigree shaped into finely worked brambles clustered around a tree. Generations old, it had been left to Marie Ravenne by her father, whose wife had given it to him. Marie had given the amulet to her son, and since then it had passed from husband to wife, from mother to first-born son, and thence to his wife. Jenny had worn the amulet, but she had died before Joseph was old enough to receive the charm.

Tom's fingertips strayed over the surface and traced the finely worked details. What the artist had had in mind he didn't know, but the symbols for him were powerful. Oaks were strong and long-lasting, brambles were resilient and tenacious. The name Paxton had embodied those virtues for five generations. Clutching the amulet a final time before letting it slip back inside his shirt, he swore there would be a sixth.

ᑯ CHAPTER VII ᑌ

"To your good health, sir."

"Humph! Good health, indeed!" Sir Theodotus Vincent sprawled listlessly in the ribbon-back Chippendale armchair that had accompanied him to San Sebastian a little over a year earlier, and stared balefully down the highly polished mahogany pedestal table littered with the remnants of a light dinner of fruits and vegetables suitable for a hot and muggy evening. "How anyone could be healthy in this devil of a climate is beyond me."

The truth was that Sir Theodotus had rarely been healthy for the past four and a half years. The departure—the kidnapping, as he perceived it—of his beloved Jenny had robbed him of spirit. Calamity had followed calamity: less than a year later, on April the eighteenth of 1807, Jenny's birthday, Lady Eugenia's heart had failed and she had passed away. For two years Sir Theodotus had lived in a slough of despond. Luckily, he had friends with influence, and on the supposition that a total change would help, he allowed himself to be posted to San Sebastian. Recently, however, he'd received a letter from Tom Paxton—addressed to both himself and Lady Eugenia, forwarded from England—informing him of Jenny's death less than four months before. The news had devastated him.

During his first six months as governor of the tiny island, Sir Theodotus had been a changed man. He had enjoyed the climate and the people. He had discharged his duties with dispatch and governed wisely. And then he had learned of Jenny's death, and had been thrown into a depression so severe that he could hardly get out of bed.

The mind-numbing paralysis had persisted. He could accept Lady Eugenia's death, but that he should have to endure Jenny's, that he had not seen her for almost five years and now lacked the chance to mourn her decently, was unbearable. Several days had passed, during which he sat and stared at the somber gray-blue sea imprisoning the island. At last, in August, during one mad night of ceaseless pacing, the scheme to kidnap Jenny's twins had sprung full-blown into his mind. Contacting the right person for the job without informing the whole world of his intent had consumed a month, and negotiations with the pirate Sanchez another week. Now Sanchez had been gone for over five weeks, and Sir Theodotus's patience was wearing thin.

Life had become one long exercise in keeping madness at bay. At first, he had tried to occupy himself with the minutiae of government, but his interest had waned quickly and he now contented himself with signing whatever papers were thrust in front of him. He tried reading, but books quickly bored him. He let himself slip into what approached a trance. He slept, he ate, he relieved himself. He drank too much—not a good idea, but a man had to do something to fill the hours. His attention dulled by boredom and waiting, he stared at walls and furnishings, the sea and the sky, whatever took his attention at the moment.

But what was there to see, really? The room in which he sat was a prime example: silver candelabra, each with six candles, illuminating the table; waxed floors without rugs to soak up the light; whitewashed walls with windows shuttered to keep out mosquitoes and other insects and keep in the heat. Ten more ribbon-back Chippendales were arranged against the wall. A Sheraton breakfront sideboard and paintings of English landscapes reminded Sir Theodotus of a home far away from what had become a subtropical nightmare. A serving girl leaned sullenly against the wall, another lurked behind the door. Details, details, details. A candle flame reflected in a drawer knob. A quarter moon in an oil-painting sky. A moth flirting with incineration. . . .

Things, mere things. A man imbued things with life. Without meaning in a man's life, the objects that surrounded him were without meaning. If only Sanchez . . . "Damn, but I hate this place," he swore.

"Oh, San Sebastian isn't all *that* bad," Trevor Bliss said from the far end of the table, where he lounged contentedly and sipped from his glass. Even seated and at ease, Bliss presented a dashing figure with finely chiseled features beneath his sand-colored hair. "Remember," he said with a chuckle. "The first snow has fallen at home by now. And I for one can do without chilblains, thank you."

"An argument without merit, Captain," Sir Theodotus said. "I'm tired of all this blasted rain and unending fecundity, not to speak of that damned sulfurous smoke that descends without warning every so often. I'm tired of unalleviated greenery everywhere I look and the ceaselessly pleasant weather. I long for a change of seasons, damn it all. I long for *contrast*."

"Nonetheless, sir, I've rather enjoyed being posted here."

"That's fine for you," Sir Theodotus snorted. "You're young yet. You can make something fine for yourself in a place like this."

"Yes," Bliss agreed softly. "The Caribbean is ripe with opportunity if one dares to reach out and grasp when the chance presents itself." He leaned back in his chair and considered both the wine and the situation. His rise in the Navy had been, if not meteoric, at least steady. He had distinguished himself under fire, committed no glaring blunders, and had made friends in the right places. And then, in a move that stunned him, the Admiralty had slapped him in the face with the command of a mere eighteen-gun sloop of war and posted him to an utterly insignificant island. Once again, he had been denied the prominence and riches he deserved.

Fortunately for Bliss, Napoleon Bonaparte, that diminutive madman who ruled France, kept stirring up trouble. The continuing hostilities between England and France during recent years had led to a situation in the Caribbean that was replete with potential for profit. The reason was simple, really. Since France, like any other country, rose or fell according to the world trade she generated, the British Parliament and crown had adopted the American Embargo Act and the Nonintercourse Act to hamper that country's trade whenever and wherever possible. As a result, all ships flying the flag of a nonbelligerent nation were forbidden under threat of seizure to sail from any foreign port to any French or French-held port without an intermediate call at a British port. Of course, enforcement required a British naval presence in virtually all corners of the world, including the West Indies. And Bliss's predecessor, Captain Wallingham, had been quick to teach him how being part of that naval presence could enrich him.

Sugar was king on San Sebastian. The three major planters, headed by Henri LeBusque, owned plantations on the opposite end of the island and raised cane, which, when crudely processed, yielded a dark, moist unrefined sugar called muscovado. After the muscovado was drained of molasses, it was stored in kegs for eventual shipment. The molasses, in turn, was either shipped to the United States to become rum, or distilled on the plantations and sold locally, or shipped abroad. Between them, the three owners completely controlled a moderate-sized cove that, when wind and tide were right, could accommodate a single large vessel. From this cove, at least one ship a month loaded with muscovado, molasses, or rum set sail directly for France. With Wallingham's connivance, the departures were not recorded. The scheme was elegant in its simplicity. Now

Bliss, like Wallingham before him, would assure the planters that the *Druid* would be elsewhere when the ships sailed. In return, he would receive a healthy portion of the profits, which he could either reinvest in the venture or retain for his personal use.

Bliss wasn't so naive as to think that graft didn't exist; what surprised him was how easily it was engaged in. The knowledge that he was doing no more than thousands of others before him had done—plus his bitterness toward those who had betrayed him—made his decision easy and painless. His initial meeting with the planters lasted a half-hour. Two weeks later, the *Druid* was well to the north and west of San Sebastian when LeBusque's first ship sailed for France.

The rising inflection of a question caught Bliss's attention, and the captain set aside for the moment thoughts of the wealth he was accumulating. "I beg your pardon, sir?" he asked. "What was that?"

"Damned heat puts everybody to sleep," Sir Theodotus grumbled. "I was asking what you thought should be done about LeBusque. The man has become insufferable. Just because he's the owner of the largest plantation on the island, he believes he's above the law."

Bliss smiled. "Oh, no, sir. I don't think Henri feels like that at all," he said smoothly. "I'd be glad to have a word with him, though, if you'd like. Even Monsieur LeBusque would have to admit his manner could be slightly less abrasive."

"Thank you, Captain Bliss. I'd like that very much. You seem to have a knack for handling these merchants." Sir Theodotus chuckled dryly. "How would you like to be governor?"

Bliss laughed and shook his head. "No, thank you, sir. I don't mind helping out when and where I can, but I'm afraid I'm just a simple sailor at heart."

Simple sailor indeed, Bliss thought, regarding Sir Theodotus from under hooded eyes. Simple enough to understand the potential value to the French of an island like San Sebastian, and shrewd enough to accept a most handsome reward for neutralizing British power when the moment for the French coup should arrive. Not that his task would be difficult. Sir Theodotus relied on him exclusively for advice and counsel as he became daily more removed from reality. He was not a well man. His eyes were sunk deeply in his head and the skin of his face was tight and mottled. His hands trembled as he reached for his wineglass, and his breathing was heavy and labored. All told, he looked more like a man in his seventies than his fifties. "Just give me a decent ship and a crew of stout British lads, and I'll happily leave the business of governing to you older and wiser chaps," the young captain added unctuously.

"Good thinking. Good thinking," Sir Theodotus grunted. He finished his wine, banged the glass down on the table, and motioned curtly. The serving girl, dressed in a white blouse and a bright-red skirt, hurried out of the shadows, refilled the men's glasses, and slunk away again. "Mark my words, though. You've the talent. Another twenty years of seasoning and you'll make a fine governor yourself—and of a far better place than this hellhole," he added darkly.

"Really, sir—"

"Don't contradict me, young man," Sir Theodotus growled. He sagged in his chair, then suddenly jerked upright. "Oh, damn. Contradict me if you wish. No one else does. I enjoy a modicum of contradiction from time to time." His voice slurred with fatigue and the effect of too much wine. " 'Strouble with being governor. Every mother's son agrees with every damn thing you say. A man needs someone around to contradict him once or twice a week . . ." He trailed off and focused with difficulty on Bliss. "How long did you say you'd be in port?" he asked.

"Unfortunately, not long," Bliss answered. "Time

enough to reprovision and give the men a taste of life ashore. Then I'm off on patrol again."

"Good. Good!" Sir Theodotus thumped the table with his fist, adding fatuously, "Vigilance, by God, is the watchword of the empire!"

"Suh?"

Sir Theodotus squinted into the darkness. "What do you want?" he barked at the dark-skinned servant who hurried in from the front of the house.

"News, suh," the servant said. He went to Sir Theodotus's side and spoke to the governor in such a low voice that Bliss could distinguish no more than an occasional word.

An immediate and dramatic change came over the governor. He sat up straighter and color appeared in his cheeks for the first time in days. "Good Lord," he breathed, suddenly sobered. "At last. I'd begun to lose hope. . . . Captain," he added, standing so abruptly he almost knocked over his chair, "I'd like you to accompany me, if you'd be so kind."

"Of course, sir," Bliss said, patting his lips with a napkin and standing. "Might I inquire where?"

"To meet a ship." Sir Theodotus turned to the servant. "Have my coach brought around. We'll be leaving immediately. Tell Louisa that I'll return shortly, and shall want everything prepared as ordered. Hurry, now. Get moving, man."

"Yes, suh!" the servant said, already on the move.

"And you, Captain—I'll meet you at the front door in two minutes." Discarding the lightweight lounging jacket he'd worn for dinner, Sir Theodotus hurried down the hall to his study. A moment later, he was spinning the dial of his safe, from which he withdrew an obviously heavily weighted carpetbag. In the hall again, he accepted from a waiting servant a coat more suitable for outside wear. "Where's the coach?" he snapped as the servant handed him his chapeau bras.

"Comin' roun', suh. Be here by the time you out the door."

So it was. With Bliss right on his heels, Sir Theodotus plunged out the door at the same instant the coach rounded the side of the mansion. "I hope you don't mind my saying so, sir," Bliss said after he'd helped Sir Theodotus into the coach and had climbed in himself, "but I'm puzzled."

"The harbor!" Sir Theodotus called. The coach leaped forward. "I don't mind at all, Captain, but you'll understand soon enough," he added as the motion threw him back in the seat.

The coach descended the hill where the governor's mansion perched and rolled swiftly through the streets of San Sebastian. It was not a large island. The product of twin volcanoes, it vaguely resembled two irregularly shaped coins joined by a narrow isthmus. The eastern volcano had long since sealed itself off and eroded away. The western volcano, called The Sleeping Giant, was younger and occasionally belched a cloud of sulfurous smoke or rocked the island with gentle quakes that were so much a part of life on San Sebastian that the citizens no longer took alarm. The geography of the island's two halves differed radically. The eastern half was lower and well suited for agriculture. The western was wildly precipitous and impossible to cultivate commercially because of the volcano and the thick forest that carpeted the jumbled slopes. The eastern half was populated by the plantation owners, their employees, and their slaves. The western half boasted the town and port of San Sebastian with its population of fifteen hundred, not counting sailors ashore for a night or two. Travel between the two halves of the island was limited to a single poorly constructed road, without which the plantations could not function, for the port was the entry through which most of their lifeblood flowed.

The town of San Sebastian had been a pirate haunt a

hundred years earlier, but time and economics and the British Navy had transformed it into a proper outpost of civilization. The streets were narrow and the tile-roofed buildings crowded close together. Lights from the pubs and coffeehouses provided sporadic illumination that, with a half-moon halfway up the eastern sky, lighted the way for horses and carriages.

The first view of the harbor, obscured by buildings until the coach turned onto King George Street, was a narrow slot of water that widened as they neared the waterfront. "I trust we can use your gig, Captain," Sir Theodotus said, trying not to sound nervous.

"Certainly," Bliss replied as they turned onto the broad board roadway that paralleled the harbor. "Sir?"

"Yes?" Sir Theodotus grunted.

Bliss gestured toward the harbor. There, in the center, a ship with no discernible flag and with signal lights hung fore and aft lay at anchor. Directly behind it, the *Druid* was sliding slowly into position to deliver a broadside. "We're going out to meet *that* ship?" Bliss asked tightly.

"We are, Captain. It contains priceless cargo."

Bliss ordered the coachman to stop, and no sooner had he and Sir Theodotus alighted than a midshipman ran toward them. "Sir!" the boy called. "Midshipman Holmes, sir!" Spine stiff and heels clicking, the youth snapped to attention before Bliss.

"What is it, lad?"

"It's a pirate ship, sir. The man calls himself San-chez, and says he has been given safe passage by Governor Vincent! Lieutenant Meecham told me to get you as fast—"

"Enough, Holmes," Bliss interrupted. "Who has the duty on my gig?"

"Able Seaman Stone, sir."

"Very well. Tell him to make ready to shove off immediately, if you please." Midshipman Holmes raced back to the gig. Bliss's face was indecipherable. "I find it difficult to believe," he said in a voice as cold as ice, "that the governor is engaged in commerce with a pirate. I'm sorry, sir, but I'm afraid I must demand an explanation."

Sir Theodotus hadn't divulged his plans to Bliss earlier because he knew the officer would be outraged. Now that the time had come, though, he did not flinch. "My grandsons are aboard that ship, Captain," he said in a tone of authority that Bliss hadn't heard in months, "and I am in no mood for questions and answers. You will kindly lead the way. Immediately."

Bliss opened his mouth to speak but abruptly changed his mind, turned on his heel, and strode out the quay toward his gig. His mind raced. A pirate in *his* harbor! The very idea was an affront, and yet. . . . Like a large painting being unveiled, the picture came to him. Sir Theodotus had related the tale of his daughter: her abduction by the American, the birth of her twin sons, and her death. The only possible explanation for the presence of the pirate ship in San Sebastian was that Sanchez had kidnapped the boys. If that indeed was the case—and he would know soon enough—Bliss had an unbreakable hold on Sir Theodotus. A hold, he told himself as he helped the governor into the gig, that he could exploit to great benefit when the time came.

The gig leaped across the water. "To the *Druid* first," Bliss ordered. "Midshipman Holmes."

"Aye, sir!"

"I want you to take this message to Mr. Meecham. Tell him that he's to stand by at ready and do nothing to exacerbate the situation, that I'll be aboard shortly, and that on my command of 'Fire!' he's to blow that ship out of the water. Is that clear?"

"Aye, aye, sir!"

"Now, listen here!" Sir Theodotus sputtered. "You'll do nothing of the sort!"

"You have your orders, Midshipman," Bliss said
curtly as the gig nuzzled up to the *Druid*'s ladder.
"Smartly, now."

The midshipman scampered up the ladder and Bliss
ordered the crew of the gig to make for the pirate ship.
His body aching with tension, Sir Theodotus clutched
the carpetbag to him and prayed that the twins were
safe. "I . . . I don't think I can climb a rope ladder," he
said in a subdued tone as the gig slowed and one of the
sailors caught the ladder that was dropped to them. He
thrust the carpetbag at Bliss. "If you would, Captain?
My grandsons . . ."

Bliss took the bag and glanced up. A twelve-foot
climb wasn't far, but with a heavy bag in one hand . . .

"Beggin' the captain's pardon, sir," Able Seaman
Stone said.

"Yes?" Bliss asked.

Stone's hands worked rapidly as he stepped forward
and took the seat facing Bliss. "You can hang it on this,
sir," he said, holding out a piece of line he'd fashioned
into a loop.

At the same time, a lantern floated down and stopped
a few feet above the gig. "Welcome, Governor," a
voice said from the darkness. "Welcome aboard the
Red Dog Song."

"I can't make the climb, Sanchez," Sir Theodotus
called back. "I'm sending Captain Bliss in my place."

"Captain Bliss? The scourge of Caribbean pirates,
celebrated in song and a hundred drunken tales?"
Mocking laughter floated across the water. "Come
aboard, Captain Bliss, and don't forget my gold. We'll
have a nice cup of tea."

Bliss's eyes narrowed and a grim smile pulled at the
corners of his mouth. Sir Theodotus Vincent, the em-
bodiment of the king's law and authority, was a kidnapper, and not one whit better than Captain Trevor
Bliss of His Majesty's Navy, who was, unbeknownst to
everyone except the island planters, guilty of treason.

The irony was too rich for words. He allowed Able Seaman Stone to adjust the loop around his neck and one shoulder and tie the bag so it wouldn't knock against his legs, then grabbed the ladder and stood.

"There's, ah, one other thing, Captain," Sir Theodotus said as Stone retreated to the stern of the gig. "You've got to promise Sanchez that you won't bother him for six months if he cooperates and doesn't raid any British ships. That was part of the bargain I struck with him."

Bliss stiffened. There was no way on God's earth that he could keep the events of this night secret. The word would spread and he'd be the laughingstock of the fleet. Of course, he did have other plans, come New Year's Day. . . . "As you say, sir," Bliss replied coldly. "And now, if you don't mind, I'll be on my way. I've been invited for tea, don't you know."

Bliss climbed rapidly, caught hold of a helping hand, and leaped over the rail to the deck.

"Well, well! So this is Captain Bliss!" Onofre Sanchez, wearing a British officer's hat and coat for the occasion, stepped forward. "We meet face to face at last, no? It is an honor. Not many of your officers step aboard the *Red Dog Song*. Those who do . . ." He shrugged and a look of immense sorrow darkened his face as he flicked a speck of dust from his coat. "But then, why should we be sad, eh? You, at least, will be fortunate enough to leave unharmed, no?"

"I had better," Bliss answered, his scorn for Sanchez evident. He gestured to the *Druid*, whose gun ports, even in the darkness, were obviously open. "If not, my first officer has explicit orders to blow you out of the water."

A flurry of whispers passed through Sanchez's crew. Roughly dressed and cutthroats all, they pressed more closely around Bliss until Sanchez waved them back. "Some of them speak English, Captain Bliss," he explained, "and they have translated your threats for the others. I, on the other hand, see those threats as nothing more than the words of a prudent man.'' His smile faded as fast as the light under the dark clouds of a summer squall. ''Until you have the boys, of course. And then, Captain, I too must wonder what will keep your jack-tars' hands from their guns.''

Bliss's voice was brittle with contempt. ''You have my word, Sanchez, the word of a British officer. You also have the word of the governor of San Sebastian.''

Sanchez regarded Bliss, read in his eyes the overweening pride that was the product of a code as stringent as any blood oath a pirate took. Just as he, Sanchez, would give the dead Fouchet's woman triple the share due her, Bliss, no matter how much it pained him, would keep his word.

''Very well, then,'' Sanchez agreed. ''Let us see the gold and have done with it.''

Bliss kept a firm grip on the carpetbag. ''I want to see the boys first,'' he said. ''If they're safe and healthy, you shall have your gold.''

A slow smile spread across Sanchez's face, and he rattled off something in Spanish that elicited hoots and catcalls from his crew. ''I told them, Señor *Capitan*, that they should hide their heads in shame because the noble officer of the distant English king thinks they are bad little boys, and does not trust them.''

''You can tell them that I know exactly with whom I'm dealing,'' Bliss snapped angrily. He spaced his words evenly and spoke clearly so he would not be misunderstood. ''They and their captain are scum and cutthroats. Their ship is filthy and reeks of the stench of dishonest men. They have the manners of dogs, and will die like dogs within a turn of the glass when I next set eyes on them. And now, damn your soul to hell, fetch me the boys.''

No man under the sun spoke to Onofre Sanchez that way and lived. Hatred twisted his face. His hand hovered near the hilt of his cutlass and his fingers trembled with the desire to gut the arrogant Englishman. But nine loaded guns waited astern, and a bag of gold lay on the deck not two paces from where he stood. There would come a day, though, when Onofre Sanchez would savor his revenge, and the captain would learn the real meaning of filth and stench—before he died. Abruptly, he relaxed and smiled again. "Very well, Captain Bliss," he said, gesturing behind him to two men waiting next to a hatch. "You shall see first, and then pay."

The twins had been kept immediately below deck, and no more than thirty seconds passed before they were handed onto the deck and led to Sanchez. The pirate knelt in front of them. "So, my hearties! Your voyage aboard a real pirate ship is over." He glanced at Bliss. "Did you have fun with Onofre Sanchez? Enjoy your adventure?"

"Yes, sir," Joseph piped.

"I want my daddy," Jason said.

"You'll have your granddaddy instead, and this man will take you to him. What do you say to that, eh?"

They were presentable, Bliss agreed as he inspected them briefly. "What are your names, boys?" he asked gruffly.

"Joseph . . . Jason . . . Paxton," the twins answered in unison.

"They appear not to be harmed, pirate," Bliss said, turning to Sanchez. "But know this. If you cross me in any way, you will not leave this harbor alive."

"Onofre Sanchez loves children, Captain, and would not hurt one on purpose, so no more threats are necessary."

"You are a prince among men," Bliss said sarcastically. He nudged the carpetbag full of gold with his foot. "And now, if you don't mind, we'll—"

"Not quite yet, Captain. There's a little matter of safe passage for six months. The governor—"

"I wouldn't think of disobeying a governor's orders," Bliss snapped. "But I expect you out of this harbor on the next tide."

"I need water and fresh—"

"You'll be allowed that. A boat will stand by at daybreak to lead no more than three of your men ashore. The tide goes out between nine and nine-thirty in the morning. See that you're on it."

"I understand," Sanchez said, nodding. He watched as Bliss led the boys to the rail, then lifted his hand in mock salute. "*Adios,* Señor *Capitan*, from one who will sail this sea long after the sharks have eaten your carcass."

Bliss handed the twins into the waiting arms of Able Seaman Stone, climbed down the ladder, and dropped lightly into the gig. "To shore," he ordered. "Quickly."

"Jason! Joseph!" Sir Theodotus looked as if he'd shed twenty years as he held out his arms to the boys. "I'm your grandfather. Do you understand? I'm your mother's father."

"Mama's dead," Joseph said matter-of-factly. "We want to go home."

"We already have a grandfather," Jason added as the pirate ship dropped rapidly behind them.

"I know," Sir Theodotus said, his voice choked with emotion. "I loved your mother, and now that she is gone I have you to love instead." One boy on each side of him, he wrapped protective arms around them. "But we must get to know each other. You shall call me Grandfather, and I shall call you . . . but which of you is Joseph?"

"I am. Where's O'fre?"

"Never mind him now." Sir Theodotus turned to Jason and gave him a little squeeze. "So you're Jason, then."

Jason's face tightened in preparation for an unhappy wail. "I want to go home," he cried.

"You are going home," Sir Theodotus reassured

him. He held Jason close, let go of Joseph long enough to point up at the hill that loomed over the town, and the brightly lighted grounds of the governor's mansion silhouetted against the dark slope of The Sleeping Giant. "There's your home," he said, his finger quivering slightly. "There's your new home. You'll like living there, I promise."

The water was dark and forbidding. Somewhere, far away, the greater menace of Tom Gunn Paxton no doubt sought his sons, and would one day arrive to try to reclaim them. Sir Theodotus had taken that into consideration, though, and would be prepared when that day came. In the meantime, as he gazed down at the twins, his heart swelled with pride and love and his mind reeled before the onslaught of memories. Jennifer, his lovely Jenny, was gone, lost to him forever, but now she lived again in these two boys. And as Jason and Joseph grew, they would learn to hate the man they had known as their father, hate Tom Gunn Paxton every bit as deeply and passionately and eternally as their grandfather did.

"We are together now," Sir Theodotus whispered. "There are happy days ahead of us. Happy, happy days."

And as if sensing his love, the little ones leaned into his sheltering embrace and fell fast asleep.

CHAPTER VIII

The tiny candle flame grew steadily from a wavering pinprick of light to a stable source of illumination, revealing a narrow, low-ceilinged room all abuzz with a steady dull roar from the tavern below. The walls were of drab gray plaster; the floor consisted of dark rough planks covered by a thin rug. Simple furnishings were the rule: a bed frame with no headboard, its slats covered with a worn straw-filled ticking; a rude three-legged stool that wobbled when sat upon; and an uneven table, round and also three-legged. A bright-red cloth draped over the table provided one of the few spots of color in the room. A short row of blouses and skirts hung from pegs protruding from the wall.

The candle stood in a plain metal holder in the center of the table. Adriana moved the stool closer to the table with one slippered foot, and sat in a single fluid motion. She clasped her hands together on the table and, her back straight and her breathing slowed, leaned forward slightly to look into the flame. Slowly, the tensions of the day melted. The muscles in her neck and back and legs relaxed. The sound from below swelled, but she willed herself to ignore it, and it receded beyond the edge of consciousness. Her green eyes watched intently as the night breeze, wafting through the narrow open window, stirred the orange flame that danced on the candle stem. And slowly, slowly, the walls of the room melted . . . and faded. . . .

There were waves. Waves and an angry sky. There were blinding flashes of lightning and sheets of dark rain. A storm-tossed boat rode the wild mountains of water that heaved and crashed in avalanches of foam and fury. The boat fought valiantly against the wind and water, with no land in sight.

A man appeared. Adriana was aware first of bunched muscles and of great strength contending with fatigue. The man's clothes and dark hair were plastered to his body. She could not see his face or eyes, and was denied that single route that would have allowed her to delve into his soul. Still, she wanted to cry out to him, to reach out and touch him and give him her strength. . . .

Spindrift wrapped, the vessel stood poised on the crest of a wave. The man's arms bulged as he fought to keep the tiny boat's bow into the wind. In that instant, frozen indelibly on her mind, man, boat, and sea disappeared and were replaced by a soft golden glow at whose center was an oak tree intricately wound about with brambles.

The vision of the golden tree had become familiar since it had first appeared to her on the night before Giuseppe was murdered. She no longer experienced the bone-cracking fear that had preceded the image then, but its meaning still escaped her. That it was a symbol of promise and of a destiny that awaited her seemed obvious. But of what? And when? The vision had become a nagging puzzle by day, and a mystery that haunted her sleep.

"Adriana!"

The sound of her name and a sharp rap on the door roused her. Adriana tried to ignore the distraction, but the golden glow of the vision faded and was replaced by the more mundane flicker of the candle and the noise from below.

"Adriana!"

Slowly, shaking herself awake, she swept her thick auburn hair away from her face, stood, and crossed to the door. "Yes?" she asked, without lifting the latch.

"Zebediah wants you downstairs." The voice was a

woman's, but the tone and inflection were coarse and unfeminine. "Now."

"*Oui.* I shall be down right away, Harriet. Tell him one minute to dress."

She was already wearing a long brown skirt with tiny bells sewed to the hem and a lime-colored blouse that was cut low to reveal her shoulders. Rings sparkled on her fingers, large gilt bracelets at her wrists and ankles. Moving quickly, she selected an assortment of sheer veils from the pegs on the wall, tied some around her waist, and carefully draped others about her head and shoulders in a manner that hid, save for tantalizing glimpses, the honey color of her skin and her full, curvaceous figure.

Her room was one of several that opened onto a narrow interior balcony that overlooked a vast smoke-filled chamber. The room was lighted by a quartet of wheel lamp chandeliers hanging from the beamed ceiling, and a double row of lanterns behind the bar. There were few windows, and the sluggish air with its suffocating haze was thick with the smell of cooked meat and spilled rum and seldom-washed bodies. Sawdust scattered on the floor covered planks permeated with a mixture of alcohol, grease, and blood. A hardwood bar, once polished and proud but now pocked and scarred after years of hard usage, ran the length of the wall opposite a fireplace. In one corner, a steep staircase led to the balcony where Adriana stood and watched the commotion below.

The tavern was crammed with grimy, sweaty, unshaved men who drank and ate and sang and danced and fought and pawed the serving girls who darted among them with tankards of beer and racks of beef and platters of bread to soak up the grease. In one corner, two brutes were bashing each other into bloody pulps. In the center of the floor, four sailors were trying to dance with a single girl who tried her best to please them all. A dozen feet away, a sailor had collapsed across a table; despite the fact that he was unconscious, his besotted companions were attempting to pour his share of rum down his throat. All in all, it was just another night at the Cottonmouth Tavern, a stone's throw from the Mississippi River, in the heart of New Orleans.

The riverboat men—Kaintocks, as they were called— were a burly lot dressed in rough homespun cotton shirts and leather breeches that were tucked into high boots. On their heads they wore knotted scarves or broad floppy-brimmed hats. The sprinkling of trappers wore leather from foot to head and their eyes burned with fever as they frantically packed in enough companionship and debauchery to last the next long, lonely, dreary months of solitude. Sailors from a hundred ports wore cotton, spoke a babel of languages, and tried to blot out the endless empty vistas of the world's oceans with as much alcohol as they could empty down their throats. The sailors, trappers, and Kaintocks toiled endless grueling hours in the open, risking their lives for a handful of coins and a few days and nights of nonstop celebration, and though their crude and boisterous behavior was looked down upon by the locals, no one could deny that they were vital to the survival and growth of the city. The goods they barged and rafted down the mighty Mississippi, the furs they collected from the vast hinterlands, and the cargoes they unloaded from the multitude of ships tied up at the city's docks had transformed New Orleans into one of the premier cities of the young United States.

A large man perched on a high stool behind the bar overlooked the proceedings in general and the work of his bartenders and serving girls in particular. Zebediah Gibbs, the proprietor, was as bald as a lantern globe. His heavy black eyebrows shaded eyes sharp enough to note immediately when his men failed to water down the whiskey to the extent that he required, or to spot the telltale glint of a blade drawn by one of his patrons. His skin was pasty-white from a decade spent inside. His cheeks were puffy, his face doughy-looking from too much smoke and an excess of beef and bread, but his arms were long and hard as cordwood and his shoulders were broad and knotted with muscles. He never drank, and those who did in the Cottonmouth rarely needed more than one lesson in his proficiency with hands, feet, or, his weapon of choice, the bungstarter.

Attuned to the slightest change in his tavern, Gibbs became aware of Adriana's presence the second she appeared on the balcony. Towering over lesser men, he stood on the raised step of the stool and slammed his fist down on a specially constructed heavy shelf at his side. "Play, boys, play!" he yelled to a small group of men clustered on a small dais near the bottom of the stairs. "Play, damn your souls!"

The musicians, five men clad in sailor's garb and threadbare military tunics, raised accordion, pipes, and fiddles, and launched into a strident melody that was lost in the uproar until Gibbs picked up his bungstarter and brought it crashing down on the shelf. "Gentlemen!" he roared, demonstrating that he was capable of sarcasm. "Adriana is going to dance!"

Men who had visited the Cottonmouth before and who knew what was coming growled for the others to be quiet. Someone moaned and was immediately hushed. A chair fell, and others scraped across the floor as everyone sought seats. Two bartenders carrying an oversized table hurried into the center of the room. Another pair pushed back the crowd to clear a wide circle, in which was placed the table and one chair. Within a minute, a vast and respectful silence fell over the crowd and the musicians began to play louder, if not better.

Adriana had been in New Orleans for nine months, and felt no particular fear of the men who waited to watch her dance. Sure of her power over them, she calmly descended the narrow staircase as all eyes in the room turned to her. The music changed, became softer as she neared the bottom of the stairs. By that time, she was gliding, flowing down the stairs and past the musicians to stop at the edge of the crowd. Chairs squeaked as men turned for a better view. A sigh of longing was answered by laughter, which was immediately shushed as Adriana lifted her hands palms upward, fingers spread and imploring, and began to dance.

Beer, rum, and whiskey were forgotten. Adriana's arms described the gliding flight of birds, the ripple of mountain streams, the soft flow of wind-bent grass. Swaying, undulating, her hips whispered promises of loneliness banished and passion slaked. She wended her way among the tables. Her hem brushed one man's knee, and he shuddered. A veil flicked across another's face, and he blushed furiously. When she reached the center of the room, she stepped lightly onto the chair, where, for a long, excruciating moment while the music stopped, she stood perfectly still.

Suddenly, the music began again, and a roar of appreciation erupted from the crowd as Adriana ripped one of the veils from her face, leaped onto the table, and began to dance. The tempo increased, and the desire in the spectators' eyes burned as brightly as the tavern fires as she lifted her skirt, revealing her feet and tantalizing glimpses of her calves.

The dance became a wild, frenzied display of abandonment, and to everyone there, Adriana appeared lost in the passion of the moment. She was, in truth, coldly conscious of her every move: for her the dance she performed was but a distant cousin to her dances in the Gypsy tribe's encampments throughout the English countryside. The Gypsy dances had been true and honest, and she had felt them in her soul as well as in her body. The dance in the Cottonmouth was only a performance, a show calculated to please men starved for both affection and the mere sight of a woman so that they would shower her with coins when the music ended, and later pay a visit to the table in the corner where she read palms and told fortunes. Like the dance, the palm reading was only for entertainment. And if the men liked to hear that good fortune awaited them, that fate had many wonderful surprises in store for them, she told them nothing more than she wished might come true for herself.

Fate's greatest kindness to her would be the death, at her hands, of Trevor Bliss. Ten months earlier, when she had fled England, she had feared that Bliss was beyond her reach forever. Exhausted to the point of collapse, she'd been found on board by Isaiah Hawkins and, after being given warm clothes and food, had hidden away to sleep off the effects of her ordeal. When she woke, the *Swan of Yorkshire* was in the English Channel heading west past the cliffs of Dover.

Life at sea demanded a hardheaded pragmatism and yet at the same time fostered a high degree of superstition, for no matter how practical a man might be, luck often determined success or failure. Captain Isaiah Hawkins ran a taut ship and was a man who'd survived a long run of bad luck only through unstinting diligence and determination. The bad luck, though, seemed to dissolve and become good luck the moment they cleared Land's End: for the next three days, the *Swan of Yorkshire* was driven west by winds favorable beyond his experience. The crew attributed its good fortune to Adriana, and though Isaiah was at first skeptical, he was soon convinced. On the fourth day out, the taffrail log showed over two hundred fifty nautical miles for the preceding twenty-four hours. On the fifth day, the number was still over two hundred. On the sixth day, Adriana read Hawkins's palm and predicted a speedy voyage without mishap. Six short weeks later, she was the toast of the *Swan of Yorkshire*, and was cheered by the crew as she went ashore in New Orleans.

New Orleans. Six thousand miles, an ocean and a gulf, separated Adriana from Bliss. Desire for revenge still burned in her heart, and despite the adoration of the *Swan of Yorkshire*'s crew, she had been utterly demoralized. Her salvation had been Captain Hawkins, who had proclaimed her powers far and wide and who —after obtaining her promise to have dinner with him when she repaid him on his next call to New Orleans—had advanced her enough money for a change of clothing, led her to the French Quarter, and introduced her to Zebediah Gibbs, who after a brief audition, hired her on the spot.

Her life, Adriana soon discovered, could have been worse. Zebediah Gibbs was a hot-tempered man with a propensity for dispensing quick justice where his customers were concerned, but, unlike most saloon keepers, he treated his help fairly and well. Harriet, his wife, took Adriana under her wing, and, in spite of her gruff masculinity, proved to be the perfect confidante. Within three months of her arrival, Adriana found her spirit restored, and she once again began to think in terms of finding Bliss.

Hope soared with the return of Isaiah Hawkins, though Hawkins's bad luck had assumed monumental proportions in the six months since he and Adriana had seen each other. Destitute, bitter, and uttering dire oaths that he would wreak vengeance on an uncaring world, he drank away the loan Adriana repaid and stumbled into the night—but not without first passing on the news that Trevor Bliss had been posted to San Sebastian. From that moment on, an ebullient Adriana hoarded her money and longed for the day when, finally, her knife would find its mark and Bliss would pay in full for Giuseppe's life.

In the meantime, she danced. Her skirt spun higher, her veils fell one by one. Her legs, tawny, lithe, and lovely, glowed like promises. Her arms beckoned, her fingers traced lines of fire on imaginations run wild, her breasts unloosed impossible hopes. Music, alcohol, food, and brawling receded into the dim past, leaving only the sound of bells, the whisper of slippers on a tabletop, and the hushed expectancy of the dreams of men who yearned to make her their own. It was said that a man who tasted Adriana's charms would surely die with a smile on his lips and a song in his heart.

The music and dance ended abruptly. Adriana silently, slowly turned to acknowledge the deafening cheers and applause that rocked the room, and then jumped down from the table. Someone called for more beer. Someone else laughed. An angry roar was punctuated by the sound of a chair splitting. Adriana made her way slowly across the room, stopping to say hello to a bosun mate who was an old friend of Gibbs's and to chat with an acquaintance. By the time she settled in her chair by the wall, pandemonium reigned once again in the Cottonmouth. Things were back to normal.

Giselle Depree, a coarse-featured eighteen-year-old redhead, collapsed wearily in the chair across the table from Adriana. "God, my feet hurt," she said by way of greeting.

"You should soak them each morning before you sleep," Adriana replied in the awkward French she'd been trying to learn since her arrival in New Orleans.

Giselle clutched a round wooden tray laden with clay mugs of rye whiskey to her large breasts and looked around the room. "I would, but I'm always too tired to carry the water." She sighed and arched her back in an attempt to relieve the stiffness. "Sometimes, Adriana," she went on in a discouraged voice, "I think I will never be able to leave this place. I wish some man would come in here and take me away from these Americans with their boasts and their fights. This is no life for either of us. These fellows have pinched my bottom until it is black-and-blue. And when I complain, they laugh and ask to see the bruises. We deserve better, no?"

Adriana laughed. "Naturally," she agreed. "And it will come to pass, Giselle. Two very handsome young gentlemen will someday enter this den of pestilence and make us their own. We will be married in a cathedral and live in fine homes with flower gardens and fountains. And our husbands will be devoted to us and shower us with lovely gifts every day.''

''Do you really think so?'' Giselle asked breathlessly, caught in the fantasy Adriana painted.

Adriana smiled mysteriously. ''I have the power to see into the future, do I not?'' she asked, glad that she was able to transport Giselle out of her dreary surroundings, even momentarily, into the realm of imagination.

Zebediah Gibbs broke the spell. ''Giselle!'' he roared from his perch behind the bar. ''Spread them drinks around, girl. They won't sell themselves.''

Giselle's aching back and feet would have to ache. ''Yes, Mr. Gibbs,'' she answered, reverting to English and jumping up hastily. A sad smile crossed her face. ''I know it's a dream, but I shall hold on to it anyway,'' she said, and plunged into the crowd. And the first man she passed reached out and pinched her bottom.

The smile remained on Adriana's lips as she waited for her first customer. She, too, longed for the day when she could leave the tavern, but not to the future she had spun for Giselle. There was no room in her plans for handsome strangers and fountains and flowers and love. Such things were only fantasies with which to titillate the fancies of gullible young girls, and not for her—at least until Trevor Bliss lay in his grave.

''All right, missy!'' One of the riverboat men, a thickly bearded fellow almost as broad as he was tall, jerked the other chair back and sat down. He thrust out a grimy, callused palm and grinned at Adriana. ''Tell me what ye see in that, other than twenty more years of hard work.''

Adriana ignored the dirt and the sharp smell of whiskey on the man's breath as she took his hand, leaned forward, and made a show of studying his palm. ''I see,'' she began, ''a turn of good fortune in your future, my friend . . .''

Another night in the Cottonmouth Tavern wore on.

⌒ CHAPTER IX ⌒

The first leg of the journey to San Sebastian was nearly over. They sailed upriver with Maurice handling the sheet and Tom the tiller, though either one of them could have handled the small boat alone. "There she is," Maurice called as the *Marie* cleared the last bit of land between them and the great bend of the Mississippi where New Orleans was situated. "Almost there, Tom. One long tack and another hour ought to do it."

They were too far from the docks to identify individual ships, but Tom tried anyway. When he failed to distinguish a Paxton vessel, he slumped against the bulwark. "We'll come about just past that buoy," he said tonelessly.

And that, Maurice thought sourly, looking at his listless friend, was how the voyage had gone. Ten days down the East Coast, through the keys, up the west coast of Florida. A whale of a storm had caught them during the sixth night and they'd almost foundered. They'd had a smooth run westward to the Mississippi Delta, that flat, rich plain that had grown from silt carried by untold millions of gallons of water over unreckoned years. Tom ate when Maurice handed him food. He slept when Maurice directed him to one of the two bunks in the tiny cabin. He handled the *Marie* when it was his turn. He spoke only when asked a question or when necessary. And he stared blankly across the water for hours on end. All told, Maurice had decided on the second day out, a horse was a more lively partner and stimulating conversationalist.

Coming about served as a sort of signal for Tom, and his spirits brightened as the *Marie* picked up speed. At last he could do something. There was a ship to be obtained and provisioned, a crew to be hired, a course to be set. The ten-day wait was over, and he sensed that he needed activity every bit as much as a starving man needed food. Alive now, suddenly charged with energy, he searched through the keelboats and flatboats from upriver and the oceangoing schooners, ketches, and brigs that lined the docks for a ship that he recognized. "Well," he announced at last as they wove through the thick water traffic on their way to the Paxton dock, "Barton will know. Anything that'll get us there. . . ."

Two ships, a schooner and a brig, were tied up at the Paxton docks. "Either of 'em in the family?" Maurice asked as he dropped the sail.

Tom glumly shook his head as the *Marie* drifted closer and he began to paddle. "Leasing dock space, probably. Damn!"

Maurice busied himself stowing the sail. "Don't panic yet," he counseled. "Plenty of ships we ain't seen yet. Look lively there, Tom!" he yelled, pushing them away from a splintered piling. "Keep her bow upstream long as you can."

Docking a small boat at a pier designed for ocean going vessels was a tricky job. Great care was needed to avoid being pushed between the piles by the force of the river, and by the time they'd paddled under the bow of the schooner and made fast to a ladder, both Tom and Maurice were sweating freely. "Hey, you!" a voice from above called. "This here's a Paxton dock. If you ain't got business here, stand off."

"This is a Paxton boat," Tom called back as Maurice tossed him his duffel. "I'm Tom Paxton," he added as he began to climb the ladder, "and that's the *Marie*, out of Brandborough."

A burly man covered with tattoos greeted Tom with a helping hand. "Great jumpin' Jehoshaphat," he said in wonder. "You boys sailed that little bitty thing all the way around Florida?"

"That's right." Tom turned to give Maurice a hand. "Is Mr. Barton around?"

"Yes, sir. In the office. Tom Paxton, eh?" He stuck out a gnarled and rope-scarred hand. "Jamie Ragland. Knowed your daddy from way back. Fought at Kings Mountain with him and sailed on the old *Marie*, which was a damned sight more ship than that dinky puddle-jumper."

"It got us here," Tom said shortly. "Father's told a tale or two about you. You still work for him?"

"Long as I can hoist a sail or splice a line."

"Good." Tom grinned and clapped the older man on the shoulder. "We'll swap war stories later. Right now, I've got urgent business. Can you round up someone to help you get this little bitty thing to a small boat basin? I'd hate to see her get stove up."

The arrangements made, Tom and Maurice headed for the Paxton office two blocks away. "Damn," Maurice swore when he stumbled over a sprung plank. "I'd plumb forgot about makin' the switch from water to land. Just don't hardly seem right for land to be so durn solid, does it?"

Levee Street was alive with activity. Slaves dressed in short trousers of linsey-woolsey sweated beneath bales of cotton and sugarcane. At one dock, Tom noticed with distaste, more slaves to be sold at auction were being unloaded despite the fact that importing slaves had been illegal for two years. The air rang with the shouts of men and the bawling protestations of cattle, sheep, and other livestock that had been brought down-river. Businessmen in suits mingled with rough Kain-tocks, farmers, and seamen, all haggling over the price of goods being transferred from ship to shore, from shore to warehouse, and from warehouse back to an-other hold for transportation to God only knew where.

Everywhere, excited by the sights and sounds of the busy port, boys scurried underfoot as they ran errands or searched for whatever mischief they could get into.

The Paxton warehouse and office had been moved since Tom's last visit—more than six years earlier—but, as Jase had promised, it wasn't hard to find. A half-block long, with the office occupying one front corner, the building wore a coat of fresh white paint and was trimmed with red. Three stories above the street, PAXTON SHIPPING LINES was painted in huge black block letters. Smaller white letters illuminated with gilt repeated the message on the window in the office door.

Inside, the effect was of a prestigious, well-established firm. Dark paneled walls were set off with paintings of ships under full sail. The hardwood flooring shone with wax. Mahogany captain's chairs were arranged around the periphery of the room, near the center of which sat an enormous secretary's desk of the same wood. Nearer to the rear wall, three clerks' desks were piled high with paperwork.

"May I help you?" a pale, emaciated young man seated at the secretary's desk asked as Tom and Maurice entered.

"We're here to see Mr. Barton," Tom said.

The young man peered disdainfully over his pince-nez at the disreputable pair facing him. Neither had shaved for over a week, and both wore the filthy, salt-stained garb of common seamen. "We're not hiring at the moment," he sniffed. One fluttering hand shooed them toward the door. "You may try dock eight-B sometime next week. All hiring is done—"

"What's your name?" Tom asked, unceremoniously leaning on the desk.

"Varner," the secretary said curtly, glancing down in dismay at the dirty hands soiling his desk. "William Varner. Now, if you'll be so kind as to—"

"My name is Paxton," Tom interrupted in a low

voice. "Tom Paxton. You do recognize the name, don't you?" he asked, pointedly tapping a ledger whose cover was marked Paxton Shipping Lines.

"Oh," Varner said in a tiny voice. A sickly smile crossed his face as he scrambled to his feet. "I see. That is, I'm sorry, sir. I didn't know . . . that is, I didn't expect—"

"That's all right, Varner. Just take me to Thad Barton. I don't have all day."

"Yes, sir. Of course." Trying to maintain some dignity, Varner led the way to a door with a ground-glass window on which was printed Thaddeus Barton, Manager. He knocked twice, and poked his head in without waiting for a response. "Mr. Barton? A Mr. Tom Paxton and, er, companion to see you, sir."

"Well, send 'em in, damn it," a deep bass voice answered. "What're you waiting for?"

"Yes, sir." Varner pushed the door open and stepped aside. "You may go—"

"Tom! What the devil!" A diminutive man, no more than five feet tall, thin and delicate-looking in utter contrast to his voice, came around the desk to shake Tom's hand.

"Hello, Thad. Good to see you again."

"And what's this thing? A Leakey?" Barton's eyes twinkled as he looked up at Maurice and shook his head. "Damned if it isn't still growing, looks like."

"Well, you ain't, that's for sure," Maurice growled, happy to see Barton again.

Barton laughed, indicated a pair of chairs in front of his desk. "Have a seat," he said, returning to his own chair. "You look tuckered out. When'd you get in? How's Jase? What the hell are you doing in this neck of the woods, anyway?"

"I need a ship, Thad," Tom said, all traces of levity gone from his voice. He pulled a waxed canvas packet from his shirt, broke the seal, and pushed it across the desk. "It's all in there."

The letter from Jase was short and to the point. "By the Jesus!" Barton swore softly as he finished reading. "Take a man's little boys away from him like that. Son of a bitch needs to be hanged, you ask me. Christ, I'm sorry, Tom."

"I don't need sympathy, Thad. I need a ship, and I need one now."

"Yeah. I know." Barton leaned back in his chair, ran his fingers through his hair. "Only trouble is, the only one in port is the *Cassandra*, and she's stove up so bad there's no chance of using her."

"How bad is bad?" Tom asked.

"She tangled with a hurricane and limped in holed and minus a mainmast two weeks ago. I've got her scheduled into the yards, but it'll be another two, three weeks before they can get to her, and still another week or two to make the repairs. You could lease, maybe, but you'd have to find a fool or lie about what you're up to. Which, come to think of it, ain't a bad idea anyway. If word gets out, somebody could pick up some easy gold for passing it along—and besides, ain't nobody gonna think a run like that'll be a pleasure cruise. You can be sure this Vincent bastard ain't gonna hand you back them boys for the askin'. Along with everything else, there's an eighteen-gun sloop of war that runs out of San Sebastian. You'll be lucky to get out of there alive."

If Maurice thought Tom would react with anger to these difficulties, he couldn't have been more wrong. The trip from Brandborough to New Orleans had been unbearable for Tom precisely because he wasn't doing anything concrete. Being given a difficult set of problems to solve brought out the best in him, though, and he set to work with determination. By the time an hour had passed, the basic decisions had been made and the wheels were in motion. The object was to get the *Cassandra* under way in ten days at the most, preferably a week. To that end, they would pay the shipyard a premium for space, the use of its tools, and such foremen as could be spared, with craftsmen hired from the waterfront doing the bulk of the work. Asking for an immediate answer, Barton sent a note to the owner of the shipyard requesting his cooperation, explaining why it was needed, and sent a runner to Jamie Ragland, who was put in charge of hiring the men needed to effect the repairs.

"Well, there's not much more we can do this afternoon," Barton announced after they'd spoken with Jamie and he'd read the return note from the shipyard. He looked Tom and Maurice up and down, and grinned. "Best thing I'd say you can do now is get cleaned up, get some decent food and whiskey in you, and get a good night's sleep in a bed. The suite at the Paris is open, if you want to stay there."

"I suppose so," Tom said, suddenly tired. "The company's paying for it anyway, so we might as well use it."

Maurice sheepishly rubbed his jaw. "Is that the place with the red velvet on the walls?" he asked. "I'm not sure I'm welcome there after that ruckus in the lobby when we were there the last time."

Tom laughed, a welcome sound to the other men. "That's the place. The Hotel de Paris. The golden days of your youth. Let's just try to make this stay a little more peaceable, all right?"

"Well, I'll try if they will," Maurice promised solemnly, " 'cause I guess I was kind of rowdy. Rowdy or not, though, I didn't mean to break that mirror. But you know what, Tom?"

"What?"

An irrepressible, impish grin spread across Maurice's face. "The sound of that glass breakin' sure was pretty." He sighed, and the impish grin became almost beatific. "One of the prettiest things I ever heard in all my life."

Appropriately enough, the Hotel de Paris was on

Dauphin Street in the French Quarter. Tom and Maurice followed the narrow, unpaved boulevards that ran between two- and three-story buildings. Despite the area's name, the architecture was predominantly Spanish and the stucco-covered structures were topped with roofs of slate or red tile. Balconies guarded by railings of iron wrought into myriad designs overhung the streets. More wrought-iron gates protected the courtyards the two men occasionally glimpsed at the ends of slender alleys. Due to the scarcity of stone in the area, the streets were surfaced with black loamy soil that became as treacherous as quicksand in heavy rain. Wooden poles, topped by cross beams fitted with oil lamps that cast a feeble light at night marked alternate corners.

Traffic on the streets was heavy. Kaintocks and sailors streamed in and out of taverns and bordellos and cheap hotels. Men of commerce hurried on their way to and from important engagements. Men and women of every race intermingled as they bustled about. Orientals and American Indians paraded solemnly. Negroes from Africa and Caribbean Indian–Negro mixed-bloods ranged from the deepest black through mulattoes, quadroons, and octoroons, who were indistinguishable from Caucasians. Tall, blond, blue-eyed Scandinavians rubbed shoulders with lean, dark-haired French Canadians known as Creoles, and ruddy Englishmen contrasted with olive-skinned Castilians. One and all, from the impoverished immigrants in rags to the haughty Creole ladies in silks and satins riding in carriages pulled by expensive high-stepping horses, they flowed, bustled, paraded, yelled, haggled, argued, and minded their own business in one vast potpourri of humanity that made New Orleans the most exciting city in the area that stretched from the northwestern frontier to New York and Philadelphia in the East, and all of the Caribbean to the south.

Tom and Maurice dodged a carriage, then forced

their way through a knot of sailors. "There it is," Tom yelled, pointing at a magnificent building of white stucco surrounded by gardens and enclosed by a wrought-iron fence.

Maurice nodded. "I recollect the place, all right. From that fountain there in front. Seems I tried to move it once."

Together they fought their way to the gate, identified themselves to a skeptical guard, and were admitted. The fountain was situated in the center of an open courtyard. A pool of white Georgian marble accepted a stream of water from a carved jug held by a beautifully sculpted female figure who wore a loose gown that only partially concealed her loveliness. Maurice thought she was the most magnificent woman he had ever seen, and he gazed up at her with reverent awe. "Onliest gal I ever proposed to," he said with a sad shake of his head. "Turned me down cold, she did."

"I remember," Tom said dryly. "You were disconsolate—until that French girl came along a half-hour later."

"Not just French," Maurice corrected. "French and Spanish and African and Injun, by God. Four of the best kinds all rolled into one. If I could find another one like her—"

"She'd tell you you needed a bath." Tom laughed, giving him a shove toward the front of the hotel. "Come on. Let's see if the Paxton name will get us in."

It did, of course. And by the time ten o'clock rolled around, Tom and Maurice had bathed in hot fresh water, had paid for shaves and haircuts, eaten both splendidly and voraciously, drunk some of the finest Kentucky sour mash bourbon ever to pass the lips of man, and had collapsed into real beds with real sheets, which—even Maurice had to admit, in that brief moment before he lapsed into snores—beat a horse blanket on a forest floor.

The next day further proved that action was the best

cure for Tom's doldrums. Jamie Ragland had indeed
found a work crew, and Tom met the men shortly after
daybreak and led the way to the Hutchinson Shipyards.
George Hutchinson had done business with Barton and
the Paxtons before, and, as promised, had freed a corner of the yards where the *Cassandra* could be careened.
He'd also made available the necessary foremen to oversee the work she needed. That day the men were as-
signed their jobs, supplies were bought, and the *Cassandra* was brought to the yards. The next day would
see her stripped of rigging and readied for careening,
after which they could begin the actual repairs.

Tom had been fine as long as he'd been busy, but
once back in the suite at the Paris, all he wanted to do
was sit and stare at the walls.

"That's a pile of crap, Tom," Maurice said, toweling
dry after a bath.

"What?"

"Sittin' there and brooding ain't gonna help. All
you'll do is get your brain goin' in circles until you can't
do anything right when the time comes."

"That's easy for you to say. It isn't your boys who
are missing."

Maurice busied himself saddle-soaping the new boots
he'd bought earlier in the day. "Knowin' that don't
make anything I said less true. 'Sides, you'd be sayin'
the same thing to me if the shoe was on the other foot,
and you know it." He dropped one boot and started on
the other. "Now, the way I see it, we're workin' as fast
as we can, so let's get out of this room and latch on to
some of the good life around here. There's more to the
French Quarter than this hotel."

Tom wasn't to be swayed easily. "You go on if you
like," he said. "I'll stay here."

"The hell you will," Maurice growled. He took two
long steps, grabbed Tom's arm, and pulled him out of
his chair. "You're actin' like you're dead inside, and
that's gonna stop. Now, get in there and take a bath and

put on some of them fancy duds you bought so we can eat some of that fancy French cookin' and find us a place to do a little serious drinkin'!''

Anger flared in Tom's face as he jerked his arm free. "And if I say no?" he asked coldly.

Maurice lifted a hand and slowly closed his thick fingers into a fist. "Then I'll have to persuade you. And that's liable to make that prissy peacock of a manager downstairs right unhappy again."

Tom stared at Maurice for a long moment. "All right," he finally said. "All right. You win. But only," he shot over his shoulder on his way to the bath, "because I don't want to get us kicked out on our ears."

The café on Chartres Street was tiny, with tables that were crowded together and a ceiling so low they had to duck to miss the beams. Maurice was dubious about eating orange duck, but the first bite won him over, and by the time he'd finished he'd gone through two complete birds, along with enough rice and gravy for three normal men and a bottle and a half of red wine that the waiter described as "amusingly presumptuous." "Now for some real drinking," he announced as he and Tom sauntered back to the street an hour later. "That French wine ain't bad, but it lacks kick."

Tom heaved a mock sigh. "I suppose I'll have to go along to help you stagger back to the hotel when you've drunk enough whiskey to kill a mule."

Maurice rubbed his hands together in anticipation. "You know what, Tom? You're just gooder'n anybody. C'mon." He gave Tom a shove toward the nearest tavern, just down the street. "Let's get movin'. I don't want the rest of the world to get too far ahead of me!"

The Fifth Ace was full of celebrating Kaintocks out for a good time, no holds barred. The air was filled with a constant babel, the harsh smoke of cigars and pipes, and the fumes of whiskey and beer. To judge from the parade of gaudily dressed women and eager men on the narrow stairway at the rear of the room, another business was thriving upstairs. "You ought to feel right at home here," Tom said as the two shoved their way through the crowd to the bar, where they each claimed a brimming schooner of beer.

Maurice snagged a tumbler of Monongahela rye and downed the fiery liquid in one swallow, then happily licked his lips and sipped his beer chaser. A smile of pure bliss lit his face. "You gotta admit this beats sittin' around that stuffy hotel room."

"I'm not so sure," Tom yelled above a sudden uproar of obscenities as a fight broke out behind them. "Let's at least find a place to sit down."

The one remaining empty table was against the far wall. "I don't want to stay out too long," Tom said as he rested his tankard on the scarred tabletop. "Come morning, the *Cassandra* will be waiting for us."

At the mention of the *Cassandra*, a man sitting alone at the next table turned until he was looking directly at them. *"Cassandra?"* he croaked. "You lads from the *Cassandra*?"

"And what business is it of your'n if we are?" Maurice asked sourly.

The man lifted a knobby finger and pushed his cap back, revealing a pink scalp crossed by a few strands of greasy hair plastered across the gleaming expanse. He was older than either Tom or Maurice, in his late forties, perhaps. The flesh around his eyes was wrinkled by years of sun and salt water, and he sported the veined, protuberant nose of a heavy tippler. His coat and trousers were threadbare, and his shirt was a curious color that once had passed for white. "What business o' mine!" he exclaimed. "Well, they was hirin' for work on the *Cassandra* last night, and the word got around that one o' Jase Paxton's boys and his Kaintockish friend was in a big hurry to take that bad luck schooner to San Sebastian. So I just naturally figgered you was them, if you get my drift."

"If we are," Tom said, irked that their destination was known, "where we're bound is our own affair."

The man wasn't about to be dismissed so easily. "Used to sail for Jase," he said, hitching his chair around before either Tom or Maurice could protest. "Ran a little brig o' his in and out o' San Sebastian many a time. Reason I mention that," he went on, his words taking on a confidential tone, "is that I'm needin' a berth pretty bad right now, though how a Christian man and a master o' the seas like ol' Slurry Walls got hisself into this position is beyond my knowin'."

Maurice was watching the sailor with narrowed eyes. "So you claim to know San Sebastian, eh?"

"Claim?" Slurry echoed. "Claim! Hell's own fire, lad, I know that island and the reefs and currents 'round about it like the back of me own hand."

"The back of your own head sounds more likely to me," Tom snorted. "I'd bet you've no more been to San Sebastian than you have to Barataria."

Slurry leaned forward and lowered his voice conspiringly. "The truth is, I been there, too. Sailed with the renowned Jean Laffite hisself fer two voyages when times was hard in oh-two, though it's nothin' I'm proud of. And as for San Sebastian," he said, his voice returning to normal, "you can ask me anything you want about it or the whole damn Caribbean. Go ahead. Ask."

Tom remembered a little about the harbor at San Sebastian, and asked the first question. Slurry responded with a complete description of the main harbor, as well as the cove on the far side of the island, which neither Tom nor Maurice knew about. And then, before they could ask, he added a wealth of information about the reefs and currents in the vicinity of the island, and how a smart man could best evade pursuit, should he be followed.

"You sound as if you might be a good man to have

aboard," Tom admitted when Slurry had finished. "I'll talk to a couple of people tomorrow and let you know. Good enough?"

"I'll drink to that," Slurry said, raising his mug.

"But not on board," Tom warned, raising his mug in return. "This is going to be a dry voyage. Dry as a foretops'l in a calm, you hear?"

Slurry grinned and pounded a fist against Tom's shoulder. "I hear," Slurry acknowledged. "An' don't you fret 'bout my tipplin'. I only indulge myself in port when there's nothin' better to occupy me. You'll see what a dandy job I can do."

"Whoa!" Tom laughed. "You're not hired yet, remember?"

"Close enough to celebrate," Slurry whooped. One eyelid dropped in a wink. "Wha'd'ya say, lads? I know a place that's a hell of a lot better than this rattrap. You game for followin' ol' Slurry?"

"Sounds good to me," Maurice rumbled, finishing off his third beer and tossing a coin to the serving girl.

"Come along, young Paxton," Slurry said, bouncing up. "You're in for a sight, if you do. You'll see a by-God charmer who dances prettier than anything. She's the loveliest creature these old eyes have ever seen, but she'll carve the man who lays a hand on her. Somethin' strange about her, aye, but damn, she's beautiful. Lord, beautiful."

"All right, all right. I'm convinced," Tom said, rising to join Maurice and Slurry. "What's the name of this den of iniquity?"

"Ain't no iniquity," Slurry said, leading the way to the door. "It's called the Cottonmouth."

∾ CHAPTER X ∾

Nearer, ever nearer. The glow intensified in Adriana's mind. Involuntarily, her hands moved to shade her eyes, though there could be no shade from that pinprick of ghostly light that came from within.

The light expanded and became the now-familiar vision of the golden oak tree surrounded by brambles. "Who are you?" she whispered, aware that her voice might banish the vision. "Where do you come from? Why do you plague me? When? When will you reveal yourself?"

Abruptly, the vision vanished, leaving only darkness. Slowly, she opened her eyes to the soft glow of the candle, placed her elbows on the table, and rested her head in her hands. "Who?" she whispered again, consumed by the mystery. "When? How? Why?"

"Adriana? Adriana? Are you there?"

Another hour had passed: it was time to dance again. "Coming, Harriet," she called, rising wearily from her chair. "Coming. Three minutes."

The Cottonmouth Tavern appeared to be one notch above the Fifth Ace, but not a large notch. Outside, the threatening figure of a coiled cottonmouth snake was painted on a cracked signboard that hung above the tavern entrance, which was crowded by a continuous procession of revelers. Inside, a tidal wave of noise and aromas—almost painful in its intensity—washed over Tom and Maurice and Slurry as they entered. Slurry took in the room at a single glance and turned to Tom. "Many a seafarin' man in here tonight," he yelled over the uproar. "If you think your ship needs more hands, 'twould be a good idea to talk to some of these lads."

"I'll keep that in mind," Tom shouted back noncommittally.

"Right now, you just lead the way to that fine liquor you was talkin' about," Maurice said, almost literally picking up Slurry and shoving him into the crowd. "I'm ready to do a little howlin'!"

They elbowed and pushed their way through the maze of tables and chairs, around dancers, past two fights, and ended up at last at the bar in front of Zebediah Gibbs's modified perch.

"Hallo there, Zebediah!" Slurry yelled. " 'Member me?"

Gibbs stared malevolently down at Slurry, let his eyes slide no more amicably to Tom and Maurice. "I remember you well, Slurry Walls," he boomed, "and I remember having to throw you into the street more than once. Not to mention the last time you were in and neglected to check your pockets for coins before drinking my liquor." One hand closed around the handle of his bungstarter, which he tapped menacingly on the shelf. His gaze snapped from Tom to Maurice and back to Slurry again. "So I hope you gents don't take offense when I ask to see the color of your money before you see a drop of my spirits. An understandable precaution, considering the company you're keeping."

Gibbs's tone was cordial enough, but his eyes were as hard as the bungstarter, which he now slapped into his palm. Tom saw Maurice's hands tighten on the edge of the bar and, sensing trouble, quickly dug a ten-dollar gold piece out of his pocket and tossed it to Gibbs. Zebediah caught the coin, tested the metal with his teeth, and gestured sharply to one of his barmen. "Give these high spenders whatever they want," he ordered.

A smile that never reached his eyes stretched across Tom's face. "Thanks," he said, politely but coolly.

The hidden message wasn't lost on Gibbs. The young American wasn't going to take offense this time—but he wanted no further aspersions cast on the character of either himself or his friends. "The first one's on me," Gibbs added to the barman, conceding the point in a gesture of conciliation as he set aside his bungstarter. "Welcome to the Cottonmouth, boys."

A free drink freely given didn't often come Slurry's way, and he wasted no time holding up three fingers before Gibbs could change his mind. "Three Cottonmouths," he said, beginning to drool in anticipation.

The barman complied by filling three mugs with a combination of Jamaican, Honduran, and the house rum. Into this concoction, he measured a spoonful of pepper juice and a hint of what Slurry explained was snake venom, for "body." "These'll open your eyes," the old seaman added as the barkeep topped each drink with a mound of whipped cream, from which the drink got its name.

"Or close them," Tom said, taking a sip. "Phew!" The rums were flavorful. The pepper juice burned like fire, after which the whipped cream soothed the throat. The so-called venom, whatever it really was, had no taste, but Tom could feel his fingertips going numb.

"Hard to believe this is your first visit to the Cottonmouth," Slurry said, his glass already half-empty. "I'll lay you a day's wages you've never tasted a drink like this."

"You'd win," Tom gasped, watching in awe as Maurice finished his first and, a beatific grin plastered to his face, ordered a second. "My only question," he said, jerking a thumb in Maurice's direction, "is, who's going to carry him home?"

The answer was drowned in the sudden tattoo of Gibbs's bungstarter beating on the shelf. "Gentlemen!"

the bar owner roared. "Gentlemen! Adriana is going to dance!"

In a remarkably short time for a situation that bordered on absolute chaos, the large high-ceilinged room quieted enough for the band to be heard. All around, men scurried for chairs or vantage places along the walls. "Looky there! Looky there!" Slurry said, nudging first Tom and then Maurice with a bony elbow and then pointing to the opposite corner. "It's the Gypsy girl, by God!"

A rhythmic cry of "Adriana, Adriana, Adriana" swelled from the crowd, and as if in response, a figure that could barely be seen in the haze moved along the balcony and stopped at the top of the stairs. Slowly, as she gazed over the crowd, the chanting subsided. Only then did she deign to begin her descent.

"She's the one I told ye about," Slurry whispered, again jabbing Tom in the ribs. "Aye, she be the one. Just watch her, now!"

Tom didn't hear a word Slurry said. The very word Gypsy had conjured up images of seductive mystery and exotic pleasures that were confirmed by Adriana's every slightest move. She didn't walk, she glided. The slight tinkling of bells accompanied her. Her long purple skirt, the color of the sea before a storm, flowed around her, and her low-cut white blouse strained to conceal the inviting swell of her bosom. Her sultry features were partially hidden by veils of yellow and amethyst-colored silk, diaphanous as clouds. When she reached the bottom of the stairs, she gestured and the music stopped, making the silence total.

The air was charged with electricity. The tension, the expectancy that filled the room, were almost palpable. Exuding animal magnetism, Adriana let the suspense build to the breaking point, and then magically broke the spell with a toss of her head and the slow rise of her arms.

Time began again. A sigh of longing and relief swept through the crowd as the musicians began to play. Mesmerized, Tom couldn't take his eyes off Adriana's hands, and was only dimly aware when she moved off the dais and began to work her way toward the center of the room. Kaintocks and sailors stumbled out of her way. A serving girl sitting on a trapper's knee fell to the floor when the trapper stood, swept off his hat, and bowed deeply as Adriana passed him. A moment later, as the tempo of the music suddenly increased, the Gypsy leaped onto the table placed there for her and began to dance.

Had any woman ever danced before? Were those arms only arms, those legs only legs? Adriana danced secrets. The swift secret of young love blooming in an explosion of petals. The slow, provocative secret of mysterious womanhood. The soft secret of femininity, as fragile as the aroma of orchids. The sultry, seductive secret of arousal, the fast, panting secret of lust. Hers was the dance of new life discovered, a dance of promises and desire, a dance of beginnings and climaxes and endings.

His drink forgotten, Tom braced himself against the bar and shook his head to clear his senses. His skull throbbed. The spacious drinking hall seemed stifling and claustrophobic. A drop of sweat trickled down his back, another down his side. He wanted to turn away, to turn and face the bar again, but he couldn't tear his eyes away from Adriana. A blur of color floated away from her, gently descended onto a pair of outstretched hands that seemed to come from nowhere. A second veil slipped down her arm and he found himself staring at her shoulder until one of her hands caught his attention, and then he was staring at that as she slowly twined the veil through her fingers and then withdrew it. He couldn't see all of her at once. A flash of copper flesh caught his eye and he was staring at her legs until he realized he was following the motion of her hip, then the whip of her auburn hair that tossed before her face and, a moment later, floated as softly as one of her veils down her shoulders.

And then, before Tom was fully aware that she had stopped, the dance was over and Adriana was bowing, turning slowly to acknowledge the applause, stepping lightly down from the table and working her way across the room to a small table in the corner. "What now?" Tom asked Slurry. "Is that all she does?"

"That's all the dancin' for now," Slurry answered. "She'll do another turn in a couple hours. Between now and then, she reads palms for a while and then disappears upstairs—for a rest, I s'pose."

"Reads palms?"

"That's what Gypsies do, ain't it? Cards, too, if you ask her. Good at it too, so they say, for there's men who'll swear by what she's told 'em. Why, one feller, Johnny Spingle it was, ast her one night if he—say, are ye listenin' to me, mate?"

Maurice followed the direction of his friend's gaze. "I'd say he's more interested in someone else right now, Slurry, and don't know that I blame him. What say we try another one of them Cottonmouths? Tom, what about you?"

Tom didn't answer, so absorbed was he in watching Adriana. Gypsy, dancer, reader of palms, she sat quietly like a queen in repose as riverboat men and sailors and men from the frontier flocked around her like a retinue of rustic courtiers about a queen of mystery and fire. Tom watched her speak and knew from her customers' expressions that they were pleased with her predictions. And what, Tom found himself wondering, would she say to *him*? He didn't really believe in palmistry, but the urge to ask if he would get his sons back was almost irresistible.

"What the hell are you doing?" Maurice asked, breaking into his thoughts.

Tom glanced up guiltily from looking at the meaningless jumble of lines traced in his own hand. "Oh, nothing," he said lamely, and, to cover his embarrassment, "Where's that drink you were going to order for me?"

"Slurry's had his paw wrapped around it for the last five minutes. Look, why don't you just go on over there and get it read, 'stead of tryin' to read it yourself? Don't look like it hurts none. Leastways, them other fellers don't appear to be in pain. Slurry says it only costs a couple of bits."

"Those other fellows are damned fools," Tom said, knowing full well that he wanted nothing more than to join them. "The only way we'll find out what the future holds is to go about our business and set sail as soon as possible."

"Maybe so, but I'd feel a heap better if that gal told us everything was goin' to work out all right."

"Aye, go ahead, mate," Slurry put in. "Maybe ye won't learn anything, but what harm can it do? And ye'll have your hand held by the prettiest lass in all of New Orleans."

"Well . . ." Tom finished his drink and wiped his mouth with the side of his hand. "I guess maybe it wouldn't hurt," he agreed reluctantly. "But if my fortune turns out to be bad, I'm holding the two of you responsible."

" 'Tis a risk I'll take," Slurry said. "Go on, lad."

The press of men around Adriana had eased by the time Tom arrived at her table, and he had to wait only a moment before taking his seat in the rough wooden chair across from her. Feeling shy and a little foolish, he handed her a dollar coin and saw it whisked into a pocket in her skirt, with no hint of an offer of change. "Can you see what the future holds for me?" he asked lamely as he laid his hand palm up on the table.

"If the fates allow, I can," Adriana said, looking at him with a faint, enigmatic smile.

Her voice was soft, tinged with mystery and an accent

Tom didn't recognize. For the first time, he could see her face clearly. Her features were bold, yet seemed softened by an inner light. He marveled at her smooth, high cheekbones and strong, sensual lips. The strange fascination that he had felt earlier rushed back even stronger to snare him as he gazed into eyes as green and deep as the ocean.

The coin was the first hint. Inexplicably, it seemed to burn her hand with an otherworldly heat, and she could not let it go. Beneath the table she withdrew it from her pocket and laid it in her lap. Adriana was certain she had seen the man who sat across the table from her before, but where she couldn't recall, and it was impossible to concentrate with all the hullabaloo surrounding her. Biding her time, for time would tell, she reached out and closed her hand over his—and in that instant, felt a spark more secret than fox fire, quicker than thought itself, pass between them. Her mind stumbled and reeled, and though she tried to distance herself from him, the feeling intensified as she lifted his hand and tightened her hold. She knew this man! Knew him intimately, though he seemed not to recognize her. They were connected, from another life, perhaps, another time, another place she knew only in the dim recesses of memory, which were hidden even to those with the gift of inner sight.

There was a power at work Tom didn't understand. Warmth flooded through his hand and up his arm. Of what was happening he hadn't the foggiest notion, but he knew that he couldn't have broken the contact between him and the mysterious Adriana even had he wanted to. His earlier prejudices to the contrary, the longer she cradled his hand, the more certain he became that she was no charlatan and that she did indeed probe straight to his heart and soul.

Adriana had been taught the meaning of the lines by her grandmother, then taught to forget the lines and read the feel of the hand, to let go and open herself to the essence of self that every man or woman emanated. Many times had she done this, but never had the essence so compelled her, so consumed her. Adriana's breath came faster. She stared at the lines of his palm in an attempt to bring herself back to reality, and a puzzled look came over her face, as if she saw something there that she could not understand, or dared not believe. "I see . . . I see much passion in your future, monsieur," she whispered haltingly. "There is . . . but no. I. . . . The mists of the future are thick—"

A heavy hand clamped down on Tom's shoulder and broke the spell. "Looks like you better take that hand somewheres else, boy," a harsh voice thundered, " 'cause the little lady here's gonna tell me what I got to look forward to." The interloper, a Kaintock by the sight and smell of his buckskins, swayed alarmingly from all the Cottonmouths he'd poured down his throat. "Mebbe a dance with her, if'n she's lucky."

Adriana let Tom's hand go, caught his eyes, and gave him a warning look.

"I don't know who you are, friend," Tom said mildly, ignoring Adriana's glance, "but you're interrupting here. The lady'll be through in a minute. You'll get your turn."

The man stood well over six feet, had huge shoulders, long arms, and a chest like a barrel. He wore a fur cap, beaded shirt, greasy trousers, and the calf-high moccasins that were common to the men who roamed the wilderness. His mouth, almost hidden beneath a heavy beard, parted in a snarl. "You don't understand, boy," he growled, jerking Tom out of his chair. "I'm Bull Hallam, and I want my fortune told now!"

"You tried your way with me last night," Adriana interrupted in an attempt to avert a fight. "The answer is still the same." She rose and faced Hallam without fear. "Read your palm? Ha! I spit on your palm!"

"I think you'd better leave the lady alone," Tom said, stepping between Adriana and Hallam.

"And I think I do not need your help—or your death on my conscience," Adriana snapped at Tom. "Leave us!"

"Or face Bull Hallam," the riverboat man threatened.

Tom didn't need a fortune-teller to predict what would come next. Many, many months had passed since he'd last been in a brawl, and though it was probably the wrong time and the wrong place and the wrong man, he was suddenly ready. "And just who the hell," he asked deliberately, "is Bull Hallam?"

Hallam's eyes widened in disbelief and the men around him backed away and quieted. "Who?" he sputtered. "Who!"

"Must be *deaf* Bull Hallam," Tom goaded, to the delight of the crowd.

"I'll tell you who I am, boy, and then I'm a-fixin' to kill you! Wah-hooo!"

A half-circle of spectators crowded around the contestants. Behind them, men stood on chairs in anticipation of seeing one of Bull's famous rages and the mayhem he wreaked.

Never one to disappoint a crowd, Hallam leaped into the air, cracked his heels together, then slapped his chest as he landed. "I'm a child of the snappin' turtle, pilgrim, raised by 'gators and weaned on panther milk! I can wrassle a buffalo and chaw the ear off'n a grizzly! I can outrun, outjump, outshoot, throw down, drag out, and lick any man up or down the Mississip'! I'm a roarin' ripsnorter and chock-full of fight, and this is my night to howl, boy!" And as he screamed the last words, he drew back a hamlike fist and prepared to send a killing blow into Tom's face.

"Howdy, friend," Maurice said as he stepped behind Bull and grabbed his wrist to stop the blow before it got started.

"Wha—?" Bull glanced over his shoulder.

Tom stomped the heel of his right boot onto Bull's

moccasin-covered instep, then followed that with double-fisted sidearm blows to the face. Almost as if they'd practiced, Maurice released Bull's wrist, and the Kaintock flew backward and crashed straight through a table to the floor.

Mugs, bottles, harlots, and customers scattered. A bandy-legged Irishman howled at the top of his lungs and leaped onto Maurice's back. "You can't do that to a mate o' mine!" he screeched as he and Maurice went careening across the floor.

Maurice's feet tangled with an overturned chair, and he and his rider fell to the floor. "Hold on a durned minute!" Slurry cried as he grabbed at the Irishman. "Ye ain't bein' fair! Hallam started it."

"Who gives a damn about fair?" another man asked as he drew back a foot and kicked Slurry.

Slurry yelped in pain and somersaulted over Maurice and the Irishman, and when the riverboat man followed to finish the job, Tom crashed a bottle over his skull. The riverboat man crumpled in a heap next to Slurry, who proceeded to bite a chunk off his ear.

There was nothing like a good brawl to stir the blood. The ring of spectators widened, cheered on the participants, and laid bets. Maurice struggled halfway to his feet and fell again, this time purposely, knocking the breath out of the Irishman. Tom grabbed Slurry and heaved him onto the dais vacated hurriedly by the musicians, then gave Maurice a helping hand before Bull's crew could regroup.

Adriana had fled. Tom, Maurice, and Slurry, their backs to the wall, occupied the dais and faced a dozen riverboat men led by a still groggy and confused Bull Hallam. "C'mon, ye apes!" Maurice howled gleefully. "Twelve agin' three. Almost even odds!"

A blast from a gun stopped the brawlers in their tracks. Zebediah Gibbs dropped the pistol he had just discharged, snatched up a shotgun, and leaped over the bar. "There'll be no more fightin' in here tonight!" he bellowed as he forced his way through the crowd and trained the shotgun on Tom, Maurice, and Slurry. "You three. Out, and out quick, before I have you pitched out!"

"Out?" Maurice protested indignantly. "Hell, we ain't drunk up our ten dollars—"

"You broke up fifteen worth," Gibbs interrupted, at the same time gesturing.

A half-dozen bartenders armed with bungstarters charged from behind the bar. Bull's crew cleared a path for them.

"Lay hands on us and you'll wish you hadn't, fellers," Maurice warned.

"Throw 'em out!" Gibbs snapped. "And you boys stay out of it," he added, turning to train the shotgun on Bull's crew.

The bartenders leaped to the attack. Tom, Maurice, and Slurry tried to defend themselves, but the odds, the bungstarters, the booze they'd drunk, and the punishment they'd already taken were too potent a combination. Slurry was out of action in a few seconds. Tom avoided the first flailing bungstarter, but a second connected with his shoulder and sent him spinning into the grasp of two other bartenders. He heard Maurice's battle cry and then saw a body come flying through the air at him. A second later, a boot came out of nowhere and clubbed him in the forehead, and the world went dim.

He was aware of being dragged, of faces swimming past him, then of flying through the air to land in the dust of the darkened street. Dirt filled his mouth. He raised his head and spat, got his hands underneath himself, and tried to push up. Before he could, Slurry, his arms and legs pinwheeling ludicrously, was pitched from the tavern and landed with a dull thud in the street. Maurice, propelled by at least four hefty bartenders, came last.

Tom climbed to his feet, adjusted his eye patch, and

realized that the sight in his good eye was fading rapidly. "Oh, shit," he whispered in horror. Tentatively, afraid of what he'd find, he explored the damage and discovered a deep gash on his forehead that was bleeding into his eye. Relieved, he pulled out his shirt-tail, wiped his face, and found he could see again. "Are you all right?" he asked the writhing and moaning Slurry. He bent over and shook the older man's shoulder. "Come on, Slurry. Get up."

Slurry took Tom's hand and allowed himself to be pulled to his feet. Swaying unsteadily, he spit out blood and a piece of tooth. "Tol' you the Cottonmouth was a hell of a place, didn't I, mates?" he said, a silly grin spreading over his face.

"That you did, Slurry," Maurice said from flat on his back. He rolled over, climbed to his feet, and brushed himself off. "I purely hate," he said, "for them fellers to think they got the best of us. 'Specially when I only got to drink two of them Cottonmouths." His eyes went to the door of the tavern and a devilish look appeared. "Wha'd'ya say, Tom?"

The bleeding was slowing. Tom flexed his shoulder, found it still operable, and realized that he felt better than he had since the night he'd learned that the boys had been kidnapped. He ripped a strip from the bottom of his shirt and tied a makeshift bandage around his head so the blood wouldn't blind him again. "I say we pay those gents another visit," he said. "Only this time, throw them *away* from me, not *at* me. I was doing just fine until—"

"Ye must be joking, lads," Slurry cried as he caught at Tom's sleeve. "We got out alive the first time. There ain't no need to tempt fate again. It'd be a Christian thing to forgive them lads."

Tom pulled off his belt, wrapped it around his right hand while Maurice did the same. "I'll forgive 'em, all right," he said.

"We've forgave roisterers like that before," Maurice agreed, starting toward the door. "After we've read 'em from the book."

"No!" The soft, feminine whisper came from a narrow alley that separated the Cottonmouth from the coffeehouse next door. A slender figure emerged from the deep shadows and entered the faint illumination that came from the door of the tavern. "Please. Do not go in there again."

"Adriana?" Tom asked, astonished.

"Yes. You must not go in there a second time. Zebediah will turn Bull Hallam and his friends loose on you, and you could be killed. You must leave and not come back." She stepped closer and saw the bloody bandage wrapped around Tom's forehead. "*Mon Dieu!* You are hurt!"

"A cut," Tom protested. "It'll heal."

Adriana lifted one edge of the bandage. "It is filled with dirt from the street," she announced. "You will get blood poisoning if it is not cleaned."

She smelled faintly of wood smoke and lilacs, and the touch of her hand befuddled him. "I've ah . . . had worse," Tom said lamely, aware that Maurice was staring at him. "But . . ." He took a deep breath, and decided. "We don't want to cause any more trouble where you work," he said firmly. "We'll leave."

Maurice snorted in disappointment, but signaled his acceptance of Tom's decision by moving back toward the center of the street. A look of total relief crossed Slurry's face.

"Good. And now, you must allow me to see to your injury." Adriana glanced at Slurry. "And yours, too, monsieur," she added, noting the blood running down his chin. "I live here at the tavern, but a friend nearby will let us use her house."

"I assure you that's not necessary, Adriana. We can—"

"I wish to help," Adriana insisted. "And gentlemen like yourselves would not refuse, eh, messieurs?"

Slurry gulped and shook his head.

Tom grinned. "Since you insist, how can we refuse? We'll go wherever you want."

"And you will accompany us, my valiant warrior?" Adriana asked Maurice.

"Well, ah . . ."

"Good. Come along, then. I must dance again soon. There is little time."

Tom gave Adriana his arm as she led the way. "You never finished telling my fortune," he reminded her.

"That is true," Adriana admitted. "And you never told me your name. Or those of your friends, for that matter."

Tom introduced Maurice and Slurry. "And I'm Tom Paxton. Thomas Gunn Paxton, really."

"Tom. Thomas Gunn Paxton." The name flowed from her tongue, and the mysterious accent made the words sound lovelier than Tom would have dreamed possible. "And you know that I am called Adriana."

"Adriana—?" Tom prompted, waiting to hear her last name.

She almost told him, came closer than she had to telling any man since Giuseppe's death. Why, she wasn't sure. Something about him, though, some quality that other men lacked. . . . "Just Adriana," she said simply. Sadness and anger were mixed in her voice, but the message was clear: Tom should not ask again.

"A lovely name. One that suits you, I might add," Tom said hurriedly. "You dance beautifully. Slurry tells me that you're a Gypsy. Was that a Gypsy dance?"

"It was the dance I dance."

"It was marvelous. I've never seen . . ." He felt foolish making small talk, but couldn't seem to stop. Fate certainly had a liking for strange circumstances, he mused. Otherwise, why was he flirting with this woman in the street while blood oozed from a cut on his head?

His hand on the hilt of his knife, Maurice kept a sharp eye out. Adriana didn't look like the sort of woman who would lead a man into a trap, but dark and unfamiliar streets made him wary. "You mind tellin' us where we're goin', miss?" he asked.

"As I said, I have a friend who lives near here," Adriana said over her shoulder. "She'll let us use her kitchen."

The old and elegant house to which she led them was half-hidden behind an iron fence and a thick hedge. When Adriana knocked, the door was opened by an elderly lady holding an angry tomcat by the scruff of its neck in one hand and a lantern in the other. Her face was a record of beauty faded, of time that had stolen her youthful loveliness, leaving in its place understanding and wisdom. "My goodness, Adriana, whatever are you doing here at this hour?"

"Some friends need help, Madame Villon," Adriana answered simply. "May we come in?"

They could, and, without a moment's hesitation, did. "This is awfully kind of you, ma'am," Tom said. "Most people wouldn't open their doors to strangers in the middle of the night."

"Adriana is no stranger. She is my friend whose youth and beauty bring back many wonderful memories. Her friends are my friends, Mr.—?"

The introductions complete, Madame Villon, regal in her dressing gown, her long white hair let down for the night, led them through the house. The front parlor smelled faintly of musk and jasmine, the dining room of lavender and mint. Tom glimpsed a montage of oil lamps and green growing plants and vases topped with peacock feathers as he passed through the house.

"We sure are grateful," Maurice said as Madame Villon opened the kitchen door. "We got in a little ruckus over at the Cottonmouth, is how we got banged up."

"I can imagine," Madame Villon said. "I have seen

a few ruckuses in my time, monsieur. Oh, heavenly days!'' she exclaimed to the cat, which had become thoroughly outraged. She put down the lantern and cuddled the animal briefly before setting him free. "Poor Edward. I'm afraid he simply doesn't understand."

"Understand?" Tom asked, mystified.

Madame Villon busied herself collecting a basin and rags and water. "Why, his usefulness, of course. I'm an old woman, and sometimes very bad men come to my door. But they always leave when I throw Edward in their faces."

Slurry's eyes widened; Maurice stifled a guffaw. "I sure hope," Tom said, somehow keeping a straight face, "that you never forget I'm a friend."

The hour was late and Adriana had to leave soon. She cleaned Slurry's cut lip, washed and bandaged Maurice's knuckles in spite of his protests, and then turned both men over to the tender mercies of Madame Villon, who led them to the parlor for a glass of her homemade scuppernong brandy.

"She's quite a woman," Tom said as Adriana turned to him.

His face, now in the light, now darkened by her shadow, still seemed familiar. Adriana wet a cloth in fresh water and laid it on the bandage to soak it loose. *But where have I seen him? In England? In New Orleans? In my dreams?* She forced herself to focus on the task at hand, and peeled the bandage from his forehead. "I'm sorry," she said when he winced.

" 'S'all right. Reminds me of the time when . . ."

He talked, but she didn't hear. In her dreams, then? The oak tree and the brambles? She worked swiftly and efficiently, scrubbing, using tweezers to pluck out more stubborn bits of dirt. That eye—only one eye—so soft and yet so piercing.

"There," she finally said. She gently dried the skin around the cut and closed it with strips of adhesive, then bound a small wad of moss to it with a fresh bandage.

"There should be only a small scar now."

"Thanks," Tom said, looking up at her and realizing with a rush how beautiful she was. Even more beautiful close to him than when she'd danced. "You . . ."—his voice sounded distant, strangely different— ". . . didn't have to do this. I appreciate it."

Men! How many over the years had stared at her and desired her? And yet this one, handsome for all his scars, a man of conflicting violence and gentleness. . . . Something had drawn her to him, some force too powerful to be denied. "I did only what I wished to do," she said, making herself speak in the hope that words might break the spell that bound her. She touched his shirt and grimaced. "Your shirt will be ruined. Give it to me now, before the blood dries, and I'll rinse it."

"All right." Tom stood, removed his coat, began to unbutton his shirt, and then stopped when Adriana gasped and backed away from him. Confused, he looked down at himself, but saw nothing out of the ordinary. "What's wrong?" he asked. "I don't understand."

The vision became real! An amulet of gold . . . an oak tree entwined with brambles! It was he, the man she had seen in her dreams! The hair on the back of her neck prickled and her blood went cold. Thomas Gunn Paxton was the man for whom she had been waiting! Awed by the confluence of vision and reality, unable to tear her eyes away, unable to resist, finally, the urge, she reached out and touched the amulet.

Tom stared at her. The amulet was obviously significant to her, but why, he couldn't imagine. Inexplicably, her hesitation and the wonder on her face made her seem terribly vulnerable, and Tom found himself wanting to gather her in his arms, to hold and comfort her. "What do you see, Adriana?" he asked.

Adriana closed her eyes and shuddered violently.

Unnerved, afraid she would fall, Tom reached to support her. "For God's sake, what do you see?"

"Nothing." Her eyes opened. Her voice sounded normal. Matter-of-factly, she began to rebutton his shirt. "It's too late. The blood is dry." She was careful to keep her eyes from his. "I must return to the Cottonmouth. Can you and your friends find your way home?"

"I think so." He shrugged into his coat. "Adriana, I—"

Her voice was cool and distant, a wall between them. "Yes?"

"I . . ." Something told him that pressing her about her reaction to the amulet would be a grave error. "I would like to see you again, if I might," he said instead. "Perhaps we could take a carriage ride tomorrow. I can hire a team and rig . . ."

She needed time to contemplate all that had happened, to sort out her thoughts, her fears, her hopes. "I would love to go for a carriage ride with you, Thomas Gunn Paxton," she said. "But you shouldn't call for me at the Cottonmouth." She reflected a moment. "We can meet at the Cabildo. Do you know where it is?"

"I'll be there. Early afternoon. One o'clock, say?"

"That is fine." The look on her face was dazzling in its loveliness as she hurried to the back door. "I must run. Madame Villon will let you out the front way." She hesitated, half-in and half-out the door. "Good night," she whispered. "Until tomorrow."

⤳ CHAPTER XI ⤳

The Cabildo had housed the city's government under Spanish rule, and had retained that role during the brief occupation of the French and, more recently, under American authority. Adriana arrived an hour early at the porticoed edifice with its wrought-iron decorations, sculpted facade, and impressive array of arches and cut-glass windows. She had arrived early in order to think—although that was virtually all she had done for the past twelve hours.

The amulet had been a shock for which, despite the warnings, she was unprepared. So great had been her confusion that she had returned to the Cottonmouth, danced, read palms, and danced again without any memory of doing so. First light was softening the sky when, at last, the Cottonmouth closed and she found the time she needed. Alone in her room, she lighted her candle, stared deeply into the flame, and found—nothing.

Nothing! The vision had deserted her! Panic-stricken, she lay on her cot and forced herself to relax by taking slow breaths and imagining the beauty of a sunset . . . and still no vision. At last, she was forced to conclude that her powers had failed her. One thing she knew, though: whatever else the future held, Thomas Gunn Paxton would play a part. She slept fitfully, dreamed of Giuseppe and Trevor Bliss, but never of Tom. And when, at ten, she rose to bathe and dress, she had reached a decision. The amulet and Thomas Gunn Paxton were inextricably entwined, and she had no choice but to attach her fortunes to Tom's and have faith that he would somehow, eventually, lead her to Trevor Bliss.

The morning was cool, with a high layer of light clouds drifting up from the gulf and slowly burning off. By noon, when Adriana found a seat in the small park across the road from the Cabildo, it was warm enough to remove her shawl. She waited calmly and confidently, sure that he would arrive, for though her visions might not reveal everything she wanted to know, neither did they lead her astray.

She felt his presence before she saw him, and saw him long before he saw her. Dressed in formal black and driving a quietly elegant one-horse shay, he looked the very image of a man of substance despite the blood-stained bandage on his forehead and the black eye patch. A man of substance, and one who had been attracted to her. His face the night before had told a familiar story. He had seen her dance, and the sight had kindled a fire in his blood. He wanted what all men wanted of her, and, had it not been for the overriding imperative of her vision, she would have slipped away unnoticed, never to see him again.

That he wanted no more than other men wanted of Adriana was a simple explanation Tom would have rejected out of hand. He had dreamed erotically of her, it was true; but, more important, he was intrigued by her reaction to the amulet, and also curious about what she had seen but not had time to say about his future. He was instinctively certain that, for whatever reason, he could reveal his innermost doubts and fears and hopes to her without fear of censure or ridicule.

"Tom? Thomas Gunn Paxton."

He had thought he'd never forget her voice, but hearing it then was like hearing it for the first time, and the sound shook him to the core. Tom pulled the team to a halt and swung around to see Adriana coming up alongside him. He immediately jumped to the ground and took the hand she extended. "Good afternoon," he said, the words inadequate to express the way he felt about her. "I'm glad to see you again."

"And I to see you. How is your wound today?"

"I barely notice it. You did an excellent job, Madame Surgeon."

Her laugh was soft and throaty, but her smile was quickly replaced by a look of concern. "You must be careful with such injuries," she said with a glance at his eye patch.

"I know. If anything were to happen to the good one, I wouldn't be able to see at all. And after meeting you, I realize what a shame that would be. Think of all the beauty I'd miss."

The compliment was one any gentleman would offer, yet Adriana liked hearing it from Tom. "You are a flatterer, sir," she said, a slight blush coloring her cheeks.

"On the contrary. I speak only the truth. Now, if I may assist you?"

Daylight enhanced her beauty. She wore a long white skirt with green swirls that complemented the bright emerald of her eyes. A dazzling white blouse accentuated the warm honey tones of her skin, and an equally white lace shawl gave her hair the soft depth of a polished chestnut. Numbed, Tom took her arm and led her around the carriage, and as his hand fell to her waist when he helped her to her seat, his touch lingered a moment longer than necessary.

They rode in silence. Graceful homes, the grande dames of New Orleans architecture, lined their way. Spacious and elegant in the immaculately landscaped grounds they dominated, they gave way to the lesser, though still neatly kept, cottages and slave houses of those who served the wealthy. Slowly, the city fell behind them, and after an hour's ride they were alone in the open countryside on a wide path that cut through November-idled fields of cotton stubble.

The area around Lake Pontchartrain was low and marshy, and Tom was reminded of South Carolina in the fall when the air was crisp and clear and the first cold nights had set the trees to turning. Moss dripped from cypress and live oak. Birds of every hue, like living blossoms, flitted from branch to branch and filled the world with song.

It had been a peaceful, tranquil hour, an hour given to the sky and the land, the gentle rocking motion of the shay, and the steady clip-clop of the mare. An hour given to the turning trees and moss and bird song, to the flight of geese, the whisper of wind, the shifting shadows. And an hour given to that silence, deeper than words, in which two people strive to know each other. One elbow touches another. A glance followed, a burst of wood ducks from a hidden marsh. A smile given and returned. All the wondering hours of the long night and morning were forgotten in the sudden mesh of two minds. The thought, unspoken, that there will be time enough for words, but that the magic of this first hour alone will surpass time.

Wordless still, Tom turned the mare off the beaten path, then followed a faint trail to a completely secluded glade of cypress on the shore of the lake and stopped. Lake Pontchartrain lay before them. A hundred yards offshore, a solitary catboat ran across the south wind. A flight of pelicans wheeled gracefully and then, one by one, plummeted comically into the choppy water. "Why, then, *did* you fight?" Adriana asked suddenly, breaking their silence.

"Why? Oh, anger, I suppose. Frustration. One of those crazy urges to lash out—" He stopped and stared at her. "How'd you know what I was thinking?"

Adriana studied his face, saw the merriment in the grin that exposed his even white teeth, and the strength and determination written in the lines around his eyes. "I do not know," she finally admitted. "Sometimes, not often, with the right person, thoughts come to me as clearly as if they had been spoken. It is a gift."

"Then you know—?"

"Very little more, for the gift is flawed, thank God." She shrugged, decided to lie, and then quickly changed her mind. "I have seen in my dreams the amulet you wear."

"Then that's why you—?"

"Yes. Seeing it frightened me. All I could think of was to run." She smiled and touched his arm. "I'm glad you asked me to come with you today."

Tom laughed in an attempt to make light of her unease. "I couldn't let you get away without finishing my fortune. Here." He held out his left hand. "Want to try again?"

Adriana took his hand, glanced down at it, then looked up and stared into the distance across the water. Calluses. A small white scar crossing his heart line. A broken fate line. All, and more, she remembered vividly from the night before. "There are . . . troubles," she finally said in little more than a whisper. "You are a worried man who carries a great load. But—"

"I thought I was concealing my problems better than that," Tom said with a nervous laugh.

"I'm a Gypsy," Adriana answered with a shrug. "More important, I'm a woman, and know when a man has much on his mind." She turned his hand over, held it concealed in both of hers in her lap. "I listen at least as well as I dance," she said simply.

It was Tom's turn to stare across the water. Strange about lakes. When a lake was too large to be seen across, it might be an ocean for all the casual observer knew. One might think the water went on for thousands of miles, and yet, if one took to the water, one discovered soon enough that land and trees began again just over the horizon. What that had to do with anything, he didn't know, but something, surely. What women had he talked to beyond casual or formal conversations in his life? His mother, of course, when he was younger, but otherwise only Jenny. And there was the crux of the problem. What did he really know of Adriana? How much of himself should he share? He wanted to know her and her to know him, found himself captivated by her beauty and the depth of feeling she displayed in her dancing, and yet at the same time he was plagued by a sense of betrayal of Jenny—and an equally disquieting sense of dishonesty toward Adriana. He wasn't aware how, but thoughts became words, and he was talking.

"My wife died last spring," he began, "and left me with our twin sons, Joseph and Jason." A wistful look fleetingly crossed his face. "They're a little over three years old."

The story was sad, sometimes humorous, poignant, but no more so than myriad others that might be told. Adriana listened intently, sympathized as he spoke painfully of the loss of Jenny, marveled at the strength of their love, and silently admitted her envy, not of Jenny, but that she herself had never been so loved. And as the story unfolded from the couple's meeting in England to their elopement and marriage, from their first idyllic months together to the birth of the twins, it slowly dawned on Adriana that the amulet in her vision might have had nothing to do with Giuseppe or Trevor Bliss, but that it had been meant to lead her to Tom. The revelation left her with mixed emotions. On the one hand, she was dismayed, because vengeance in Giuseppe's name had been so important for so long and her hopes for an ally were dashed. On the other, she liked Tom and found herself hoping that their initial attraction might lead to something more, something she had denied herself since Giuseppe's death.

". . . on San Sebastian."

The name struck like a thunderbolt, and rendered all Adriana's suppositions meaningless. San Sebastian! Getting to San Sebastian had been her single goal ever since Isaiah Hawkins had told her Bliss was stationed there. Her first assessment of the vision's meaning had been correct: Tom had been sent to help her. How else to explain the absurdly improbable coincidence that two strangers should both be bent toward the same tiny spot in the wide world?

". . . and nothing will stop me," Tom swore, his right fist pounding his thigh. "No thing, no person will stop me. I *will* have my sons!"

Adriana had almost spoken, so great was her excitement, but she clamped her mouth shut.

"Well?" he asked, thrusting his hand at her again. "What do you think? What does my palm say? Are they safe? Will I find them and bring them home?"

If she told him about Giuseppe and Trevor, if she asked to accompany him and requested his aid, he would surely refuse her. Coldly, she calculated how she might best change his mind or maneuver him into a position where he could not refuse. As precisely as a navigator plots his course, she determined her own. "I will tell you a secret," she answered, covering his palm with her hand. "Palms aren't that precise. The adept palmist reads the lines that nature has traced in a palm, and then, through her own insight, leaps from those lines to the person himself. This line," she said, indicating the life line, "hints how long a life will be, but says nothing of how that life will be lived. This finger, how it is inclined, speaks of the strength of a person, but says nothing about whether that strength will be used for good or for evil. Here we read of love, but whether gentle or tortured we cannot tell." She folded his hand, counted lines along its edge. "You will have two more children, but whether they will be boys or girls, whether they will live long lives or die at an early age, is not shown. You will marry again, but whether that wife will be beautiful or plain, whether you will love her as deeply as you loved Jenny or merely tolerate her, I cannot tell.'' She shrugged. ''Do not expect, my newfound friend, too much from a reader of palms.''

''Then you know nothing?'' Tom asked, disappointment in his voice.

Adriana shook her head and smiled. ''I didn't say that. I said I know nothing *precisely*, and that you shouldn't expect too much. What I do see is happiness and great love, and when I read the person, when I see his strength, his great capacity for love, his determination, his intelligence, and his loyalty, when I feel these qualities through the touch of his hand, I surmise that he will succeed, for fate rarely stands in the way of the man who challenges fate and wills his own success.''

The prediction was heartening, but not what Tom wanted. ''And that's it, then? You can only surmise?''

''No. In some ways I can be quite exact.'' She hid her brief impish smile by concentrating over his palm. ''I see,'' she went on, her tone intentionally mysterious, ''that we have been sitting in this carriage for two hours, and that our legs will fall off if we don't get out and move around, and that our stomachs will shrivel and we will die of starvation if we don't eat. And is that, Mr. Thomas Gunn Paxton,'' she asked, looking up at him, ''precise enough for you?''

Tom bridled momentarily, but then, understanding that she wasn't mocking him, allowed himself to relax. ''You and Maurice,'' he said with a self-deprecating grin, ''make quite a pair. Both pulling me out of myself when I get too glum. And do you know what?''

''No. What?''

''You're right. I need a good kick in the seat every once in a while. Come on. Let's see what they packed for us.''

The tension broken, Tom jumped down from the shay, circled the horse, and helped Adriana down. The afternoon had warmed pleasantly. Sunlight cut through the trees and danced on the water. A heron stalking the shoreline fled in ungainly flight. The glade was quiet and warm, a friendly place untouched by the city so few miles away.

The picnic lunch packed by the hotel staff was simple but elegant. A red-and-white checkered cloth served as a spread, on which Adriana set out fried chicken, fresh rolls, a potato salad garnished with cucumber, parsley, and pimiento, and a bottle of white wine, each wrapped in thick towels to keep it warm or cold as needed. They ate ravenously and, when finished, lay back on the soft grass and stared into the trees and sky.

Tom yawned and blinked to keep his eyes open. "That was good," he finally said, as much to keep awake as to converse. "I feel better."

"Mmm. I do too."

A pause, another yawn. "Care to go for a walk?"

Silence, and then a drowsy, "No."

"I wouldn't either."

A wren landed on the wicker picnic hamper, regarded them quizzically, and flitted away.

"Adriana?"

"Mmm?"

"I . . . that is, you . . ." He found her hand near his and squeezed it gently. "Thank you."

"For what?"

"Just listening, I guess. We've only known each other a little while, but for some reason I think you were truly interested. That's rare."

Adriana propped herself on one elbow and looked down at him. "You are a foolish man, Thomas Gunn Paxton. What else are friends for if not listening?"

Her eyes, deep-green, bored into his and invited an answer. Suddenly uncomfortably aware of how close he was to betraying Jenny, Tom avoided them. "Working," he answered, trying hard to sound nonchalant. "Fighting, drinking—you know, things like that. Racing horses."

"Then a woman cannot be your friend?"

"Well, sure she could, but . . ."

"But what?"

The thought of having a woman as a friend had never occurred to Tom. Men loved, cherished, and married women, but *friends* were other men. "You have to admit it would be kind of different," he said, pointing out the obvious. "After all, women are women, and men—"

"Are men. Of course," Adriana said, lying down again.

"So what's wrong with that?" Tom asked defensively, rising in turn on his elbow. "It's true, isn't it?"

"Yes," Adriana sighed, and closed her eyes. "It's true."

Tom waited for more, but she lay without moving. Puzzled, at a loss for words himself, he lay back down and watched, for a long, silent moment, a blue jay trying to break open a pecan. "I guess," he finally said in a voice that sounded tiny in the vast emptiness that surrounded them, "that you must think me a silly ass."

Adriana spoke sternly, but gently. "I think you are a man who loved a woman very deeply. I think you are a man who is afraid to believe that life goes on because he fears he will betray that love. But I tell you this. Life does go on, and your Jenny—you see, I dare say her name—could not have loved you as deeply as you say and yet wish you to live as half a man because she is no longer with you."

Tom's eyes stung, and he had to clear his throat before he could speak. "I wish I could believe that," he said.

Adriana sat up, and her hair made a tent over his face as she leaned over him. "You will," she whispered huskily. Her fingers traced the line of his jaw, floated, light as a feather, to touch his good eye, and then his lips. "I will teach you to believe."

Her hands were magic wands that soothed the tension from his face. Patiently, Adriana gave him time, first to remember, and then, bit by reluctant bit, to forget. As his jaw relaxed and the hard lines around his mouth smoothed, her hands moved down to massage, ever so gently, his neck. And almost without his knowing, she undid his tie and unbuttoned his shirt so she could massage his chest.

Tom was confused at first, even frightened. Jenny was watching, he was sure, and he was embarrassed to be seen with another woman. Jenny wept, and tears came to his eyes, to be kissed away by ghostly lips bidding him goodbye and whispering in his ear, *live, my love*.

His throat burned and hot tears scalded his eyes. *No! Don't go, Jenny. Don't leave me. I love you!*

But I already have left, my darling, don't you see? Our forever is over. Such a lovely forever. . . . Her voice faded, became weak with distance, receded beyond his grasp. *You must live, my love. Do not be afraid. . . . You must live. . . .*

He was empty. Drained, he lay in the sun, and only gradually became aware of the gentle insistence of hands giving him the gift of life. At first, there were only the hands, for he dared not look. The hands, fingers combing the hair on his chest, slid across his nipples, ran lightly down his sides, and kneaded the muscles ridging his abdomen.

"Take off your clothes."

Tom's eyes popped open. "What?"

"You're tense as a board." Adriana reached behind her for the checkered cloth, then stood and spread it on the ground at his side. "Take them off and lie on your stomach."

"I don't think—"

She knelt, pressed a finger to his lips. "We won't do anything you don't want to do," she promised, and then turned her back. "Take them off."

He felt foolish, like a child. Awkwardly, he struggled out of his boots and socks, stood to remove his trousers, coat, and shirt, then lay down with his head on his hands. "Are you sure—?"

"Hush," Adriana said, turning back to him. "Relax. Empty your mind."

She placed his arms at his sides and then, starting at the back of his head, began to work the tension out of him. Her fingers kneaded, caressed, stroked, and teased, easing, like a magic potion, the stiffness as they worked. His shoulders succumbed next, and as she manipulated each hand and arm, a sweet lassitude crept through him. Her hands worked down his spine, now gently, now probing muscles he hadn't known he had. She kneaded his buttocks, massaged his thighs. His calves felt like knotted ropes that she untied one by one, and so adept was she that he actually dozed off while she was massaging his feet.

How long he slept, he had no idea, but not long, certainly, for the sun had barely moved when he woke. In the months since Jenny had died, sleep had been a physical need to which he gave in only when he was exhausted, and when he had slept long enough, he would awaken instantly. On this afternoon, though, he was aware of a slow awakening, a pleasant swimming ascent from the depths, and a feeling of refreshment, as if he'd slept for many, many hours.

"You slept."

Her voice was like a dream that comes between sleeping and waking, not quite dream, not quite real. "Ummm," he grunted. "How'd you do that?"

"It doesn't matter. Roll over."

Tom lifted his head and turned to look at her. "Now, wait a—"

She was naked. Her hair, alive with light from the sun, streamed down her shoulders. Her breasts, perfectly shaped, swelled enticingly to end in large, deeply pigmented areolae and dark thick nipples that begged to be touched. Her skin was clear, the hue of honey gold. Sturdy thighs, pressed together as she knelt at his side, protected the dark, luxuriant hair where they met.

Tom's breath caught in his throat as, in spite of himself, he rolled onto his side. "You are . . . *beautiful*," he said, his voice filled with wonder.

"I am Adriana. Only . . . Adriana. Roll over. Onto your back."

Strangely enough, Tom was no longer embarrassed. This time, Adriana started at his feet, and as she worked her way up each leg, Tom felt the first faint stirrings of desire. He hadn't thought about sex for months. A woman had been the furthest thing from his mind, but now, as her hands moved closer to his loins, he felt himself begin to fill and swell.

He was disconnected from himself. He watched her hands slide up his hips, along his sides. She licked her palms and slowly, lightly, rotated them on his breasts.

Adriana's breath quickened in time with Tom's, and, as if imbued with a life of their own, her hands strayed down his torso to enfold his now rapidly rising sex. She hadn't planned on being so affected herself. The seduction had been calculated, a way to win his heart, to make him so dependent on her that he would have to take her to San Sebastian. She had, instead, been caught in her own web. His honesty, his touching display of loyalty to a woman long dead, his single-minded devotion to his children, engendered in her a tenderness that, fired by the touch and sight of his tumescence, rapidly became ardor. Her breasts swelled achingly and her nipples hardened. She could feel herself becoming warm and moist in anticipation, and at last understood that she wanted him—wanted him more than she had known it was possible to want a man. "Tom," she whispered hoarsely. "Thomas Gunn Paxton. Make love to me."

His heart singing, Tom reached for her and pulled her down to him. Hungrily, their lips met and his tongue explored her mouth. So long without the touch of a woman, his hands swept over her body. Flare of hips, rise of breasts. Caress of moist, parting lips ready for his entrance. The musk-sweet smell of arousal . . .

Moaning, gone wild, Adriana rolled off him and he was quickly on top of her. His sex, rigid against her, seared her flesh. Eagerly, near her climax already, she tilted her hips to accept him, and guided him to her with her hand.

Suddenly, he was inside her. A beast untamed, his length pierced and filled her. His sweat mingled with hers. The touch of his chest against her breasts electrified her. Rhythmically, he withdrew, hung poised above her, and then entered to her depth.

She wanted to wait, to savor the exquisite friction, the maddening pressure as, already large, he seemed to grow and harden even more inside her. "Thomas!" His name was ripped from her throat. Her legs wrapped around his waist and she drove herself against him as the first spasms racked her.

His teeth clenched, his lips parted. His back arched, his body shuddered and stiffened. Adriana threw back her head and gasped. Her eyes, wide with surprise, locked with his, and the slow, fierce explosion hurled them into that measureless void in which two hearts, two souls, two bodies meld and expand to become one distinct being, whole and timeless, without beginning or end.

∽ **CHAPTER XII** ∼

Three days passed all but unnoticed by Tom and Adriana. Tom had never known a woman of such fire; Adriana had never met a man so gentle and yet so forceful. Their lovemaking was extravagantly impetuous. A knowing glance, a smile, the merest hint of invitation sent them tumbling into bed to explore each other's sensuality, and join themselves in ageless ecstasy. They spent hours on end in the exquisitely appointed suite— Maurice had thoughtfully moved elsewhere— and the delicate furnishings, draperies, and silks seemed the perfect setting for romance. Tom reveled in hedonistic bliss. He glutted himself on passion, and only occasionally succumbed to guilt about Jenny. Adriana discovered within herself a desire long held dormant. She had been a child of love—for the Gypsies are a race bred out of a passion for love and life—yet that part of her able to give love had until now existed as one asleep, like a seed in the earth awaiting spring.

But it was nearly winter. How ironic! And did she dare come alive before she had fulfilled her solemn vow to Giuseppe's memory? She knew the answer, and the answer shamed her even as vengeance cried in the dark night of her soul. Fate had provided her with the means to bring herself once more within a dagger's length of Trevor Bliss. Fate had brought her Tom Paxton and his ship, the *Cassandra*. No matter how honest her growing love for Tom, he was also the means to an end. Guilt ridden, she held her tongue and let sweet passion rule—

the passion whose wild tide she planned to ride all the way to San Sebastian.

Not that Tom had forgotten the ship or his mission. Early every morning, he went to the yards to inspect the previous day's progress. Her hull now repaired and scraped clean of barnacles, the *Cassandra* had been floated free the afternoon before, and rode gently in a wet dock. She was a sleek three-masted cargo schooner, and her speed was evident to any experienced seaman who took the trouble to study her lines. Fore-and-aft rigged, with two jibs, she presented a breathtakingly beautiful picture. An adjustable centerboard eighteen feet long, six inches thick, and eight feet deep when fully lowered enabled her to navigate waters too shallow for a ship with a fixed keel. Her seventy-foot length and eighteen-foot beam allowed ample cargo space below decks in addition to three cabins and the other necessary working and living spaces for the crew. Lashed securely to the deck were a small catboat and a longer rowboat which would serve the double function of harbor lighters and lifeboats. The hull of the *Cassandra* was painted a brilliant white, with her name in black script against the bright background.

"Well?" Tom asked as he climbed aboard at first light and met Jamie Ragland. "What do you think?"

"Ready to go tomorrow morning," Jamie said, proud of his accomplishment. "Want to take a look?"

They inspected her from stern to bow. The patch in the hull was indiscernible from the outside, and watertight. The new mast appeared to be sound, and a fresh set of lines had been rove. Half the sails were being replaced with new canvas, a job that would be finished by late afternoon. Below decks the ship had been fumigated and thoroughly aired. Later in the day, ballast, food and water, powder and shot and rifles would be loaded aboard.

Maurice was waiting with Slurry Walls when Tom emerged from the yard offices after a busy half-hour of signing papers. "Jamie says you took the tour," Maurice said by way of greeting. "Any problems you can think of?"

"Everything looked shipshape to me," Tom said. "You find any cannon?"

"Couple of three-pounders is all, which is about as good as tryin' to piss out a forest fire. Nobody wants to part with what they have."

"Damn."

"She's sailed for three years without cannon," Maurice noted with a shrug. "I guess she oughta make this trip without 'em."

Tom's eyebrow rose a notch. "You want to sail near that island and try to get the twins out of there with nothing bigger'n a rifle aboard?"

"Well . . ."

"I still think our best bet's Barataria," Slurry interjected. "You can buy damn near anything you need there if you've got the cash in your pocket and the iron in your spine to deal with the men who live there."

Maurice snorted. "Pirates!"

"If you want to call men like Laffite brothers and Dominique You pirates, suit yourself. As for meself, I like to refer to 'em as enterprising businessmen."

"Businessmen, my arse," Maurice growled. "You ask me, everything about 'em stinks. A thief's a thief, and no way around it."

"So who's askin' you?" Slurry said. "It's Tom's ship and Tom's boys, so it's up to him to say."

Tom rubbed his jaw and considered a moment longer. "You're sure you know some of the people there?" he asked Slurry.

Slurry held up two fingers. "Me and the Laffites are like this."

"That don't surprise me none," Maurice grunted sarcastically.

"Me either," Tom agreed, "but what choice do we have? Which settles the matter as far as I'm concerned.

We stop at Barataria to buy cannon. Anything else?'' he asked, eager to return to Adriana.

. "The crew," Maurice reminded him.

"Oh. Well?"

"Pease says he won't go. Says one captain aboard is enough, and he doesn't want anything to do with this voyage, that he has enough troubles with the British Navy without sailing into one of its harbors an' askin' to be sunk. Most of the rest of the crew is waitin' to hear what you have to say, though."

"Any of them I know?" Tom asked, leading the way through the yards.

"The first mate, Simeon Larkin, that big feller with the red hair," Maurice said. "Barton says he's a good man, one of the best, and I believe him. Couple others you've met. Blaine, little bitty guy built like a marlinespike, was in charge of the rigging. Engle, the one with that big birthmark on his face, is the sail maker. The rest'll be checkin' in for the first time this morning. Barton vouches for 'em all."

Tom crossed the gangplank with Maurice and Slurry behind him. As promised, the crew waited midships. "Here he is, boys," Maurice called as Tom hopped up on a keg to address them. "Gather 'round."

"Beggin' your pardon, Mr. Paxton," one of the men said, stepping to the fore. "We can cut this short, if I can have a word."

"Certainly," Tom replied. "What is it, Larkin?"

Simeon Larkin was a thick-bodied, bandy-legged man whose feet were more at home on the heaving deck of a ship than they were on land. Red hair curled around his ears and hung long in the back, but the top of his head was completely bald. His once-fair skin had been burned to a deep-brown and was wrinkled from years of being battered by the elements. He twisted his cap with gnarled, work-scarred fingers as he cleared his throat for the speech he'd prepared for the man whose family owned the ship he'd called his home since the day she had first slipped down the ways.

"Mr. Barton told us last night what you was up to, sir, and Jamie and Leakey here both explained the details. We just wanted you to know that we're with you every cable length of the way, an' come hurricane or calm, we'll do everything a crew can do to get them boys of yours back." He cleared his throat again and looked around for support at the men behind him. "Which is what I had to say."

"Those are fine words, Mr. Larkin, and I appreciate them." Tom's gaze swept the crew, then lingered for a moment of eye contact with each man. "You understand," he said, "that I'll be the captain."

"Yes, sir," said Larkin. "It was explained to us why Captain Pease don't want to go."

"And were your wages explained to you?"

"Yes, sir," he said, adding, "and every man here agrees the terms is generous."

"Good." Tom made a show of counting, then glanced around the rigging. "Fourteen men can handle her?"

"Beggin' the captain's pardon, sir, but there'll be seventeen, countin' you, Leakey, and Slurry here." His look was determined and there wasn't a trace of doubt in his voice. "We can handle her, sir. Easy as a mother with a babe in her arms."

Maurice caught Tom's attention, mouthed the single word, "Barataria."

"Oh, yes," Tom said. "There's a new development you don't know about. After you hear about it, I'll hold no ill will toward any man who changes his mind about sailing with us. This isn't company business, and those who stay behind are assured a berth on any other Paxton ship."

Much to his surprise, not a man faltered when told of the side trip to Barataria, despite all that carrying cannon implied. "It looks to me," Tom said as he and Maurice headed for the ship's chandler's to make sure that the last of their provisions would be aboard by nightfall, "that we have a damned fine crew."

"Far as it goes, I suppose so," Maurice agreed.

"What's that supposed to mean?" Tom asked.

"First, seventeen's cuttin' it thin, given the cannon. Second, them boys're merchant men. How many of 'em know how to aim and fire a cannon? An' third, how many of 'em can fight—an' I mean down an' dirty, banshee an' she grizzly bear fight—if an' when the time comes?"

Tom stopped, stared into the distance as if picturing San Sebastian and all that could befall them there. "Done," he finally said. "How many do you want?"

"Four," Maurice said without pause. "One for each cannon. I seen two of 'em already, and heard of two more who sound like they'd be right."

The decision made, there was no hesitation in Tom's next words. "We sail at sunup," he said curtly, and turned to enter the chandler's. "Get 'em."

Tom returned from the yards to find Adriana waiting for him by the hotel fountain. Her shoulders, bare and inviting kisses, were dappled with sunlight. Her breasts pressed enticingly against the cotton overlayers of lace on her blouse. "Be careful, my dear Thomas," she warned as he embraced her. "They are watching us from the terrace."

Tom glanced toward the terrace crowded with diners enjoying a late breakfast. "This will give them a good reason to arch their eyebrows," he said, kissing her anyway. "Don't worry about them. They're just jealous; the men because I'm with you, the women because you're more beautiful than they are." He took her arm and led her along the cobblestone walkway. "Have you eaten?"

"I was going to wait, but I was ravenous. Last night

. . . *mon Dieu!*'' She squeezed his arm, reached up to kiss his cheek. "You will wear me away to nothing, Thomas."

"No chance of that," Tom retorted unhappily, his mind leaping ahead. They rounded the corner of the hotel, skirted a stone-rimmed pond with lily pads resembling emerald islands afloat in an inland sea, ducked under the sheltering branches of a weeping willow, and seated themselves on a crescent marble bench set close to the trunk where they were free from the prying eyes of the other guests.

Adriana sighed, leaned back against the tree trunk, and looked upward to the dappled sunlight filtering through the thick foliage. "You have news?" she asked, sensing that Tom was having trouble telling her something.

Tom sat next to her, took her hand, and stared at it as if he wished he could read the lines. "Who are you?" he asked, his voice as soft as the rustling leaves.

"A woman."

"No, more than a woman. You've placed a spell on me."

Adriana laughed. "Foolish one. You have placed a spell on yourself. Why blame me? I'm a woman. Nothing more." She fixed him with eyes of green fire. "Nothing less," she added pointedly.

"I'm confused," Tom said, leaning forward, his elbows on his knees. "Ah, hell! I guess the only way is straight out. With a rapier I admit no master. I've fallen off a horse but once in my life, and that when I was twelve. Maurice is the only man I know who can outshoot me, and I can sail a ship through wind and storm. But words—such simple things—words fail me." He took a deep breath and looked her directly in the eye. "The *Cassandra* is ready," he said bluntly. "We sail in the morning."

"Dear Thomas, was that so hard to say?" Adriana brought his hands to her lips and kissed his fingertips.

"We both knew you'd be leaving."

"That isn't it," Tom said, and then blurted, "It's the Cottonmouth. I don't want you to go back to dance there."

"Oh?" Adriana asked, thinking that she had never intended to anyway. "Why not?"

"Because it's . . . dangerous."

"For others, perhaps. Not for me."

Tom's cheeks reddened and he was unable to look at her. "Still and all, I don't want you to go back."

"But why?" she asked again.

"Because . . ." Tom's voice faded, and he coughed nervously. "I don't want you to."

"Oh?"

"What's 'Oh' supposed to mean?" Tom retorted, trying to remove himself from the defensive. "It's wrong, is why. A woman shouldn't—"

"Dance? A Gypsy is *born* to dance. I earn my bread and board by dancing."

"I don't want you back there," Tom repeated doggedly.

Adriana stood and moved away from him. "You would have me starve then, *n'est-ce pas?*" she asked, gesticulating angrily. He had no idea she was going to sail with him, but before she told him, he would pay for his assumption that he could determine what she might or might not do. "Or," she hissed, "sell myself the way other women do?"

"Of course not," Tom protested, cursing himself for being such a bumbler. "I'd see that you had enough to live on comfortably, and—"

"You'd *keep* me?" Adriana's eyes flashed with anger. "You dishonor me, monsieur! What is this? You take me for some harlot on the streets? I gave myself to you, Thomas Gunn Paxton, not sold myself. And as for your gold, you may keep it instead of me, for every shiny coin you own could not buy me."

"I didn't say—"

"You said more than enough," Adriana spat, turning to leave. "So good day, monsieur!"

Tom sprang after her, caught her by the arm, and dragged her back to the bench. "That isn't what I meant to say, damn it." Angry himself, he seated her on the bench and made sure she stayed. "I hate to think of you dancing on that tabletop for all those men. I hate to think of the way they look at you," he explained, striving to find the right words to salvage the situation.

To his surprise, the outrage and indignation left her face. "Tell me how those men look at me, Thomas. Tell me how, and I will tell you that I have seen that same look on your face."

"I know," Tom agreed glumly. "I know all too well. I don't want you to dance, but I do want to leave you with enough to live on because . . ." His mouth felt dry and he had to wet his lips and take a deep breath before he went on. ". . . because, after I get the twins back to Solitary, I'd like to see you again."

"Oh, Thomas, Thomas." Adriana stood and went to him, wrapping her arms around his waist and resting her cheek against his chest.

"Well?" he asked hoarsely. "Will you?"

A tiny inner voice told her the time was not right to tell him of her plans. "You were right about spells," she said gently. "We've both been under one. But a week isn't long enough, dear Thomas, to ask me to deny what I am." She looked up at him, and her eyes softened as she spoke. "Go to your sons, my friend, and after you have taken them safely home, we will speak again. In the meantime"—she was careful not to lie—"I will live as I must, do as I must."

"But—"

"You know I'm right," she insisted. "But as a token, I make this pledge. No man at the Cottonmouth will touch me until then."

"That's a promise?" Tom asked.

"I say so."

Tom paused. She was right, of course. The week had been a whirlwind of lovemaking, of passionate excesses, and after his long celibacy following Jenny's death, even he had to wonder whether his heart might have been moved more than he liked to admit by his loins.

"Well, Thomas?" Adriana prompted.

"What?"

"Will you kiss me? To seal our pact?"

She smelled of spiced tea, Tom thought, and cinnamon. And though a kiss wasn't the resolution he'd had in mind, it was a beginning.

They planned the rest of their last day together carefully. In the afternoon, they hired a carriage and rode into the country. The day was suffused with an afterglow of autumn, and the air lay warm and lazy on fields of unpicked cotton and tassel-topped stalks of ripened sorghum. At peace with each other and the world, they picnicked on cheese and apples and white wine, and fell asleep in each other's arms beneath the shading branches of a solitary magnolia.

Not mentioning their imminent separation, they made love slowly after their return to the hotel. Afterward, while Adriana dozed, Tom shaved and dressed, then slipped quietly out to summon the maid he'd requested earlier. Adriana was awake when he returned. "Where were you?" she asked with a yawn.

Tom sat at her side, pulled the covers down, and kissed her breast. "An errand. You slept?"

Adriana stretched luxuriously. "You've spoiled me, Thomas. All I've done for the past four days is eat, sleep, and make love with you."

Her skin looked as warm as sun on autumn leaves. Her hair lay in auburn tangles against the pillowcase. In the lantern light, her eyes glowed with a mysterious deep-green fire. He would sail away from her in the morning . . . "I have to run by the yards," he said, his voice harsh with self-discipline. "There's a little present waiting in the hall for you. It's seven now. I'll meet you downstairs at nine, all right?"

"I'll be there," Adriana promised, adding as he strode toward the door, "Thomas?"

His shoulders and neck were tense, and he answered without turning. "Yes?"

"No other man ever touched me at the Cotton-mouth." She wanted desperately to tell him then the whole truth, about Giuseppe and Bliss and San Sebastian, but, as afraid of his response as she had been that afternoon, and not wanting to ruin their evening, she held her tongue. "Do you understand?"

"I understand," Tom said curtly, opening the door and motioning in the maid. "Remember, nine o'clock."

All was quiet at the yards. The extra gold Tom had ordered from the bank that morning had arrived and was safely stowed. Maurice was off finding the additional men. The crew was putting the final touches on the quarters and making everything else shipshape. Larkin had overseen the loading of provisions and fresh water; he gave Tom the bills of lading for signing.

It was eight-thirty by the time Tom returned to the hotel. After a quick drink at the bar he checked in with the maître d'. All was in readiness: a secluded table, the flowers he'd ordered, the wine opened and breathing. Ignoring the stares of the other patrons—their curiosity would be rewarded soon enough—he retired to the lobby to wait for Adriana.

No queen ever made a more stately entrance. Precisely on the stroke of nine, Adriana appeared at the top of the main stairs to the lobby and began her descent. Tom's breath caught in his throat. All activity in the lobby came to a standstill. Resplendent in a gown of white satin and crinoline, with a bodice adorned with a myriad of tiny white bows, she seemed to float as lightly and gracefully as a cloud. Her hair was piled high atop her head in an elaborate coiffure, and the tawny luster of her skin contrasted sharply with the shining purity of her gown.

"My God!" Tom whispered in awe.

Adriana stopped in front of him and curtsied. "Such a gift you have given me, dear Thomas," she said in a voice as soft as a cat's purr. "The gown is lovely. Maybe too much so for me, no?"

"Hardly," Tom said, and though he tried to think of something else to add, the sight of her had momentarily robbed him of speech.

The dining room was abuzz with conversation and the soft clink of utensils when they entered. Adriana on his arm, his heart swelling with pride, Tom followed the maître d' through the hushed and envious whispers of the other diners to their table. The waiting sommelier tipped some wine into Tom's glass and stood back. The color was like rubies shot through with moonlight, the taste light and subtle, hinting of romantic evenings spent on the terrace of a château hidden on a French hillside. "Very good," he said with a nod of approval.

The sommelier poured, and withdrew discreetly.

Tom raised his glass, Adriana hers, and the crystal chimed as the two met. "To our week," Adriana said.

"To our week," Tom repeated—and drank, with the unsettling impression that she had left a great deal unsaid.

A moonlit floor. A flickering candle. Slippers. A frock coat draped carelessly over the French love seat. And there, near the bed, a mound of brilliant satin and tiny white bows. Bed covers in disarray. Flesh joined—sweet joining—in the moonlight. The bed trembles and the flesh separates, melds anew, becomes two, becomes one. His body drives down into hers, pours its strength and fierce heat into hers, cries to hers, shudders while she claws his back and sobs and clings to him, surrenders to the final svelte plunge, to the wondrous sighing, subsiding of the fire, the ebbing of passion's moonlit silver tide.

They lay side by side, flesh warm and naked and close, as a chorus of insects outside filled the night air with song. Adriana breathed deeply, inhaling and exhaling slowly to prepare herself for the next critical minutes. "Thomas?" she said, at last composed.

"Ummm?"

"Will you listen to me?"

Something in her voice alarmed him, and Tom turned his head so he could see her. "Of course."

"I was going to tell you earlier, but couldn't."

His alarm became cold certainty that she was going to say something he didn't want to hear.

"You've picked a fine time."

"No time was the right time. Will you listen to me now?" She had relived the night of Giuseppe's death a thousand times. Every excruciating detail was clear in her mind, but putting the scene into words was a different matter. She spoke haltingly at first, starting with the life of a Gypsy and describing the small towns scattered across the English countryside. She spoke of one town and one night in particular, and of the face of Trevor Bliss, menacing in the firelight. Of the unexpected pistol shot, and of the warm blood, sticky on her hands, as Giuseppe died in her arms. And finally, of her vow to kill Trevor Bliss, of her pursuit of him, which had led—so far—to this room, this night, this man at her side.

"I don't understand," Tom said after the silence had dragged on for over a minute. "I'm sorry for your brother, and God knows I sympathize with your desire to kill this Bliss fellow, but I don't see what any of it has to do with me."

"Trevor Bliss," Adriana said, "is now the captain of the sloop of war *Druid,* which is stationed at . . . San Sebastian."

"Ohhhh!" Tom said, the pieces falling into place.

Adriana raised herself on one elbow, lifted the amulet from Tom's chest, and held it, gleaming like a miniature sun in the candlelight, in her palm. "I told you I'd seen this in my dreams." She spoke rapidly, as if speed would override any possible objection and convince him she should sail with him. "When we first met that night, something told me you were special, and when I saw this. . . . At first, I was certain you'd come to help me avenge Giuseppe. Later, I doubted; I thought that my dreams had thrown us together as man and woman. But then . . . then when you told me about your boys and San Sebastian, I knew, I tell you, dear Thomas—" She clenched the amulet in her fist and pounded lightly on his chest, as if to drive the message into his heart. "I knew that we were meant to go together. We must obey our destinies."

"Oh, Jesus, Adriana." He held her hand pressed against his chest and tried to think. With any kind of luck at all, the *Druid* and Trevor Bliss would be on patrol far from San Sebastian when they struck. And if Bliss was nearby, what would Tom do? Allow, even assist, a passenger aboard a Paxton ship to murder a British naval officer? By the time word got back to England, no Paxton ship would be safe anywhere in the world. And what of Adriana? The teeming streets of London were one thing, but a single girl stalking Bliss on a small island was quite another. He would more likely be taking her to her own death.

"I can't," he said, sick at heart.

"You *can*! Fate has—"

"Fate is nothing! For God's sake, Adriana, they'll be waiting for us as it is. I'll be lucky as hell to get my boys out of there and to escape unscathed. And in the middle of all that, I'm supposed to help execute a British naval officer who just happens to command an eighteen-gun sloop of war?"

"Just leave me there, is all I ask," Adriana pleaded. "You don't have to help."

"No. It's out of the question."

"Thomas! I'm begging you!"

"And I'm telling you *no,* damn it," Tom snapped, rolling away from her and out of the bed. "If that's what you wanted, you came to the wrong place. I'm sorry about your brother, but—"

"Sorry!" Adriana hissed. She rose to her knees and crouched, facing him, like an animal. "Your sons have been kidnapped. If I say I'm sorry, does that heal your wound? Is that enough for you?"

"That's not the point." All those words of endearment, those tainted kisses! "There's no place for you on the *Cassandra.*"

Eerily calm, Adriana settled back on her haunches. "This bed," she said, touching the sheets still warm from their lovemaking, "With you. I have given myself to you, and will again as often as you wish. For this, you will take me with you."

"So that's it," Tom said listlessly. He'd been used and deceived. He'd sullied Jenny's memory and himself. "All my shiny gold pieces weren't enough to buy you, you said." His voice was dull, his heart hurt. "And yet you sold yourself for a boat ride."

Her body glowing in the candlelight, Adriana climbed out of the bed. "Yes," she said calmly, kicking her new gown aside and reaching for her more simple blouse and skirt. She hadn't meant it to come out the way it had, but he had turned her words against her, and would pay. "With you, or with any man who would take me to San Sebastian."

"One week," Tom said, watching her dress. "To our week! What a lovely toast. But I'll say this." His voice was brittle with sarcasm. "You sure picked one hell of a way to honor your brother's death."

The pain written on his face was terrible to see, but she had to keep pressing, or she would never be free of her brother's ghost. "Will you take me or not?"

"No," said Tom, looking away from her.

"Very well." She stalked to the door and stood, nearly invisible, in the shadows. "If you won't have me, the men at the Cottonmouth will be glad to see their Adriana has returned. Bon voyage, Thomas Gunn Paxton."

The hour was late, the hotel quiet as a tomb. Slamming the door behind her, Adriana walked quickly down the hall, ran down the stairs, and woke the night porter as she banged through the front doors. He'd refused to take her. Refused! Stunned, unable to believe she'd been thwarted once again, she stumbled down the street toward the French Quarter.

And then, suddenly, the possibility dawning on her like a blaze of light, she whirled about and began to run, not toward the Quarter and the Cottonmouth, but toward the shipyard—where the *Cassandra* waited.

⟡ CHAPTER XIII ⟡

Tom spent a sleepless night, and by morning was in no mood for pleasantries. Thirty minutes after settling his bill at the Hotel de Paris, he stalked up the gangplank and brushed past Maurice without so much as a by-your-leave. Maurice took note of his friend's foul mood, but reserved inquiry. The *Cassandra* was preparing to set sail, and he had more than enough to occupy his time.

The ship was a beehive of activity. Most of the crew was busy tightening the new lines that had stretched overnight. Larkin had decided that since there was no cargo, he wanted more weight forward, and a crew of dockworkers, each bringing a hundred-pound cast-iron ingot, was filing on and off board.

"Captain?"

"What?" Tom snapped, anxious to seclude himself in his cabin.

Larkin, with a distinguished-looking gentleman smoking a pipe at his side, stood at the door to the wheelhouse. "Thought you ought to meet the pilot, sir. Pilot Randall, Captain Thomas Paxton, Paxton Shipping Lines."

"Pleased to have you aboard, Pilot," Tom said, shaking Randall's hand. "Any problems I need to know about?"

"None to speak of. Wind'll back around to the north or nor'west by noon, or I miss my guess. Should have a fairly easy run to Pilottown."

"Good. Mr. Larkin, if you'll be so kind as to call me

when you're ready to cast off?''

''Aye, sir. Shouldn't be long now.''

The captain's quarters was a ten-by-twelve cabin astern, furnished with a bunk, a pair of captain's chairs, and a mahogany table that served double duty as a desk. The walls were lined with cabinets, and also held a small-arms rack and a chart locker. Tom stowed his bag beneath his bunk and, ducking to avoid the hurricane lamp suspended overhead, sat behind the desk to look over the charts Larkin had set out. The one for the channel to the gulf lay on top, but since the pilot would be in control during that part of the voyage, Tom set it aside. Next came a general map of the Caribbean, already marked by Larkin with a suggested course to San Sebastian. More detailed charts followed. Tom scanned them in turn and then picked the one detailing the approach to their first destination.

Barataria, Laffite's stronghold and Tom's last chance to buy cannon, lay on the gulf coast to the south and west of New Orleans. The settlement was accessible from New Orleans by bayou, but not in a vessel the size of the *Cassandra,* even with her centerboard drawn up completely. Tom calculated quickly for the dozenth time. A day to Pilottown at the mouth of the Mississippi. A night in the gulf and, with luck, an arrival at Barataria by the next evening. If all went well, they'd be on their way to San Sebastian by the end of the week.

''You in there, Tom?'' The door opened and Maurice stuck his head into the cabin. ''Those men we talked about yesterday just came aboard. You want to meet 'em before we sail?''

Tom sighed and folded the Barataria chart. ''I guess I'd better. What do you think of them?''

Maurice grinned. ''I'm damned if I'd want to tangle with 'em, but you can judge for yourself.'' The grin disappeared, replaced by a look of concern. ''You all right?''

''Sure,'' Tom replied, a hint of venom in his voice.

"Hell, no," he corrected himself, edging past Maurice and heading for the deck, "but what does it matter?"

A quartet of some of the hardest cases Tom had seen in a long time waited with Jamie Ragland near the mainmast. "They're ready to sign on soon as you talk to 'em," Ragland said, gesturing with a ledger toward the four. "Boys, this is Tom Paxton, the captain of the *Cassandra*. Tom, this first one's August Benet. There's a price on his head from New York City north into Canada. The posters say for murder, but I wouldn't ask for details, was I you."

Benet, a tall, fair-skinned Frenchman whose smile had all the warmth of a winter night, stepped forward. He looked wiry, very trim, and his eyes were those of a mercenary. If men could be likened to blades, Benet was a stiletto. *"Bonjour,"* he grunted, thrusting out his hand.

Tom nodded, smiled with approval at the strength of Benet's grasp. "You know how to handle a cannon?" he asked.

"Mais oui," Benet answered shortly. "With cannons and beautiful widows, I have vast experience."

"Very well," Tom said, clearing his throat. "Welcome aboard."

"Next is Jim Strickland," Ragland continued. "He has a deep and abiding hatred for the English ever since he was pressed off an American vessel and spent six years as a gunner aboard a British frigate before being released."

Strickland was swarthy and solid, wide-shouldered and compact, with a face of which the most striking feature was a battered lump of cartilage that served as a nose. "Cap'n," he grunted.

"Can you sail?" Tom asked.

"Not as good as I can shoot," Strickland said, "but good enough to help when needed."

"Good enough for me," Tom said, shaking his hand. "Welcome aboard."

"Third one's Tom Fairleigh," Ragland went on. "He looks a little worse for wear 'cause he tried to clean out the Cottonmouth last night."

Fairleigh wore a blood-caked stocking cap. His hands were swollen and cut, his great muscle-knotted arms black with bruises. "Came damned close to it, too," he mumbled through split lips.

"Better luck next time," Tom said, with a sidelong glance at Maurice. "Can you shoot a cannon as well as you clean out bars?"

"Take a crab out of a sea gull's beak at a quarter mile, sir."

Tom gingerly shook the big man's hand. "Hope you don't have to," he said. "Welcome aboard."

"Last one here is Topaz," Ragland concluded. "He's a Carib."

Dark-skinned and slightly built, Topaz was impeccably dressed from the waist up in a frock coat, elaborately stitched waistcoat, and beaver skin top hat. From his waist down, he wore nothing but a tattered and frayed pair of loose shorts. The effect, ludicrous at first glance, was on a more studied appraisal altogether ominous, especially when he grinned and revealed his teeth, which had been filed to points. "Good morning, suh," Topaz said, tipping his hat and bowing shallowly. "Most pleased to make your acquaintance, suh!"

Tom wasn't sure what to make of Topaz, and his glance in Ragland's direction said as much.

"Tell 'im a little bit about yourself, Topaz," Ragland said.

"Yes, suh! There was a missionary on my island. He was a good man, cured illnesses, so my people did not kill him. He taught me English, so when he leaves, I go with him to protect him, all the way to New Orleans. But he get sick and die, so now I wear his clothes and make my living among his people."

"That's very, ah, commendable," Tom said, "but can you—"

"Fairleigh teach me shoot cannon," Topaz interrupted. "All Carib know seas. This Carib"—faster than the eye could follow, Topaz produced and threw two knives, which stuck with a dull thud no more than an inch apart in the mizzenmast— "can fight good."

"Jesus!" Tom whispered in awe.

"I seen it but I don't believe it," Maurice said. "You throw tomahawks like that?" he asked Topaz.

The Indian shrugged. "Knife, tomahawk. All the same. Many dead men."

"You want my advice," Maurice told Tom, "we take him—all the way back to Brandborough. And if Jase can beat him, I'll by God bow down and kiss that old man's foot."

"You've made a believer out of me," Tom said, shaking Topaz's hand. "Welcome aboard." He stepped back, looked them over collectively. "Mr. Larkin's your first mate," he announced. "After Ragland gets your signatures on the log, you can stow your gear below and turn topside to help get under way. Any questions?"

There being none, Tom and Maurice headed aft. "You sure pick 'em," Tom said with a shake of his head. "A wanted murderer, a deserter, a brawler, and a cannibal. A couple dozen more like them and we could take the whole damned island."

"No sense in hirin' 'em half-bad," Maurice pointed out. He pulled a gold coin out of his pocket and found that it barely fit between Topaz's knives. "Would you look at that! Feller wouldn't have much chance goin' up against—" He stopped, looked around, and located Tom standing at the rail and staring toward the city as if expecting to see someone at the last minute. Which explained, he thought, why Tom had come aboard in such a foul mood. But that was the trouble with men like Tom. Couldn't let a woman be what she was meant to be, a roll in the hay, a quick tumble, and a quicker goodbye.

"Beg your pardon, suh." Topaz had come to retrieve his knives.

Maurice pocketed his coin and stepped aside. "You ever consider givin' lessons with them things?" he asked.

Topaz showed his teeth in a wide grin. "Sell, suh, for a price."

"What about a trade? Know anything about Indian leg wrasslin'?"

"Suh?"

"Trade you even. Lesson for lesson."

Topaz started to respond, but stopped short as Slurry Walls fell to his knees half a dozen paces away and lifted his eyes to the mainmast and its multiple crosses. In his right hand, he held a worn leather-backed Bible, which he placed over his heart. "Oh, Lord," he cried, "we set sail to do Thy will!"

Sailors paused and snickered. Topaz and Maurice stared.

"Though we be not all Christians here," the old man went on in pointed reference to Topaz, "we be just and honest men, fearing only Thy wrath, seeking only Thy divine mercy. Grant us a fair wind and clear sky, and bring us home again both safe and sound! Amen!"

"Might better ask for a pint of rum, Slurry," a voice called down from the mainmast.

Slurry stood, stowed his Bible in his coat pocket, and wiped his mouth on his sleeve. "I could use a drink," he admitted to general laughter, "but I got my standards, and I'm dry till we touch land again."

Topaz went back to his knives. "Interesting," he said, slipping the first one into a sheath sewn into the inside of his coat collar. "I find white men a source of amusement."

"Oh, yeah?" Maurice asked. He watched as the second knife disappeared up Topaz's left sleeve. "Fine with me," he added. "Just as long as you don't find us a source of nourishment."

Topaz didn't find that particularly amusing, but was nonetheless sufficiently intrigued with Maurice's earlier offer of a trade to accept the deal before hurrying below to stow his gear. A quarter hour later, all was in readiness for sailing. The gangplank was secured, the mainsail raised, and one of the forward jibs unfurled to help keep them steady on course. Larkin, standing next to the pilot, bellowed orders. The forward lines were cast off, the rudder put hard to starboard. Slowly, the current swung the *Cassandra*'s bow away from the dock, and moments later they were under way.

From his place on the capstan that controlled the depth of the centerboard, Maurice watched Tom, who remained a solitary figure outlined against the growing gap of water between the *Cassandra* and the docks. Slowly, then faster as the Mississippi caught them and pushed them downstream, New Orleans slipped into the distance and lost its definition. Ships at anchor blocked their view, and when they could see, docks and warehouses and commercial buildings became an undifferentiated line of city shapes, a montage of grays and browns dashed with splashes of green. And still Tom watched, searching but not finding, until at last he turned away from the rail and disappeared below.

The wind shifted as Randall had predicted, and by the time they transferred him to the pilot boat at the mouth of the Mississippi, the *Cassandra* was running smartly ahead of a full-blown norther. The temperature dropped sharply and the men broke out their foul weather gear.

The first night was spent tacking back and forth in the darkness, well away from the treacherous shallows that spread in all directions from the Delta. Dawn found the *Cassandra* far out in the gulf, where, Tom determined, they would remain until the wind was more favorable.

Their fourth morning out, November 12, a Monday, the wind backed to a little south of east, and they began the long, cautious approach to Barataria. "You're sure you know these waters?" Tom asked for the third time as he and Slurry pored over the appropriate chart.

"Not as good as the pilot knew the Mississippi," Slurry admitted, "but good enough to get us in and out." He pointed to the thin pencil line he'd drawn. "This here's our course, Cap'n. You keep that center-board no deeper'n four feet, and we'll make her slicker'n gull shit."

The chart was old, and as useful as a blank piece of paper as far as Tom was concerned. "You know this water well enough to take us in now, or do you want to wait until morning?" he asked, not wanting to waste a day, but more than willing to do that rather than run aground.

Slurry had gone four and a half days without a drop to drink. His eye was clear, his hand steady, and his voice sure. "Time's a-wastin'," he said by way of answer. "You want to get them boys of yours or not?"

Tom took a deep breath and decided to try for it. "I want them, Slurry."

"Then bring her to nor'east by north," Slurry called immediately. "And get that durned centerboard up to four feet, an' ready to go to three when I call for it."

The water shallowed perceptibly for the next two hours, and the crew was noticeably nervous as the *Cassandra* crept toward the line of green that was Grand Isle. "Sure looks peaceful for the reputation it has," Tom said as the tree line edged closer.

Slurry called for more mainsail, ordered the center-board raised to three feet. "It wasn't so peaceful a couple of years ago," he said, "Laffite's got those boys in line now."

"Still and all, I never trusted a pirate, and don't plan to start this afternoon," Tom said, almost to himself.

"Privateer, Cap'n, not pirate," Slurry corrected. "There's a difference. All of Laffite's captains fly the flag of the republic of Cartagena. They're duly licensed

—got letters of marque, and everything. 'Course, there's still them that consider 'em to be pirates, but I'd be careful about usin' that word when we get there."

Three bells; one-thirty. Another five and a half to six hours before sundown. One man high up the foremast kept an eye out for hidden shoals ahead. Two more forward alternated throwing lead lines and calling out the depth of the water. Tom kept a close eye, but left the navigation to Slurry and hoped for the best.

Laffite and his cohorts had chosen the location of their headquarters with great care, and wisely. Located on one of the Grand Terre islands, their community was protected from all but the worst of hurricanes by the islands between it and the gulf. Approach from inland was impossible except by small boat; approach by sea was readily discovered long before an attacker could bring his guns to bear. And once an enemy entered the bay, the shallow waters and unpredictable winds forced him to navigate at a crawl past Barataria's concealed shore batteries.

The facts were known to Tom and the crew of the *Cassandra* as they negotiated the narrow tide-scoured channel between Grand Isle and the first of the Grand Terres, but their position took on added meaning as the dull boom of a cannon rang out across the bay. The first island fell astern. "We'll be goin' hard to starboard once we get past the second one," Slurry called. "Be ready on them sheets, and then ready again to spill the mainsail on my call!"

"You heard 'im," Larkin bellowed. "Look lively, lads!"

Benet, Strickland, Fairleigh, and Topaz waited by racks of loaded and primed rifles concealed by the rail. The cook had doused the galley fire and waited below with more weapons for the crew, should the need arise. Ready to move in any direction, Maurice stood by Tom's side, and Tom, armed with a brace of pistols and Raven's rapier, stood ready to take over from Slurry.

"Hard to starboard!" Slurry yelled.

The rudder caught, the bow swung to starboard. The crew hauled on the mainsail sheets to catch the wind abeam, and adjusted the jib. Slowly, majestically, the *Cassandra* slipped through the gap between the two islands and emerged into what amounted to a large, sheltered lagoon. And there in front of them lay Barataria.

The pirate stronghold was a miniature city in the middle of nowhere. Dominating the scene on a rise a hundred yards from the beach was a pillared two-story mansion with glass windows. Beyond the mansion, a cluster of thatched-roof cottages provided housing when their inhabitants weren't at sea. A row of bordellos, gambling houses, saloons, and cafés that looked as if they might have been lifted whole from the French Quarter provided entertainment. A single long dock stretched into the water; near it were clustered a half-dozen warehouses made of imported planks. Not far from them was another warehouse called, Slurry explained, the barracoon, where hundreds of Africans were chained in fetid darkness until they could be smuggled into New Orleans and sold at auction. Scattered around the lagoon lay at least a dozen ships, anchored fore and aft to present a broadside to any outsider who dared enter, all with gun ports open and guns run out.

"Jesus," Maurice whispered in awe to Tom. "Now I know how it feels to be a sittin' duck."

"You sure worry a lot for a big feller," Slurry cackled. He pointed out a line of small boats tied along the beach. "See? They belong to them merchants from New Orleans I was tellin' you about. We ain't the only ones here to buy."

"They ain't here to buy cannon, though, I'll bet," Maurice pointed out. "There's a difference."

"Well, you'll just have to take my word for it," Slurry said. "Ain't nobody gonna shoot a payin' customer. Oops." He pointed to the dock, where a catboat was casting off. "Welcoming committee on the way. Spill that air, boys!"

The welcoming committee was surprisingly civil, though blunt about the *Cassandra*'s chances should Tom try anything suspicious, and a half-hour after they boarded, the *Cassandra* was tied up at the dock.

The men who had greeted them told them to wait on the dock and then set off at a run for the mansion.

"You sure made an impression on 'em, Slurry," Maurice noted.

Slurry rubbed his jaw and grinned sheepishly. "That's 'cause them fellers is new an' don't know me. Now, if we'd been met by Cap'n Dominique You or Cap'n Rene Beluche, or even Laffite hisself, the reception would've been different."

"Looks like you might get a chance to prove that," Tom said. "Who's he?"

A large man who emanated an aura of power that was felt even at a distance had emerged from the mansion and was unhurriedly making his way toward the dock. He wore a lightweight suit and a plain white shirt, and clenched a long, thick cigar between his teeth. "That's Laffite, all right," Slurry said in a subdued voice.

Tom's pulse quickened. Jean Laffite hadn't become one of the most notorious pirates in history by taking foolish chances, and Tom wasn't about to jeopardize his mission by challenging him. "Keep an eye on the *Cassandra* and let me know if anyone shows a weapon," he told Maurice. "I'll do the talking."

Laffite's skin was fair and his broad features were dominated by dark eyes, heavy brows, and a thick moustache. *"Bonjour, messieurs."* he said in a deep, sure voice as he approached. "Welcome to Barataria. Allow me to introduce myself. I am Jean Laffite, at your service."

The punctilious observance of drawing room formalities took Tom by surprise. "The honor is mine, sir," he said, stepping forward to shake hands.

"Thomas Gunn Paxton, at *your* service."

Laffite returned the handshake and, his eyes wary, smiled. "Many years ago, in this part of the world, a man named Jason Brand sailed with the woman called Raven, he noted, lifting his eyebrows in curiosity.

"I'm descended from Raven, whose name was Marie Ravenne," Tom said. "The rapier I wear was hers."

"Then you come from a fine, proud family, my friend. I've heard many stories about Raven, and am honored to meet one of her descendants." His tone became brisk and businesslike. "How can I be of assistance?"

"I need to purchase certain items," Tom said. "One of my men suggested that you might be able to help."

Again the lift of the bushy eyebrows. *"Oui?* And who might that be?"

Maurice gave Slurry a shove that sent him forward. Slurry quickly caught his balance and ducked his head. "Me, Monsieur Laffite. Slurry Walls. I sailed with you in oh-two."

A smile lighted the privateer's face. "But of course! So good to see you again, Mr. Walls. How are you?"

"Just . . . just fine, Monsieur Laffite," Slurry mumbled.

"Wonderful. We must talk about old times with you and your friends here." Laffite turned back to Tom as Slurry shot a triumphant leer at a frankly disbelieving Maurice. "Now, Monsieur Paxton. I have some excellent brandy you might care to sample. If you'd accompany me to my house, we can discuss your requirements."

They had passed the first test. Laffite lifted one hand. On his signal, orders could be heard being called aboard the pirate ships and Tom could see guns being run in and gun ports closed. At the same time, people emerged from doors onshore and began going about their daily business. Chatting comfortably, Laffite escorted his astonished visitors to the front verandah of the mansion, where they were met by an elderly black man in butler's livery.

They might as well have been visiting a plantation in South Carolina as a pirate's den in Barataria Bay. Luxurious carpets cushioned their steps as they entered the foyer, and the high-ceilinged parlor was furnished with delicate, expensive furniture. "You are surprised, gentlemen?" Laffite asked.

"It's a far cry from what I expected," Maurice admitted.

"Doubtless." Laffite smiled thinly and clapped his hands. Immediately, a side door opened and the butler entered with a crystal decanter filled with brandy, and four crystal snifters on a silver tray which he placed on an elaborately carved table that had at one time belonged to the king of Spain.

Laffite himself poured, then raised his glass in a toast. "To your good health, gentlemen."

They all raised their glasses and drank. "And to the successful conclusion of our business," Tom added pointedly.

Laffite allowed himself a polite chuckle. "You are impatient, my friend, but I quite understand. Gentlemen," he said to Maurice and Slurry, "please feel free to help yourselves to more brandy, if you wish, while Mr. Paxton and I discuss our business." He steered Tom across the room to a large window with a view of the settlement. "And now, Mr. Paxton," he said in a low voice, "you may speak bluntly. What is it you wish to buy from us?"

"Cannon," Tom said simply. "I want to buy four nine-pounders, and I have gold with which to pay for them."

Laffite's hand tightened around his snifter. "Your proposal is a difficult one for me to answer," he said with a frown. "As a privateer, my business is selling whatever my customers require, but I'm placed in an awkward position when you ask for large weapons."

"And why is that?"

Laffite's eyes were cool and thoughtful. "I know that your family owns a shipping line, my friend. Perhaps you wish to buy these cannon so that someday you can turn them against the men of the brotherhood."

Tom shook his head. "That isn't my desire. I have no quarrel with you or your men. Paxton ships are fast—you have seen the *Cassandra*—and are seldom molested. I intend to use those guns far away from here."

"For—?"

"That, Monsieur Laffite, is none of your business. Unless, of course, you want to sell the information to someone who might be interested."

Tom realized at once he'd gone too far. Few men had eyes so hard and piercing. With those eyes alone, Laffite had cowed men far more savage and bloodthirsty than Tom.

"No offense meant," he added quickly, giving ground, "but that's a factor I have to take into account."

"You dare much, my friend. I can believe that the blood of Raven runs in your veins. And you have," Laffite conceded, "a point well taken." He sipped his brandy and stood in contemplation for a few seconds. "I'll tell you what I'll do," he finally said. "A decision such as this must be made in consultation with my lieutenants. After dinner—you will dine with me, I trust?—we'll meet with them and you may present your request in person. Is this agreeable?"

Tom knew he had no choice. "Of course," he said, hiding his disappointment.

"Good. Dinner will be at eight. And, oh, yes." Laffite chuckled, and once more his eyes were open and friendly. "I've a small confession to make, Thomas—I may call you Thomas, may I not? You should know that you took a very great chance when you came here. Were it not for your ancestry and audacity, you and your men would be prisoners by now. You see, you might have made a better choice when you picked someone to serve as your introduction to my little colony. No doubt he *has* been here before, but I have no memory of that scrofulous creature called Slurry. No memory of him at all."

Acting on impulse as she had, Adriana had been ill prepared when she boarded the *Cassandra* after leaving Tom at the hotel. Her plan had been simple: hide until Tom was too far into the gulf to turn back, and then take her chances.

The hold where she'd hidden was dark and deserted. She'd obtained bread and cheese and water before coming on board, but her supplies had been depleted two days earlier. Unable to see, and unaware of the side trip to Barataria, she hadn't the foggiest notion where they were when, to her surprise the *Cassandra* entered calm waters and came to a dead stop. But where? Back in New Orleans? Why? Cuba? How long did it take to get to Cuba? Her questions remained unanswered because she dared not come out.

The darkness intensified. It was night. Hungry and thirsty, she waited for the ship to quiet, and at last crept out of the hold. Below decks was deserted, but she could hear occasional footsteps and the murmur of voices above her on the main deck. If she could find the galley and slip inside before she was discovered . . .

"Here, now! What's this?"

Adriana froze, then turned calmly to see a young sailor in the doorway. "Oh, hello," she said, as if she had every right in the world to be there. "What's your name?"

The sailor blinked and shook his head. "Huh?"

Adriana dropped the dipper into the water bucket and walked toward him. "My name's Adriana," she said with a smile. "What's yours?"

"Uh . . . Crane, ma'am. Jeffrey Crane."

"How nice to meet you, Jeffrey. Would you excuse me, please?"

Still not sure he wasn't seeing a ghost, Crane stepped aside.

"Thank you."

"Hey!"

A second was all she'd needed. Adriana slammed the door behind her and had darted down the passageway and up the ladder to the main deck before the sailor's cry of alarm was heard. Surprise was her ally. She sprinted across the deck and was halfway down the gangplank to the dock before anyone knew what was happening. Seconds later, unpursued, she dived into the cover of some bushes and lay panting on the cool earth.

The dinner with Laffite seemed endless. Although— or perhaps because—they assiduously avoided discussion of the guns, Tom's nervousness increased as the meal proceeded. Under other circumstances, he would have enjoyed the delicately seasoned chicken and rice and the choice wines, but on that evening his thoughts were full of the precarious situation in which he and his men found themselves. Laffite was no stranger to the social graces, but beneath his veneer of civility, he was a man who would unhesitatingly kill if he felt threatened.

The meal finally finished, Laffite stood, lighted a cigar, and took his hat from the butler. "The time has come, my friend. If Mr. Leakey would care to wait?"

"He goes where I go," Tom answered without hesitation. "We're ready when you are."

The sky was overcast and a warm, moist breeze from the south rustled the trees as Tom and Maurice followed Laffite to a brightly lighted tavern near the beach. Music floated through the open door into the night, but silence fell abruptly as Laffite entered. Quickly, as if all had been prearranged, the tavern emptied save for five men seated at a large round table.

"My friends," Laffite said to the seated men, "let me present Monsieur Thomas Paxton, whose unusual request you've had the chance to ponder. His companion is Maurice Leakey." Laffite moved around the table and stood behind the seat that had been saved for him. "Thomas, starting at my far right, Captain Gambi and Captain Nez Coupe. To my left, Captain Dominique You, Captain Rene Beluche, and Captain Isaiah Hawkins. The floor is yours."

Laffite's announcement that his lieutenants knew what Tom wanted came as a surprise, and Tom realized with a sinking feeling that he'd be doing well simply to get the *Cassandra* and her crew out of Barataria in one piece. "I'm not sure what I can add to what Monsieur Laffite has already told you," he said, looking each man in turn in the eye. "I need four guns, I need them now, and I have gold to pay for them."

The air reeked with hostility and distrust. "Why?" Nez Coupe asked, an ugly smile splitting his face.

Tom and Maurice had discussed whether they dared reveal their mission, and had decided that Tom's initial reticence was correct. "I'm not at liberty to discuss that," he said, knowing the answer wouldn't help his cause.

"Fagh!" Gambi spat on the sawdust-covered floor. "Are you at liberty to discuss what's to stop us from just taking your gold? And maybe your pretty ship, too?"

"The honor of Jean Laffite," Tom replied, noting the pleased expression that crossed Laffite's face. "Monsieur Laffite expressed the concern that the cannon would be used against his own men and ships. I give you my word that this is not my intention, and that it will not happen. My mission is my concern and mine alone; it does not threaten the brotherhood. However, any man jack of you is welcome to try to take what belongs to me. Men have tried it before. But know that I came to conduct a fair transaction, to your benefit and mine.''

Gambi shook his head. "I say no! No cannon for this fancy rich man." He looked at Tom with a savage leer. "Why you come to us anyway, Paxton? Your family got plenty money. You can buy cannon damn near anywhere.''

"If I could have, I would have," Tom answered honestly. "We scoured New Orleans, and there were none to be had.''

"So what made you think you'd find any here?" Nez Coupe asked.

"I was told you were my best bet.''

"Then you was told wrong," Gambi snarled, "and lost your bet, too.''

Tom smiled. "You speak for all of Monsieur Laffite's men, when not even he does?''

"Not for me," Hawkins allowed. He glanced at Gambi, and it was apparent that no love was lost between them. "But I don't like the idea of selling guns to a merchant, either.''

"Nor I," Dominique You added softly.

Captain Beluche did not speak, but nodded in agreement with Captain You.

The room was suddenly filled with a heavy silence, and Tom felt his skin begin to prickle with alarm. Without looking at Maurice, Tom knew that he, too, was evaluating the now-charged atmosphere of the tavern.

Adriana had no earthly idea where she was. She could make out a mansion on a hill. A row of taverns lay to her right, what looked like warehouses to her left. Behind her, the *Cassandra* was strangely quiet. How long she lay hidden she wasn't sure, but she soon spied Tom and Maurice emerging from the mansion in the company of a third man. All three descended the hill and entered one of the taverns. Curiously, the tavern emptied immediately. After a short wait to make sure the coast was clear, Adriana slipped away from her hiding place and edged close enough to hear.

Tom had spoken of his desire to buy cannon, and when Adriana heard the name Jean Laffite, she knew where she was. Stunned and frightened, wanting only to get back to the *Cassandra*—better to take her chances with Tom than with a horde of pirates—she backed stealthily away from the window, even as she heard Laffite's final answer to Tom's request.

"The vote is five to nothing. I am truly sorry we cannot do business, Thomas. The best I can do is offer you safe passage out of Barataria on the morning tide, and wish you luck on your mission, whatever it may—"

"Gotcha!"

An arm encircled her waist. A hand grabbed her hair and pulled back her head. Adriana struggled silently as her captor muscled her onto the porch. "Animal! Pig!" Her nails found his face and clawed his flesh. "Let me go, you—"

"Owww! Gaw damn!" The pirate kicked open the door, dragged Adriana inside, and unceremoniously dumped her on the floor. "Sorry to interrupt," he croaked, "but look what I found listenin' at the window."

"Great jumpin' Jehoshaphat!" Maurice whispered as Tom stared speechlessly at the auburn hair, honey-colored skin, bright-red skirt, and torn white blouse.

"Adriana!" gasped a voice from the table.

Tom's gaze whipped around. Stunned though he was by Adriana's appearance, he was even more surprised to hear her name from a stranger. Isaiah Hawkins looked every bit as surprised as Tom.

For someone who had just been caught spying, Adriana displayed a remarkable degree of self-possession. Her eyes touching Tom's for only an instant, she looked up and pushed the hair out of her face. "Hello, Isaiah," she said, coolly rising and ignoring the way her captor grabbed her arm. "It's good to see you again, though I'm surprised to find you here."

"You know this girl?" Laffite asked Hawkins.

"Aye. She's the one I told you about, who dances in New Orleans."

"*That* Adriana?" Dominique You asked, suddenly interested.

"Damn!" Gambi interjected with a leer. "Maybe she dance for us, no?"

She stowed away. Stowed away! "She's with me," Tom said, hiding his anger and stepping quickly to her side. *How does she know this Hawkins? Pretend that it's no surprise. Cover up as best I can and get us the hell out of here.* "I thought I told you not to leave the ship," he said sternly.

The role of a petulant mistress, Adriana decided, made the most sense. "I was bored," she said with a shrug. "I meant no harm, but this . . . animal!" She jerked away from the pirate and took Tom's arm.

Neither Tom nor Maurice knew what to think. Tom kept an eye on the lecherous Gambi and tried to concoct a graceful way to make an exit. Maurice shared a glance with Tom, decided Tom had had no idea Adriana was aboard, and mentally took inventory of the arkansas toothpick in his boot. If it came to a fight, he'd take out You and Beluche on his way to Laffite, let Tom handle Gambi and Nez Coupe, and hope that Hawkins would remain neutral for a few seconds.

No pirate woman would have dared be caught eavesdropping on Laffite and his captains. That this woman had done so reflected badly on Tom. "I suggest, Mr. Paxton," Laffite said coldly, "that you return your woman to your ship. Gambi? Nez Coupe? This . . . gentleman . . . has my permission to leave the island without harm to him or anyone with him. I hope I make myself clear. And now, if you'll excuse me—"

"One minute, Captain Laffite." Hawkins stood, met the challenge in Laffite's eyes, and didn't quail. "I know what you're thinking, and it's true, but this is no ordinary woman. I ought to know, because I'm the man who brought her to America.''

Tom groaned audibly. *So that's it. He's the one she told me about.*

Hawkins glared at Tom, then turned back to Adriana. "You're bound for San Sebastian, aren't you?"

"How the hell did you know?" Tom interrupted.

"I asked Adriana," Hawkins snapped. "Well?"

"Yes, Isaiah."

"Very interesting, Captain Hawkins," Laffite said. Obviously intrigued, he took a seat between Nez Coupe and Dominique You. "Don't stop now. Please go on."

Hawkins briefly related how Adriana had brought him good luck and the story of her brother's death and her determination to avenge him. "I trust her," he finished simply. "She brought me luck and was my friend when I needed a friend. I owe her, and can't believe she'd bring harm to me or mine." He drew a deep breath. "So I'm changing my mind, and voting to let them have the cannon."

"No!" Gambi roared. "One vote don't make any difference."

Laffite ignored him, sat silently and drummed his fingertips on the tabletop. His respect for Tom was restored. Any man with the courage to sail into a British-held port with four guns deserved respect, after all, and under the circumstances not wanting to announce his intentions was a reasonable precaution. But still, there was something about the whole mess that smelled of rotten fish. Something in Paxton's eye—a man with one eye was harder to read than a man with two—told Laffite that part of the story was being left out, and he wanted to know what.

"You say the girl brings good luck," he finally said. "Maybe, maybe not. She's not lucky right now. You say she reads the future. I can believe that, because there are those who can. But that is not the issue. The question is: can we trust Mr. Paxton? Tell me, girl.'' His eyes turned to Adriana and bored into hers. "If we sell him the guns, will he use them against us? And why should we believe that he won't?''

Adriana felt a slight nudge from Tom. A warning? Had Laffite laid a trap for her? And what should her answer be?

"You are in no danger from this man,'' she said boldly, deciding, because she had no idea of what had been said earlier, that only the truth would do. "Thomas Gunn Paxton is a man of honor whose only intention is to rescue his sons from their kidnapper, the governor of San Sebastian.''

Laffite and the other captains exchanged looks of bewilderment. "I don't understand,'' Dominique You said. "I thought you were going to kill this Bliss.''

"Well, ya see,'' Maurice began with every intention of straightening out what had become an impossible mess, "it's like this. Tom . . . that is . . .'' He paused and threw up his hands in despair. "Ah, hell, you explain it.''

"It's pretty simple, really, I was—''

"No, Thomas,'' Adriana interrupted. "Let *me* explain.'' The words tumbling out, she addressed Laffite. "*He* is going to get his sons back. *I* was going to avenge my brother, only Thomas wouldn't let me go with him because it's too dangerous, so I stowed away on his boat and—''

Hawkins erupted in laughter. Wounded, Adriana watched as the others joined in, one by one. Maurice looked as if he hoped he was dreaming, and Tom looked as if he wished he could sink out of sight through the floor.

"But, Monsieur Paxton,'' Laffite said as the merriment finally died, "why didn't you simply tell us the truth in the first place? We're all men here. We would have understood.''

Gambi's glare was fierce as he leaned across the table.

"You think Gambi would let a British pig—*any* man—take his sons?"

"I didn't say that," Tom protested, his face reddening. "But would *you* announce to all the world that you were planning to—"

"Thomas, Thomas." Laffite waved him to silence. "You wanted us to trust you, but you didn't trust us, eh?" Disconsolate, he shook his head and sighed. "That was wrong, my dear friend. But—" The sad look disappeared, to be replaced by a wide smile. "We forgive you, eh? And grant your request. Four nine-pounders shall be yours."

"Thank you" wasn't quite enough, but it was a good beginning. An hour later, the price negotiated, Laffite's men began loading the cannon aboard the *Cassandra,* and Adriana began reading palms, starting with Jean Laffite's. Three hours later, the *Cassandra* was ready to sail on the morning tide and the party was in full swing. Not until after Adriana's second dance did Tom have a free moment with her. "You're an amazing woman," he said as she nestled in his arms. "The only problem is, what am I going to do with you now?"

Adriana looked up at him, at the fierce face gentled by moonlight and shadows. "I know exactly what you're going to do," she told him, the amulet he wore warm against her chest. "You're going to take me with you."

~ CHAPTER XIV ~

Midnight, starlight. The wind had died with the setting of the sun. The *Cassandra* had long since slowed to a dead stop, and lay rolling gently on the long, shallow swells. When the moon rose, they noted the first faint glimmering of the phosphorescence that, common in the wake of a ship, was rarely seen in a sea so calm. By midnight, the glow had become a bright, ghostly, dazzling light that covered the dark sea.

"It's doomed we are," a shaking voice announced fearfully. "We be dead men afloat on hell's black belly."

Someone guffawed. "How can a man be afloat on a belly, you damned fool?"

"You'll see. We'll all see. That's my fear."

"Enough of your heathen rumblings," Slurry shouted, his voice sounding frail despite his determination to be brave. He crossed to the starboard rail where Adriana stood and stared across the silent water. "Tell us, Gypsy, what it is you see in store for us. Read that, if ye will."

Adriana looked past the old sea dog to the careworn faces that turned as he spoke and drew closer to listen to her reply.

"Now ain't the time for secrets or holdin' back," Strickland said from the shadow of the mainmast.

"Each man must read for himself," Adriana said.

"Not good enough, wench. You're hiding the truth as plain as can be." Strickland loomed out of the darkness and his solid, rough-hewn form blocked Adriana as she

208

turned to walk away from her unwanted audience.

"Now, looky here," Slurry protested, putting out a hand to restrain Strickland.

Strickland brushed Slurry aside. "Stay out of it, old man. I want an answer."

"Somebody get Tom or Maurice," a new voice whispered hoarsely.

"Don't disturb them," Adriana ordered, to the surprise of the men slowly gathering around her. "What exactly is it you wanted to know?"

"What you see," Strickland growled, stepping closer. He liked the smell of her, liked the way the heat seemed to emanate from her body, the swell of her breasts against her cotton bodice. "Out there, pretty one . . . pretty wench . . ."

His eyes glittered and he smelled of tobacco, of rum and salt and sweat. Adriana had heard of the madness that temporarily seized some men when the ships they rode lay becalmed and helpless. A ship had only speed and mobility to escape the black sea's predators, and without a breeze to fill the sails, it had neither.

Danger fired Strickland's senses and filled him with excitement. Fear of the unknown fed his lust, and he could feel himself growing. "What do you see out there, pretty one?" he repeated, his arousal complete as he lifted a hand to touch her breast.

Adriana smiled seductively to draw attention from the sudden blurred movement of her hand and leg. Without warning, a razor-sharp sliver of steel pressed against the crotch of Strickland's cloth breeches. "I see you spending the rest of your days as a gelding if you don't stand aside," she said as sweetly as if she were asking him the time.

Strickland's lust vanished as quickly as his courage. Tamed in a second by a mere slip of a Gypsy girl, he lowered his hand and head and allowed her to pass. The rest of the crew parted to let her through, and more than one man suppressed a laugh at Strickland's expense.

Adriana turned to them and gave them a glimpse of her calf as she returned the dagger to its sheath. "If you must know," she said quietly, "I see nothing but vapors and will-o'-the-wisps. I see nothing but your fear." Her gaze swept over the crew. "You men have taken Tom Gunn Paxton's gold. You can earn it by putting away your fear. The wind goes, the wind returns as God wills. No man, no woman can say why, nor see anything beyond the coming and the going. Your time is better spent thinking of the good days past and those to come. Which of you can play a pipe?"

"Why, I can," Jeffrey Crane said.

"And I've a fiddle stowed away," another voice called.

"I heard a squeeze box the other night," Adriana prompted.

"You'll hear it again," said Joe Reese, the old-timer of the crew, already on his way below.

Crane played his pipe to the accompaniment of Slurry Wall's rhythm on an empty water keg. Before the fiddle could sing or the accordion wail, Adriana began to dance. Her hair flew like the wind, her hands dipped and dived like seabirds. Her hips emulated the undulating waves, and her slippered feet sounded like the whisper of rain on the deck. Her smile seeming a promise of better days to come, Adriana danced by Fairleigh, caught him by the wrist, and dragged him into the center of the clapping, cheering circle of men. They danced the hornpipe, and when Fairleigh fell winded to one side, Engle, the sail maker, took his place. No tonic could have worked better, for as the men danced and laughed and sang, they forgot the listless air and the sea's tricks. Even Strickland forgot his fear, because Adriana danced.

The dancing ended with the arrival of the wind. Chilled by its passage across the Atlantic, the breeze sent everyone scurrying for warm clothes. By the time Adriana returned to the deck, the sails had been set and the starboard watch had gone below to get some sleep. On deck, the seven men left to tend the ship clustered around the wheel, drank hot coffee, and spun yarns.

Wrapped in her shawl, Adriana strolled forward and, finding a perch on a crate that held a half-dozen chickens, sat and stared out at the black sea and the star-spangled sky. To be alone was a luxury. Rarely had she felt more alive in the past two years. She listened to the slap of waves against the hull, the hiss of the bow cutting through the water, the low, intermittent hum of lines vibrating in the wind, the rhythmic creaking of straining timbers—and, in her mind, the incessant buzz of unanswered questions.

Did she love this man, this Thomas who made her heart sing? The song said yes. She liked being with him, liked the way his voice sounded, the way his skin felt, the way his hands felt on her. She wanted to be with him, to nurture him and be nurtured by him, to live her days and the long nights through with him.

And yet, he had never spoken of love. Was it his natural reticence, his doubts, his ghosts that muted him? Or was it simply that he didn't love her?

She stared at the stars, wished they could supply her with answers, and realized that stars, for all their cold beauty, knew nothing. What did stars, after all, know of vengeance and retribution, of loneliness and love? Better to be a star burning brightly to light a lover's night, yet never have to know a lover's doubts or pains. Or joys?

And there lay her answer, in all its bright ambiguity. There was no answer; there was only love's desperate gamble: grief and pain on one side of love's coin, and on the other, joy and ecstasy.

To dare to play was to chance remorse, but having played was to live for love.

I would have it no other way. I have him now, and whatever dear pleasure I find, I will take and cherish.

And if tomorrow comes and love is gone?

Then I shall dance, as I always have.

Feeling Tom's eyes on her, Adriana turned. He stood behind her, and opened his arms as she went to him.

A cannon thundered and the sound jarred Tom awake. He sat up, yawned, and tried to stretch the kink out of his shoulder. Adriana's hand snaked up his side to massage the muscles around his neck. Tom groaned, then sighed in relief. "Hand's asleep," he explained, flexing his fingers into life. "Damned bed's built for one."

"Poor Thomas," Adriana teased. She kicked the covers aside and, sleek and tawny, stretched luxuriously. "You suffer so. Perhaps you'd rather sleep alone?"

He leaned down and kissed each nipple into tautness. "You'll stay right here," he ordered gruffly, lowering his head and nibbling at her tummy.

Adriana closed her eyes and shivered, ran her fingers through his hair. "Don't be silly. You probably need a good night's sleep. Anyway, I shouldn't continue to take advantage of your gentlemanly nature. I can always find somewhere . . . oh . . . else . . ." Her legs parted at his touch. ". . . to . . . Tom? Don't do—oh!—sleep . . ."

A cannon roared. Adriana jumped and bumped Tom away from her.

"Just practice," he said, calming her with his hands. He lay back, then turned onto his side to face her. "You're jumpy. You should be used to them by now."

"I know. Every time I think I am, they take me by surprise all over again." As she looked down at their naked bodies entwined, her eyes grew misty and her voice husky. Gently, she held him, arranged him so he lay between her legs. "And this?" she whispered huskily. "Is this just practice too?"

"Practice is important," Tom said. His tongue found her ear, dallied on her throat. "You know what they say?"

Adriana moaned, tilted herself against him, and, when she could stand it no longer, opened herself to him. "No, what?"

The cannon roared twice more in rapid succession—unnoticed as Tom entered her. "Practice makes perfect."

"All right! Listen up, you whoreson bastards!" Strickland bellowed. "I know you think you're pretty good, so I've arranged a little test to see just *how* good. Where's that tub, Crane?"

"Right here, sir," Crane called, pulling up a tub half-filled with sand.

"Good. Now, you may be wondering what's in this tub, and I'm gonna tell you." He lighted a piece of pitch-soaked line from a lantern and dropped it into the tub. As he talked, dark tendrils of smoke began to rise from the tub. "It's easy enough to load and fire a cannon when nothin' else is happening. In a battle, though, there's gonna be smoke and pain, and that's what this'll give you—and plenty of both!"

"Target coming up," Larkin called from the quarterdeck.

Strickland peered out over the water. A half-mile ahead and as far off their beam a brightly flagged keg buoy they'd thrown overboard bobbed up and down on the waves. "You should come close on the first shot," Strickland said, his attention returning to the two starboard crews. "How far you miss on the next four will give you a measure of just how good you ain't."

"Five in all?" someone groaned. "Jee-sus!"

"Be glad you ain't in the Navy," Strickland said. "Then we'd have enough powder for ten rounds and you'd learn what sweatin' and chokin' really is. Ready? Remember, I'll be timing you."

The fire had caught hold, and a dense black cloud billowed from the tub. "Ready!" Strickland roared.

The already-loaded cannon were run out.

"Aim!"

Chocks elevated the muzzles, which swung toward their target.

"Fire!"

Two cannon roared as one. Immediately, Strickland and Crane pushed the tub into a position where the thick, oily smoke rolled over the crew. "What in the *hell*?" Tom asked, picking that moment to come on deck.

A chorus of coughs and heartfelt curses came from inside the smoke as the crews labored to swab the barrels and reload.

"Strickland's idea of simulatin' battle conditions," Maurice explained, joining Tom at the rail. "Told me they'd be ready for anything if they could pass that test."

"I imagine," Tom said, laughing. "Where's Larkin?"

"Catchin' three winks."

"Who knows where we are, then?"

"Me. We came about at two or three this morning, and are on a long reach toward Tortola. Right now I'd say we're somewhere around the middle of Anegada Pass. Another two days at the most, the way Larkin makes it."

"If the weather holds," Tom said.

"Which is why Larkin's sleepin'," Maurice explained. "The glass is down and he says he smells a squall. Shouldn't last too long and we got plenty of sea room, so it shouldn't be a big problem. Slow us down a day, maybe."

"Damn!"

Maurice grinned. "Larkin said to tell you, when you said that, that we're better off gettin' a blow now instead of when we're off San Sebastian. All things bein' equal, we'll have a week or so of good weather after this one has passed."

"I suppose so . . ." One cannon roared, followed

by the other. The smoke from Strickland's burning tub passed between Tom and the flagged target keg. "Well?" he shouted forward.

"Close enough for a hit," Strickland called back, peering into the smoke. "Get a move on, lads! Swab 'em out, load 'em up, and run 'em on out!"

There wasn't much point in watching any longer. Whether the men were capable of hitting a keg at a quarter mile had little bearing on anything except, perhaps, their confidence; the real test—if it came— would be at close quarters, and aiming would not count nearly as much as the grit to continue in the face of grave danger. Pensive, Tom chatted a moment with the man at the helm, then headed below for coffee.

All in all, he thought, alone in the galley, the voyage had gone remarkably well. The crew had worked hard with little supervision and had remained in good spirits. The men had taken to Adriana and had restrained themselves to an occasional bawdy comment. A large scale map of the island—the details filled in by Slurry and two other crew members who'd spent time there—had been prepared. It had been decided that Tom, Maurice, Strickland, Benet, Fairleigh, and Topaz would constitute the landing party, and the six men spent hours poring over the map and devising a loosely drawn plan on which they could improvise once ashore. They spent more hours trying to manufacture a good reason, in case they ran into the *Druid* before they reached the island, for being in those waters without a cargo. It had been Fairleigh who'd finally suggested a solution: simply tell what, in a pinch, could be the truth —that Tom was on his way to negotiate with the governor for the return of his sons. That, in turn, prompted the suggestion that negotiation first might not be a bad idea, but Tom vetoed this alternative in favor of their surprise attack, which he felt stood a greater chance of success.

Not all their time was spent at work. Every member

of the crew had his palm read by Adriana. Gunnery practice turned into a competition that Topaz's crew won, and for its proficiency was rewarded an extra five dollar gold coin per man. Maurice and Topaz spent at least an hour each day together trading fighting secrets in one of the holds. Though Maurice's hands were cut in a dozen places and Topaz's legs were covered with bruises, each man appeared pleased with his progress. As for Tom himself . . .

As for me, what? he brooded. Uppermost in his mind, of course, had been his sons. Were they alive? Had the pirate Sanchez transported them safely to San Sebastian? Were they being well treated? Were they accessible? What defenses had Sir Theodotus prepared against Tom's arrival? Should he have negotiated, gone through diplomatic channels and legal procedures instead of taking the law in his own hands?

No, damn it, no! That could take years. They're my sons. Mine and Jenny's. And we will get them back!

"We." The thought jarred him. He wasn't thinking of himself and Jenny, but of himself and Adriana. Adriana had replaced Jenny.

That's not true. No one can take Jenny's place. Adriana's just . . . a woman who . . .

What? Shared his bed? Listened to his dreams and told him hers? Laughed with him? Ate at his side? Loved—?

No. Not that. I love Jenny. Jenny alone is . . .

"Captain? Begging your pardon, sir."

Tom sloshed his coffee as he jerked around. "Yes, Crane?"

"Mr. Larkin's on deck, sir, and would like a word with you."

The interruption was a godsend. Tom hurried topside to find Maurice and Larkin waiting for him on the quarterdeck. "Morning, Larkin. What is it?"

"Thought you ought to take a look, sir," the first

mate answered, pointing to the northeastern horizon, where a low, dark bank of clouds had appeared.

"Well, shit."

"The glass is still on its way down. 'Fraid it'll be a little bigger than I expected."

"How long do we have?"

Larkin checked the sails, the angle of the flag, and glanced again at the clouds. "Another two and a half to three hours is my guess. We'll want to take in everything but a bit of a jib and a spot of the mains'l. We should have a sea anchor ready in case we need one, and we'll need to get everything battened down." He nodded in the direction of the cannon. "Especially them. Triple ties at least."

"Very well," Tom said, disappointed but resigned to the impending delay. "We'll keep full sail on for now, but you may start on everything else."

No one had to be told anything twice. Most of the crew had sailed together for over a year and every man knew his job. Within minutes, the galley fire was out and safety lines were being rigged on deck. Topaz, Fairleigh, Benet, and Strickland were busy tying down the cannon. Two men were dispatched to double-check below decks; another three were readying a sea anchor so it could be cut free with two well-placed blows of an ax. Tom hurried below to prepare his cabin and to warn Adriana to stay put once the storm hit. No sooner had he stowed and tied down all his gear than Crane appeared again with another summons from Larkin.

"What now?" Tom asked.

"A sail, sir. Hull down to the nor'-nor'east. There's a man on the way up the mainmast now to take a better look."

Tom left Adriana to finish readying his quarters and ran topside. "Well?" he asked, joining Larkin.

Larkin jerked his head toward the tops. "You'll hear it at the same time I—"

"Headin' straight toward us, Cap'n!" Slurry shouted down. "Every sail on, and goin' large with the wind abaft her beam."

"What is she?" Tom yelled.

Slurry closed the glass, dropped it in its pouch, and scrambled nimbly down the shrouds to the deck. "Fast as she's goin', you'll be able to see for yourself in a few minutes," he answered ominously, holding the glass to Tom. "But unless me sight's playin' tricks on me, she's a sloop-of-war."

"Well, Midshipman Holmes," Bliss snapped at the young man who stood nervously at attention in front of him, "what do you make of it?"

"A cargo schooner, sir," Holmes replied, "flying the American flag."

"We've long ago ascertained that, Mr. Holmes." Bliss's sarcasm had a steel cutting edge. "I was interested in the name of the vessel, if you please."

Able Seaman Stone spoke up before Holmes was forced to admit that he hadn't been able to hold the glass steady enough to read the name. "The *Cassandra,* didn't you say, Mr. Holmes?"

"Yes. Ah . . ." Holmes's face was beet-red. "The *Cassandra,* sir."

"Thank you, Mr. Holmes," Bliss said, giving no indication he had heard Stone's remark. "And now, please be so kind as to convey the name *Cassandra* to Mr. Meecham and ask him to look it up on the list. I'll be waiting here for his reply."

Bliss stared across the water at the *Cassandra,* then appraised the line of clouds looming high over the horizon abaft his starboard beam. Aloof and remote, he watched with a practiced eye as the crew scurried about preparing the *Druid* for the storm to come. "Yes, Mr. Williams?" he said as the navigator appeared on the edge of the quarterdeck.

Williams approached, then showed Bliss a chart

tacked to a board. "Their course, sir, and ours," he explained, pointing to two converging lines. "I estimate two hours, sir."

Again the quick glance at the sky. "Just about the time the weather hits, right?"

"Aye, sir."

Bliss considered. He could run before the storm, but he would still have to contend with it eventually. He could turn into the storm immediately, and get through the worst part before nightfall. Or he could decide after he knew more about the *Cassandra*. "Very well, Mr. Williams. We'll continue on our present course for the time being."

"Aye, sir."

The wind freshened, the minutes wore away. At long last, Meecham, the first officer, hurried up. "Well?" Bliss asked shortly.

"Yes, sir." Meecham looked at a slip of paper. "The *Cassandra*, sir. An American cargo schooner owned and operated by the Paxton Shipping Lines. The firm is known to conduct business with French firms, and the *Cassandra* herself is listed as having called at numerous French ports, in contravention of the American Embargo Act and the Nonintercourse Act."

Bliss concealed his delight behind a razor-thin smile. His first potential prize in over three weeks, the *Cassandra* was a plum in its own right. That it was a Paxton ship, and that there was little doubt who was on it and why, was an added piece of luck. A substantial sum in prize money and the undying gratitude—Bliss would see to that—of Sir Theodotus would make this a profitable trip indeed. "Very well, Mr. Meecham," he said in the flat, emotionless tone most becoming to a captain. "We'll intercept, if you please. Use every yard of canvas you can crowd on. I should like to put a boarding party on her deck before the storm hits."

"It's the *Druid,* all right," Tom said. He slammed the

telescoping glass closed and handed it back to Slurry. "Damn! That's the last thing we need."

"Him!" Adriana said, her fingers clutching the rail. "It's he, Thomas. Fate has delivered him to us."

"Not if I can help it. What we're going to do is hope to hell we can get away."

"But you can't run!" Adriana insisted. "I tell you, Thomas, you can't fight destiny."

"But we can an eighteen-gunner, right?" Maurice asked sarcastically.

"He's right, Adriana. I told you I'd do whatever I could to help you, but that doesn't include getting us blown out of the water while we're still a good three days from San Sebastian. You'll get another chance."

"Thomas!"

"It's settled, Adriana," Tom said, turning angrily on her. "Finished. The end. No more discussion."

"I won't—"

"You *will,* damn it!" His eye blazed with fury as he gripped her shoulders. "You'll go below before you're spotted, and when I pass the word, you'll hide in the rope locker until this is all over. And if you don't agree to that—if you don't give me your word—I'll by God have you bound and gagged. I'll not jeopardize the lives of the crew or my chances of getting my boys back just so you can kill a man, do you understand?"

Two years, Giuseppe! Two long years! Adriana opened her mouth to speak, but then, distraught though she was, closed it in resignation. *You will be avenged, my brother. Somehow, I swear.* "As you wish, Thomas," she said dully, turning away from him and walking slowly toward the door that led to his cabin. "As you wish . . . for now."

"Slurry!" Tom snapped.

Awed by a side of Tom he'd never seen, Slurry answered fast. "Aye, Cap'n?"

"Keep an eye on Adriana. Make sure she stays in my cabin. If we're boarded, hide her quick."

"Aye, sir."

"What do you think, Larkin? Which gets to us first, him or the storm?"

The first mate had been thinking of little else in the hour that had passed since they'd sighted the *Druid*. "He'll have to take in sail a little before we do because he's upwind of us, but even so, with all the canvas he has spread now, I'd say it's a dead heat." Larkin shrugged apologetically. "We don't have anyplace to run to, Cap'n. Tough it out, is all I can think of. We ain't doin' nothin' wrong."

"Maurice?"

"If we try to evade him, we'll look suspicious. There's no law against one man goin' to talk to another one."

Tom watched the looming cloud bank, then cast his eye back at the *Druid*. "Can we pick up speed without looking too much like we're trying to?" he asked Larkin.

"I can fall off the wind a tad without trimming sail. Might give us five minutes or so."

"Do it. If we make it into the storm, we'll come about as soon as we lose sight of them, make for St. Martin, and come up on San Sebastian from the southeast. If they get to us just before the storm hits, we'll try some sloppy ship handling and see if that gives us enough time. If there's no way out, we'll let them board as planned and see what happens. Any questions?"

"Just in case," Maurice rumbled, "you mind if we get them starboard cannon ready?"

"In this weather?"

"Strickland says no problem. He's got some fancy way of tyin' them down, I guess."

Tom considered briefly. A full-fledged fight was foolhardy, but if it was a question of holding out for a minute or two before the full fury of the storm hit . . . "Done. But no one fires until I give the order. *No* one. Make sure they understand."

Half an hour wore away. Forty-five minutes. Seconds became critical. The *Druid* was brig-rigged, with square sails, making it necessary for her crew to furl the royals, topgallants, and upper topsails early. On the *Cassandra,* fore- and aft-rigged, Larkin waited for the *Druid* to slow, and then gave the order for his topsails to be furled. The tactic gave them two minutes, during which they pulled ahead a few yards.

Fifty minutes. Fifty-five. The *Druid* pulled to within less than half a mile, but was forced to furl its topsails when the first fingers of cloud closed about the sun.

One hour. Mid-afternoon had become as gloomy and dark as dusk. Ready to let them go the moment the wind died, the *Cassandra*'s crew loosened the fore and mainsail lines.

Aboard the *Druid,* men on the yards waited for the order to start taking in canvas.

The tension was so thick it could have been stitched into a sail. "Remember," Tom called, "No one fires unless I give the order! We will *not* fight unless they fire first!"

Less than a hundred yards away, the *Druid* changed course to sail parallel to the *Cassandra.* And at that precise instant, the wind died.

Larkin barked an order and the crew dropped the sails. On board the *Druid,* a similar order rang out and the frantic task of furling sails began.

Resplendent in his uniform, Bliss stepped to the rail and raised a speaking horn. "Heave to!" he shouted. "By the authority of His Majesty's Royal Navy, heave to and prepare to be boarded!"

"No!" screamed a hoarse voice behind Tom.

A small mistake, like the failure to ask a crucial question, can have disproportionally dire consequences. No one had thought to ask why Strickland was never seen shirtless, and he hadn't felt it necessary to reveal the cat-o'-nine-tail scars on his back or the tattoo "HMS *Swiftsure*" on his upper arm, much less that he was a mutineer and a deserter, which fact would be duly ascertained were he taken. Neither—so closely was everyone watching the *Druid*—had anyone noticed the sweat that had beaded Strickland's brow or his increasing agitation until that single syllable electrified the air like a thunderbolt.

"Strickland!" Tom shouted in shock and horror as the gunner's torch descended. "Don't—"

"You'll never take me back, damn your souls to hell!"

Maurice flung himself across the deck toward Strickland, but too late. The *Cassandra*'s cannon belched flame and smoke, and a roar shattered the calm. A hundred yards away, English sailors desperately leaped out of the ball's deadly path. One, too slow, felt a tug on his arm, and looked down uncomprehendingly at the blood spurting from his severed wrist.

Why? Tom's mind churned, seeking a way out, but as the first flash of fire from the *Druid*'s cannon registered, he knew there no longer was one. Time seemed frozen. A rolling thunder of sound washed over him. He could see the black dots of twelve-pound shot, their trajectory flat at that range, float toward the *Cassandra*. Marines stationed in the *Druid*'s shrouds pointed muskets at him that blossomed tiny puffs of smoke.

The *Cassandra* shuddered. Someone screamed. Snapped standing rigging lines whipped like snakes through the air and the mainmast tilted alarmingly. *Where is the wind?* Tom wondered. *This is impossible! Where is the wind?* And with no alternative, he shouted at last, "Fire, damn it! Fire!"

It wasn't impossible. The single loaded cannon, sounding pathetic in contrast to the *Druid*'s nine, roared. Two of the *Cassandra*'s crew fell, but the others—the coming storm forgotten for the moment—began to return the small-arms fire. Strickland, in the midst of shouting orders to his gun crew, suddenly gave

a strangled cry, spun around, and clutched his throat in
an attempt to stop the spurting blood. Topaz dropped
his rifle and took Strickland's place. Maurice stood
fearlessly at the rail, firing, reloading, firing his Kentucky long rifle again with calm precision, dropping one
by one the marine sharpshooters on the *Druid*. Once
more the *Cassandra*'s cannon spoke, once more they
were answered by a deadly broadside from the *Druid*.

The *Cassandra* shuddered again. The foremast,
sheared off six feet above the deck, toppled against the
already weakened mainmast and both went down in a
hopeless tangle of snarled lines.

His mind racing, Tom loaded his rifle and fired as the
first tendril of wind caught his hair. He could see a wall
of rain bearing down on them. *Another minute. One
more minute! We can still make it! Can't give up now!*

"Fire!" he shouted as a musket ball splintered the rail
and ricocheted into the deck between his feet. "Fire!
Fire! Fire!"

The impertinent fools! Had they no sense at all? His
prize being destroyed before his very eyes, Bliss watched
coldly as the *Cassandra*'s fore- and mainmasts fell. "A
prize under a hundred fathoms is no prize at all, Mr.
Meecham," he said coolly. "Tell Guns to belay another
broadside until I give the order, and then call for their
captain to strike his colors."

"Aye, sir."

The distance between the two ships had shrunk to
fifty yards. Bliss felt the wind, glanced behind to the
rapidly approaching storm. *What will they do when it
hits? What would I do?*

Meecham's cry was being ignored. Bliss scowled. He
couldn't wait much longer. "Ready to come into the
wind, Mr. Meecham."

"Ready helm hard to starboard!" Meecham called.

A scream from above. Bliss glanced up in time to step

aside as the body of a marine crashed to the deck. "I'll have the marines down now, Mr.—"

Bliss screamed as a ball from the *Cassandra* shattered a section of gunwale and drove a jagged two-foot-long splinter through the muscles of his chest. Bliss staggered, grabbed the rail for support, and groaned in agony as he sank to his knees. "Broadside," he gasped through the pain. "Quickly, man. Broadside!"

White-faced, Meecham leaped to support him.

Bliss slapped his first officer's hand away. "I'll shoot you myself if you touch me again, Meecham," he snarled. "You have your orders. I want a broadside. As soon as it's off, come into the wind, and then send for the surgeon. Move! Now!"

Meecham hesitated only a split second, then relayed Bliss's orders and darted off to find the surgeon.

Slowly, torturously, Bliss pulled himself to his feet. Dazed, he looked down, saw that the splinter had sliced him open. Blood welled from the long, jagged cut, but his breathing seemed normal. If he could stop the bleeding. . . .

The *Druid* reeled under the impact of the recoil of nine guns firing as one. A dreadful smile pulled Bliss's lips back as the first raindrops hit him and the *Cassandra* leaped sideways through the water under the impact. A slow, dreadful smile. . . . He would live, but the *Cassandra* would die.

Dead. Tom stared down at the face of the young seaman and tried to remember his name. *Crane. We laughed at him because he thought Adriana was a ghost. And now he's a ghost.*

Tom felt driven to the edge of madness. *Two minutes. All we needed was two minutes.* Three men were dead, four more lay dying. *My sons! Jason, Joseph.* And across the water, the face of the *Druid*'s captain— Bliss, the murderer!—stared implacably back at him.

"Fire!" he had howled against the building wind. "Fire, goddamn you!"

Still manned, the two cannon had roared and Bliss had fallen, struck down by a splinter. Seconds later, the *Druid*'s nine had answered, and splinters whirred angrily over Tom as he fell to the deck and scrambled frantically to avoid the toppling mizzenmast. Dazed, Tom looked around. One of the cannon had disappeared, the other lay upside down on top of Benet.

"We're on fire!" Slurry shouted.

Adriana! Tom staggered to his feet in time to see Slurry emerge from below decks. "Where's Adriana?" he shouted.

"Your cabin, last I saw. Fire right next to the magazine. We gotta get outa here!"

The *Cassandra* lurched and rolled slightly to starboard. The cannon tilted off Benet and skidded across the deck. Tom could see Maurice and Topaz and two others struggling to free the boats. "Help get the boats in the water!" he shouted over the rising wind. A drop of rain, then another and another stung his face. "Get everybody off. I'm going for Adriana!"

The deck tilted. Tom worked his way through the maze of tangled lines and splintered wood into the short passageway that led to his cabin. Below decks, the air was acrid and thick with smoke. Choking, he found the door to his cabin and burst in. "Adriana! Where are you?"

"Tom?"

She was crouched in a far corner, wedged between a chest and the bulkhead.

"We're abandoning ship." He crossed the cabin in three strides and pulled her out of her hiding place.

"But—"

"There's no time, damn it. The *Cassandra* is—" His eye caught a glint of steel and, hardly thinking, he grabbed Raven's rapier from the wall and buckled it on. "We're done for. We're sinking!"

Smoke billowed into the cabin. Bent double, Tom led Adriana onto the deck in time to meet Maurice coming after them.

"Both boats're in the water," Maurice bellowed over the hiss of rain. "Let's go!"

A more difficult twenty feet couldn't be imagined. Flames shot from the forward hatch to light their way. The full fury of the storm now upon her, the *Cassandra* bucked and heaved wildly even as her list increased and she settled in the water. Jagged spears of wood jabbed at them, reached for them, ripped their clothes. Lines snared their legs, tripped them in the blinding rain.

Topaz stood midships at the rail. Below him, the wind held the small boats against the wounded hulk of the *Cassandra*. Tom leaned over the rail, saw Slurry in the catboat, Larkin and three others in the dory.

"Give her to Larkin!" Maurice shouted in Tom's ear.

"Right! Larkin!" Tom pointed to Adriana, down to the first mate. "Take her!"

"Thomas, no!" Adriana gasped.

Ignoring her protests, Tom and Maurice took her arms, lifted her over the rail and, when the dory rose on a wave, deposited her in Larkin's arms. "Make for the *Druid*!" Tom shouted. "They'll take us as prisoners. We'll follow in the catboat."

Topaz sliced into the water in a graceful dive. Maurice cautiously followed, feet first. Tom hesitated, waiting for a glimpse of the dory carrying Adriana toward the rain-shrouded outline of the *Druid*.

Slurry put his back to the oars and rowed frantically to put distance between the catboat and the doomed *Cassandra*. "Jump!" he screamed. "Before she blows!"

Jason . . . Joseph . . . two minutes . . .

Beam to the seas, the *Cassandra* rose dizzily on each wave, plunged to wallow helplessly in the succeeding trough. Smoke poured from cracks in her deck. Timbers creaked and groaned. All hope of saving her long gone, Tom took one last look—the proud lines, the hiss of

water as her hull cut the waves, the beauty of her sails—
and jumped.

The water was warm. He sank, then kicked furiously
until his head broke water. Lightning crackled overhead
in a sky as black as night. The rain was so heavy that the
air seemed as wet as the sea. He heard his name, pushed
the hair out of his eye, and spotted Slurry and the catboat a few yards away. Topaz was already aboard,
Maurice just pulling himself over the gunwale.

Tom swam hard, bumped against the catboat. The
hilt of the rapier caught on the gunwale. Maurice freed
it, grabbed his arm and yanked him aboard. Flames had
burst through the deck of the *Cassandra*, and the four
men rowed to get away from her before the magazine
blew.

"The rain's stopped over there," Slurry yelled, pointing. "They're gonna make it."

Muscles quivering, Tom peered through the slacken-
ing torrent and saw, in the flickering glare of the lightning, the dory approach the *Druid*.

The price is too great.

Behind her, a wall of water obscured the burning
Cassandra. Ahead of her, the rain thinned and then
abruptly stopped as the trailing edge of the storm passed
over the dory. The *Druid* lay scant yards away. Sails
trimmed, bow to the wind, it rose and fell gracefully on
the twenty-foot waves that tossed the dory about like a
cockleshell.

Larkin approached from the *Druid*'s starboard side,
watched the crew fling over a rope ladder and paused to
read the waves and the motion of the *Druid*.

"There they are," said Engle, pointing in the direction of the *Cassandra*. "They made it!"

Adriana followed his finger, saw nothing, then a brief
glimpse of a wave-tossed boat before it disappeared.
The price is too great, Thomas. I did not wish for this.
"Three or four?" she asked.

"Four. Don't worry. He's aboard too."

"Now!" Larkin said, jamming the tiller to his right. "Pull . . . pull . . . and ship oars!"

Engle grabbed the rope ladder and steadied them. The man in the bow used his oar as a fender to keep them from smashing against the *Druid*'s hull. A line snaked down from the deck. Larkin fixed a loop on the end with a bowline. "Under your arms," he said, slipping the loop over Adriana's head. "If you fall, grab the line and they'll pull you up."

"Tom—"

"Don't worry about him. Go!"

The ladder swayed dangerously but she held on, and when she reached the top, hands waited to help her over the rail.

"Well, damn my eyes," a voice rasped.

Bliss's face was pale, drained by shock and loss of blood. He was coatless and shirtless, his breeches were stained with blood, and a blood-soaked bandage bound his chest. Adriana, exhausted by fear, soaked, and soot-stained, stood slack-jawed and stared at him. She had known he would be there, but hadn't been prepared for the reality of standing face to face with him.

"You . . . !" He stopped short, and fear showed in his eyes. *How? It's uncanny. She's a sorceress!* "Boatswain! Cut that ladder free!"

In sixteen years at sea, the boatswain had seen floggings, hangings, one keelhauling, and innumerable other acts of official brutality, but never had he heard a commanding officer of a naval vessel consign survivors of a defeated ship to the sea. Neither, in sixteen years, had the boatswain ever questioned or disobeyed an order. Unhesitatingly, he drew his knife, slashed the lines as ordered, and carefully avoided looking down at the hapless, uncomprehending men below.

"Mr. Meecham, I'll have a squad of marines with rifles, loaded and primed, on the double."

"No!" Adriana gasped as the first officer gave the

order and she realized what was about to happen. "You
can't!"

"I am the captain of this vessel, and will do as I
wish," Bliss said coldly, his fear now in check. "As, my
dear, you shall have occasion to learn."

"Murderer!" Adriana hissed.

"Boatswain, bind her and take her—"

Adriana sprang. The boatswain caught one arm, but
couldn't prevent her other hand from striking Bliss in
the chest.

Bliss's mouth opened in a silent scream and he turned
white as a sheet as he reeled backward into Meecham.
Red-hot pokers seemed to sear his chest. His knees felt
like water. The sky darkened and closed in on him, but
he stood. "Boatswain," he said in a voice that Bliss
himself could barely hear, "bind her, and when I am
finished here, confine her to the brig. Mr. Meecham."

"Aye, sir."

Bliss tapped hidden reservoirs of strength, and his
voice rang loud and clear. "I'll have those men shot, if
you please."

Meecham blinked in astonishment. "Sir?" he said.

"Are you questioning my order, Mr. Meecham?"

"Ah . . ." Meecham sought aid, met only blank
stares, and capitulated. "No, sir. Of course not, sir."
He drew back his shoulders, and when he spoke, his
voice was thin and reedy. "Sergeant!"

"Aye, sir!"

"Form your men in a line at the gunwale, and on my
command, shoot the men in the boat below."

"No," Adriana sobbed helplessly as the sergeant
moved his men into position. "Please—"

"I'm waiting, Mr. Meecham," Bliss said, ignoring
Adriana. "Please proceed."

"Ready."

Eight marines moved as one.

"Aim!"

"What the hell are you doing?" Larkin yelled as he

spotted the muzzles pointing down at him. "Wait a—"

"Fire!"

The roar of the muskets sounded strangely attenuated in the brisk wind. Unable to help herself, Adriana looked down, then quickly away from the four bodies in the dory. "Murderer," she whispered faintly. "Murderer!"

"Very good, Mr. Meecham," Bliss said with no more emotion than had he just snuffed out a candle. Trembling with the effort, his right arm rose and indicated the catboat poised on a wave some hundred yards away. "And now, them."

Speechless, Adriana sagged against the rail. *Oh, my God, no! Thomas! Beware, my love!*

Again the horrid litany. In the distance, the catboat rose into view, disappeared, rose again, bobbed like a cork . . .

"Fire!" Eight muskets roared as one.

. . . disappeared again, and rose . . . empty.

⤎ CHAPTER XV ⤏

Tom woke and stared into a hazy white sky that resolved into a linen shirt shielding him from the blazing sun. His mouth was dry, thick with the residue of fear and sleep. A patch of blue shone through a ragged hole in the fabric. He was moving up and down, up and down and sideways. Queasy, he eased himself into the open and blinked as his eye adjusted to the blinding glare of sun reflecting off numberless planes of water. Overhead, the catboat's single sail was bellied out by a gentle breeze that propelled the little craft through the heaving waves.

"Well, I see your highness is up." Maurice grinned through bruised features and handed Tom a brown bottle. "Slurry's emergency supply. Helps to settle the stomach. There's rainwater in another jug, but that'll have to last us till the next squall."

Tom swallowed, then shook his head to clear the cobwebs. "What happened?"

"You hit your head when we boarded the catboat. I caught you. About then, the magazine of the *Cassandra* blew, and the *Druid* sailed off a few minutes later." Maurice nodded toward Tom's rapier, lying next to him in the bilge. "I sure as hell hope you appreciate that sword. The damned thing almost got you drowned."

"That damned thing is over a hundred years old," Tom flared, his anger peaking like the waves, then falling sharply. "Ah, hell. I'm sorry. But Jase would kill me if I went home without it." He picked up the rapier, wiped it on his shirttail. "Larkin, Crane, Blaine, Engle,

Benet, Fairleigh, the others. Maybe Adriana, for all we
know . . ." The thought sobered him. He wrapped his
fingers around the hilt, turned the blade so the sun
caught it. "We'll have need of this. It has some killing
to do before it hangs on a wall again—or sinks to a
grave of its own."

The day was young. Slurry was handling the boat,
steering them northeast, in the general direction of Tortola. Topaz sat hunched over a length of wood he was
carving into a crude two-pronged spear. His precious
frock coat lay folded in the bottom of the boat, and his
blue silk vest had been torn into bandages that circled
his right shoulder where one of the rifle balls had torn
through the flesh. A pink stain oozed through to the
outer layer of cloth, but his shoulder had suffered no
lasting damage. From time to time, the Carib scooped
up a handful of seawater and soaked his bandage.

"Just us four, then," Tom finally said. "The
rest . . ."

"Food for sharks," Topaz remarked in an offhanded
way. "Like me, soon."

"You don't need to sound so happy about it, you
bloody savage," Slurry growled.

"Not happy, not sad," Topaz said with a shrug. "I
die, you die. All die one day."

"I hope you'll forgive us if we don't try to rush
things," Tom said.

"It is not in your power to go fast or slow. The gods
claim us when they will," Topaz said, his blade demonstrating the steady, unvarying pace he ascribed to the
gods.

Slurry wouldn't let the matter drop. "If you're so
sure we're done for, then why carve that spear? Why try
to bring in food for a boat full of corpses?"

"Those words are yours, Slurry Walls," Topaz said.
"Not mine."

"The hell! What you said was, we're a bunch of
corpses. So why don't you give up and roll over?

Answer me that if you can!''

"I could be wrong. I don't say what the gods will do or when, only that they will do what they will do when they please.''

Slurry snorted in disgust. "Ain't bad enough we gotta fry out here, without listenin' to the likes of a pagan cannibal as well.''

"Or,'' Maurice grunted, tired of the chatter, "a whiskey-drinkin' Bible spouter. Why don't you both shut up and save your strength for when you need it.''

The advice was practical if not popular. Slurry hunched over the tiller and stared at the horizon. Topaz whittled. Maurice curled up in a ball with his head in the shade of a seat, and slept. Tom crawled back into his shade and tried to sort out his thoughts. Three days until land, Slurry had said, if they were lucky. But then what? Brandborough to New Orleans to Barataria to nowhere. He'd traveled thousands of miles and might as well have stayed home. Never in all his life had he felt so desolate, so incompetent, so useless, so crushed. Seventeen men had died, and three more—plus himself—were in grave jeopardy. Adriana, in his care, had been captured and, if not already dead, was undoubtedly suffering unspeakable indignities. He was a fool and a failure, and though the sun beat down on him with all the power of a sledgehammer, he had never known a darker night.

Jason, Joseph . . . forgive me. I tried. God knows I tried. I loved . . . I love you so much.

Hidden, bitter, scalding tears coursed his face. A man alone, defeated, shamed. Like a wounded animal seeking the shelter of a cave, he twisted and curled into a tight ball.

He winced, lifted his arm, and gently fingered the new bandage around his head. *Don't even remember hitting it. Christ, it hurts . . .*

And out of pain came hope, for if he could feel pain he was alive, and as long as he lived he had a chance to rescue his twins.

And Adriana? His heart ached. *I never told her that I loved her. Never said the words, even to myself. But someday, one day sooner or later . . .*

There was a time to weep, and a time to stop weeping. There was a time to hide, and a time to stand and face the world. Careful not to rock the boat, Tom made his way forward, then stood spread-legged in the bow, and gazed upon the hopelessly vast seascape. First Jenny had been taken from him, then his children, and then Adriana. But all was not lost. Not yet. Slowly, one hand reached up to touch the golden amulet at his throat.

The day passed. "God, it's hot," Maurice said. The sound of his voice hung listless on the air, faded unanswered. Night fell.

The second day dawned. Faces blistered. Tempers flared.

Another night passed, and at noon on the third day they doled out the last of the fresh water.

Tom was awakened in the middle of the fourth night by the sound of Topaz singing. Eyes blank and staring, the Carib was crooning a strange and unearthly song. "What the—?"

"Shhh," Slurry whispered. "Don't ye have any respect for a man's religion?"

"It's his death song. Kind of like a prayer," Maurice explained. "Just like Injuns everywhere, I reckon."

"I make a prayer for all of us. Your God, my God, all same. It is all one prayer," Topaz said, and, after a moment of silence, continued singing.

"Is that so?" Tom asked. He found his rapier and knelt before Topaz. "Listen to me, Topaz," he said. "I spit on your prayer. Keep your death chant to yourself. I have no use for it."

"Lordy," Slurry whispered, grimacing and drawing back as far as the boat allowed.

Maurice braced himself and wondered where Topaz's knives were.

The chanting slowed, and stopped. Shadows in the starlight, the two men faced each other. "I will not die," Tom said, raising the rapier hilt-first. "I swear by the blood of Raven and by the steel of this, her talon, that I will live to rescue my sons and my woman. I *will* live, and so will you."

Tom lowered his rapier. Topaz closed his eyes and remained silent. The sail flapped listlessly in the faint breeze and tiny wavelets slapped against the hull. Tom crawled back to his place, laid the sword at his side, folded his arms, and closed his eyes.

And the fourth night passed.

Maurice was the first to wake and find Topaz missing. "Damn," he muttered. "What the hell happened to Topaz?"

Tom and Slurry bolted awake. The wind had died to a dead calm and the sail hung lifeless against the brilliant blue sky.

"Topaz?" Tom stood and held the mast for balance as the catboat rocked. "Topaz?" The flat, glassy expanse of water and space swallowed his voice. Nothing broke the surface of the blue-green sea.

"Not a trace," Maurice said, leaning over the side.

Slurry hurriedly shifted his weight to starboard to keep the boat from capsizing. "Blast it, Leakey, sit down!" he shouted. "I can't swim!"

"He gave up," Tom said bitterly. "Just gave—"

The water exploded right under Slurry's head. Slurry screamed in horror and fell backward. Maurice almost fell out, barely managing to throw his weight to the center of the boat. Tom dropped to his knees and grabbed for his rapier as a wriggling sea snake skewered by a crude spear plopped into the boat, followed a moment later by Topaz, glistening and dripping.

"Shit!" Slurry bawled. "You no-good man-eating son of a bitch! You just scared the living bejesus out of me! Here we was, feeling sorry for you and all, and . . ."

His speech trailed off as he stared at the thrashing gray snake in the bottom of the boat. It was at least six feet long. "What the hell is that thing?"

"Breakfast," Topaz said, nonchalantly grabbing the snake behind the head with one hand and a few inches down its body with the other. "Cut," he ordered, holding it toward Maurice.

"We thought you were dead," Tom said, grinning in relief.

Topaz flung the snake's head into the water, pinned its tail to the gunwale with Maurice's knife, and reached for one of his own. "I cut and drained my wound last night. The pain was great, but when I was finished, I was hungry." He held the snake so its blood drained into the water. "I told the spirit of my mother's father that if he did not come and carry me away, I would go fishing this morning."

"That ain't no fish," Slurry pointed out as the serpent's death throes gradually subsided.

"Maybe not," Topaz agreed, "but it is food."

Topaz slit the snake along the belly, cleaned it in the sea, stripped the skin, and cut the carcass into six-inch segments. "Better cooked," he said, tossing the first chunk to Maurice, "but good enough raw. My people eat many times."

Maurice snatched his piece out of the air and began to eat immediately. Tom followed suit. When he bit into the gray meat he found it had a not unpleasant smoky taste.

"I don't know," Slurry said, hastily dropping his piece on the seat next to him. "Eating snake don't seem Christian. I may take a drink from time to time and I know I ain't perfect, but I'd rather starve than lose my soul. A God-fearin' man don't eat no devil serpent."

"You'd eat a piece of pig that's been in a barrel of brine for six months," Maurice said, spitting out a bone, "but not a fresh snake? That's stupid."

Tom made his way to the stern, skewered Slurry's

piece with his knife, and peered into the mariner's eyes. "Slurry," he said, the voice of reason, "you have a point. But I want to ask you something."

"I ain't gonna eat no snake."

"I'm not asking you to. What I want to know is, are you baptized?"

"I am. My ma took me down to the water and dunked me herself."

"You're sure it took—your ma not being a preacher?"

Slurry's faith couldn't be shaken. "Baptizin's baptizin'. Don't matter who does the dunkin'."

"Good. Then you do believe in the power of baptism and the changes it can work?"

"Of course."

Tom dipped the piece of snake in the sea. "I baptize thee beef," he proclaimed in his most stentorian tone, "in the name of the Father and the Son and the Holy Ghost, amen."

Slurry stared at Tom, at the snake-become-beef, at Tom again, then at the meat. "Kind of determined to keep me alive, aren't you?" he finally said.

"That's right," Tom said. *"Bon appétit."*

"I gotta admit, that beef looks pretty good right now, raw or not," Slurry said, gingerly removing it from Tom's knife. "Thank ye, I guess." And without looking at the others, he said a silent prayer and began to eat.

The wind returned, as it always must, on the fifth night, and brought with it rain from the northeast. Hour after hour, they kept the bow to the wind and rode out the storm. At last, the gale died to a stiff and shifting wind and the last of the clouds swept by, leaving the sky clean and sparkling with stars. Slowly, the wind steadied, and while the others slept, Tom sat at the tiller and guided the small boat over the waves—and toward land. Just as slowly, as he watched, new light from the east blended with the starlight and edged aside the velvet hold of night.

From the east. . . . At least a hundred miles to the east, his sons slept while the sun rose. Did they wait for him? Just three years old when Jenny died, they had essentially forgotten her soon enough. Did they remember him? Were they old enough now to understand he would move heaven and earth to have them at his side? Once he had thought he could never love another human being as much as he loved Jenny, but the boys had taught him that love knew no such limits. And then Adriana had come along to teach him that he was alive, even if Jenny was dead, and that his love for her in no way diminished his love for Jenny.

If only he had spoken the words! *I love you, Adriana.* Was that so hard? Did she know anyway? She had seen his amulet in her dreams and had predicted his arrival. Perhaps, wherever she was, she heard him at that moment. Perhaps, if he concentrated. . . . Determined, he clutched the amulet in his fist. *Adriana. I love you, Adriana. I will be with you. Not long now. Not long—*

The thought broke off abruptly. His breath catching in his throat, he shielded his eye and saw . . . a speck of white in the first budding rays of golden sunlight. Spellbound, he watched the speck grow and become a swirling, diving sea gull that spilled its screeching song over the empty sea. The sweetest song a man had ever heard: the song of land.

"Virgin Gorda," Slurry said as the island rose out of the sea three hours later. "The Fat Virgin."

"What happened to Tortola?" Tom asked.

Slurry pointed to the west. "Over there. It's hell gettin' there from here in this thing, though, 'cause of the currents."

"What are our chances of finding a way off?"

" 'Bout the same as on Tortola," Slurry said, receiving a confirming nod from Topaz. "Plenty of food an' fresh water on both islands. Ships pull in from time to time, though who or where is a matter of luck. Best places are on the south side, but who knows? I'd say that, since we're here, we land, rest up for a day or so, and then decide what we want to do.''

It made sense. By nightfall, Maurice had a fire going and the smell of roasting turtle filled the air. Fresh water from a stream plunging down a nearby hillside tasted better than the rarest wine. And for dessert, the sweet soft meat of green coconuts brought smiles before they all drifted off to their first good sleep in five nights.

Oil pressed from coconuts soothed their blistered skin. Plenty of water, fresh fruits, meat, and sleep restored their strength. On the morning of their third day ashore, they pushed the catboat into the water and worked their way west, stopping at sundown to camp near the western tip of the island. "We'll try the north side tomorrow," Slurry said. "If there's nothin' there, maybe we ought to think of Tortola, or even St. John or St. Thomas.''

The wait was beginning to get on Tom's nerves. That night, after the others had fallen asleep, he stole away from the campsite and, rapier in hand, walked down to the water's edge. There, feet embedded in the cool, moist sand, he slashed the air, thrust and parried with a vengeance until his chest and shoulders glistened with sweat.

There's Bliss! Run him through, dance away. Marines? Hah! Dodge, leap, thrust once, twice, again and again until. . . . Well, well. If it isn't Sir Theodotus. On your guard, old man. I've come for my sons. I'll beat past your blade and thrust home!

The fantasy remained unfinished, ended prematurely by a faint but distinct rumble. Poised in a position of full thrust, Tom froze and strained to hear. *No, not thunder. No clouds in the sky. Again?* Every nerve taut, he listened without moving until his muscles protested and he sank, exhausted, to his knees. Nothing. Nothing but the wind and the endless crash of breakers.

But he *had* heard.

"It's possible," Slurry admitted the next morning. He studied the crude map of the northern side of the island he'd drawn in the sand and poked a twig in two indentations that indicated bays. "A cannon shot here or here . . . well, the wind could carry it this far."

"Let's get goin', then," Maurice said. "What the hell we waitin' for?"

"To think," Topaz said, not budging. "Men shoot guns for two reasons. To signal or to kill." He looked at Tom. "Which did you hear?"

"How the hell should I know?" Tom asked, peeved.

Topaz drew a line parallel to the coast. "This is wind." He held out the twig to Tom. "You draw the line of how we get from here to there without them seeing us—just in case maybe they're not so friendly."

"He's sure got a point," Maurice said. "Last I looked, we didn't have nothin' to shoot back with."

A mile to the northeast, a point jutted out into the water. "The first bay's the other side of that?" Tom asked, pointing to a low ridge.

"Yup."

"And the next one's how far?"

"Two, three miles up the beach, I'd guess."

"Good. See what you think about this, then. . . ."

It was late afternoon by the time they checked out the first bay, found it empty, sailed past it, and landed out of sight of the second bay. "We ain't gonna walk that shoreline, are we?" Slurry asked apprehensively.

Scoured by the nearly constant trade winds and heavy wave action, the coastline was an inhospitable jumble of rocks and boulders and coral that would require hours to negotiate. "That way," Topaz said, pointing to the ridge that separated them from the next bay. "Jungle not too bad, I think. Maybe one hour to top."

"Well, time's a-wastin'," Maurice said. He slung the

thong that held their water jugs over his shoulder, then pulled his arkansas toothpick out of his boot and stuck it in his belt. "It's your kind of country, Topaz. Lead the way."

By the time they reached the top and flopped down on the jungle floor for a rest, they were soaked with sweat. "Great view," Tom snorted, gazing in dismay at the wall of green that confronted them. "Any more bright ideas?"

Topaz tested a vine and began to climb. "Only one," he said. "Keep going to the very top."

Maurice watched Topaz until he disappeared in the foliage, then helped himself to some water and passed the jug. "I'll tell you one thing for sure," he said. "This ain't nothin' like Tennessee or Kentucky. Nothin' at all. You can forget that ashes to ashes and dust to dust business. All that's gonna be left of me is a puddle of sweat."

"I got dibs on your boots when you go," Slurry said, inspecting what remained of his. "Mine ain't worth much more'n a puddle o'—"

Silently sliding down the vine, Topaz appeared suddenly at Slurry's side.

"Jesus God, Topaz! Can't you—"

"Stow it!" Tom ordered curtly. "Well?"

Topaz's smile revealed rows of pearly pointed teeth. "I have found your cannon."

The descent was precipitous and dangerous, and became more so as the light faded. At home in the jungle, Topaz went ahead to reconnoiter while, far behind him, Tom, Maurice, and Slurry followed the trail he marked.

"Stop." Topaz materialized in front of them and spoke quietly. "One hundred feet," he said, pointing behind him, "to the beach. Fifteen men. Three tied. Six went off just now for water before dark. Six watching. Their ship is in the bay. French make, six or eight guns. The captain is one of the prisoners."

Silently, they crept to the edge of the vegetation and peered out. "So who'd they shoot at?" Maurice wondered.

"I went that far," Topaz said, pointing to a mammoth piece of driftwood, "and listened. One of the captain's men is still aboard. He fired at the mutineers last night and they're waiting until tonight to try to take the ship again. The new captain, the one with the hat with the red feathers, has a crew but no ship."

"Pirates?" Tom asked.

Topaz nodded.

"Anybody mind tellin' me how we got so lucky?" Maurice asked dryly.

"The question is," Tom said thoughtfully, "how are we going to get those three loose and get to the boat?"

"Why the bound-up three?" Slurry asked. "Hell, we go with the twelve—"

"Plenty of reasons," Tom said. "One, I don't want to sail with mutineers of any kind. Two, the others outnumber us. Three, how am I supposed to pay them? Four, if we free him, the captain will owe us. And five, the odds are good."

Slurry snorted in disgust. "You call twelve to four good odds?"

"Six to four if we hurry," Tom pointed out.

"So? Them guns they're carryin'—"

"The hell with the guns," Tom said. "We have something better."

"If it's luck you're talkin' about, forget it. You can count me out."

"I'm talking about surprise," Tom said.

Boisterous laughter exploded from the six mutineers. Two of them fired their flintlocks into the air and waggled their empty pistols at their prisoners. One of them danced a drunken jig, and another toppled facedown in the sand.

"And plenty of rum."

∽ CHAPTER XVI ∽

It had not been the best of days for Onofre Sanchez. In truth, his future looked as bleak as the night-shrouded sky. The beach was black and forbidding and a chill wind blew off the Atlantic. Sanchez strained at his bonds and lamented his dismal predicament. A quarrel with Crow Johnny. Outright mutiny. The ignominy of being trussed like a lamb waiting for slaughter. And worst of all, the supreme indignity: Crow Johnny had stolen the hat and crimson feather of Onofre Sanchez.

"I should never have listened to you," LaFrocque said. A small, wiry Frenchman, Gabriel LaFrocque had stood by his captain and now sat beside him, a prisoner.

"And I shouldn't have," said Ruiz, a portly olive-skinned Spaniard from Barcelona who served—who *had* served—as surgeon and cook. " 'Take arms with me,' " he continued, mimicking Sanchez. " 'Crow Johnny is a misbegotten dog with no following.' "

"But who now wears your hat," LaFrocque added unkindly.

Sanchez glared in response, and said nothing.

" 'But who now wears your hat,' " Crow Johnny echoed. The new self-appointed captain squatted in front of Sanchez, who pretended not to see him. Crow Johnny took off the hat and tickled Sanchez's foot. "That is what the first crab will feel like, no, Señor Sanchez? They tickle before they bite, but I think you will not laugh." He cackled and replaced the hat on his head. "But that is not my problem, eh? Soon the others will return with water and fruit and maybe a little fresh game. Then, a nice supper, a drink or two, and it's off to see if your friend Walsh can be persuaded to let us come aboard.'' Crow Johnny smiled, but the word *persuaded* carried an ominous tone.

"Too bad about Walsh," a new voice broke in as a weasel-faced, emaciated man named Lupe stumbled away from the campfire. "A nice boy. At least he'll die fast. Not like some, right, LaFrocque?''

Not wishing to attract any more attention than necessary, the Frenchman lowered his eyes.

"Yes, *sir!*" Lupe screamed. "Say it to me, you slime!"

LaFrocque mumbled something unintelligible.

Lupe backhanded LaFrocque across the face. "Say it, you miserable scum, just like you said it to *him* when he told you to tie me to the mast."

Blood oozed from the corner of LaFrocque's mouth. "Yes, sir," he mumbled.

"So you could take the cat to me," Lupe slurred, turning to Sanchez. "You liked that, didn't you, Sanchez?"

"You raped the girl in Martinique," Sanchez said quietly.

"And for that you peeled my back like a piece of fruit?"

"She was only a child. A whipping was a mercy. I should have cut off your ears. Or something else!"

Lupe pulled his knife, then stopped as the alcoholic fog rolled back far enough for him to remember the treat he'd prepared for Sanchez. "And I should cut out your eyes," he said, shoving the knife back in its sheath, "but I won't. Instead, I've brought you something to drink—so you'll live longer and have a day more in which to remember what you did to Lupe."

Squatting, he uncorked the bottle he carried and tilted it to Sanchez's lips. Sanchez smelled the mouth of the bottle and jerked his head sideways at the last moment, then gritted his teeth as the warm liquid poured down his chest and soaked his breeches.

"Sacrebleu!" LaFrocque snorted, recognizing the stench of urine.

"I warned you," Ruiz said as Lupe, choking with laughter, staggered back to the campfire. " 'Trouble is coming,' I said. 'The men are unhappy. We should take that ship.' Are we not raiders? And Lupe—what of him? Girls have been taken before, and that one was no exception."

"The girl was too young," Sanchez snarled. "And he cut her. And the ship was British."

"She wasn't too young, and she had been cut before," Ruiz said. "You took the cat to Lupe for what I have seen you do yourself."

"Shut up, Ruiz," LaFrocque growled. "Your advice is of no help to us now."

"Maybe mine will be," a voice whispered from the shadows behind the prisoners. "Be quiet and pretend nothing is happening."

A moth fluttered out of the firelight to dash itself against Sanchez's nose. The pirate captain snorted at the insect as it darted away. *God in heaven, I am hearing insects speak!* he thought mournfully, and then stiffened as the point of a knife scratched his back and the blade began to saw at the rope securing his hands.

Sanchez cast a wide shadow, but not so large that he could move about without Tom being discovered. "Be quiet!" Tom ordered in a harsh whisper. "Don't look!"

As if sensing something, Crow Johnny turned from the fire.

Sanchez smiled beatifically. "He's looking this way," he whispered without moving his lips, and then, a moment later, "Safe."

"What's that?" a voice at the fire asked.

"You're too damned drunk to see," Lupe said, shoving the other man over with a hand to his face. He lurched out of the firelight and squinted down the beach.

"What is it?" Crow Johnny asked. He booted one of his companions. "Wake up, Cipriano. On your feet. Damn it, Lupe, what do you see?"

"I don't know. Maybe they come back. It's time."

Cipriano, a razor-thin brown man with a stubbled, scarred face that looked as if it had never known a mother's love, propped himself up on his cutlass. "Maybe it's Caribs." He chuckled. "They smell Sanchez and come to put him in a cook pot. Or maybe wild dogs," he added, that idea so appealing that he bayed comically and, sniffing like a dog, followed an imaginary scent toward the prisoners.

"That you, Pelter?" Crow Johnny called. "You bring back plenty of fruits like I told you?"

The darkness offered no response.

Tom worked his knife under the last length of rope and peeked past Sanchez's elbow at Cipriano. Drunk and playing the fool, the pirate whined and scratched the sand and sniffed. "They'll like you, Captain. Oh, yes. Put you in a pot and boil all that fat away and . . ."

The rope parted.

". . . all that'll be left is a big chunk . . ."

Tom placed the knife in Sanchez's fist.

". . . of nice pink meat." Cipriano bent over and leaned on the basket hilt of his cutlass. "Captain Long Pig." He laughed. "Do you hear, Crow Johnny? A new name for him. Captain Long Pig!"

In a single swift motion, Sanchez grabbed Cipriano by the hair and thrust the knife completely through his throat, then quickly into his heart.

Cipriano gurgled once, then dropped silently to the ground. His death might have passed unnoticed had not Sanchez risen from the ground and, roaring loud enough to wake the dead, pulled Cipriano's cutlass from the sand and charged straight for Crow Johnny. "My hat, you scum-fed whelp of a Barbary she-bitch, fathered by the cream of a hundred lepers!" he howled. "I'll have my hat!"

"Damn," Tom cursed, their surprise attack obviously thwarted. "Maurice! Topaz! Slurry!" Rapier in hand, he rolled to his feet and yelled to attract the attention of Lupe, who turned, wide-eyed with surprise. The other three mutineers roused themselves from a rum-induced stupor to claw for their weapons.

Crow Johnny grabbed for the pistol at his waist, but the revolver caught in the material of his coat and then snagged on a button. And for a button, he lost his head. Sanchez, with one terrible swipe of Cipriano's cutlass, retrieved his black hat and crimson feather in a most gruesome manner.

Tom moved swiftly. He knocked aside one man, pummeled a second with his rapier's silver guard, then leaped the campfire to parry the thrust Lupe had started toward Sanchez's back. The rapier's thin steel rang on the heavier cutlass blade and knocked it aside. Lupe turned, switched opponents, and slashed twice—missing both times—before Tom could check his momentum. Remembering his father's advice that any two fools could bang blades together, Tom dropped the tip of his rapier to draw a thrust and lunge. Lupe took the bait and, in the soft sand, threw himself off balance by the lack of resistance. It was all the advantage Tom needed. Almost casually, he stepped outside Lupe's thrust, lunged over his extended arm, and sank his rapier into the pirate's chest.

"Who are you?" Lupe gasped, his visage contorted with pain and his cutlass sliding from his grasp.

"The man who killed you," Tom said simply, pulling the rapier free.

The other three pirates, unable to decide whether to attack or defend themselves, broke and ran when Maurice, Topaz, and Slurry came barreling into the light. "What took you so long?" Tom asked.

"Why'd you start so soon?" Maurice retorted.

"Hey, little rabbits!" Sanchez bellowed. "Run, my little *conejos*!" Glowing, he turned to his benefactors, bowed low with a sweeping gesture, and placed his feathered hat on his head. "My friends!"

"Oh, my God," Slurry muttered, recognizing the pirate captain for the first time. A glance told him that Tom was ignorant of Sanchez's identity.

"You have made a friend for life of—"

"We better get outa here," Slurry shouted, eliciting a glare of annoyance from Sanchez. "Them others is bound to be back before long."

A flurry of musket fire confirmed his prediction. Blossoms of gunfire bloomed on the edge of the jungled hillside to their right and gouts of sand erupted around the campfire.

"To the boats!" Sanchez yelled.

"Wait!" LaFrocque screamed, still bound. "Don't leave us. *Mon Dieu*, we will be killed!"

Topaz reached them first, sliced through their bonds, and helped them to their feet.

Tom sheathed his rapier, took a pair of flaming brands from the fire. "Grab a couple jugs of that rum and let's get!" he shouted to Maurice.

The musket fire was coming closer. Scrambling, ducking, everyone ran for the two boats pulled up on the beach. Tom and Maurice had worked and fought together too long to need to resort to words. "Take that one into the water," Tom ordered the others as Maurice splashed rum over the interior of the second boat.

As the first boat slid farther into the water, Tom fired the second. Knees high, he and Maurice splashed through the water and dived into the first boat, now pulling away from the beach.

"Row, you slackards!" Sanchez bellowed. "We aren't free yet."

Five minutes later, a hundred and fifty yards off the beach, they rowed behind the *Red Dog Song*. "Walsh!" Sanchez called.

"That you, Captain?"

"Aye, lad, so hold your fire. I've settled accounts

with Crow Johnny. Light a light. We're coming aboard.''

Lines snaked down to them as the small boat scraped the hull of its mother ship. Tom reached for one, but LaFrocque stopped him. "Pardon, *mon ami,* but the first face Walsh sees better be one he knows. You understand?''

A tow-haired young man, not much more than a boy, helped LaFrocque over the side. Last to board, Sanchez embraced the youth with a bear hug, admiringly held him at arm's length. "How'd you do it, lad?''

"Played dead," Walsh said with a shrug. He touched a huge knot and bruise on his forehead. "It wasn't hard to do at first, and then when Gustav wasn't watching, I hit him over the head with a full water keg.''

"Magnificent!" Sanchez roared with delight. "A water keg. What a weapon!" He bent and picked up the dead Gustav in his arms, then balanced the body on the rail between boat and burial. "You hear that, boys?" he shouted into the darkness. "Done in by a wounded lad. Gustav was no better than you or Crow Johnny. Listen carefully, boys. Maybe you'll hear his corpse hit the water. Maybe you'll hear the sharks tear him to pieces, eh?''

Ruiz sighed in satisfaction as Gustav's body hit the water. "He never did like my cooking," he said, evidently pleased that such a heinous crime had at last resulted in an appropriate punishment.

Tom scowled. "Where we come from, we say words over a dead man no matter what he did.''

"We're not where you come from," Sanchez retorted. He swaggered to the middle of the deck, his face bronze in the lantern light, then stared up at the furled sails as a particularly large swell rocked the ship. "By heaven, the *Red Dog Song* is mine again! I have dared the fates and won. Aye, and rid myself of a mean and cowardly crew. And you, my friends, will not go unrewarded,'' he added, turning to the four men who had saved his life. ''And what reward, you wonder? Aye, and well you should. This day, you have won the undying gratitude of Captain Onofre Sanchez, scourge of the—''

''Oh, shit,'' Slurry mumbled, ducking for cover.

''You!'' Tom roared, the name striking him like a thunderbolt. With a roar of hatred and fury unleashed, he leaped forward. Before Sanchez could even realize he was being attacked, Tom staggered him with two vicious blows to the face. Sanchez tried to back away, but tripped over a coiled line and fell over backward. ''You bastard!'' Tom roared, landing on Sanchez's chest and throttling him. ''It's you, by blessed fate. You!''

LaFrocque and Ruiz started to go to the aid of Sanchez, but, unarmed and weakened by their ordeal, they stopped at the sight of Maurice and Topaz's knives. ''Stand and live; take a step and die,'' Maurice said. ''Keep track of the boy, Slurry. Tom, wait!''

Sanchez's face was contorted in pain and his eyes bulged with fear as he tried to pry Tom's hands from his throat.

Maurice knelt facing Tom, grabbed his wrists, and gradually pulled his hands from Sanchez's throat. ''Wait,'' he repeated gently. ''You can kill him later, but not now.''

''Bastard!'' Tom panted, fighting Maurice's restraining hold. ''I'll kill him *now*—''

Faster than a man his size should have been able to move, Maurice was on his feet, behind Tom, lifting him off Sanchez with a double nelson. ''Later. We need him now.''

Sanchez scrambled out of harm's way and fought to regain his breath.

''We need to ask him some questions first. Use your head, man.''

Reason fought its way through a mind clouded with

fury. In the hurricane of his terrible anger, Tom found again the calm center and slumped in Maurice's embrace.

With a look of wounded innocence, Sanchez managed to haul himself to his feet. "Was it something I said?" he rasped.

Tom shrugged off Maurice's hold and walked slowly forward until he stood squarely in front of the pirate captain. "The boys you kidnapped in South Carolina were *my sons*."

Horror spread across Sanchez's face. His bluster and rowdy energy drained, he found the nearest barrel and sat heavily. He seemed to shrink. And most important of all, he removed his black hat with the crimson feather. "Oh," he said.

"You're damned right, 'oh,' " Tom said. "You have about three seconds to start at the beginning. I want to know what happened every step of the way, and especially where you left them and with whom."

"And if—"

Tom's hand moved and his rapier, singing a high, steely note of death, pressed lightly against Sanchez's Adam's apple.

"I won't stop him this time, pirate," Maurice rumbled.

The sound of creaking wood, of lapping water, of wind on taut lines. "Put away your steel, Thomas Paxton. I'll talk without it."

A half-hour later, Sanchez slumped against the rail and stared at the restless sea. "And that's it," he said listlessly. "They're fine lads and brave. I hope that old man's taking good care of them."

"You hope!" Tom snorted. "What do you know about—"

"I have three sons of my own, señor. I harmed you, I agree, and your father. But not the boys."

"How come the mutiny?" Maurice asked from the shadows.

"Hah!" Sanchez spit into the water. "Four days ago, a fat prize minus a foremast wallowed before our very noses, but it was British and I kept my word to the governor and Bliss and refused to take it. For this, Crow Johnny led the men against me." He stared at the hat in his hands and gazed lovingly at it. "That and my hat. He was jealous of my hat and feather, and wanted them for himself."

After the silence stretched on, Maurice turned to Tom. "What do you want to do?"

"Ah, hell," Tom sighed. He sat, rubbed his eyes. "See if we can get this tub to San Sebastian. It's only a hundred and fifty miles." He glanced at the rigging. "Shouldn't be too hard if the weather holds for a day or two."

"And once you're there, señor?" Sanchez asked.

Tom shrugged. "I don't know. Tie up somewhere, get the kids and Adriana—"

"I have a better idea," Sanchez interrupted. "You think maybe I apologize for taking your sons. Well, I don't. I'm sorry they were yours, but I don't apologize, because that was a job and I do it like a job."

Tom bridled but Sanchez cut him off.

"No, you wait. You are not truly mad at Onofre Sanchez. You are mad at someone who took your sons. But now that you know Onofre Sanchez, you are no longer going to be mad, because Onofre Sanchez is going to help you get those sons back."

"You're crazy as a loon!" Tom said. "He's crazy, Maurice."

Maurice loomed out of the shadows. "Maybe not," he said quietly. "Go on, Sanchez."

"You were trying to hurt that old man when you took his daughter?" Sanchez asked.

"Of course not. Jenny and I—" Tom stopped and sagged visibly. "All right, Sanchez. Don't stop now."

Sanchez shrugged. "It's simple. I don't know you when I take those boys, so I just take boys, not *your* boys. But then a real man—Thomas Paxton, who I can see with these eyes—saves my life, my ship, and my hat. And for this I owe a debt." Very formally, Sanchez removed his hat and handed it to Tom. "It is no joke, *hombre,* when I tell you. Onofre Sanchez swears by his black hat and red feather that he will help you get your sons back."

Tom stared at the hat in his hands, at Sanchez, back to the hat, and at last at Maurice. "Well?" he asked. "What do you think?"

"I think," Maurice said, a slow grin spreading, "that you aren't gonna get a better offer in a long, long time."

The amulet was cool against his chest. In a house on a hill a hundred fifty miles away, his sons waited. Somewhere nearby, he would find Adriana. "I still think you're crazy," Tom finally said, "but . . ." He stood, handed Sanchez's hat back, and held out his hand. "You've got yourself a deal."

A wild light gleamed in Sanchez's eyes as he clamped the hat on his head and shook Tom's hand. "Let's sail," he said. "As soon as we're under way, I'll tell you my plan."

The *Red Dog Song* had a crew once more.

⤙ CHAPTER XVII ⤚

. . . love you. I love you, Adriana . . .

The voice faded and disappeared. Struggling out of a deep sleep, Adriana bolted upright in bed and pressed her fingers to her temples. *Thomas? Is that you, Thomas?*

It had been his voice, she was sure, but try as she might, she couldn't bring it back. Concentrating, she thought she heard the dim echoes of the sea, much like the roar heard when one places a shell to one's ear, but that, too, disappeared within seconds, leaving only silence. *He was calling me, trying to tell me. . . .* Or had the dream been nothing more than wishful thinking? Bleakly admitting the possibility, she lay back on the lumpy straw-filled ticking and recalled the events of the past five days.

The storm . . . fight . . . the Cassandra *afire . . .*

The trip across the heaving water filled her with terror, but was nothing compared to the fear that clutched her stomach when she saw Bliss and heard him give the unbelievable command to shoot Larkin and the others. What followed was worse, and when she saw the tiny catboat that held Tom pitch emptily atop the waves, she lost consciousness.

When she came to, she found she was a prisoner in the ship's brig, she was still in shock when the *Druid* dropped anchor at San Sebastian later that night. Defeated, her will beaten into submission by an overwhelming sense of loss, she was taken by carriage

through winding streets and up the gradually rising
slopes of The Sleeping Giant. The carriage passed
through wrought-iron gates into a well-tended courtyard alive with flowers. "Where are we?" she asked her
escorts.

"Captain Bliss's residence, miss," answered one,
"and I shouldn't like to be in your shoes if the captain
dies. Or if he lives, for that matter," he added with a
shudder. "Out you go, now. And no sense tryin' to run
for it."

They were greeted by a muscular, dark-skinned native
who listened impassively to the instructions passed on
by the sailor and then, without a word, took Adriana by
the arm and led her into the house. Inside, the residence
was airy and spacious, well lighted, and luxuriously appointed with imported furniture that glowed richly in
the lantern light. Not that Adriana had time to see
much. The native whisked her down a hall, up a flight
of stairs, down another hall, and finally had stopped in
front of a heavily barred door. "Inside," he grunted—
the only word he'd spoken during the entire proceedings
—and pushed her into darkness.

Slowly, Adriana's eyes had adjusted to the dim light.
Her prison was a room no more than eight by ten feet. It
was furnished with a simple bed, a chair, a small table,
and nothing else. The only exit, other than the door
through which she had just come, was a window choked
by wrought-iron bars fashioned into vines that were, she
immediately discovered, impossible to budge. Alone,
disconsolate, and frightened, she slumped onto the bed
and, feeling for the first time the weight of her predicament, wept her only tears since Giuseppe's death. She
grieved for Tom, she grieved for his sons who would
never again see their father, and she grieved for herself.
Not until some hours later did the sobs subside, and she
lapsed into the deep sleep of total exhaustion.

Nothing but her state of mind had improved by morning. Telling herself she had to remain calm, she used the
chamber pot supplied by her captors, drank some of the

fresh water left her, and used the rest for a modest toilet. Refreshed, she inspected her surroundings and discovered little new of interest. The door and window were as impregnable as they had been the night before: the only way out was the way she had come in. The view through the window was restricted to what, she calculated from the angle of the morning shadows, must be the western and southern slopes of The Sleeping Giant. Straight ahead was a wall of steeply rising jungle. If she lay her head against the left edge of the window, she could see a profile of the mountain and, perhaps a couple of hundred yards away and higher up, most of a large and elegant mansion that she guessed was the governor's residence.

Her inspection was interrupted by the sound of the bar being lifted from the door. On guard immediately, she turned and found herself face to face with the man who had locked her in the night before, this time accompanied by a woman who carried a tray holding a teapot and a basket woven of split cane. The woman set the tray on the table and gestured curtly. "Food," she said simply. "You eat."

Adriana didn't have to be asked twice. Famished, she attacked the slice of fried pork and still-warm corn bread while the woman watched impassively. "Who are you?" she asked when the first hard edge of her appetite had been assuaged.

"I am Carlotta. He," she added, pointing, "is my husband, Ramon. We are Captain Bliss's people."

Adriana sipped her tea, then slowly peeled the banana. "Is Captain Bliss . . . all right?" she asked. "That is," she added hurriedly as disapproval darkened the servant's eyes, "I hope he is well."

"We will watch you," Carlotta replied without answering the question. "Bring you food, take you to wash. Make sure you stay. You are finished?"

"May I keep the orange for later?"

Carlotta checked quickly with her husband and, when he grunted his approval, nodded. "Soon come back," she said, taking the tray. "Take you to wash, give you clean clothes." And without further comment, she and Ramon slipped out the door and were gone.

Adriana's hunger was satisfied, but not her curiosity, for she knew little more than she had the night before. Bliss was wounded, but how badly was a mystery. She was under guard on the second floor of his house, but had only the foggiest notion of where the house was in relation to its surroundings, and where in the house she was. Of her keepers she had learned little. Both appeared to be mixed-bloods of Indian and African extraction. Both were dark-skinned and had jet-black hair. Ramon was at least six feet tall, and the strength in his massive shoulders and thick arms and legs was not hidden by his loose-fitting light cotton pants and shirt. His scowl appeared permanent; his eyes without expression but all-seeing; his voice, when he spoke, was a hollow rasp. He was armed with a knife that was almost long enough to be called a machete. Adriana didn't need to read Ramon's palm to know that Bliss would have had to search long and far to find another man as obdurately trustworthy as this one.

Carlotta was of the same height as Adriana and perhaps a few years older. Her features, more Indian than Negroid, were sharper than Ramon's and her skin was lighter, like the soft brown of an aged coconut shell. All told, softness seemed to characterize Carlotta in spite of her terseness. The soft brown of her eyes; the softness of her breasts, no doubt from nursing; the softness of her voice; the softness of her hands, which, though large and callused, moved deftly and competently.

Adriana passed the next four days in a stupor. Carlotta and Ramon brought her meals twice a day. Every morning, she was escorted to an enclosed room built over a stream, where she was allowed to bathe under the watchful eye of Carlotta. She was given a change of clothes. Only twice did something happen to break the stultifying boredom. Once at night the earth shook and the stench of sulfur filled the air. The next morning she understood why when, after a series of mild shocks, a cloud of smoke billowed from the top of The Sleeping Giant. Her concern, however, was short-lived when Carlotta shrugged and explained that the giant was only snoring, as he had for as many years as anyone could remember, and that there was nothing to fear.

The following day, Adriana experienced a shock of a different sort. While watching out her window, she saw two small boys—who she was certain were Jason and Joseph—playing under the watchful eye of a servant on the grounds of the governor's mansion. The sight almost broke her heart. That night, she resolved to somehow reach the boys to tell them of their father— that he loved them, and had tried to come for them.

And perhaps still would, she now dared hope. Perhaps. . . . Her spirits rising, she sprang from the bed and clutched the wrought-iron vines barring her way to freedom. At that moment, the sun, long risen on the far side of The Sleeping Giant, edged above its towering heights and the first rays, shining through a cleft in the rocks, struck her in the face. Why, she did not know, but she watched a few seconds too long before she averted her face and closed her eyes. And then saw, in the white glare that lingered, the explosion of light shift and soften and transform itself into the unmistakable outline of an oak tree wound about with brambles.

Oh, Thomas, Thomas. It was your voice. Thank God you're alive. I love you, too. Thank God. . . .

Calmed, she sat at the table and waited patiently for her breakfast. Thomas was alive. He loved her. And she had no doubt he would come for her and rescue her.

As if in confirmation that this particular morning was unusual, breakfast arrived later than expected and Carlotta appeared pale and drawn. "Carlotta?" Adriana asked when the servant handed her the tray and turned to leave without speaking. "Are you ill? Is something wrong?"

Carlotta hesitated, tension apparent in her shoulders.

"Is it Ramon? If he's ill, perhaps I can—"

"The master burns with fever," Carlotta said, distress in her voice. "His wound stinks of corruption."

Adriana's mind raced. *An infection! Do you hear, Giuseppe? It's an ugly death. He'll pay! He'll pay dearly for taking your life.* "But you said yesterday that he was mending," she said aloud, with no trace of the exultation she felt.

"As did the English doctor, but the master weakened during the night and now the doctor bleeds him. Fah! I fear that will not help." She whirled on Adriana. "You take pleasure in this, eh, foolish one?"

"Why, no," Adriana stammered. "Of course not. I—"

"Then know if our master dies he leaves orders for Ramon to kill you. My husband is devoted. He will obey."

"Carlotta!" Ramon called impatiently from outside the door.

Panic rushed like ice water through Adriana's veins. She couldn't die. Not with Tom somewhere alive and coming for her and the boys. Bliss's death would have to wait: she had to live no matter what the cost. "Listen," she blurted, stopping Carlotta at the door. "I've told you I have the gift of healing, and it's the truth. I know many secrets from the old times."

"Ramon called. The doctor—"

"You said yourself the bleeding will not help," Adriana rushed on. "I can cure him. I swear it!"

Carlotta frowned and shook Adriana's hand off her arm. "Do not say such things, girl. You are a prisoner here."

"I know that, but I will take the pain from your master and save him from the death that waits for him —in exchange for my freedom. Go to him and tell him that."

Fearful, Carlotta glanced over her shoulder at Ramon, who now stood in the doorway. "I cannot," she whispered, backing away. "I cannot."

"Carlotta!"

The door closed, the bar dropped. Alone, Adriana sat wearily on the edge of her bed and stared at the wall. There was nothing to do but wait. The seed was planted, and though there was no way of knowing what fruit would spring from it, at least there was hope . . . *if* Carlotta spoke, and if Bliss didn't wait too long to decide.

The results came sooner than Adriana had expected. Early in the afternoon, footsteps approached her door and stopped. An instant later, with an indecipherable look on his face, Ramon appeared in the doorway.

Adriana froze. *To my death, or to Bliss? Please, God . . .*

Ramon's hand rested lightly on the handle of his knife as he pushed the door wide open and stared at her. "You come," he said, gesturing for Adriana to precede him. "See master."

Adriana's knees felt like water and she had to hide her hands to conceal how they shook. Steering her with a series of grunts and prods, Ramon guided her down the hall and stairs, across the foyer, and to a door at the end of an undecorated whitewashed stucco corridor where Carlotta waited.

"Carlotta. Is he—"

"Worse." Carlotta's eyes glittered with a ferocity that burned away all traces of softness. "If you lied," she said, knocking on the door and stepping aside, "I swear I will help Ramon slit your throat. Do not fail."

The door opened to reveal a portly silver-haired gentleman in a rumpled frock coat. "You're the Gypsy?" he asked, looking Adriana up and down disdainfully.

"Yes, sir."

"I'm Dr. Fraser, and I don't like Gypsies." He wiped the perspiration from his forehead and gestured curtly for her to enter. "But you're to come in anyway."

The room was large, airy, and well lighted, with netting over the windows to keep out the flies and mosquitoes. A large dresser flanked by two wardrobes occupied most of one wall, bookcases another. A large desk with a Chippendale wing chair behind it and a pair of walnut captain's chairs flanking it sat in front of the windows. An extra table that held pitchers, basins, a mound of fresh bandages, and the doctor's surgical instruments sat at the end of an immense canopied bed.

"I believe," Fraser said with sarcastic gentility, "that you're acquainted with Captain Trevor Bliss?"

My God! This is impossible! Bliss looked more dead than alive. Already weakened by the infection, he had been bled only moments earlier, to judge by the blood-stained basin of water that sat on the bedside table. He was naked from the waist up; a blanket covered him from the waist down. A thick bandage swathed his chest, and a smaller one covered the wound on his forearm where he'd been bled. His face was flushed with fever and drawn with pain. His eyes were closed and his head moved slowly from side to side as his fingers clawed weakly at the sheets. "You . . . you've bled him," Adriana said inanely, shocked by Bliss's condition.

Dr. Fraser considered himself a man of science and had no use for the charlatan practices of the Gypsies, practices that he knew were based on nothing more than superstition and witchcraft. "Of course," he said, his contempt evident. He turned and walked to Bliss's side. "The girl is here as you ordered, Captain," he announced stiffly.

Bliss opened his eyes and looked around as if in a daze. "Girl," he croaked. "Come here."

Adriana approached the bed, stood silently, and waited for him to speak again.

"You told . . . Carlotta that you . . . can cure me," he gasped. After a moment, he added, "Accomplish that, and you shall go free."

Impossible though the odds might be, it was no time

to appear indecisive. "I can cure you," Adriana said simply. "My grandmother and my mother schooled me in the old ways. You will live."

"The old ways?" Fraser exploded. "This is idiocy!"

"Bleeding is new?" Adriana retorted angrily. She pointed to the open astrology book lying on the table. "Astrology is new?"

Fraser's face turned purple with rage, but he spoke with exaggerated patience. "Every reputable physician in the world knows—"

"Quiet!" Bliss's voice was barely audible, but it rang with authority. "I have seen . . . the Gypsy cures," he rasped. "They work." His hand shaking with the effort, he pointed at Adriana. "I . . . I do not trust you, though, girl." His hand fell to the bed and he was forced to rest before continuing. "Everything you do . . . will be watched. And remember . . ." A death's-head grimace was intended as a smile, but there was nothing amusing about it. "Remember. If I die . . . you follow me . . . on the instant."

Adriana's journey to his side had spanned years and oceans. How ironic that, when she had at last been presented with a perfect chance to kill him, a twist of fate had placed him at her mercy. She would cure him. To live, she had to heal her brother's murderer. She would kill him when he was once again fit. Bliss would die knowing she was responsible not from the wounds of battle. "I'm not ready to die yet," Adriana said without emotion. "I won't forget."

"Good," Bliss whispered. "Then begin."

"Just what do you intend to do?" Fraser demanded.

"I won't know that until I see the wound, will I?"

There wasn't a moment to lose. Action freed her from indecision. Working quickly but gently, she untied the outer bandage and began to remove the inner compresses. Bliss winced, and groaned in pain when the last one stuck. "I'll try not to hurt you any more than necessary," Adriana promised, looking under the bandage and wincing herself, "but there will be pain."

"Well?" Fraser asked.

"Is there laudanum?"

"I gave him a dram an hour ago," Fraser said with a smirk. "I shouldn't give him any more, if I were you."

He was right. Bliss was on a tightrope strung across the chasm of death. The shock resulting from too much pain could kill him; any more laudanum, in his debilitated state, could have equally disastrous results. Her only chance was to take a chance; her only consolation, that Bliss would surely die soon under Fraser's care. "Carlotta," she called, ignoring Fraser and crossing the room to talk to the woman, "I'll need your help, and I'll need Ramon, too."

The master had spoken, and Carlotta dipped her head in deference to Adriana's newly acquired authority.

Adriana's list of supplies was short, but required time to fill. "Water that's been boiled, and a box of salt. Fresh linen for bandages, and you must boil them, too. Is there a cook available?"

"Yes."

"Put him to work making a clear broth from fresh beef, and make sure there's hot sweetened tea ready at all times. And lastly, you must send someone to find a good-sized piece of spoiled meat or a dead animal infested with maggots."

"Maggots!" Fraser exploded.

"His flesh is putrefying," Adriana said. "So long as that flesh remains in his body, he cannot be healed."

"But my God, woman!" Fraser protested. "They'll eat him alive!"

"Maggots eat only dead flesh," Adriana explained curtly. "There's little time to spare, Carlotta. The water and salt first, and quickly."

Fraser, his eyes narrowed dangerously, interposed himself between Adriana and Bliss. "You're mad, girl. Get out of here before I have you flogged."

"Dr. Fraser." Bliss's voice was weak, but the words

cut through the doctor's protests and silenced him. "I am still in command of my own house, sir, and of my own body. The girl will . . . proceed with her treatment, whatever it may be."

Fraser drew himself up to his full height. "As you command, Captain. But I shall not remain to witness such mummery. Good day, sir!"

"Carlotta. Ramon. Come here," Bliss ordered in the silence that followed the slamming of the door.

Obediently, the two servants approached and stood at his side.

"One time," Bliss began haltingly, "my father owned a mastiff that was tusked by a boar. When the wound became infected, the houndsman treated it with maggots. The dog lived to hunt again." He lay quietly, collecting his strength before he could go on. "Do as the girl says. But if I die . . . remember. She must die, too."

"The water and salt, Carlotta," Adriana said, moving back to the bed. "Hurry."

Bliss opened his eyes and focused with difficulty on Adriana. "So you think a trick that worked on a dog will cure a man, eh?"

"If it's not too late, yes."

"Too late . . ." What started as a feeble attempt at laughter ended in a cough. Perspiring profusely and racked with pain, Bliss lay silently for a long moment. "Tell me. Is it too late to apologize for killing your brother?"

"It isn't a question of too late," Adriana said, wondering, but not really caring, if he was serious.

Bliss sighed. "I was afraid that might be the case. Well, what . . . are you going to do?"

"The wound must be opened first, and then cleansed. It will be very painful, but once it's done, you'll be past the first hard part." She took a deep breath. "Then I shall place maggots in the wound and hope that we can arrest the infection. From then on, it's a question of time and your constitution. I'll be asking you to drink a great deal of broth to fortify your blood. You must cooperate if you want to live.''

''I'll cooperate.'' He closed his eyes, and a shudder racked his fevered body. ''Ramon, see that I do as she says. And see that you or Carlotta are always close by.''

''Yes, master,'' Ramon replied, his face hard and watchful as he looked at Adriana.

Another half-hour was spent in preparation. Buckets of fresh water and piles of bandages arrived. An extra bed and clean linens were sent for. Bliss drank a cup of tea laced with honey, plus as much beef broth as he could hold, and was transferred to the new bed. Finally, when all was ready, all the servants except Carlotta and Ramon were sent out of the room, and Adriana, a sharpened knife in her hand, stood over Bliss. ''I'm ready,'' she announced grimly. ''Are you?''

''Begin,'' Bliss said, and gritted his teeth against the pain that he knew would follow.

Time hung suspended as Adriana ministered to the limp form in the bed. Bliss gave one short scream when she opened the festering wound, and then fainted from agony. The stench was almost overwhelming and threatened to gag her, but Adriana swallowed the sour taste in her throat and called for water. Working quickly, she laved the wound with dipperful after dipperful of salted water and, as gently as possible, removed the last pieces of splinter. At last, the wound thoroughly cleansed, she took a bundle from Carlotta and unwrapped it, reavealing a chunk of decayed meat wriggling with maggots. With teeth clenched, she scraped the larvae into the open gash on Bliss's chest, then quickly covered the wound with a light layer of dampened linen and bound it loosely. As a final step, Ramon transferred the unconscious Bliss back to his own bed.

''He will live?'' Ramon asked as he stepped back.

''I don't know,'' Adriana admitted, feeling completely drained. ''Have someone clean up that mess and bring more fresh clean water. He must have cool baths.

I don't want the fever to climb too high before it breaks."

Carlotta nodded and disappeared. Moments later, with Ramon standing guard at the door, the room was filled again with bustling servants. Adriana pulled a chair close to the bed, sank wearily into it, and studied her patient. Bliss hadn't regained consciousness during the procedure, an occurrence for which he might have been devoutly thankful. But then, he might never regain consciousness.

Day turned into night and night again to day, and the grueling work continued without pause. Hourly, the bandages were changed. Whenever Bliss roused, Adriana and either Ramon or Carlotta fed him spoonfuls of beef broth. He was bathed regularly with cool water, and his bedding was changed every four hours. Sometime during the following morning, Carlotta entered with a basketful of leaves that a native *curandera,* or witch doctor, had told her would lower a fever. Grasping at straws, Adriana prepared an infusion, gave some to Bliss to drink, and saturated his bandages with the rest.

The crisis came late that night. Adriana had awakened from a short nap and Carlotta had just fallen asleep when Bliss's fever started climbing. Within a half-hour, his forehead felt blisteringly hot. He tossed wildly and moaned in delirium. He ranted and cursed in his madness. Occasionally, a word or phrase was intelligible. Adriana recognized the governor's name during one long, incoherent speech. In another rambling, mumbled monologue he spoke of shipments to France, of treason and vast sums of money, and of a man named, she thought, LeBusque, who he was afraid would cheat him. Over and over again, he referred to a journal, which he seemed to fear losing.

The fever broke early the next morning, and as Bliss's temperature plummeted and the sweat poured from him, Adriana knew she had won. The damage to the muscles of his chest was significant and his strength on that side would be diminished, but he would live. From then on, it was a matter of time and Bliss's own recuperative powers. Revitalized, Adriana worked silently. She replaced the bandages, bathed her sleeping patient, and changed his bed linens. And at last, weary but ebullient from her accomplishment, she sat by the bed for a well-earned rest.

Bliss slept peacefully. Across the room, Carlotta snored lightly as she, too, slept. For the first time in two days Adriana had time to think beyond the immediate problem at hand. And for the first time, too, she realized that she wasn't altogether sure she wanted to take Bliss's life anymore. Everything was so confusing. It was as if Bliss's life had taken on a separate identity from Bliss himself. Bliss had killed her brother and deserved to die. Yet she had saved the life that belonged to Bliss, and—having fought so hard and expended so much energy—she couldn't imagine now taking it.

It isn't fair, damn it. If there was justice . . . but how ridiculous even to think of justice. There was a time when Adriana would gladly have given her life to avenge Giuseppe's death—would have let Bliss die in the most gruesome manner possible. But things had changed so much. There was Tom, and the boys . . . Bliss's death had become a matter to be resolved in the future. Adriana's immediate problem was how to survive long enough for Tom to rescue her. Even after he regained his strength, Bliss would never trust her—as well he should not, she admitted to herself. With the typically cavalier attitude of the high-born, he considered her life inconsequential in comparison with his own. If only she had some hold over him. . . .

Journal. The word, repeated so often in his delirium, hung in her mind. *Shipments to France. LeBusque.*

A Gypsy who couldn't smell graft—or worse—from a mile away didn't deserve the name. Adriana moved away from the bed and to the desk in utter silence. The drawers were closed, but unlocked. Her movements measured, her eyes constantly shifting from the desk to Carlotta to Bliss, she began her search. The center drawer held paper, sealing wax, ink, and extra blotters and quills. The three drawers on the left held nothing resembling a journal. At last, in the bottom drawer on the right, her fingers traced the rectangular shape of a book. Hands trembling, she removed it from its hiding place, closed the drawer, and returned to her seat at Bliss's side, where there was enough light to read by.

The journal was perhaps eight inches by ten, and looked more like a lady's diary or a religious text than the journal of a naval officer. The binding was of fine-grained leather, the pages gilt-edged. Adriana easily opened the delicate brass catch and lock and began to skim through the beginning pages. Bliss had written about his arrival and early impressions of the island. He described the island's geography and people. He discussed his duties. The first hint of anything untoward came on the thirteenth page. The French plantation owner, LeBusque, along with two other planters, had approached him with a scheme that involved illegal shipments to French ports. Bliss's predecessor had evidently been happy to oblige. Twenty pages later, in a shaking hand, he recorded a conversation in which LeBusque revealed his true colors: as an agent of Napoleon Bonaparte, he was prepared to offer Bliss fifty thousand pounds sterling and a percentage of the profits from the island's trade with France at such time as, with Bliss's connivance, the island of San Sebastian fell into French hands and a French flag flew over the governor's mansion. Less than a week later, Bliss became a traitor.

Adriana had scarcely slept in the last two hectic, nerve-racking days. The neatly penned tiny letters blurred, but she had seen enough: the journal was damning evidence of high treason and, were its contents revealed, would lead Bliss to a gibbet and the hangman's noose. *If* they were revealed. But how? Bliss would be bedridden for at least a week. If, during that time, she could contrive an escape and, once free, seek an audience with the governor, she could present him with the journal and beg his protection. And as a bonus, she'd then be in a better position to help Tom when he arrived.

But again, the nagging question: how? Escape was an iffy business at best. And if she stole the journal and Bliss missed it before she escaped, he'd soon discover that she was the thief and would have no alternative but to kill her.

Both Carlotta and Bliss slept on. *Of course!* Congratulating herself on her cleverness, Adriana moved stealthily to the table at the foot of Bliss's bed. The blade she had used to open and debride his wound was razor-sharp. Cutting as close to the binding as possible, she excised three of the most damning pages.

Surely he doesn't check every page every day. Surely. . . . She replaced the journal and quietly slid the drawer closed. She folded the pages and bound them to her thigh with a strip of linen bandage. And then, ebullient but reeling with fatigue, Adriana woke Carlotta and took her place on the cot. The last thing she remembered before she slept was the glow of a candle that became, in her exhaustion, an amulet in the shape of an oak tree wound about with brambles. *Hurry, my love*, she thought as her eyes closed and sleep overtook her. *Hurry. . . .*

✑ CHAPTER XVIII ✑

Bliss and gratitude were strangers. Adriana was called to his room the afternoon after he weathered his crisis, but not to receive thanks. Closemouthed, she cleaned the rapidly healing wound, pulled the ragged edges together with a row of neat stitches, and ordered him to remain on clear liquids, plenty of them, for at least another day. The next afternoon she was back to check his progress, and acquiesced to his demand for something more substantial to eat. The third day she found him still weak but restlessly prowling his room. He allowed her to change the bandages and then ordered her to return to her room. He made no mention of her promised release.

Adriana could do little but bide her time—and worry that Bliss would discover that someone had tampered with his journal. That night, she stared into the candlelight and sent herself into a deep trance, but her dreams failed her. *Because I couldn't concentrate properly* she thought the next morning as she checked the tightly rolled cylinder of stolen pages tied out of sight behind one of the wrought-iron vines choking her window. The slanting rays of the sun spilling over the summit of The Sleeping Giant brightened the room. A breeze kissed her naked skin as she stretched. *When, Thomas? When shall I expect you? I ache to be free, to walk in sunshine with you and your sons. . . .*

The bar on the door rasped as it was lifted and Adriana hurried back to the bed, wrapping herself in the coverlet. "Is that you, Carlotta?"

The servant stepped in the door and looked disapprovingly at Adriana. "Not dressed yet?"

"I couldn't get to sleep until late. And now I'm starved. What's—" Realizing that Carlotta wasn't carrying the usual breakfast tray, she stopped in mid-sentence. "I don't understand," she said, tensing. "Is something wrong?"

Carlotta's laugh was soft and dusky as she picked up Adriana's skirt from the chair and tossed it to her. "Nothing," she answered. "The master's in a good mood, and wishes to see you."

"To let me go?" Adriana asked, taking hope.

"I do not question the master. He tells me to bring you to him, and that is what I do. So hurry, girl, and get dressed."

Adriana pulled on the ruffled blouse given her the day after her arrival, stepped into her flowered skirt and calfskin slippers, and dashed water on her face. "He didn't say anything?" she asked, following Carlotta along the familiar route to Bliss's room. "Not even a hint?" she persisted, as Carlotta knocked on the door.

Carlotta pushed open the door and gestured for Adriana to precede her. "Do as master says," she whispered. "All will be good."

"Come in, come in," Bliss called cheerfully from behind his desk. "Good morning. If you'd wait outside, Carlotta?"

Adriana's knees turned to jelly as the door closed behind Carlotta. *He knows! He's missed them and knows I took them. Dear God. . . .*

"You're well, I trust?" Bliss asked politely.

His color was good and his voice had regained its strength. More important, he didn't look angry or out of sorts, and Adriana could detect no hint of sarcasm in his voice. *Don't antagonize him. Act civilly.* "I am, thank you, sir," she said with a shallow curtsy. "You're looking much better today."

"You think so, eh?" Bliss said with a chuckle. The

chuckle stopped abruptly as he closed his eyes and winced in pain. "I'm not so sure," he gasped.

"The pain is part of the healing process. You're well enough to be up and about. And to give me my freedom, as you promised," Adriana pointed out.

Bliss's pain receded with the memory of the promise he'd made. "All in good time," he quipped with a wave. His eyes played over Adriana's body and his lips curved in a lustful smile. "I need you here to oversee my recuperation. You are, after all, the angel of mercy who saved my life."

Adriana shuddered under his stare and remembered another time when he had looked at her that way. "Then you should be grateful and release me," she said, feeling naked and vulnerable.

Bliss started as if awakened. "Soon enough for that, my dear. Tonight, though, I'm having guests. Some friends of mine, planters from the other end of the island. Quite well off, I might add."

Friends like LeBusque? Adriana wondered, hiding her fear. "What have your guests to do with me?" she asked.

"I have never forgotten the Mumford fair and how you looked as you danced in the firelight," Bliss said, folding his hands below the bandage on his chest.

Red flames of insane rage burned before Adriana's eyes. For herself that night would always represent pain—the cruel destruction of one life, and the warping of another. "How flattering," she said with poisonous sincerity.

Bliss chuckled. "Tut, tut, my dear. Sarcasm doesn't become you." His voice hardened. "In any case, I should like you to dance for them, after which you shall have your freedom, as promised."

Adriana wasn't fooled for an instant. Bliss would find another reason to keep her, and then another, until he was strong enough to take what he really wanted from her. But there was no point in arguing with him.

"Very well," she agreed, already planning how she might turn the performance to her advantage. "I will dance."

Bliss clapped his hands. "Excellent! There'll be musicians, of course, and I'll have Carlotta see to some new clothes for you. We should have quite an evening. Carlotta!" He rose as Carlotta entered and went to his bed. "Let's get this dressing changed. And then there's work to be done. You've seen to the beef, I trust. And Ramon to the musicians? There's no time to be lost, no time . . ."

Adriana spent a dark and gloomy afternoon altering the new clothes Carlotta brought her. Twice, the earth shook, and the air was thick with the stench of the sulfurous smoke that spilled from The Sleeping Giant.

Carlotta came for her long after night fell. "For you," she said, handing Adriana a small dark-blue bottle and a large sweet-smelling white flower. "The master likes you, I think," she volunteered.

"The only person in this world Trevor Bliss likes is himself," Adriana answered. She pinned the flower in her hair, opened the bottle, and discovered it held a rich perfume that smelled of musk and jungle flowers. "At least I'll smell nice," she said, dabbing some on her neck and wrists and between her breasts. "But I have no mirror." She turned slowly. "How do I look?"

Carlotta held the lantern high and stepped back. Adriana's hair fell in gentle deep-auburn waves past her shoulders. Her blouse was of white silk embroidered with tiny, delicate flowers of red, blue, and yellow. It was cut low in front, revealing much of her breasts, and was thin enough for her nipples and the dark circles of her areolae to show through provocatively. Her skirt was the bright blue of the Caribbean on a sunny day, and swirled around her legs as she turned. She wore soft slippers of brushed deerskin. If her skin had been a shade darker, she might have passed as a native girl.

"You do not have to dance good," Carlotta said with a smile. "I think maybe they be happy only looking. But now they ask for you, and you must come."

Even Ramon, who had waited in the hall, was impressed, for he actually smiled and, Adriana thought, almost said something more than his usual noncommittal grunt. The sound of rattling dishes floated up the stairs to meet them as they descended. "Have they been drinking much?" Adriana asked.

"Wine," Carlotta said. "You be nice," she added by way of a friendly warning. "Master sometimes gets mean when drinking too much."

No one knew that better than Adriana. "I'll be careful," she promised, and then steeled herself for the task that lay ahead.

The foyer was empty. To the left lay the corridor that led to Bliss's bedchamber, to the right a set of double doors that Ramon threw open with a flourish.

"Aha!" Bliss exclaimed, his voice stilling a burst of laughter from the others. "At last, gentlemen, the goddess I promised you. Come in, Adriana. Don't keep us waiting, my dear."

Her eyes flashing, her shoulders back to deliberately accentuate the thrust of her breasts, Adriana entered as bidden and found herself in a large ballroom to which the men had retired after their dinner. The room was illuminated by a trio of matched crystal chandeliers that hung from a high ceiling, which was decorated with pastoral murals of an English countryside. French windows on the wall opposite the main doors looked onto a verandah, now brightly glowing with lanterns, and, beyond and below, the lights of the town. To her left, in the far corner, a half-dozen musicians in tight breeches and beaded uniform jackets occupied a dais and waited to play. To her right, the room stretched away to a large arch that separated it from the dining room proper.

Bliss and his companions were seated in four huge armchairs that had been placed near the center of the room. Behind them, attended by servants, a long table held crystal decanters and stemware and a silver service fit for royalty. A wineglass, a plate of cheeses, and another of fruit sat on smaller tables placed at each man's immediate right. The effect was ludicrously pretentious, but no one, Adriana noticed, was laughing.

Seated in the second chair from the right, his legs propped on an ottoman, Bliss held court. He was dressed in loose white breeches, his shirt partly concealed by an elaborately embroidered turkish robe of black silk. His face was pale, his eyes feverish. The wineglass in his hand trembled, and it was only with great effort that he managed not to spill his Madeira. A man in his condition shouldn't have been drinking at all, and Adriana guessed that he'd pass out within an hour. Two men sat to his right, one swarthy and moustachioed, with a pockmark-scarred face, the other sallow, with thin pale lips and a sharp nose on which rested rimless spectacles. The third guest, a young, brooding fellow with jet-black hair, thin moustache, an immaculately trimmed goatee, and a full, sensual mouth, sat to Bliss's left.

"See?" Bliss crowed drunkenly. "What did I tell you? What did I tell you, eh? When's the last time you saw such a beauty? Come give us a curtsy, my dear, and I'll introduce you around."

Adriana approached as directed.

Bliss gestured to his right with his glass. "This is Señor Hernandez . . ."

The man with the sweeping moustache inclined his head as Adriana curtsied.

". . . and Mr. Will Hadlock."

The man with the spectacles nodded stiffly.

"And to my left, a roué, my dear. Should you ever find yourself alone in his presence, you must be very, very careful. Monsieur Henri LeBusque."

"Really, Trevor," LeBusque drawled in heavily accented English. "You exaggerate!"

Adriana curtsied and smiled demurely. *This one. This is the one.* "I'll be sure to remember, sir," she said. *And now to bait the hook.* "Although I doubt that will ever happen."

LeBusque was darkly handsome. His smile spoke of lust and sensual gratification, of cruelty and the harsh tyranny of a man used to having his way. "A pity," he said, undressing Adriana with his eyes, "because you're such a lovely creature."

"And all mine," Bliss said with an ugly laugh. He drained his glass and waved for a refill. "Well?" he barked impatiently. "Go tell the band what you want them to play," he told Adriana. "We're waiting."

The band's repertoire was limited. Adriana outlined the tempos and rhythms she wanted while simultaneously plotting her seduction of Henri LeBusque. That he had wanted her from the moment she had stood before him had been evident, and his desire had only increased with Bliss's implicit warning to stay away from her. The trick would be to extend an unmistakable invitation to LeBusque without arousing Bliss's suspicion. She would entice him to search her out later.

The first tune started out slow and throbbing. Adriana glided to the center of the room and knelt in the bright light under the central chandelier. Slowly, her hands rose over her head and then, as if she were a girl waking from sleep, her arms extended sideways in a languorous stretch which became an almost imperceptible undulation as her shoulders began to move. *I do this for you, Thomas. For you alone. . . .* Swaying as the tempo increased, she rose as effortlessly as a wish or a dream, and began to dance.

There comes to every girl a moment, a single moment, when love becomes real and all the world is transformed. All things assume a new reality. Dawn becomes a sunrise that bursts with full-blown radiance in the heart. The sky is a mantle that wraps her and her love in a world inhabited by themselves alone. The air smells sweeter, the grass underfoot feels softer. Time becomes as a wild horse, now plunging out of control, now standing motionless and trembling with impatience. The setting sun brings tears, until she realizes that darkness is a welcome cloak to hide kisses and sweet embraces from prying eyes. Love fills her heart until she feels she will burst from sheer exultation.

Adriana's dance was true and real, for dancing cleansed her and gave her the strength she would need for that which would follow. For if a girl awakens innocently to love, surely that innocence is left behind when the girl becomes a woman, and the dance that follows is the dance of a sensual woman who inflames men's passions.

Her audience of four applauded as Adriana sank to the floor in her characteristic finish. "Marvelous!" Hernandez shouted, clapping enthusiastically. "*Dios mío*, Captain Bliss. She is magnificent!"

"But surely there will be more," LeBusque said, affecting a nonchalance that the glint in his eyes belied.

"Of course there's more," Bliss slurred. "Well?" he asked peevishly. "What're you waiting for, girl?"

Adriana's mind flashed back to that horrible night in Mumford when his eyes had held that same glazed, dangerous look, and the recollection fueled her determination. Haughtily, she rose and snapped her fingers for the band to begin.

The rhythm was sultry, the driving beat of unabashed sexuality. Brazenly, her breasts straining against the fabric of her blouse, her legs flashing sleek and lithe and tawny, she danced closer and closer to her audience. Bliss reached out drunkenly to touch her and spilled his wine on his legs as she darted out of reach. Hernandez beamed as she danced around him and feigned a kiss to his forehead. Hadlock, even when she brushed close by him, displayed all the enthusiasm of a fish.

The moment of truth. LeBusque's eyes locked with hers as she danced behind Bliss. He watched narrowly as her tongue licked out to wet her lips. She shaved the distance between herself and LeBusque as the music rose to a fever pitch. Wildly uninhibited, her hands locked behind her head and her pelvis swaying inches from his face, Adriana danced at LeBusque's side, then disappeared behind him. Her breasts near the back of his neck, she dipped and whispered into his ear, "I know another dance, if you're interested," and was gone.

It was done! The seed was planted. A woman gone mad, she leaped and whirled and, as the music climaxed, sank exhausted to the floor.

"Brava!" Hernandez shouted, leaping to his feet. "Brava! *Bravissima!*"

Hadlock applauded politely.

LeBusque stood and applauded, and nodded to her ever so slightly.

Without a word, the glass slipping from his fingers and crashing to the floor, Captain Trevor Bliss passed out.

He will come. I can feel it in my bones. He must come!

Adriana stared into the candle, repeating the incantation over and over again. The candle had burned down to a nubbin in the time that had passed since Carlotta had hurriedly escorted her back to her room. But how long had it been? An hour? Two? How long would she have to wait? Until the candle guttered and went out? Until the moon was lost behind the roof of the house?

He will come. I can feel it in my bones. He must come!

Everything was ready. She had untied the rolled pages and tucked them under the ticking at the bottom of the bed. She had emptied the pitcher in preparation for . . .

Wait!

Certain she had heard the scrape of wood on wood, she tensed and held her breath. Silently she moved the

candle aside and stared at the door as the hinges creaked
and a crack of light shone through the narrow opening.

Victory! Her heart leaped. She could feel her pulse
pound in her temples. *Lord, give me the strength . . .*
"Carlotta?" she whispered. "Is that you?"

The door opened wider. "Hardly," Henri LeBusque
said, slipping inside.

"You!" Adriana gasped, rising and stepping away
from the table.

LeBusque had divested himself of his coat and boots,
and was wearing only breeches, an open shirt, and soft
moccasins. "You expected someone else?" he asked
wryly.

"No," Adriana admitted. "But you took so
long . . ."

Wary, he held his candle high and briefly inspected
the room. "These things take time," he explained.

"Captain Bliss?"

"Is sound asleep, as far as I know."

"I warned him not to drink to excess." She let a slow
smile warm her face as her eyes roamed down his body.
"A man in his condition has only himself to blame if
another . . . takes his place." Quickly, she checked the
hall and pushed the door closed. "The others?" she
asked. "Hernandez? Hadlock?"

LeBusque placed the heavy brass candlestick he carried on the table next to the water pitcher and basin,
then sat casually on the bed and began to remove his
moccasins. "Returned to their plantations. I pleaded
indisposition, and begged a room for the night to sleep
off the effects of too much wine and rich food." He
grinned wolfishly. "I feel better already."

"And the servants?"

"You worry too much."

"The servants!" Adriana hissed. She shuddered and
wrapped her arms around herself as if chilled. "If Bliss
learns that you . . . that I . . ."

"The servants are like faithful dogs," LeBusque

snorted. "The woman sleeps in his room to be near him, the man on the floor in the corridor outside his door. The others went to their quarters an hour ago, which left me free to prowl about and find you. You needn't worry. No one will disturb us. We might as well be alone in the house. As we shall be," he added, his fingers beckoning her, "in this bed."

Adriana approached with mock reluctance. "I was told to beware of roués . . ."

"And I was told to beware of witches, but know better than to listen to foolishness." He ran his fingers up her arm, let them slide fleetingly over her breast. "You dance divinely, Adriana. You are beautiful, you excite me . . ."

Adriana caught his hand in her teeth and softly bit the tender skin between his thumb and index finger. "No more," she said huskily, "than you excite me."

"Damn you!" LeBusque rasped, grabbing her wrist and pulling her into his lap.

Thomas! Thomas! It was all she could do not to fight him off. Almost sick with revulsion, Adriana returned his embrace and, a low moan rising in her throat, his kisses. Her arms circled his neck, her fingers entwined in his hair. "You are a forceful man," she whispered when he finally released her. "One who knows how to turn a lady into a wanton."

His hand cupped her breast, his lips caressed the swell of warm flesh above the fabric of her blouse. "And *you* are a wanton who knows how to turn a man into a satyr."

"Yes." She moistened her fingertips with her tongue and traced his lips. "As you shall see. But . . ." Coyly, she pushed away from him and stood. "I promised you a dance."

"There is no music . . ."

"I need no music," she said, backing away from him until the table stopped her, "except that which plays in my soul."

Her hands slid up her thighs and across her abdomen, then pressed her breasts together as her fingers undid one button, then another and another as she turned away from him. Slowly, she pulled the blouse from her shoulders, let the slick fabric slide down her arms and whisper to the floor. "Come," she purred, turning to face him. "Come to Adriana, my satyr. Come and . . . dance . . . with Adriana."

Mesmerized, as awkward as a bumbling schoolboy, LeBusque rose and, unable to tear his eyes from her breasts and the deep rose of her nipples, walked toward her as one in a trance.

"Come," Adriana repeated, her arms out, her hands beckoning him.

Only in his wildest dreams had LeBusque expected anything like Adriana. A conquest, yes. Acquiescence, of course, for women often gave themselves to him in the hope of future favors. But outright seduction by one so beautiful. . . . Her eyes burned with a desire no less than his own. Her breasts were firm and high and soft and he imagined them against his chest, in his mouth. Her hands, so supple, so smooth . . . hands that would enfold him and guide him to her. . . .

Confined by his breeches, he was almost painfully hard. "We shall dance," Adriana whispered, her fingers tracing the rigid line of his arousal. Her hands went to her waist and began to undo the tie that held her skirt. Modestly, in the moment of truth, she turned her back on him and, instead of the pitcher she'd planned to use, grasped the heavy brass candlestick.

Now!

Her face transformed into a mask of hatred, Adriana whirled and swung with all her strength. LeBusque looked up, had time to realize what was happening and try to duck aside, but not time enough before the candlestick thudded into the side of his head.

The world exploded into shimmering fragments that, like fireworks on an autumn evening, quickly faded.

LeBusque blinked and tried to reach for her, but his arms wouldn't function. "Why?" he asked, unable to comprehend, and dropped, unconscious, to the floor.

Warily, holding the candlestick ready to strike again just in case, Adriana knelt at his side. The pulse in his neck was strong; he was breathing lightly but without difficulty. Working quickly, she removed his belt, rolled him tightly into her coverlet, secured the belt around his chest, and tied his shirt around his legs. It wouldn't hold him forever, but neither would he escape easily.

The hall was empty; the house quiet. Adriana pulled on her blouse, tied the pages to her thigh, and, tapping on wood for luck, slipped out the door and barred it behind her. A single lantern burned at the head of the stairs, another in the foyer. She paused at the corridor to Bliss's room, checked to see that Ramon was asleep, and darted to the front door. A moment later, fresh air cool on her skin, she ran, a free woman, through the night.

Sir Theodotus Vincent stood at the window of his study and regarded the slight red glow at the summit of The Sleeping Giant. The glow matched the one in the bowl of the pipe that was firmly clenched in his teeth, and smoke drifted around his head in the same manner as the sulfurous clouds eddied around the volcano. *Damned stinking smoke anyway*, he thought, sick of the smell and personally affronted by its frequency during the last two months. There hadn't been any when he'd arrived at San Sebastian, and he'd be damned glad when it stopped its infernal spewing again—as the islanders assured him it soon would.

But it was too late in the evening to worry about a little smoke. Sir Theodotus polished off his bedtime glass of sherry, tapped out his pipe, and set about extinguishing the lanterns for the night. It had been a good day. He and the boys had taken an excursion to the port that morning and had lunched with his friend Charlie

Waite at the Captains' Club. The afternoon had been quiet, with only one minor altercation—something of a record, given the ability of the twins to turn the merest frustration into a calamity, or a squabble over a trifle into a pitched battle. Even dinner had gone well—both boys had eaten without balking for a change—and they'd played quietly together until bedtime, a little over three hours earlier.

Time for one last peek in at them before he went to sleep. There was so much about them he enjoyed: watching them play, watching them grow; watching them sleep, their faces twin studies in innocence. They were Jenny all over again, he thought, and if there was any trace in them of their father, he chose to ignore it. The house was quiet. Yawning widely, he closed the study door and started down the hall toward the stairs, and then stopped when his butler appeared out of the darkness at the rear of the hall. "Is that you, Juan?"

"Yes, suh," a deep, mellow voice answered. "There's a woman out back wants to see you."

Sir Theodotus frowned. "At this hour? And out back? I don't believe I want to see anyone who comes calling in such a manner. Who is she, anyway?"

"Don't know, suh. Looks like an island girl, but says she don't be." He paused. "Say she came from Cap'n Bliss's house, suh."

Vincent's frown deepened. "Good Lord, why would Bliss be sending a girl to see me? One of his trollops, no doubt, though I'd have thought he was in no shape for that sort of thing yet." He waved a hand in dismissal. "Send her away. If her business is important, she can return in the morning at a decent hour."

"My business is too important to wait for morning, sir," Adriana said from the end of the hallway. "Or manners. I'm sorry about the hour, but it wasn't of my own choosing."

Sir Theodotus looked past his butler and saw a figure silhouetted in the doorway that led to the rear of the mansion. "Go away, girl," he said. "I've no time for you, whatever you want."

"No time to discover that a man you trust is a traitor, a thief, and a murderer?"

"What the devil are you talking about?" Sir Theodotus demanded, brushing past the butler and stalking toward Adriana. "I could have you thrashed, you know."

Adriana held her ground. "You could, but you won't. Not after you hear what I have to say."

Her beauty was spellbinding. Her breasts, dimly visible under the sheer fabric of her blouse, rose and fell in a delicious rhythm. "Who are you?" Sir Theodotus asked, mesmerized.

"My name is Adriana. And as far as I know, I'm the only survivor of the *Cassandra*, a ship that Bliss sank last week."

Sir Theodotus's breath caught in his throat. The *Cassandra*! He'd read Bliss's dictated report. The *Cassandra* was a Paxton ship, and he had no doubt that Thomas Gunn Paxton had been aboard her, bound surely for San Sebastian in an effort to steal back his sons. "You lie," he rasped. "The *Cassandra* exploded and burned, and went down with all hands."

"According to whom?" Adriana asked. "Captain Trevor Bliss?"

"Do you question him, girl? Do you dare impugn the honor of—"

"He lied," Adriana said flatly. "Rather than take them prisoner, Trevor Bliss ordered his crew to murder eight surviving members of the crew of the *Cassandra*. I alone was saved, and brought here to be kept prisoner in Bliss's house so he could toy with me and torment me when he regained sufficient strength."

"But . . . but I *know* Bliss," Sir Theodotus protested. "Why in heaven's name would he do something like that?"

"I don't know," Adriana said, judiciously omitting

the story of her attempted murder of Bliss, "but I do know that he tried to rape me three years ago, and that on the same night he murdered my brother."

"This is preposterous!" Sir Theodotus snorted. He gestured angrily to Juan. "Throw her out," he ordered. "And see that she doesn't return."

"No," Adriana said, reaching for the pages with a casual disregard for the amount of flesh she revealed in the process.

Juan stopped short and, unsure of himself in the face of Adriana's strange behavior, looked back at Sir Theodotus for advice.

"Not before you read these." Adriana untied the piece of linen holding the pages to her thigh. "Does the name LeBusque mean anything to you?" she asked.

"You must know it does," Sir Theodotus snapped. "What's that you have there?"

Adriana unrolled the pages so Sir Theodotus could see the writing. "They are pages from Captain Bliss's journal, and they indicate treason. Are you interested?"

"Of course I am," Sir Theodotus said, reaching for them. "Let me see that!"

"Not quite yet, Governor." Adriana moved the pages just out of his reach. "I'll give them to you to study, and you may draw your own conclusions—in return for your promise to shield and protect me from Captain Bliss."

She was definitely British, to judge by her speech, so there *was* a possibility that she and Bliss had met before. Bliss and LeBusque were as thick as thieves—the irony of the idiom struck him at the same time as the thought —so her accusations might have some substance. In addition to which, she was bold as brass, especially for a woman, and her boldness intrigued him. "Very well," he conceded. "Give them to me. If you're telling the truth, I'll see that no harm comes to you. Be warned, though, girl: if you're lying, you'll come to grief."

Adriana almost handed the pages to him, and then,

belatedly cautious—Sir Theodotus was, after all, the man who had kidnapped Tom's sons—she hesitated. "Do I . . . that is . . ." Embarrassed and fearful of offending him, she blushed and rushed on. "Forgive me for seeming to doubt you, but do I have your word, sir?"

"Ye gods, girl, I've said as much!" Sir Theodotus thundered.

Adriana shrank away from him. "I'm sorry, sir. I didn't mean—"

"Now, now, miss." The angry frown became a paternalistic smile. "I once had a daughter your age, and I assure you I'm not going to allow Bliss or anyone else hurt you." He held out his hand. "So let's take a look, eh, and get down to business?"

Reassured, and having little choice in any case, Adriana surrendered the pages. And for the first time in what seemed an eternity, she felt safe.

Sir Theodotus ambled back to the light at the bottom of the stairs and scanned the first page. "Damn!" he grunted. The penmanship was Bliss's. LeBusque's name leaped off the page. Fifty thousand pounds . . . a percentage of profits. Sir Theodotus's stomach churned. "Does he say when?" he asked.

"Not exactly," Adriana said. "But soon. It's on the third page."

The governor scanned the third sheet and then, his face turning white, folded the pages and thrust them in his pocket.

"Prepare a room for the young lady," he said, his voice faint and shaking. "Upstairs, I think, in this case. And tell no one she is here, do you understand? No one. Her presence must be kept a secret for the moment."

"Yes, suh!"

"Then you believe me?" Adriana asked in a voice weak with relief.

The hour was late and he needed time to contemplate the information that had fallen into his hands. "Please be so kind as to accompany Juan and follow his instructions," he answered. "You have sanctuary for the present. Afterward . . ." He rubbed his eyes and looked bleakly at the journal pages. "Afterward, we shall see. Now, run along. We'll talk again in the morning."

Adriana followed Juan as ordered. Behind her, alone in the foyer, Sir Theodotus Vincent, His Majesty's governor of San Sebastian, lighted a taper from the lantern and trudged down the hall to his study. A long night lay ahead of him, and not at all a pleasant one.

~ CHAPTER XIX ~

". . . I have assured LeBusque that we need not fear Vincent's finger spoiling the pie: with those two brats of his in our—"

Hands? It has to be hands, Sir Theodotus thought, wishing for the dozenth time that he had the following page. If only the girl had taken. . . . No. She'd done well, had chosen wisely. The last thing he wanted Bliss to know was that his journal was missing.

But how could Bliss have become embroiled in such an unsavory venture? He was young, personable, and had friends in the Admiralty. Surely fifty thousand pounds and a minuscule percentage from an island as small as San Sebastian couldn't compare to the long-term rewards he could expect in the British Navy. Fifty thousand pounds was all well and good, but at the expense of being a wanted man for the rest of his life and never being able to return to England? What would he do when he ran through those fifty thousand pounds? Where could he go that his infamy would not precede him? No one esteemed a traitor; no one trusted a man who had sold his soul and sold out his country. More heinous yet, he had compounded his crime by stooping to threaten harm to children. A man who could do that was beyond salvation—and more important to Sir Theodotus, acutely aware who the children were, also dangerous in the extreme.

The night was filled with fears for the boys' safety and doubts about his ability to quash the imminent coup attempt. The hours dragged. Restless, alarmed by every unidentifiable noise, he prowled the house in search of imaginary intruders. Morning found him dozing fitfully in an armchair in his study, and waking abruptly with a sense of urgency that he couldn't dispel. There wasn't a moment to lose: Bliss was presently laid up, but even so, his absence probably wouldn't stop LeBusque if the planter was ready to move. The third page had been dated over three weeks earlier. The coup attempt could come at any time.

The first order of business was to protect the boys, to which end he wrote—and almost sent, before good sense prevailed—a note to the captain of the marine contingent on the island. Tearing it up, he sent instead for his friend Charlie Waite, the harbor master, and asked him to come immediately to the mansion on a matter of some urgency. Only then did he take time to make his toilet, say good morning to the boys, and choke down a bit of breakfast.

Sir Theodotus had passed the previous night in astonishment and alarm, but by late morning he had marshaled all of his thoughts and was clear-eyed and determined. He was interrogating Adriana when Charlie arrived. Waite was shown into the study and sworn to secrecy. "Just listen for now," Sir Theodotus said, showing the burly harbor master a chair, "and get the gist of things. I'll answer questions later. Now," he continued, turning back to Adriana. "You're sure, you're *positive*, that Hernandez and Hadlock aren't involved?"

"Not positive," Adriana admitted. "I was reading fast, the light was bad, and I'd scarcely slept for over two days, so I might have missed something. But I believe the only thing they're involved in is the illegal shipping."

Waite's eyebrows rose. "Illegal—"

"Try to remember," Sir Theodotus said to Adriana, interrupting. "Were there any other names mentioned?"

"Someone named Andre? A clerk? I think—"

"One of my clerks," Charlie said. "Would you mind telling me just what exactly's going on here?"

Half an hour later, after Adriana had been dismissed, Charlie knew as much as Sir Theodotus, and by the time the mariner's clock on the mantel chimed at noon, the two men had decided on a course of action. Because word would surely get back to Bliss if the marines were used, Waite promised to find two dozen trustworthy men who would be well paid to keep their lips buttoned and to guard the mansion and the twins. A trusted clerk on Sir Theodotus's staff would be sworn to secrecy and would begin all the necessary paperwork: a compilation of evidence and the drawing up of formal charges and other legal documents. LeBusque would be placed under surveillance, and certain members of the crew of the *Druid*—still in port—would be interrogated about the alleged murders of the survivors of the *Cassandra*. Last but by no means least, the boys were to be restricted to the mansion grounds, and Sir Theodotus would become officially indisposed and in seclusion until such time as the conspirators' plans were better known.

The days passed at a maddeningly slow pace. The sun crept into the eastern sky, reluctantly set in the western. The Sleeping Giant belched and grumbled, spewed its dyspeptic stink over the island, and rested again. The nights passed with the speed of a ship becalmed. Sir Theodotus tried to read to the boys but, irritated by their unending stream of questions, turned them over to Adriana, to whom they had taken a liking the moment they'd met her. At long last, on Friday, December 14, one of the men Sir Theodotus had sent to the eastern end of the island returned, and the plot was made clear. A French warship due in those waters had been ordered to lay out of sight off the coast until New Year's Eve. At morning's first light, the ship would enter the harbor and two companies of French marines would capture

the crew of the *Druid* as well as the British contingent
ashore while they were still in their cups after a large
party—arranged by Bliss—to welcome in the New Year.
Within an hour of the warship's arrival, if all went well,
the flag of France would fly over the governor's mansion, which would be occupied by LeBusque, who was
to be the new French governor. The evidence was plain;
there was no disputing the culpability of Bliss or Le-
Busque. All that remained was to arrest the conspirators
and bring them to the bar of justice. With luck, daring,
and a good deal of preparation, Sir Theodotus could
even hope to take the French warship and so turn the
tables completely.

For Sir Theodotus, once again, the sky was clear, the
sun bright. A light breeze, all that remained of the Atlantic trades after their passage over the island, per-
fumed the air as he stood on the front verandah and
watched the harbor master's carriage disappear down
the drive. The clock in the foyer struck noon as he
walked back inside, removed his frock coat, and handed
it to Juan. "The twins?" he asked, not having seen
them all morning.

"Yes, suh. In the parlor, suh, playing with Ariadna."

"Adriana," Sir Theodotus corrected automatically.

"Yes, suh. Ariadna."

The governor sighed and, once again, gave up. "Very
well, Juan. We'll want something to eat shortly, if you
please. I'll be with the boys."

Their laughter met him in the hall, and as he stood in
the doorway and watched them, Sir Theodotus wondered that he should ever have thought the parlor or the
mansion itself a drab and dreary place. All it had ever
lacked was the laughter of children. And also, he had
been forced to admit as the days had passed, the gentle
magic of Adriana.

The affection that Joseph and Jason felt for Adriana
had been instantaneous. In her they found the tenderness, the laughter, the warm caring touch all children

need, especially those whose mothers are dead. That Adriana had fallen in love with the twins at the same time had been obvious. She ate with them, played with them, and saw them to bath and bed. She regaled them with stories of life among the Gypsies. She spoke of unicorns and fauns and wove tales of magic out of the world's ordinary fabric. By the end of her week in the governor's mansion, she was their friend, confidante, and surrogate mother, and Sir Theodotus couldn't have been more pleased.

Or touched, he thought, feeling his throat tighten. She was wearing a long lace-trimmed white gown that he'd borrowed from Charlie Waite's wife. Jenny had worn such a gown once, and though Adriana bore absolutely no physical resemblance to Jenny, he imagined for a fleeting moment that she was his daughter.

Such nonsense! You're a fool. An old fool, sir! Jenny had been fair; Adriana was dark. Jenny's hair had been like spun gold; Adriana's was the deep brownish-red of ripe chestnuts. Jenny had been an aristocrat, high-born, refined, cultured; Adriana was a Gypsy, a commoner with no education.

And yet . . . Adriana was the same age Jenny would have been, had she lived. She was infected with that same spark of life that kindled warmth and affection. Her laugh was as light and as carefree as Jenny's, her hands as tender, her eyes as bright, her demeanor as charming. *I should have gone to Jenny. Just once to have seen her playing with them like this, loving them . . .*

"And that, my little friends, is the story of the first rabbit, and how he lost his long and beautiful tail."

"Aw, you made that up."

"Made it *up*? Why, shame on you, Jason Paxton! Whatever—" She stopped in mid-sentence and beamed at Sir Theodotus. "Well, there's your grandpa come for lunch. I suggest that you ask *him*."

"Grandpa!" Joseph yelled.

"She says the rabbit gave his tail to the squirrel so he could keep his nose warm," Joseph complained.

"It's true enough," Sir Theodotus said, nodding sagely.

"Awwww . . ."

"I'm hungry," Joseph interjected, not caring how the rabbit lost his tail.

"Then run along and wash up," Adriana said, rising from the floor and smoothing her skirts. "It's time for lunch, and afterward a nap."

"Can we play more then?" Jason asked.

"And will you tell us more stories?" Joseph chimed in. "I want the one about the magic bear."

"Yes to both of you, but first lunch and naps," Adriana said with a laugh. Then, clapping her hands and making a comical buzzing sound, she chased them out of the room.

"So *that's* how the rabbit lost his tail." Sir Theodotus chuckled, sinking into an armchair. "They love you, you know."

"And I love them," Adriana replied. "They're quite a pair. Their mother would have been proud of them."

"Damn it!" Sir Theodotus snapped as he slammed his fist onto the arm of the chair. "Why do you persist in reminding me of Jenny? No, never mind. Don't tell me. I know exactly what you're about, witch."

"I'm a Gypsy, sir, not a witch."

"Gypsy, witch, what's the difference?" he grumbled. "You're trying to complete the ruination of my day by sneaking the subject around to that bloody Paxton."

Adriana smiled sweetly. "You mentioned his name, not I."

"Well, your tactics won't work. I'll never change my mind about him. Anyway, he's dead, so precious little it would do."

Adriana's face fell. Sir Theodotus would have taken back his harsh words if he hadn't become so exasperated by her constant references to Paxton. First Jenny and then her. Was he doomed to be plagued by Paxton alive *and* dead?

"Thomas may be dead," Adriana said, "but he loved his children and wanted only what was best for them."

"And you think I don't?" Sir Theodotus asked. "Why do you think I had them brought here?"

"I don't doubt your love for them," Adriana answered. "That's written plainly on your face. But if you'd truly been concerned with what was best for them, you'd have gone to them instead of taking them from their father."

"*He* by God took my—"

"You saved my life, Sir Theodotus, and I'm more grateful than I know how to say, but the truth's the truth. You brought them here because you wanted to hurt and punish Thomas." Her voice dropped, became softer and sadder. "If you'd seen his pain as I did, you'd know how well you succeeded."

Sir Theodotus took a deep breath and wished the conversation had never begun. "All right, all right," he said, throwing up his hands. "I'll concede the point. I'm an ogre and a villain."

"I didn't say—"

"You might just as well have. Good Lord Almighty, girl! Have you no concern for another's sensibilities, no rein on your tongue? Have you never wished for revenge? What about Bliss? He took your brother's life, you say, and yet you never once dreamed of repaying him in kind?"

"I . . ." The truth had been fine when Sir Theodotus's motives were being discussed, but she had been less than honest regarding herself. She had never let one word of her vow to kill Bliss slip. Not once had she put herself in Sir Theodotus's place. "I tried to kill him once in London, and set out for here to try again," she admitted in a voice that was barely audible. "I didn't

tell you because . . . I was afraid you'd forbid me to care
for the boys if you knew I'd done . . . something like
that.''

Sir Theodotus sat silently for a long moment. At last
he rose and crossed to her side. ''And so I might well
have,'' he said, patting her shoulder. ''But you didn't
and I didn't, and I have no regrets. As for Paxton,
though . . .'' His jaw set in a firm line and his voice
hardened. ''As I said, he's dead and that's that. The
boys are here, and here they'll stay, no matter what happens.''

''And Bliss?'' Adriana asked, wisely changing the
subject.

''Bliss. Ah, yes, Bliss. Another matter entirely, eh?''
He paced the floor, stopped at a window overlooking
Bliss's house. ''I'd wager he knows you're here—
impossible to keep that sort of thing a secret in a place
the size of San Sebastian, after all. The trick is . . .''
He scratched his head, wondering how much to tell
Adriana, and decided he could trust her with everything. ''I received a rather enigmatic note from him
yesterday that suggested we meet in the near future to
discuss a venture that might prove profitable to me.''

''He wants you to join him?'' Adriana asked.

''It sounds like it, but I don't know. I'm letting him
cool his heels until tomorrow, at which time I shall
plead a continued indisposition and suggest that we find
a moment to slip away for a word or two at the ball next
Tuesday.''

''Ball?''

''The annual governor's masked ball that ushers in
the Christmas season. An island tradition, I'm told.''
Pleased, he beamed at Adriana. ''Well? What do you
think?''

''I think that if I were he, I'd be far away by next
Tuesday. I wouldn't trust you for—''

''But it isn't a matter of trust, my dear; rather, of ex-
pectations. He'll expect me to be as greedy and unscru-

pulous as he is. He'll be in for a bit of a surprise instead,
I think. All the pertinent documents will be prepared by
Tuesday night, and within an hour of our talk, he and
LeBusque and two or three others will embark on a merchant vessel bound for London, where I expect they'll
stand trial. Of course," he added dryly, "that will mean
you won't be able to—"

"I know," Adriana interrupted. "I do hope, however, that I'll be permitted to see him before he leaves."
A small smile played across her face and her voice took
on a dreamlike quality. "To see the look on his face
when he learns that I brought him to his downfall."

Sunlight melted through the emerald canopy of the
forest and warmed the world around Adriana as she
walked the corridor of trees and vines, past gay splashes
of color that were the flowers of a dozen strange and
wondrously beautiful species previously unknown to
her. Petals red as rubies. Petals orange as fire. Bright
yellows, whispering lavenders, flamboyant magentas.
And white! Dazzling, pristine white as pure as a virgin's
veil; muted and creamy white flecked with the delicate
blues and browns and pinks of the hidden eggs of
songbirds.

The path curved through the forest and emerged,
some two hundred yards behind and above the mansion,
in a tiny, secluded, but well-tended glade in which the
previous governor had built a gazebo. In need of solitude, Adriana climbed the wooden steps, sat in the
shade of the thatched roof, and tried to clear her mind.
The wood against her back was warm, the air balmy. A
light breeze sifted through the surrounding foliage and
played with her hair. Butterflies—bright, living blossoms against the green of the forest—floated through
the sun-drenched glade. Somewhere out of sight, a
gold-tailed grackle squawked.

Over a week had passed since her dreams had told her
Tom was alive, but he had yet to appear. She had no

doubt that he would, eventually. The question was, when? How many days, each a lifetime, did she have to wait? And what might happen before he did arrive? A thousand possibilities, most of them admittedly remote but nonetheless alarming enough, flitted through her mind. If only it were all over! Not even Bliss's demise mattered. All she wanted was to be somewhere safe with Tom and his sons, whom she had come to love.

"Adriana."

She closed her eyes and recalled the soft sweetness of his voice in her ear.

"Adriana!"

Yes, my Thomas. I am here and waiting for you. I love . . .

"Over here, damn it!"

Oh, dear God! Adriana's heart leaped as she looked about wildly and spotted a hand beckoning from the edge of the glade. "Tom?" she whispered. "Is that you?"

"Yes. Careful! Can anyone see you?"

She knew no one had followed her, and a quick check proved that the path was still empty. She ran down the steps, across the manicured grass, and into the opening Tom made in the shrubs. "Thank God you're here," she cried, throwing herself into his arms. "When they shot at you and I saw the empty boat, I thought . . . I thought . . ."

Tom cradled her in his arms, savoring the sensation of holding her once again. Suddenly, he pushed her to arm's length. "The boys," he said, his voice hoarse with emotion. "I've seen them. Are they all right?"

"They miss you, but otherwise they're perfect." She wrapped her arms around him and pressed her cheek to his chest. "God, I missed you. I was so frightened. How did you get here? And when? Where have you been? How long—"

"Whoa!" Tom laughed. He tilted her head back, inspected her as if seeing her for the first time. "You're beautiful," he finally said. "I missed you, too. Come. There's a better place."

Adriana followed him around giant *poro* trees, over exposed beds of sharp lava, through mazes of thick dangling vines. Tom looked lean and dangerous. Wherever he'd been, whatever he'd been doing, he'd been toughened during the weeks they'd been separated. His belt bristled with a brace of pistols, a dirk, two heavy knives, and his ever-present rapier. His rust-colored breeches and white linen shirt were torn and frayed and faded, and hung loose on him. His hair was bleached and tangled, his skin tanned to a deep, deep bronze.

"Maurice, Topaz, and Sanchez—" he began.

"Sanchez?" Adriana asked, almost tripping over a vine. "*Onofre* Sanchez?"

"It's a long story," Tom said, leading her into a tiny clearing. "Anyway, we found this hiding place last Tuesday. We can see the mansion and grounds, but no one there can see us."

A better spot would have been hard to find. Evidently uprooted by a storm, an ancient star-apple tree had fallen toward the governor's mansion. By walking along the trunk, one could sit completely unobserved behind a thick veil of vines and watch, less than a hundred fifty yards away, the north and west sides of the mansion. At the base of the tree, a camp had been set up behind the ten-foot-high wall of dirt-packed roots. Tom shook out a blanket and spread it on the ground for Adriana. "The others left for town just about the time I saw you start up the path. Wait here a minute." He disappeared around the wall of roots and returned a moment later. "All clear as far as I can tell. Well, what happened? What are you doing at Vincent's place?"

Adriana talked while Tom paced and, occasionally, interrupted with a question. "You're sure he thinks I'm dead?" he asked when she finished. "Sure he's not laying a trap for me?"

"Dead and gone," Adriana assured him. "The plot's

his main concern right now. The only time he talks about you is when I mention your name. Or say something about Jenny. I think . . ."

"What?" Tom prompted.

"I think he regrets his actions . . . the kidnapping. He won't admit it in so many words, of course. He's a proud man. Like you. Maybe too proud, my darling."

"Whose side are you on, anyway?"

"Yours, of course," Adriana flared, resenting the implication that she was disloyal. "I'm simply telling you what I think."

"Well, he'll regret it a lot more when this is finished."

"What are you going to do?"

"Do? I'm—we, that is, the four of us—are going to take the boys back, for starters." Legs spread, hands clenched into fists, he stood facing the hidden mansion where his sons were kept from him. "If it weren't for the guards, we'd have them already. As it is, we've had to spend time preparing a few surprises along our escape route so they won't catch us before we get back to the boat. Tomorrow night, though, at the latest . . ."

"I think you'd be better off waiting until—"

"*Waiting*? What do you mean, waiting? Do you have any idea what it's been like sitting here for four days, knowing they were there, being able to see them but not touch them or talk to them or hold them?" He crouched at her side and gripped her shoulder. "I want my sons, Adriana. I want them *back*!" A shuddering sigh racked his body and, as if the spring that had held him coiled and ready to strike had been released, he let go of her arm and sagged to the ground next to her. "The truth is," he said, subdued, "that I want you back, too. We heard in town that you'd disappeared and that Bliss was looking for you. I was scared stiff wondering what had happened. And then, two days ago, Maurice spotted you. You were gone by the time I got there, but later, I caught a glimpse of you in an open window, and . . ."

His fingers touched her cheek, slid through her hair to cup her head and gently pull her to him. "I missed you, Adriana. God, but I missed you so much . . . knowing you were so close . . . wanting you . . ."

Their kiss was the cry of souls longing to be together. Adriana's hand slid under his shirt; his hand pulled her blouse from her skirt and sought her breasts.

"Thomas . . . Thomas . . ."

He sat up, removed his belt with its warlike implements, and cast it aside. "I want to look at you," he said, his voice deep and husky as his fingers fumbled at the buttons on her blouse.

Adriana stiffened, looked around apprehensively. "The others—"

"Won't return until sundown. This time . . ."—her blouse fell open and his hands held her breasts as he bent to kiss the soft, warm valley between them— ". . . is ours."

Time lost, time suspended in a flood of sensations that left her weak and trembling. He untied the laces that secured her skirt, slipped it under her hips and lay it to one side, then rose to shed his shirt and breeches, and to gaze down at her.

Adriana lay in the sun, one hand behind her head, the other at her side. Her breasts rose and fell with each breath, her nipples swelled in anticipation of his touch. Her stomach lay flat, then sloped up to meet the twin planes of her hips and, between them, that softer padded mound of Venus rich with auburn hair that glinted in the sun. Her right leg lay straight, her left was bent slightly. "If it were given me to see you only once in this life," Tom said, kneeling at her side, "it would be like this. I would touch you everywhere, know every sweet hill and valley of you. You are my world, Adriana. My world."

He stroked her feet, her calves. His kisses warmed the hollows behind her knees. "I dreamed we were together like this, the sun warm on us . . ." More kisses, soft as the touch of a butterfly's wings, wrote the name of love on her thighs and set her to trembling. Two fingers, oh, so gently, spread her, caressed the moist inner flesh that swelled and darkened with her arousal.

"How beautiful . . . how fitting . . . that we are made so . . ." His breath warmed her, his lips caught and held her, his tongue touched her with fire.

Adriana arched her back and fought to keep from crying out. Sweat beaded her forehead and a low moan began deep in her throat. Her hand sought him, felt his heaviness, his growing hardness, the sweetness of his passion. "Thomas . . ."

Hungry, unashamed, she opened herself to him, watched with hooded eyes as he moved to kneel between her legs, as he caught her hips and lifted her to him. Forgotten the sun, forgotten the wind and the world. Unable to restrain herself, she moved against him to moisten and ready him, then spread herself and guided him into . . .

Teeth clenched, hands holding her hips to keep her from moving, Tom rocked back, fighting the coming explosion he knew he couldn't stop. "Don't move . . . I . . ."

"I don't care," she whispered. "I don't care, Thomas. Now . . . please!"

He pitched forward, his weight on his hands, then held himself over her and stared into her eyes as he plunged deep inside her, as her legs circled his waist, as her hands clawed his back, as, together, they were seized by the rolling, thundering spasms that held them paralyzed and only . . . slowly . . . released them to sag, spent and dizzy and breathless, in each other's arms.

The sun laved them with its warmth, the slight breeze cooled them as they lay quietly in the sweet, shimmering afterglow. Adriana lay on her side, her head cradled by Tom's arm, her right leg resting on his abdomen. Tom's hand stroked the side of her breast, ran lightly up and down her side, played across the small of her back.

"Strange," he said quietly, his first words in a quarter of an hour, "how sometimes it seems like . . ."

"The first time?"

"That." He turned to her, kissed her forehead. "More, though. The only time, maybe? I don't know . . ."

"The first time in the history of the world. No one else ever . . . we're the only ones." She sighed, reached to kiss his neck. "How could I not have known you were so near? These dreams of mine have a life of their own. Just when I'm beginning to believe I'm learning how to control them, they trick me and humble me." She paused, looked up at him. "Was it terrible?" she asked hesitantly.

"The terrible part was thinking about all those who'd died on my account—and about you, and about never seeing the boys again. For the rest of it, we were too busy staying alive to think about survival being terrible or not." His voice soft, he related the story of their days in the open boat, their rescue of Sanchez, and the journey to San Sebastian. "Slurry knew about a small cove—a cleft in the rocks, really, but safe enough if there's no heavy weather. We tied up there Sunday afternoon and left Slurry to wait for us while we went to see about you and the boys. San Sebastian's like any other port town in the world: you can learn all there is to know by going to a bar or two, asking leading questions, and then listening. We spent Monday nosing around some more and then, that night, slipped away. Tuesday morning we found this place, and here we are. But not," he finished grimly, "for long."

Adriana sat up and combed out her hair with her fingers. "I still think you'll be better off waiting for—"

"I told you—"

"No, let me finish," she insisted. "Vincent is having a masked ball Tuesday night. Why," she asked pointedly, "fight your way past the guards when you can walk in by invitation?"

"By invitation, huh?" Dubious, he tried to envision the scene, and found himself liking what he saw. "Maybe." He rose and paced back and forth across the clearing. "Have to find some decent clothes, of course . . . get inside and . . . stay there!" he snapped suddenly, and disappeared around the wall of roots.

Frightened by his tone and acutely aware of her nudity, Adriana reached for her skirt and was just stepping into it when Tom reappeared. "Whatever—?"

"They're looking for you. Hurry."

They dressed quickly and in silence, plunged into the forest along the broken path they'd followed earlier. "I'll tell them I fell asleep," Adriana said, stopping just short of the glade with the gazebo. "I'll get away tomorrow afternoon sometime and bring you a diagram of the house. Do I look all right?"

"A little disheveled, but otherwise . . ." He stopped and plucked a twig from her hair. "I love you, Adriana. In the boat . . . all I could think of was that I hadn't told you that I loved you."

Tears sprang to her eyes. Her fingers trembling, Adriana reached out to touch the amulet nestled against his chest. "Thomas, Thomas," she whispered, embracing him, not wanting to leave him.

Tom's heart swelled with the fullness that only love can bring. He was ten feet tall, as strong as a dozen men. All things were possible. No one could stop him. "Just don't tell me you knew already," he said gruffly. "That you heard it in a dream."

"I won't," Adriana promised, her smile a secret against his chest.

"A man likes to have a surprise or two to spring on his woman now and again."

"I know. A woman, too." She looked up and, her eyes glistening, touched his cheek. "I love you, Thomas. I have for a long time now."

Far down the path, a man's voice called her name.

"Tomorrow?" Tom asked, holding back a branch so she could pass.

"Tomorrow. Be careful."

"I will." She was gone, running across the glade, pausing to wave to him before she started down the path. Alone, Tom wondered about the future, and hoped he'd never have to watch her walk away from him again. Then he turned and disappeared into the forest.

~ CHAPTER XX ~

The fire was small, barely large enough to cast a dim light and keep a pot of water at a low boil. Maurice, Topaz, and Sanchez had spent the day finishing a deadfall that would effectively block the narrow trail they'd take on their flight around The Sleeping Giant. Tom had spent part of the afternoon with Adriana, the rest keeping an eye on the governor's mansion and dozing so he could stand watch during the night.

"I feel better," Maurice said, adding a monstrous belch for emphasis. "Gotta admit you were right, Topaz. Hate to think of old Slurry having to stay aboard ship and make his meal of biscuits and salt pork."

"Iguana good meat," Topaz grunted sleepily.

Sanchez wiped his hands on his breeches and took a pull from a jug of rum. "Damn land," he wheezed. "The best thing about the ocean is that there are no damn trees and no damn rocks. Shit."

"You talk too much," Maurice rumbled. He looked across the fire at Tom. "You gonna tell us what we're gonna do, or not?"

Tom reached inside his shirt and pulled out a piece of paper. "A diagram of the house," he said by way of preamble. "We go in Tuesday night at that party. Or I do, anyway, and here's how.

"The party begins at eight. Dinner will be served at nine-thirty. At nine, Bliss will be summoned to Sir Theodotus's study to hear the charges against him and to be placed under arrest. At the same time, LeBusque will be lured outside by a messenger and arrested. Shortly after that, without anyone at the ball knowing what's happening, they'll be placed in irons aboard a merchant ship which will sail on the midnight tide.''

"So what's all that have to do with us?'' Maurice asked.

"You two,'' he said, nodding at Maurice and Sanchez, "will wait until dark and then work your way down to the tree line and find a good place to wait and watch near the entrance to the path that leads to the gazebo. By that time, Topaz and I will be waiting outside the house of a fellow named John Pelty, who's a ship's chandler and the assistant harbor master. He's a bachelor, he lives alone, and, bad luck for him, he's about my height and build. When he leaves for the ball, Topaz and I will take him and his servant, switch clothes, tie them up, and go in their places.

"Now, here's where the diagram comes in.'' He held up the paper, pointed to the northeast corner of the mansion. "This is the study. I'll be waiting outside on the verandah, and as soon as Bliss has been taken away, in I go and take Sir Theodotus. The boys' room is right above the study. Adriana, Sir Theodotus, and I go upstairs and get the boys. You, Topaz, will be out here on the south lawn with the rest of the servants. As soon as we have the boys, Adriana will signal from the corner window. We're going to give you five minutes, then you'll start a fire in the carriage house, spook as many of the horses as you can, and then make your way around to the back of the house, where we'll meet you. From then on, it's just as we talked about earlier. Up the path to the gazebo, through the forest to the trail, to the deadfall, which we trip just in case anyone's following us, and on to the cove, where we'll row out to the *Red Dog Song,* which by that time Slurry will have in deep water.''

His companions stared at Tom, at the diagram of the

house and grounds, back at Tom. "Just like that, huh?" Maurice asked, dumbfounded. "You mind tellin' me what happens if—"

"You have a better plan?" Tom snapped.

"Well . . ." Maurice looked around for support. Topaz was near sleep. Sanchez was busy honing his knife against the side of his boot. "C'mon, Onofre. Hell, you're the pirate. What's a good pirate plan for gettin' them boys?"

"Sounds like a fine plan to me," Sanchez said with a shrug. He sheathed his knife, stretched, and yawned. "After all," he added, lying down and closing his eyes after a long day's work, "he's the one who has to go in the house."

The Sleeping Giant rumbled angrily, and belched a cloud of yellow-gray smoke that the wind carried out to sea.

"He will sleep again now," Carlotta said, nodding wisely.

Bliss turned away from the window, then strolled to his desk and the open journal that lay there. "And just how do you know that?" he asked.

"It is the Giant's way."

"I fervently hope so." He looked up as the sound of the front door knocker echoed through the house. "See who that is and have him wait in the front parlor. I'll be out as soon as I finish dressing."

"Yes, sir."

Bliss closed and put away the journal, took off his robe, and stepped into the breeches Carlotta had laid out for him.

"You get a late start on the day, my friend," a voice said from the doorway.

"Henri!" Bliss said. "Come in, come in. It's all right, Carlotta," he reassured the distraught servant. "Some tea? Chocolate? Tea it is, then, for Monsieur LeBusque and me. And what, my friend,'' he asked LeBusque, ''brings you to town so early?''

LeBusque made himself at home in the chair behind Bliss's desk. ''You're looking fit,'' he said without answering. ''When did you discard the sling?''

''Yesterday. With the last of the stitches.'' Bliss extended his left arm, flexed his fingers. ''Whatever else she has to answer for,'' he said with a grimace, ''I'll have to give her credit for this. She did a good job.''

''She's still a bitch—with whom I have a score to settle.'' LeBusque gingerly touched the bandage that covered the still-healing wound on his head. ''Any word yet?''

Bliss finished buttoning his shirt, began to tuck it into his breeches. ''How would you like to meet her tomorrow night at the ball?''

The Frenchman's eyebrows rose. ''She's with him? How do you know?''

''One of my servants saw her playing with his grandsons. And I have no doubt she'll stay right where she is for the next two weeks.'' Bliss's smile would have chilled lava. ''Can you think of a better way to begin the new year?''

There it was! Over there, a speck of light a little to the left . . . no. Not there, either. Only a figment of the imagination. Somewhere on the steep slope behind the house. *Oh, Thomas. Only twenty-four hours from now.*

'' 'Driana?''

No mistakes, Thomas. Not after we've come so far and endured so much.

'' 'Driana!''

''Mmm?'' she asked, pulling closed the shutters against the night air. ''What?''

''What're you looking at?''

''Just the stars.'' She tucked in Jason, tousled his hair, and kissed him on the forehead.

"Can we look at the stars 'fore we go t'sleep?"

"Not tonight," she said, moving to Joseph's bed.

"Tomorrow night?" Joseph asked.

She tucked him in, repeated the ritual exactly as she had with Jason. "Yes," she answered, blowing out the lantern. "I'll remember. Tomorrow night."

Night dragged on interminably. The governor swore he couldn't sleep. Sleep was out of the question with so much turmoil afoot. In the middle of his complaint, he fell asleep, then—in what seemed moments—woke to the sound of morning chimes, of the clock ringing nine. "Twelve hours," he said aloud to the empty bedroom. "Twelve hours and it'll all be over."

His brain awhirl with a mixture of anticipation and apprehension, he eased out of bed and padded barefoot across the floor to throw open the shutters. The morning air was fresh, without a trace of the sulfurous odor he detested so. The sky was clear and as blue as the vast sweep of Caribbean that stretched to the horizon. "A good day," he said, quite pleased with himself and with the way things were going to turn out. "A fine day on which to catch a traitor."

Shakespeare's "precious stone set in the silver sea, . . . This blessed plot, this earth, this realm, this England . . ." was far away across a wide and hostile ocean, but Sir Theodotus had outdone himself in evoking her memory. Royalty might have demanded greater sumptuousness, but no one could have asked for a more convivial atmosphere. Lanterns and candles lighted the mansion bright as day. The best crystal gleamed on sideboard and tables, with three pieces of stemware for each place setting. The band was ticked out in its resplendent best, and was augmented by a pair of violinists who played light and romantic tunes in the side rooms. A dozen masked island boys dressed identically in pages' uniforms carried trays of wine and hors d'oeuvres.

The governor's annual masked ball in San Sebastian was an egalitarian affair by necessity, for of that tiny island's inhabitants, only Sir Theodotus and Captain Trevor Bliss could be counted as high-born. To make up the difference, everyone with any status at all was invited. Every planter, down to the smallest freeholder. All government functionaries above the level of clerk. All captains and first mates of ships in port. All businessmen, save tavern owners and saloon keepers. All these, along with wives, and children above fourteen, crowded the verandah, ballroom, and parlors of the mansion. And if their manners and speech weren't as sophisticated and erudite as those of the lords and ladies attending similar functions in London, they made up for this lack with high spirits and good fellowship.

Of expensive silks and laces there were few, but cotton was bright and colorful and every bit as flattering to the complexion and as pleasing to the eye. Among the fifty or so men, only a half-dozen wore coats of velvet, but none of the others complained or felt himself a pauper. The climate was inimical to the keeping of wigs, the want of which had long ago been forgotten by most of the ladies, who were elegantly if simply coiffed, with their own hair complemented with ribbons and bows and native flowers. As if to make up for all these supposed deficiencies in finery, the guests had outdone themselves with their masks. Every material available— shells, bones, feathers, skins, wood, jewels, and fabrics —had been utilized and combined in a creative outpouring. A veritable bestiary, colorful, grotesque, and beautiful, walked and danced the floors of the governor's mansion. All in all, a more festive or gay masked ball couldn't have been found in all the empire.

As for Adriana, her shoes were too heavy, her breeches too tight, her wig too irritating. How men wore such cumbersome apparel was a mystery; she supposed they got used to it. Feeling awkward and out of place in her page boy's costume, she traded an empty tray for a full one and reentered the ballroom. Tom, she was virtually certain, had yet to arrive, and she was growing more apprehensive by the moment. If anything had gone wrong, if he'd been caught, perhaps harmed . . .

"Here, boy. My glass is empty. What's that you have?"

"Madeira on this side, suh, spiced cider all the way from England on this," she answered in the stilted, lilting English of the natives. "Plenty more, suh. Yes, suh! Thank you, suh!"

The great clock by the door chimed the first four notes of the Westminster tune. Eight-fifteen. Three quarters of an hour. . . . Her breath caught in her throat as Trevor Bliss, haughty in full dress uniform and wearing a simple black half-mask, strode through the door accompanied by an equally elegantly dressed and plainly masked Henri LeBusque. The crowd parted deferentially for the two second most powerful men on the island, who made their way across the room and paid their respects to Sir Theodotus. Adriana followed and arrived at Bliss's side just as, the amenities over, the captain turned away from Sir Theodotus to survey the ballroom.

"Wine, suh?" Adriana asked, her heart hammering.

Bliss reached out absentmindedly, then stopped abruptly. "What'd you say, boy?" he asked.

"Wine, suh?" she repeated.

"Oh." Sensing something was amiss, yet preoccupied with other matters, he studied her intently for a moment, then gave up and took a glass for himself and one for LeBusque. "Yes, of course . . ."

Perspiration ran down her forehead and into her eyes. Her hands shook so badly she had to steady the tray against her abdomen. She had taken a foolish chance. Had he recognized her, he might have become suspicious and . . . and what, after all? Certainly nothing violent in the middle of the party. Her fears were groundless. In another—she shot a glance at the clock—thirty-five minutes he would be hearing much worse news.

Four more Madeiras, three more ciders, two more minutes. Where was he? That one? No, too short, and with a wife on his arm. That one? Too portly, and the wrong hands.

"You have a well-turned leg for a boy," a low voice said in her ear. "Looking for someone?"

"You!" The empty glasses on her tray rattled as she turned to see the face of Pan, impish, devilish, sardonic, leering down at her. "I've been worried half-sick."

Tom shrugged. "The chandler wasn't happy about parting with his clothes. I'll be black-and-blue all over tomorrow. Is everything all right? Any problems?"

"None that I know of." Adriana looked around to make sure no one was paying undue attention to them. "Bliss and LeBusque arrived about ten minutes ago. They're over there under the chandelier."

"LeBusque is the one in green velvet?"

"Yes."

"Anyone else I should know about?"

"Not in here. There's a guard at the top of the main stairway, another in the hallway leading to Vincent's study. Is Topaz—"

"Right where he should be, I imagine. We made a slight change in plans. He's going to bring my belt and a brace of pistols around to the side for me so I'll be armed." He grinned underneath his mask. "Topaz makes a hell of a driver. He kind of forgot to tell anyone he'd never handled a team before. I had to take time to show him how."

Adriana needed to keep moving. She showed Tom the fastest way to the french doors outside Sir Theodotus's study and explained that they were unlocked. "Just pretend you belong," she said, leaving to replenish her tray. "I'll see you a few minutes after nine."

The heat was becoming unbearable. Glad for a moment's respite, Adriana slipped into the hall and hurried to a side room for a new tray. Tom had disappeared by the time she returned. Bliss and LeBusque hadn't moved. Sir Theodotus was talking to a guard who. . . . *Dear God! Bliss's journal!*

Across the room, Sir Theodotus's mask couldn't hide his distress. "Good God, man! You were supposed to wait until nine o'clock to get this."

"Don't know nothin' about that, Gov'nor," the guard answered. "Just did like I was told."

"What about his servants?"

"Under lock and key, sir."

"Good. Good." Sir Theodotus looked around, spied Bliss and LeBusque. Neither seemed perturbed, so there was evidently no harm done. "Very well. Return to Bliss's residence and make sure none of his servants is set free until you receive explicit orders to do so."

"Yes, sir."

Nothing had changed, yet everything had changed. Adriana saw Sir Theodotus excuse himself and leave the room. Unnerved, she managed to catch Tom's eye and gesture surreptitiously toward the back of the house and then, as naturally as possible, headed for the study. No sooner had Adriana disappeared than Tom slipped out the side door and, ascertaining that he was alone, whistled quietly for Topaz. Thirty seconds later, Topaz had helped him buckle on his belt and he was hiding in the shadows outside the governor's study. None of them saw Ramon slip past the guard at the gate, make his way up the drive, and insist that he be allowed to enter with an important message for Captain Bliss.

"Isn't that your man?" LeBusque asked, interrupting Bliss's cynical remark about the airs put on by commoners.

Bliss glanced over his shoulder, caught sight of Ramon, and blanched. "What're you doing here?" he asked as the servant hurried up to him. "What's happened?"

"Men come, take book from desk," Ramon said. "Lock others up. I get away, come."

"Damn!" Bliss swore. "My journal! How'd they know it was—?"

"The Gypsy girl," LeBusque hissed. "Fool! You left a journal out for anyone to read?"

"Of course not. She must have read it when I was unconscious. I've written in it since. Ramon, let me have that knife."

"Yes, suh."

LeBusque's eyes widened. "And just exactly what do you think you're going to do with that pig sticker in this crowd?" he asked.

"Nothing," Bliss said. "Boy, come here."

One of the servants hurried over. "Yes, suh?"

"Where's the governor? I need to see him immediately."

"Don't know, suh," the servant said. "He go out that door two, three minute now."

"Good. Off with you. Ramon, go outside and tell the boy to make sure my team's ready, then wait there for me. And we," he told LeBusque, "are going to pay our beloved governor a private call to discuss the safekeeping of his darling grandsons. Ready?"

LeBusque had no choice. His face grim behind his mask, he and Bliss worked their way through the crowd to the rear of the ballroom and out the door into the hallway.

"All due respect, sirs," a young man posted there said, "but this part of the house is closed to visitors. Governor's orders . . . oof!"

LeBusque struck again, and as the youth doubled over in pain, Bliss hit him on the back of the head with the hilt of Ramon's knife. "Fool," he said to the crumpling body. "Come along, Henri. The second door on the right."

Rarely had Sir Theodotus read a more fascinating document. So intent was he on the flow of Bliss's perfidy that he did not hear the door open or know he had visitors until Adriana cleared her throat in warning. "What?" he grunted.

Adriana dared not answer, for Bliss and LeBusque strode directly in.

"Speak up . . ." His mouth felt dry, his pulse hammered in his temples as he glanced up and saw Bliss. He folded his hands so they wouldn't shake and tried to look stern. "May I ask—"

"Interesting reading?" Bliss interrupted harshly.

"More so than you might imagine," Sir Theodotus answered at last, having remembered that there were guards nearby and that he was in no real danger.

"Oh, I can imagine well enough," Bliss drawled.

"Boy!" he snapped, jerking his head in Adriana's direction. "Go fetch us some wine. We may be here a few minutes and I'm dry."

Her eyes boring into those of the man who had murdered her brother, Adriana remained motionless.

"Are you deaf, boy? I said, go fetch us some wine."

His lips were compressed into a thin pale line that she found revolting. His eyes were cold and hard, without compassion or even a modicum of kindness. Hating him and tired of the charade, Adriana slowly raised her arms and, with one quick motion, removed mask and wig and threw them at Bliss's feet.

As if already linked by chains, both Bliss and LeBusque leaned forward and stared.

"Get your own damned wine," Adriana said. "I'm staying right here."

"Bitch!" LeBusque grunted.

"That's an excellent idea," Bliss said, and pulled out Ramon's knife. "I'm sure that you and Monsieur LeBusque will have a great deal to discuss while the governor and I take a little trip upstairs to see about his grandsons."

Sir Theodotus's eyes hardened. "You propose to add kidnapping to high treason?" he asked, holding up the journal.

"Why not?" Bliss asked with a hollow laugh. "Do you have a better idea? Come, come . . ." Knife at the ready in his right hand, he beckoned to Sir Theodotus with his left. "We don't have all night. Slowly around the desk, if you please. What about you, Henri? Think you can handle the girl alone this time?"

LeBusque smiled lazily, like the hunting cat who knows his kill cannot escape. "Your sarcasm is unnecessary, Trevor. The mademoiselle and I will share a tender moment—" He stopped in mid-sentence when the french doors swung open.

"Who's out there?" Bliss snapped, having to divide his attention between Sir Theodotus and the doors. "Speak up, damn you!"

A faint rumble filled the air and the room shook ever so slightly.

"Just another tremor," LeBusque said, returning his attention to Adriana.

"Not quite," said a cold voice.

"My God, it's Paxton!" Sir Theodotus blurted. "But you're dead!"

Bliss stared uncomprehendingly at the figure brandishing a brace of handguns in the doorway. Never having heard of Paxton, LeBusque looked to Bliss to see what he should do. Adriana took advantage of the distraction to crouch and draw the knife she carried in the sheath strapped to her calf. *This time! Now. Now for Giuseppe!*

"Watch out, Trevor!" LeBusque grabbed for Adriana as she hurtled past him, but missed.

Bliss caught the motion out of the corner of his eye, twisted and dropped to one knee just in time to shove Adriana past him and avoid the thrust of her knife.

The last thing Tom wanted to do was fire and bring everyone running. "Stop right there!" he yelled before

Bliss could strike Adriana from behind. "Now, all of you listen. I don't give a damn about whatever it is you're fighting about. I want my sons and that's all. Now, you—"

The world itself seemed to explode and the light in the room turned red as fiery rock geysered into the sky from the torn summit of The Sleeping Giant. The floor tilted crazily. Adriana tripped over a chair, rolled, and slammed into a bookcase. Sir Theodotus disappeared behind his desk. Bliss and LeBusque somehow collided and, looking like a pair of confused dancers, found themselves pitched out the door into the hall. Tom, feet planted, pistols held out before him, skidded halfway into the room before the floor tilted back again and, as a hundred books flew at him from the bookcase, he managed to stop.

"Tom!" Adriana screamed from beneath the pile of books.

Sir Theodotus crawled from behind the desk and flinched as a lamp crashed to the floor by his side. "My grandsons," he croaked, appealing to Tom. "The boys! Oh, God, the mountain's coming apart."

Dust choked the air as Tom dragged Adriana to her feet. "Upstairs," she yelled. "They're upstairs!"

The rumbling from the earth continued, became a deep hammering roar that leached courage from the bravest of hearts. The ceiling cracked and pieces of plaster fell. A tongue of flame from the fallen lantern caught in the coal oil–impregnated rug and began to spread. "Lead the way," Tom shouted over the uproar, pushing Adriana toward the door.

They stumbled into the hall and groped their way to the ballroom. Inside, all was chaos. The main chandelier had fallen and had pinned two unfortunate party goers. Food and drink and broken glass littered the floor, and the smells of wine and food mingled with those of sulfur and smoke and dust. Though less than a minute had passed since the initial eruption, the room was empty save for the wounded. The foyer was another matter, as guests and servants and guards all attempted to crowd through the main door.

The earth shook again. A lantern in the foyer crashed. Burning coal oil spread across the polished wood floor, and what had been panic became sheer terror as the crazed mob, ignoring a half-dozen windows in the adjacent rooms, fought to exit through the door.

"Is there another way?" Tom shouted.

Adriana pulled him back into the ballroom and led the way to a second door that opened into the hall behind the foyer. The foot of the stairway still inaccessible, Tom grabbed the railing and vaulted onto the stairs, then reached over and pulled Adriana up. The guard posted at the top of the stairs was gone. In his place, another fire from a broken lantern had spread to a tapestry and flames licked up the wall. His face grim in the lurid light, Tom ripped the fabric from the wall, covered the burning part with that which had yet to catch fire, and stamped it out, so that at least that fire wouldn't block their way when they left.

"This way," Adriana called, already halfway down the hall.

The whole building swayed sickeningly. Lurching from wall to wall, Tom rushed to catch up to Adriana, and burst into the room where the boys were supposed to be. "Jason! Joseph!" he roared.

A single lantern hanging from the ceiling swung from side to side. Grotesque shadows danced like mad demons on the walls.

"Jason! Jos—"

"Daddy?" Terrified, the boys had taken refuge under Joseph's bed. "Daddy!" Jason piped, rolling into the open.

Tom wrapped one arm around Jason, helped Joseph out from under the bed, and held them both.

"Where you been, Daddy?" Joseph asked, his arms wrapped around his father's neck.

"Time for that later," Tom said. "Are you all right?" He held them at arm's length and looked them over briefly. "Jason?"

"Yes."

"Joseph?"

"Yes."

"Good." *No time. No time to rejoice. Hurry. . . .* "Stay with Adriana a minute." He rose, went to the window, and threw open the shutters. "Damn," he swore, reeling away from the blast of heat that burned his face.

Behind him, Adriana pressed the boys' faces to her breast so they couldn't see the horror that was descending upon them. The top of The Sleeping Giant was hidden in a huge cloud of smoke that blotted out the sky. Below it, the forest was afire and, creeping through the fire, a white-hot tongue of lava oozed down the side of the mountain toward the mansion.

"Listen to me," Tom said, taking a precious moment. "You're going to have to be very brave boys, do you hear?"

"Yes, sir," two small, frightened voices said in unison.

"Do exactly *what* I say, *when* I say, all right?"

"Yes, sir."

"Good." He helped Adriana to her feet, handed Joseph to her, and picked up Jason. "Our only chance is to make it to the water," he told Adriana. "Stay close. Don't get separated."

The temperature was rising alarmingly. The hall was choked with fumes and smoke, illuminated feebly by a fire at the far end. Keeping low, below the heaviest layer of smoke, they scuttled down the hall and then stopped at the stairs where, four steps down, Sir Theodotus held a pistol aimed at Tom.

"Pa-paw Theo!" Joseph squealed. "See? My papa's come!"

"Aren't you glad?" Jason added. "Now we don't have to be afraid."

Sir Theodotus's coat was torn. He'd lost his wig and tears tracked through the soot and dust covering his face. "They're all I have of her," he sobbed. "All—"

"No, Topaz!" Tom yelled suddenly. "Don't! It's all right!"

Sir Theodotus looked around and saw an Indian at the bottom of the stairs. Both the man's arms were raised, and each hand held a knife ready for throwing. Slowly, his wits recovered, Sir Theodotus turned so the Indian could see that his gun was no longer aimed at Tom, then carefully took if off cock and lowered it. "Very well, Paxton," he said as Topaz sheathed his knives. His eyes met Tom's, and he read in that single implacable eye the message of love and conciliation he'd refused to read there five years earlier. "You win. I've a boat in a small cove below the house. With luck . . . at least we won't be trapped in town with everyone else. Follow me!"

Tom supporting Adriana, they took the stairs two at a time, tried to turn left, but were blocked by a wall of fire. "You want me to carry boy?" Topaz asked Adriana.

"No," Tom shouted above the roar of the flames. "She can handle him. Keep your hands free just in case. Here. Take this, too," he added, thrusting one of his pistols into Topaz's hand.

The front door was blocked by a dozen dead and wounded victims of the earlier crush. Sir Theodotus, ignoring one man's plea for assistance, turned right, into the ballroom. "Help me!" he yelled, pointing to a chair and then to one of the windows.

Topaz picked up the chair, heaved it through the frames, and broke out the remaining glass at the bottom. He stepped through, helped Adriana, then Tom, then Sir Theodotus just as the ceiling gave way and

buried the room in chunks of plaster and wood beams.
"Which way?" Tom yelled.

"Tom!"

"It's Maurice," Adriana cried.

Maurice and Sanchez hurried toward them from the
front of the house and joined them on the verandah.
Behind them, the forest was an inferno and the white
tongue of lava advanced ever closer. "No goin' around
that," Maurice shouted. "Jesus, you ever see anything
like it?"

"We've got to get around the house," Sir Theodotus
interrupted.

"He's on our side?" Sanchez asked in astonishment.

"You weren't either, once," Tom pointed out.
"C'mon, let's go."

"Not around front," Maurice said as Sir Theodotus
started that way. "It's an unholy mess. Here," he said
to Adriana. "Give me that young'un."

The heat was growing painfully intense and the noise
was becoming deafening. Shielding themselves and the
boys as best they could, they followed Sir Theodotus to
the relative coolness at the far side of the mansion and
stopped to catch their breath and take their bearings.
Lighted as bright as day by the surrounding fires, the
south lawn looked as if a battle had been fought there.
The horses were trapped by fire on one side and high
walls on all the others. Some, hauling conveyances,
plunged about madly, others with broken legs lay
thrashing and screaming in pain. "The gate's over
there," Sir Theodotus explained, his voice weak from
exhaustion and fear. "If I fall, a path winds down—"

"You won't," Tom said, nodding for Sanchez to lend
the older man a hand. "Hold on to my belt," he told
Adriana as he started across the lawn, "and everybody
keep an eye out for the horses."

Time stood still in that plunging, headlong flight
from the fires of hell. Mercifully, Topaz paused to slit

the throats of three screaming horses with shattered legs. Behind them, the mansion caved in as yet another strong tremor shook the ground. Tom tripped and fell, but somehow managed not to crush Jason; Adriana helped him up and started him in the right direction.

The gate had been torn from its hinges. Single file, they entered the forest and forged quickly ahead through the shadows. To their right, a massive white-hot chunk of lava fell from the sky and set the trees afire. Behind them, a tremendous explosion rocked them almost senseless, and more trees caught fire and crashed to the ground. Adriana's eyes streamed tears, her cheeks felt parched, her mouth was dry as chalk. The path was treacherously narrow and sloped sharply. Running blindly after Tom, she stumbled, willed her numbed legs and feet to obey, and somehow kept her balance and cheated death.

Down from the governor's roost with its view of the sea, away from the port now obscured by the intervening hills, away from the inexorable pursuing flow of deadly lava, down to the water's edge . . . a gale of fresh air, sucked in to replace the heated air rising from the conflagration, cooled her face. Her lungs seared, her sides splitting, her legs cramping, Adriana staggered down the last few feet of incline and almost fell as the ground leveled and her feet dug into soft sand.

The cove was small, its waters shallow. To the east, a waterfall dropped over a sheer rock wall that jutted into the Caribbean and protected the cove from the Atlantic trades. "I'm not much of a sailor, so it hasn't been in the water very often," Sir Theodotus shouted against the unnatural wind. He pointed out an overturned hull that had been pulled far up the beach. "The sail and mast are underneath."

"It'll have to do. You two take the boys," Tom yelled, and hurried off to help turn over the boat and haul it into the water.

Adriana looked back the way they'd come. The

green, wet subtropical forest was no match for the temperatures generated by the volcano. Dried and withered by the heated air sucked into the fire storm, tree after tree, each one closer to the shore, exploded into flames.

"You knew he was alive, didn't you?" Sir Theodotus yelled as he and Adriana led the boys toward the water.

"Yes, but only a few days ago."

"So while I was preoccupied with Bliss . . . ahhh, never mind. Maybe it serves me right."

"Are we gonna die, 'Driana?" Joseph asked tearfully.

"Of course not." She almost choked on the words, but forced herself to smile and say them. "Your father's here to take you home. He's not going to let a little volcano stop him. Now, let's get wet so the heat won't bother us. Just lie down and stay close to the edge . . ."

"You come too, Pa-paw Theo," Jason called, his eyes wide and innocent.

"Me?" Sir Theodotus turned, shielded his eyes against the heat, and stared with stunned disbelief at the burning island. "I don't know," he stammered. "Your father—"

"—Wants you to come, too," Adriana said, taking his hand and leading him to the water. "Trust me. He does."

"Hurry, Pa-paw Theo. Get wet!"

Twenty yards away, the boat slid into the water and floated free. "We'll have to swim 'er out," Maurice yelled against the stiffening wind. "Get the others."

"But I can't swim," Sanchez protested.

"Then man the tiller, and have the sail ready when we're far enough out to use it."

Sanchez leaped into the boat, found two coiled lines forward, tied them to cleats, and threw them to Maurice and Topaz. Tom raced along the water's edge. "We're ready. Hurry!" he shouted. He tucked a boy under each arm and ran back up the beach. "You too, Vincent. Run, damn it!"

"Run, run, Pa-paw Theo!" Joseph shrieked.

A tree at the end of the path exploded. Another on the west side of the cove turned into a ball of flame and fell sizzling into the cove. Sir Theodotus trotted after the others, finally catching up at the boat. "Will it hold us all?" he asked as Tom handed the twins to Sanchez.

"It had better," Tom grunted. He picked up Adriana, set her over the gunwale, then gave Sir Theodotus a boost. "The wind is too strong to use the sail in here," he explained to Adriana and Sir Theodotus, "so we're going to swim her out. You'll have to bail. Stay low out of the heat and wind and listen to Sanchez."

Topaz and Maurice stood waist-deep in water fifty feet ahead of the boat. Tom pulled off his belt and boots, threw them aboard. "You're the middle man," Sanchez shouted, throwing him a third line he'd just tied and then jumping overboard. "I'll push from behind until it gets too deep."

"Look!" Topaz shouted, his voice barely audible over the combined roar of fire and wind.

"What?" Sanchez yelled back.

Topaz pointed. "Up there."

Adriana followed his gaze to the edge of the cliff. There, on a boulder next to the waterfall, trapped between a wall of flames and the rocks fifty feet below him, Trevor Bliss gestured in vain for assistance.

"There's no way we can help," Tom shouted to Bliss. "Swim!"

Tom, Maurice, and Topaz pulled on the lines until the water was too deep for walking, then began the long hard swim. Sanchez climbed back on board.

Do you see, Giuseppe? Do you see? He will die more horribly than you. The earth itself will avenge you. Earth and fire . . . "Watch out!" she screamed, pushing the boys down behind the gunwale and pointing toward the cliff.

Sanchez glanced up in time to see a tiny blossom of smoke momentarily obscure Bliss. A moment later, he felt a small thud as a ball smacked into the side of the boat. "Keep down," he yelled to Adriana. "We'll be out of range before he can do any damage."

Adriana ducked but, fascinated, peeked over the gunwale and watched as Bliss, illuminated clearly by the fires surrounding him, reloaded, aimed, and fired again. "Duck!" she yelled, and dropped out of sight.

The boat seemed to sink deeper in the water. Adriana looked up and saw Sanchez fling one arm over the transom. "I think," he said, his eyes wide with surprise, "he's gone and killed me." He reached up with his free hand, pulled off his hat, and glanced once, longingly, at the water-soaked, bedraggled crimson feather. "This is yours," he said to Adriana, his voice weakening. "Keep the tiller straight."

Only when he slipped from the boat and floated free in the water did Adriana see the great gaping wound in his back, and the blood that spilled from it and stained the water the color of the feather.

The wind was growing stronger and kicking up waves against which Tom, Maurice, and Topaz had to swim. Adriana was helpless. None of the men could hear her calls, nor could they have done anything if they had. Powerless, she watched as Bliss stood to reload; then she ducked when he fired again. She watched in horror as the ground heaved and the waterfall dissolved into steam and was replaced by molten lava, and watched, too, as Bliss lost his balance, threw his arms in the air, and slipped off the boulder to land feet first in the steaming lava. Bursting into flame, he was carried over the cliff. A second later, the bright spot of flame that had been the murderer of Giuseppe hit the water and winked out, quenched like the last vestige of Adriana's hatred and desire for revenge.

A second river of lava followed the path Adriana and the others had taken and hit the water with an explosion of steam. A hundred yards from shore, the swimmers felt the temperature of the water rise, stopped to look around, and only then discovered that Sanchez was missing. "Can we tack out of here?" Tom asked.

"Believe so," Topaz said. "Have to try. You stay here, be anchor to keep us from drifting in while I rig sail. Don't let go the ropes." His pointed teeth showed in a wide grin. "Otherwise, you boil like in kettle."

The wait seemed interminable. Swimming steadily but making little headway, Tom and Maurice held the tiny boat offshore until, at last, Topaz sailed past them on a tack that would take them almost due west, and they clambered aboard and lay exhausted in the bilge.

Behind them, smoke and ash settled to meet the rising steam from the ring of boiling water that surrounded the island. And all they could see was a dense cloud glowing red from within as the entire island burned . . .

And burned . . .

And burned.

⌒⌒ **EPILOGUE** ⌒⌒

The *Red Dog Song* angled up and through a cresting wave, balanced precariously on the top, and plunged down the long smooth slope on the far side. Her bow digging into the deep green of the Atlantic, she shuddered briefly, and began again to climb. On deck, half the crew settled in for its watch while the other half made its way below for a few hours' sleep.

Two days had passed since the disastrous eruption of The Sleeping Giant and the destruction of San Sebastian. Already at sea when the volcano blew, Slurry had circumnavigated the island and begun a frantic search for his friends. At first light, when he finally spotted the tiny overladen craft, he actually wept with relief. Exhausted and fearful of being taken by relief ships that would surely come to investigate the source of the enormous cloud that drifted downwind, they had lingered only to pick up two more boat loads of survivors and, luckily, a cow that had stayed alive long enough to be brought aboard and slaughtered. Their decision to leave the area immediately saved their lives. Less than an hour after the island fell below the horizon, the volcano erupted for one final time and San Sebastian disappeared from the face of the earth. All that remained was a towering cloud of gray-black ash and smoke. Even the dark cloud, driven west by the Atlantic trades, was soon lost to sight.

There was enough food for three weeks; the water casks were full. The sails were black with grime, but most of the clothes aboard had been washed in seawater and the deck had been sluiced down. The work had been arduous, doubly so because of the shock and exhaustion everyone had suffered, and the deck quieted quickly as the ship settled in for the long reach northwest to the South Carolina coast.

Adriana was tucking the twins in for the night when Tom emerged onto the deck and found Sir Theodotus sitting on a keg and gazing blankly out to sea. "Are you all right?" he asked.

Sir Theodotus blinked as if awakening. "What? Oh, yes." He stared at his hands, tried to smooth his torn coat. "I suppose."

"Not much left, I imagine," Tom said with a nod in the direction of San Sebastian.

"I imagine not."

Nervous, Tom rubbed his hands together and tried to think of something to say. "You understand why we can't drop you off sooner. I'll arrange passage to wherever you want to go once we arrive in Charleston, of course."

Worn and pale, Sir Theodotus remained silent.

"We need to talk, you know," Tom finally said.

"Why?" Sir Theodotus asked wearily. "You have your sons."

"Your grandsons, too," Tom replied. "They don't understand what happened. Only that you love them and want to be with them. There has been a war between us. Can't we have peace?"

Sir Theodotus bowed his head. He had kidnapped the twins, and in return Paxton had saved his life and was offering the olive branch of peace. "I shouldn't imagine that would be easy," he said at last.

Tom stiffened. His gesture of conciliation had been genuine, but if the old man couldn't put aside the past and start anew, so be it. "It's up to you," he said curtly, and walked away.

"Tom Paxton!"

And stopped. "Yes."

"Did you love her?" Sir Theodotus asked in a voice that cracked with anguish. "Did you love my Jenny?"

His Jenny. My Jenny. Our Jenny.

"Yes," Tom answered simply. "I loved her very much."

"They're a lot like her, aren't they?"

"Yes, sir, they are."

"Well!" Sir Theodotus drew a deep breath. The ocean air was fresh and sweet, even exhilarating. "I'll look in on them and then turn in myself, I think. We've a long trip ahead of us."

"Yes, sir." Tom turned to face his father-in-law, and for the first time exchanged with him a smile of friendship. "Good night, sir. And sleep well."

"I will, son. For the first time in a long time, I think I will."

Tom watched Sir Theodotus walk away and disappear below decks, then ambled aft.

"What was that all about?" Maurice asked.

"Making friends."

"Been a lot easier if you'd done that five years ago. Sure as hell would've saved a lot of trouble."

Tom grinned. "Sure as hell would've," he agreed, "but think of all the fun you'd've missed." He scanned the ship with a practiced eye, took special note of the compass. "Any problems?"

"Nope. Headin' straight as an arrow for home. Won't make it by Christmas, but should be there by New Year's."

"That's close e—" Tom stopped, watched as a figure emerged from below and walked forward to the bow. "Keep an eye on things, huh?" he said, starting forward himself. "I'll, ah, be back in a minute."

"Take your time," Maurice rumbled to no one in particular. "Take your time, old friend. You've got plenty of it."

The pitch of deck, the mist of salt spray, the mystery of the sea, and the dark miles that slipped past as slowly as time itself. The sound of a footstep, the turn of a head, the silence of two hands touching, of a kiss.

"The boys?" Tom asked.

"Half-asleep."

"Sir T.?"

"He is, too, I think. In a chair by the bunk."

"And you?"

Adriana nestled against him. "Here," she said. "With you."

"Sounds like a good place to me. Tell you what," he said with exaggerated seriousness. "How'd you like me to read your palm?"

"You know how?"

"Yup. Best teacher in the world." He took her hand and, bowing, kissed each fingertip, the base of her thumb, and then nibbled at the soft center of her palm, her heart line.

Streams of auburn hair tickled his cheek when he lifted his head. Adriana's eyes were pools of invitation aglow with amusement and desire. "I'm waiting," she said, gently teasing him. "My future?"

Tom's hands went to his neck and he ducked his head. A moment later, he slipped the thin gold chain over Adriana's head, opened the top of her blouse, and carefully laid the still-warm amulet in the cleft between her breasts.

"Our future," he said. "Ours."

And as Adriana came into his arms, she knew the future would be theirs together. Always together, to live for love.